LOIS McMASTER BUJOLD

BORDERS OF INFINITY

Portions of this novel have been published in slightly different form elsewhere: "The Borders of Infinity" appeared in *Freelancers*, © 1987; "The Mountains of Mourning" appeared in *Analog*, © 1989; "Labyrinth" appeared in *Analog*, © 1989. A signed, limited hardcover edition of this book has been published by Easton Press.

A Baen Books Original

Baen Publishing Enterprises
P.O. Box 1403
Riverdale, NY 10471

ISBN: 0-671-72093-7

Cover art by Gary Ruddell

First Printing, October 1989
Second Printing, December 1989
Third Printing, October 1991
Fourth Printing, November 1992

Printed in the United States of America

Distributed by Simon & Schuster
1230 Avenue of the Americas
New York, NY 10020

AN OFFER HE COULDN'T REFUSE

They were functional fangs, not just decorative, set in a protruding jaw, with long lips and a wide mouth; yet the total effect was lupine rather than simian. Hair a dark matted mess. And yes, fully eight feet tall, a rangy, tense-muscled body.

She clawed her wild hair away from her face and stared at Miles with renewed fierceness. Her eyes were a strange light hazel, adding to the wolfish effect. "What are you *really* doing here?"

"I came for you. I'd heard of you. I'm . . . recruiting. Or I was. Things went wrong and now I'm escaping. But if you came with me, you could join the Dendarii Mercenaries. A top outfit—always looking for a few good men, or whatever. I have this master-sergeant who . . . who *needs* a recruit like you." Sgt. Dyeb was infamous for his sour attitude about women soldiers, insisting that they were too soft . . .

"Very funny," she said coldly. "But I'm not even human. Or hadn't you heard?"

"Human is as human does." He forced himself to reach out and touch her damp cheek. "Animals don't weep."

She jerked, as from an electric shock. "Animals don't lie. Humans do. All the time."

"Not *all* the time."

"Prove it." She tilted her head as she sat cross-legged. "Take off your clothes."

". . . what?"

"Take off your clothes and lie down with me as *humans* do. Men and women." Her hand reached out to touch his throat.

The pressing claws made little wells in his flesh. "Blrp?" choked Miles. His eyes felt wide as saucers. A little more pressure, and those wells would spring forth red fountains. *I am about to die. . . .*

I can't believe this. Trapped on Jackson's Whole with a sex-starved teenage werewolf. There was nothing about this in any of my Imperial Academy training manuals. . . .

Books by Lois McMaster Bujold

Barrayar
The Vor Game
Borders of Infinity
Brothers in Arms
Falling Free
Ethan of Athos
The Warrior's Apprentice
Shards of Honor

For John

ONE

"You have a visitor, Lieutenant Vorkosigan." A little glassy panic twitched in the normally matter-of-fact corpsman's face. He stepped aside to let the man he escorted enter Miles's hospital room. Miles caught a glimpse of the corpsman retreating hastily even before the door hissed shut behind the visitor.

Snub nose, bright eyes, and an open, mild expression gave the man a false air of youth, though his brown hair was greying at the temples. He was slight of body, wore civilian clothes, and radiated no aura of menace, despite the corpsman's reaction. In fact, he had scarcely an aura at all. Work as a covert agent in his early days had given Simon Illyan, Chief of Barrayar's Imperial Security, a life-long habit of being inconspicuous.

"Hi, boss," said Miles.

"You look like hell," Illyan noted agreeably. "Don't bother saluting."

Miles snorted a laugh, which hurt. Everything seemed to hurt except his arms, bandaged and immobilized from shoulderblades to fingertips; they were

1

still numb from the surgical stunners. He wriggled his hospital-gowned body further into his bedclothes, futilely seeking comfort.

"How was your bone-replacement surgery?" asked Illyan.

"About what I expected, from having my legs done before. The ugliest part was opening my right arm and hand up to pick out all the bone fragments. Tedious. The left went a lot faster, the pieces were bigger. Now I get to sit around for a while to see if the marrow transplants are going to take in their synthetic matrix. I'll be a bit anemic for a while."

"I hope you are not going to make a habit of returning from your mission assignments on a stretcher."

"Now, now, this is only the second time that's happened. Besides, eventually I'll run out of unreplaced bones. By the time I'm thirty I could be entirely plastic." Glumly, Miles considered this possibility. If more than half of him became spare parts, could he be declared legally dead? Would he ever walk into a prosthetics manufacturing plant and cry, "Mother!"? Were the medical sedatives making him just a little spacey . . . ?

"About your missions," said Illyan firmly.

Ah. So this visit wasn't just an expression of personal concern, if Illyan had ever owned any personal concern. It was sometimes hard to tell. "You have my reports," said Miles warily.

"Your reports, as usual, are masterpieces of understatement and misdirection," said Illyan. He sounded perfectly serene about it.

"Well . . . anybody might read 'em. You can't tell."

"Hardly 'anyone,' " said Illyan. "But just so."

"So what's the problem?"

"Money. Specifically, accountability for same."

Maybe it was the drugs he was stuffed with, but Miles could make no sense of this. "Don't you like my work?" he said rather plaintively.

"Apart from your injuries, the results of your latest mission are highly satisfactory," began Illyan.

"They'd by-God better be," Miles muttered grimly.

"—and your late, er, adventures on Earth, just prior to it, are still fully classified. We will discuss them later."

"I've got to report to a couple of higher authorities first," Miles put in urgently.

Illyan waved this aside. "So I understand. No. These charges date to the Dagoola affair, and before."

"Charges?" Miles muttered in bewilderment.

Illyan studied him thoughtfully. "I consider what the emperor spends to keep up your connection to the Dendarii Free Mercenaries to be worth it purely from an internal security standpoint. Were you to be permanently posted at, say, Imperial HQ here at the capital, you'd be a damned plot-magnet all the time. Not just for favor- and office-seekers, but for anyone who wants to touch your father through you. As now."

Miles squinted, as though focusing his eyes could focus his thoughts. "Ah?"

"In brief, certain parties in Imperial Accounting are going over your reports from your mercenary fleet's covert ops with a microscope. They would like to know in more detail where certain large packets of cash have gone. Some of your equipment-replacement chits have been outrageous. More than once. Even from my point of view. They would very much like to prove an on-going pattern of peculation. A court-martial charging you with lining your own pockets at the emperor's expense would be gloriously embarrassing just now, for your father and his whole Centrist coalition."

Miles exhaled, stunned. "Has it gone so far—?"

"Not yet. I fully intend to quash it before it gets off the ground. But to do so I need more details. So as not to get blindsided, as I have sometimes been in your more tangled affairs—*I* still remember, if you do not, spending a month in my own prison because of you . . ." Illyan glowered into the past.

"That was part of a plot against Dad," Miles protested.

"So is this, if I'm picking up the early signals correctly. But Count Vorvolk in Accounting is their front-man, and he is depressingly loyal, in addition to having the emperor's personal, er, support. Untouchable. But manipulatable, I fear. He's been primed. He thinks he's being a watch-dog. The more he's given a run-around the more tenacious he'll become. He must be handled with utmost care, whether he's mistaken or not."

"Not . . . ?" breathed Miles. The full import of the timing of Illyan's visit now dawned on him. Not anxiety for an injured subordinate after all. But to put his questions to Miles just post-surgery, when Miles was weak, hurting, drugged, maybe confused. . . . "Why don't you just fast-penta me and get it over with?" Miles snarled.

"Because I have the report about your idiosyncratic reaction to truth drugs," said Illyan equably. "Unfortunate, that."

"You could twist my arm." There was a bitter taste in Miles's mouth.

Illyan's expression was dry and grim. "I thought about it. Then I decided to let the surgeons do it for me."

"You can be a real sonofabitch some days, Simon, do you know?"

"Yes." Illyan sat unmoved and unmoving. Waiting. Watching. "Your father cannot afford a scandal in his government this month. Not during this appropriations fight. This plot must be quashed regardless of its truth. What is said in this room will remain—must remain—between you and me alone. But I must know."

"Are you offering me an amnesty?" Miles's voice was low, dangerous. He could feel his heart begin to pound.

"If necessary." Illyan's voice was perfectly flat.

Miles couldn't clench or even feel his fists, but his toes curled. He found himself gulping for air in the pulsing waves of his rage; the room seemed to waver. "You . . . vile . . . *bastard!* You dare call me a thief. . . ." He rocked in the bed, kicking off tangling strangling covers. His medical monitor began to bleep alarms. His arms were useless weights hanging from his shoulders, flopping nervelessly. "As if I would steal from *Barrayar*. As if I would steal from my *own dead* . . ." He swung his feet out, pulled himself upright with a mighty wrench of abdominal muscles. Dizzied, half-blacking-out, he toppled forward precipitously with no hands to catch himself.

Illyan leapt to grab him before he smashed face first on the matting. "What the hell do you think you're *doing*, boy?" Miles wasn't sure himself.

"What are you doing to my patient?" the white-faced military doctor cried, plunging through the door. "This man just had major surgery!"

The doctor was frightened and furious; the corpsman, in his wake, merely frightened. He tried to impede his superior, plucking at his arm and hissing, "Sir, that's Security Chief *Illyan!*"

"I know who he is. I don't care if he's Emperor Dorca's ghost. I will not have him carrying on his . . . *business*, here." The doctor glared courageously at Illyan. "Your interrogation, or whatever, can take place in your own damned headquarters. I will not have that kind of thing going on in my hospital. This patient is not released to anybody yet!"

Illyan looked at first baffled, then outraged. "I was *not* . . ."

Miles considered, briefly, clutching artistically at certain nerve junctions in his body and screaming, except that he wasn't equipped to clutch at anything just at present. "Appearances can be so damning," he purred in Illyan's ear, sinking in Illyan's arms. He grinned evilly through clenched teeth. His body shook, shocky, the sheen of cold sweat on his forehead quite unfeigned.

Illyan frowned at him, but put him back to bed very carefully.

"It's all right," Miles wheezed to the doctor. "It's all right. I was merely . . . merely . . ." *Upset* didn't quite seem to cover it; he'd felt for a moment as if the top of his head had been about to blow off. "Never mind." He felt horribly unbalanced. To think that Illyan, whom he'd known all his life, whom he'd assumed trusted him implicitly or why else send him on a series of such distant, independent missions . . . He'd been proud to be so trusted, while still a young officer, with so little direct supervision in his covert ops . . . Could his whole career to date have been, not desperately needed Service to the Imperium, but just a ploy to get a dangerously clumsy Vor puppy out from underfoot? Toy soldiers . . . no, that made no sense. A peculator. Ugly word. What a profound slur upon his honor, and his wit; as if he did not know where Imperial funds came from, or at what cost.

The black anger sagged into a black depression. His heart hurt. He felt smeared. Could Illyan—Illyan! —really think, even for one hypothetical moment. . . . Yes, Illyan could. Illyan would not be here, not doing this, if he were not genuinely worried the charge could be proved true. To his dismay, Miles found himself silently crying. *Damn* the drugs.

Illyan was staring at him in considerable disquiet. "One way or another, Miles, I must defend your expenditures—which are my department's expenditures—tomorrow."

"I'd rather be court-martialed."

Illyan's lips thinned. "I'll come back later. When you've had a chance to sleep. Perhaps you'll be more coherent."

The doctor fussed over him, zapped him with yet another damned drug, and left. Leadenly, Miles turned his face to the wall; not to sleep, but to remember.

The Mountains of Mourning

Miles heard the woman weeping as he was climbing the hill from the long lake. He hadn't dried himself after his swim, as the morning already promised shimmering heat. Lake water trickled cool from his hair onto his naked chest and back, more annoyingly down his legs from his ragged shorts. His leg braces chafed on his damp skin as he pistoned up the faint trail through the scrub, military double-time. His feet squished in his old wet shoes. He slowed curiously as he became conscious of the voices.

The woman's voice grated with grief and exhaustion. "Please, lord, please. All I want is m'justice . . ."

The front gate guard's voice was irritated and embarrassed. "I'm no lord. C'mon, get *up*, woman. Go back to the village and report it at the district magistrate's office."

"I tell you, I just came from there!" The woman did not move from her knees as Miles emerged from the bushes and paused to take in the tableau across the paved road. "The magistrate's not to return for

weeks, weeks. I walked four days to get here. I only
have a little money. . . ." A desperate hope rose in
her voice, and her spine bent and straightened as
she scrabbled in her skirt pocket and held out her
cupped hands to the guard. "A mark and twenty
pence, it's all I have, but—"

The exasperated guard's eye fell on Miles, and he
straightened abruptly, as if afraid Miles might suspect him of being tempted by so pitiful a bribe. "Be
off, woman!" he snapped.

Miles quirked an eyebrow, and limped across the
road to the main gate. "What's all this about, Corporal?" he inquired easily.

The guard corporal was on loan from Imperial
Security, and wore the high-necked dress greens of
the Barrayaran Service. He was sweating and uncomfortable in the bright morning light of this south-
ern district, but Miles fancied he'd be boiled before
he'd undo his collar on this post. His accent was not
local, he was a city man from the capital, where a
more-or-less efficient bureaucracy absorbed such problems as the one on her knees before him.

The woman, now, was local and more than local—
she had backcountry written all over her. She was
younger than her strained voice had at first suggested. Tall, fever-red from her weeping, with stringy
blonde hair hanging down across a ferret-thin face
and protuberant grey eyes. If she were cleaned up,
fed, rested, happy and confident, she might achieve
a near-prettiness, but she was far from that now,
despite her remarkable figure. Lean but full-breasted
—no, Miles revised himself as he crossed the road
and came up to the gate. Her bodice was all blotched
with dried milk leaks, though there was no baby in
sight. Only temporarily full-breasted. Her worn dress
was factory-woven cloth, but hand-sewn, crude and

simple. Her feet were bare, thickly-callused, cracked and sore.

"No problem," the guard assured Miles. "Go *away*," he hissed to the woman.

She lurched off her knees and sat stonily.

"I'll call my sergeant," the guard eyed her warily, "and have her removed."

"Wait a moment," said Miles.

She stared up at Miles from her cross-legged position, clearly not knowing whether to identify him as hope or not. His clothing, what there was of it, offered her no clue as to what he might be. The rest of him was all too plainly displayed. He jerked up his chin and smiled thinly. Too-large head, too-short neck, back thickened with its crooked spine, crooked legs with their brittle bones too-often broken, drawing the eye in their gleaming chromium braces. Were the hill woman standing, the top of his head would barely be even with the top of her shoulder. He waited in boredom for her hand to make the back-country hex sign against evil mutations, but it only jerked and clenched into a fist.

"I must see my lord Count," she said to an uncertain point halfway between Miles and the guard. "It's my right. My daddy, he died in the Service. It's my right."

"Prime Minister Count Vorkosigan," said the guard stiffly, "is on his country estate to rest. If he were working, he'd be back in Vorbarr Sultana." The guard looked like he wished *he* were back in Vorbarr Sultana.

The woman seized the pause. "You're only a city man. He's *my* count. My right."

"What do you want to see Count Vorkosigan for?" asked Miles patiently.

"Murder," growled the girl/woman. The security guard spasmed slightly. "I want to report a murder."

"Shouldn't you report to your village speaker first?" inquired Miles, with a hand-down gesture to calm the twitching guard.

"I did. He'll do *nothing*." Rage and frustration cracked her voice. "He says it's over and done. He won't write down my accusation, says it's nonsense. It would only make trouble for everybody, he says. I don't care! I want my justice!"

Miles frowned thoughtfully, looking the woman over. The details checked, corroborated her claimed identity, added up to a solid if subliminal sense of authentic truth which perhaps escaped the professionally paranoid security man. "It's true, Corporal," Miles said. "She has a right to appeal, first to the district magistrate, then to the count's court. And the district magistrate won't be back for two weeks."

This sector of Count Vorkosigan's native district had only one overworked district magistrate, who rode a circuit that included the lakeside village of Vorkosigan Surleau but one day a month. Since the region of the Prime Minister's country estate was crawling with Imperial Security when the great lord was in residence, and closely monitored even when he was not, prudent troublemakers took their troubles elsewhere.

"Scan her, and let her in," said Miles. "On my authority."

The guard was one of Imperial Security's best, trained to look for assassins in his own shadow. He now looked scandalized, and lowered his voice to Miles. "Sir, if I let every country lunatic wander the estate at will—"

"I'll take her up. I'm going that way."

The guard shrugged helplessly, but stopped short of saluting; Miles was decidedly not in uniform. The gate guard pulled a scanner from his belt and made a great show of going over the woman. Miles wondered if he'd have been inspired to harass her with a strip-search without Miles's inhibiting presence. When the guard finished demonstrating how alert, conscientious, and loyal he was, he palmed open the gate's lock, entered the transaction, including the woman's retina scan, into the computer monitor, and stood aside in a pose of rather pointed parade rest. Miles grinned at the silent editorial, and steered the bedraggled woman by the elbow through the gates and up the winding drive.

She twitched away from his touch at the earliest opportunity, yet still refrained from superstitious gestures, eyeing him with a strange and hungry curiosity. Time was, such openly repelled fascination with the peculiarities of his body had driven Miles to grind his teeth; now he could take it with a serene amusement only slightly tinged with acid. They would learn, all of them. They would learn.

"Do you serve Count Vorkosigan, little man?" she asked cautiously.

Miles thought about that one a moment. "Yes," he answered finally. The answer was, after all, true on every level of meaning but the one she'd asked it. He quelled the temptation to tell her he was the court jester. From the look of her, this one's troubles were much worse than his own.

She had apparently not quite believed in her own rightful destiny, despite her mulish determination at the gate, for as they climbed unimpeded toward her goal a nascent panic made her face even more drawn and pale, almost ill. "How—how do I talk to him?" she choked. "Should I curtsey . . . ?" She glanced down at herself as if conscious for the first time of her own dirt and sweat and squalor.

Miles suppressed a facetious set-up starting with,

Kneel and knock your forehead three times on the floor before speaking, that's what the General Staff does, and said instead, "Just stand up straight and speak the truth. Try to be clear. He'll take it from there. He does not, after all," Miles's lips twitched, "lack experience."

She swallowed.

A hundred years ago, the Vorkosigans' summer retreat had been a guard barracks, part of the outlying fortifications of the great castle on the bluff above the village of Vorkosigan Surleau. The castle was now a burnt-out ruin, and the barracks transformed into a comfortable low stone residence, modernized and re-modernized, artistically landscaped and bright with flowers. The arrow slits had been widened into big glass windows overlooking the lake, and comm link antennae bristled from the roof. There was a new guard barracks concealed in the trees downslope, but it had no arrow slits.

A man in the brown-and-silver livery of the Count's personal retainers exited the residence's front door as Miles approached with the strange woman in tow. It was the new man, what was his name? Pym, that was it.

"Where's m'lord Count?" Miles asked him.

"In the upper pavilion, taking breakfast with m'lady." Pym glanced at the woman, waited on Miles in a posture of polite inquiry.

"Ah. Well, this woman has walked four days to lay an appeal before the district magistrate's court. The court's not here, but the Count is, so she now proposes to skip the middlemen and go straight to the top. I like her style. Take her up, will you?"

"During *breakfast*?" said Pym.

Miles cocked his head at the woman. "Have you had breakfast?"

She shook her head mutely.

"I thought not." Miles turned his hands palm-out, dumping her, symbolically, on the retainer. "Now, yes."

"My daddy, he died in the Service," the woman repeated faintly. "It's my right." The phrase seemed as much to convince herself as anyone else, now.

Pym was, if not a hill man, district-born. "So it is," he sighed, and gestured her to follow him without further ado. Her eyes widened, as she trailed him around the house, and she glanced back nervously over her shoulder at Miles. "Little man . . . ?"

"Just stand straight," he called to her. He watched her round the corner, grinned, and took the steps two at a time into the residence's main entrance.

After a shave and cold shower, Miles dressed in his own room overlooking the long lake. He dressed with great care, as great as he'd expended on the Service Academy ceremonies and Imperial Review two days ago. Clean underwear, long-sleeved cream shirt, dark green trousers with the side piping. High-collared green tunic tailor-cut to his own difficult fit. New pale blue plastic ensign's rectangles aligned precisely on the collar and poking most uncomfortably into his jaw. He dispensed with the leg braces and pulled on mirror-polished boots to the knee, and swiped a bit of dust from them with his pajama pants, ready-to-hand on the floor where he'd dropped them before going swimming.

He straightened and checked himself in the mirror. His dark hair hadn't even begun to recover from that last cut before the graduation ceremonies. A pale, sharp-featured face, not too much dissipated bag under the grey eyes, nor too bloodshot—alas, the limits of his body compelled him to stop celebrating well before he could hurt himself.

Echoes of the late celebration still boiled up silently in his head, crooking his mouth into a grin. He was on his way now, had his hand clamped firmly around the lowest rung of the highest ladder on Barrayar, Imperial Service itself. There were no giveaways in the Service even for sons of the old Vor. You got what you earned. His brother-officers could be relied on to know that, even if outsiders wondered. He was in position at last to prove himself to all doubters. Up and away and never look down, never look back.

One last look back. As carefully as he'd dressed, Miles gathered up the necessary objects for his task. The white cloth rectangles of his former Academy cadet's rank. The hand-calligraphed second copy, purchased for this purpose, of his new officer's commission in the Barrayaran Imperial Service. A copy of his Academy three-year scholastic transcript on paper, with all its commendations (and demerits). No point in anything but honesty in this next transaction. In a cupboard downstairs he found the brass brazier and tripod, wrapped in its polishing cloth, and a plastic bag of very dry juniper bark. Chemical firesticks.

Out the back door and up the hill. The landscaped path split, right going up to the pavilion overlooking it all, left forking sideways to a garden-like area surrounded by a low fieldstone wall. Miles let himself in by the gate. "Good morning, crazy ancestors," he called, then quelled his humor. It might be true, but lacked the respect due the occasion.

He strolled over and around the graves until he came to the one he sought, knelt, and set up the brazier and tripod, humming. The stone was simple,

General Count Piotr Pierre Vorkosigan, and the dates. If they'd tried to list all the accumulated honors and accomplishments, they'd have had to go to microprint.

He piled in the bark, the very expensive papers, the cloth bits, a clipped mat of dark hair from that last cut. He set it alight and rocked back on his heels to watch it burn. He'd played a hundred versions of this moment over in his head, over the years, ranging from solemn public orations with musicians in the background, to dancing naked on the old man's grave. He'd settled on this private and traditional ceremony, played straight. Just between the two of them.

"So, Grandfather," he purred at last. "And here we are after all. Satisfied now?"

All the chaos of the graduation ceremonies behind, all the mad efforts of the last three years, all the pain, came to this point; but the grave did not speak, did not say, *Well done; you can stop now*. The ashes spelled out no messages, there were no visions to be had in the rising smoke. The brazier burned down all too quickly. Not enough stuff in it, perhaps.

He stood, and dusted his knees, in the silence and the sunlight. So what had he expected? Applause? Why was he here, in the final analysis? Dancing out a dead man's dreams—who did his Service really serve? Grandfather? Himself? Pale Emperor Gregor? Who cared?

"Well, old man," he whispered, then shouted: "ARE YOU SATISFIED YET?" The echoes rang from the stones.

A throat cleared behind him, and Miles whirled like a scalded cat, heart pounding.

"Uh . . . my lord?" said Pym carefully. "Pardon me, I did not mean to interrupt . . . anything. But the Count your father requires you to attend on him in the upper pavilion."

Pym's expression was perfectly bland. Miles swallowed, and waited for the scarlet heat he could feel in his face to recede. "Quite," he shrugged. "The fire's almost out. I'll clean it up later. Don't . . . let anybody else touch it."

He marched past Pym and didn't look back.

The pavilion was a simple structure of weathered silver wood, open on all four sides to catch the breeze, this morning a few faint puffs from the west. Good sailing on the lake this afternoon, maybe. Only ten days precious home leave left, and much Miles wanted to do, including the trip to Vorbarr Sultana with his cousin Ivan to pick out his new lightflyer. And then his first assignment would be coming through—ship duty, Miles prayed. He'd had to overcome a major temptation, not to ask his father to make sure it was ship duty. He would take whatever assignment fate dealt him, that was the first rule of the game. And win with the hand he was dealt.

The interior of the pavilion was shady and cool after the glare outside. It was furnished with comfortable old chairs and tables, one of which bore the remains of a noble breakfast—Miles mentally marked two lonely-looking oil cakes on a crumb-scattered tray as his own. Miles's mother, lingering over her cup, smiled across the table at him.

Miles's father, casually dressed in an open-throated shirt and shorts, sat in a worn armchair. Aral Vorkosigan was a thick-set, grey-haired man, heavy-jawed, heavy-browed, scarred. A face that lent itself to savage caricature—Miles had seen some, in Opposition press, in the histories of Barrayar's enemies. They had only to draw one lie, to render dull those sharp penetrating eyes, to create everyone's parody of a military dictator.

And how much is he haunted by Grandfather? Miles wondered. He doesn't show it much. But then, he doesn't have to. Admiral Aral Vorkosigan, space master strategist, conquerer of Komarr, hero of Escobar, for sixteen years Imperial Regent and supreme power on Barrayar in all but name. And then he'd capped it, confounded history and all self-sure witnesses and heaped up honor and glory beyond all that had gone before by voluntarily stepping *down* and transferring command smoothly to Emperor Gregor upon his majority. Not that the Prime Ministership hadn't made a dandy retirement from the Regency, and he was showing no signs yet of stepping down from *that*.

And so Admiral Aral's life took General Piotr's like an overpowering hand of cards, and where did that leave Ensign Miles? Holding two deuces and the joker. He must surely either concede or start bluffing like crazy. . . .

The hill woman sat on a hassock, a half-eaten oil cake clutched in her hands, staring open-mouthed at Miles in all his power and polish. As he caught and returned her gaze her lips pressed closed and her eyes lit. Her expression was strange—anger? Exhilaration? Embarrassment? Glee? Some bizarre mixture of all? *And what did you think I was, woman?*

Being in uniform (showing off his uniform?), Miles came to attention before his father. "Sir?"

Count Vorkosigan spoke to the woman. "That is my son. If I send him as my Voice, would that satisfy you?"

"Oh," she breathed, her wide mouth drawing back in a weird, fierce grin, the most expression Miles had yet seen on her face, "*yes*, my lord."

"Very well. It will be done."

What will be done? Miles wondered warily. The Count was leaning back in his chair, looking satisfied himself, but with a dangerous tension around his eyes hinting that something had aroused his true anger. Not anger at the woman, clearly they were in some sort of agreement, and—Miles searched his conscience quickly—not at Miles himself. He cleared his throat gently, cocking his head and baring his teeth in an inquiring smile.

The Count steepled his hands and spoke to Miles at last. "A most interesting case. I can see why you sent her up."

"Ah . . ." said Miles. What had he got hold of? He'd only greased the woman's way through Security on a quixotic impulse, for God's sake, and to tweak his father at breakfast. ". . . ah?" he continued noncommittally.

Count Vorkosigan's brows rose. "Did you not know?"

"She spoke of a murder, and a marked lack of cooperation from her local authorities about it. Figured you'd give her a lift on to the district magistrate."

The Count settled back still further, and rubbed his hand thoughtfully across his scarred chin. "It's an infanticide case."

Miles's belly went cold. *I don't want anything to do with this.* Well, that explained why there was no baby to go with the breasts. "Unusual . . . for it to be reported."

"We've fought the old customs for twenty years and more," said the Count. "Promulgated, propagandized . . . In the cities, we've made good progress."

"In the cities," murmured the Countess, "people have access to alternatives."

"But in the backcountry—well—little has changed.

We all know what's going on, but without a report, a complaint—and with the family invariably drawing together to protect its own—it's hard to get leverage."

"What," Miles cleared his throat, nodded at the woman, "what was your baby's mutation?"

"The cat's mouth," the woman dabbed at her upper lip to demonstrate. "She had the hole inside her mouth, too, and was a weak sucker, she choked and cried, but she was getting enough, she *was*. . . ."

"Hare-lip," the Count's off-worlder wife murmured half to herself, translating the Barrayaran term to the galactic standard, "and a cleft palate, sounds like. Harra, that's not even a mutation. They had that back on Old Earth. A . . . a normal birth defect, if that's not a contradiction in terms. Not a punishment for your Barrayaran ancestors' pilgrimage through the Fire. A simple operation could have corrected—" Countess Vorkosigan cut herself off. The hill woman was looking anguished.

"I'd heard," the woman said. "My lord had made a hospital to be built at Hassadar. I meant to take her there, when I was a little stronger, though I had no money. Her arms and legs were sound, her head was well-shaped, anybody could see—surely they would have—" her hands clenched and twisted, her voice went ragged, "but Lem killed her first."

A seven-day walk, Miles calculated, from the deep Dendarii Mountains to the lowland town of Hassadar. Reasonable, that a woman newly risen from childbed might delay that hike a few days. An hour's ride in an aircar. . . .

"So one is reported as a murder at last," said Count Vorkosigan, "and we will treat it as exactly that. This is a chance to send a message to the farthest corners of my own district. You, Miles, will be my Voice, to reach where it has not reached before. You will dispense Count's justice upon this man—and not quietly, either. It's time for the practices that brand us as barbarians in galactic eyes to end."

Miles gulped. "Wouldn't the district magistrate be better qualified . . . ?"

The Count smiled slightly. "For this case, I can think of no one better qualified than yourself."

The messenger and the message all in one; *Times have changed.* Indeed. Miles wished himself elsewhere, anywhere—back sweating blood over his final examinations, for instance. He stifled an unworthy wail, *My home leave . . . !*

Miles rubbed the back of his neck. "Who, ah . . . who is it killed your little girl?" *Meaning, who is it I'm expected to drag out, put up against a wall, and shoot?*

"My husband," she said tonelessly, looking at—through—the polished silvery floorboards.

I knew this was going to be messy. . . .

"She cried and cried," the woman went on, "and wouldn't go to sleep, not nursing well—he shouted at me to shut her up—"

"Then?" Miles prompted, sick to his stomach.

"He swore at me, and went to go sleep at his mother's. He said at least a working man could sleep there. I hadn't slept either. . . ."

This guy sounds like a real winner. Miles had an instant picture of him, a bull of a man with a bullying manner—nevertheless, there was something missing in the climax of the woman's story.

The Count had picked up on it too. He was listening with total attention, his strategy-session look, a slit-eyed intensity of thought you could mistake for sleepiness. That would be a grave mistake. "Were you an eyewitness?" he asked in a deceptively mild tone that put Miles on full alert. "Did you actually see him kill her?"

"I found her dead in the midmorning, lord."

"You went into the bedroom—" Count Vorkosigan led her on.

"We've only got one room." She shot him a look as if doubtful for the first time of his total omniscience. "She had slept, slept at last. I went out to get some brillberries, up the ravine a way. And when I came back . . . I should have taken her with me, but I was so glad she slept at last, didn't want to risk waking her—" tears leaked from the woman's tightly-closed eyes. "I let her sleep when I came back, I was glad to eat and rest, but I began to get full," her hand touched a breast, "and I went to wake her . . ."

"What, were there no marks on her? Not a cut throat?" asked the Count. That was the usual method for these backcountry infanticides, quick and clean compared to, say, exposure.

The woman shook her head. "Smothered, I think, lord. It was cruel, something cruel. The village Speaker said I must have overlain her, and wouldn't take my plea against Lem. I did not, I did not! She had her own cradle, Lem made it with his own hands when she was still in my belly. . . ." She was close to breaking down.

The Count exchanged a glance with his wife, and a small tilt of his head. Countess Vorkosigan rose smoothly.

"Come, Harra, down to the house. You must wash and rest before Miles takes you home."

The hill woman looked taken aback. "Oh, not in your house, lady!"

"Sorry, it's the only one I've got handy. Besides the guard barracks. The guards are good boys, but you'd make 'em uncomfortable . . ." The Countess eased her out.

"It is clear," said Count Vorkosigan as soon as the women were out of earshot, "that you will have to check out the medical facts before, er, popping off. And I trust you will also have noticed the little problem with a positive identification of the accused. This could be the ideal public-demonstration case we want, but not if there's any ambiguity about it. No bloody mysteries."

"I'm not a coroner," Miles pointed out immediately. If he could wriggle off this hook. . . .

"Quite. You will take Dr. Dea with you."

Lieutenant Dea was the Prime Minister's physician's assistant. Miles had seen him around—an ambitious young military doctor, in a constant state of frustration because his superior would never let him touch his most important patient—oh, he was going to be thrilled with this assignment, Miles predicted morosely.

"He can take his osteo kit with him, too," the Count went on, brightening slightly, "in case of accidents."

"How economical," said Miles, rolling his eyes. "Look, uh—suppose her story checks out and we nail this guy. Do I have to, personally . . . ?"

"One of the liveried men will be your bodyguard. And—if the story checks—the executioner."

That was only slightly better. "Couldn't we wait for the district magistrate?"

"Every judgment the district magistrate makes, he makes in my place. Every sentence his office carries out, is carried out in my name. Someday, it will be done in your name. It's time you gained a clear understanding of the process. Historically, the Vor may be a military caste, but a Vor lord's duties were never only military ones."

No escape. Damn, damn, damn. Miles sighed. "Right. Well . . . we could take the aircar, I suppose, and be up there in a couple of hours. Allow some time to find the right hole. Drop out of the sky on 'em, make the message loud and clear . . . be back before bedtime." Get it over with quickly.

The Count had that slit-eyed look again. "No . . ." he said slowly, "not the aircar, I don't think."

"No roads for a groundcar, up that far. Just trails." He added uneasily—surely his father could not be thinking of—"I don't think I'd cut a very impressive figure of central Imperial authority on foot, sir."

His father glanced up at his crisp dress uniform and smiled slightly. "Oh, you don't do so badly."

"But picture this after three or four days of beating through the bushes," Miles protested. "You didn't see us in Basic. Or smell us."

"I've been there," said the Admiral dryly. "But no, you're quite right. Not on foot. I have a better idea."

My own cavalry troop, thought Miles ironically, turning in his saddle, *just like Grandfather*. Actually, he was pretty sure the old man would have had some acerbic comments about the riders now strung out behind Miles on the wooded trail, once he'd got done rolling on the ground laughing at the equitation being displayed. The Vorkosigan stables had shrunk sadly since the old man was no longer around to take an interest, the polo string sold off, the few remaining ancient and ill-tempered ex-cavalry beasts put permanently out to pasture. The handful of riding horses left were retained for their sure-footedness and good manners, not their exotic bloodlines, and kept exercised and gentle for the occasional guest by a gaggle of girls from the village.

Miles gathered his reins, tensed one calf, and shifted his weight slightly, and Fat Ninny responded with a neat half turn and two precise back steps. The thickset roan gelding could not have been mistaken by the most ignorant urbanite for a fiery steed, but Miles adored him, for his dark and liquid eye, his wide velvet nose, his phlegmatic disposition equally unappalled by rushing streams or screaming aircars, but most of all for his exquisite dressage-trained responsiveness. Brains before beauty. Just being around him made Miles calmer, the beast was an emotional blotter, like a purring cat. Miles patted Fat Ninny on the neck. "If anybody asks," he murmured, "I'll tell them your name is Chieftan." Fat Ninny waggled one fuzzy ear, and heaved a wooshing, barrel-chested sigh.

Grandfather had a great deal to do with the unlikely parade Miles now led. The great guerilla general had poured out his youth in these mountains, fighting the Cetagandan invaders to a standstill and then reversing their tide. Anti-flyer heatless seeker-strikers smuggled in at bloody cost from off-planet had a lot more to do with the final victory than cavalry horses, which, according to Grandfather, had saved his forces through the worst winter of that campaign mainly by being edible. But through retroactive romance, the horse had become the symbol of that struggle.

Miles thought his father was being overly optimistic, if he thought Miles was going to cash in thusly on the old man's residual glory. The guerilla caches and camps were shapeless lumps of rust and *trees,* dammit, not just weeds and scrub anymore—they had passed some, earlier in today's ride—the men who had fought that war had long since gone to ground for the last time, just like Grandfather. What was he doing here? It was Jump ship duty he wanted, taking him high, high above all this. The future, not the past, held his destiny.

Miles's meditations were interrupted by Dr. Dea's horse, which, taking exception to a branch lying across the logging trail, planted all four feet in an abrupt stop and snorted loudly. Dr. Dea toppled off with a faint cry.

"Hang onto the *reins*," Miles called, and pressed Fat Ninny back down the trail.

Dr. Dea was getting rather better at falling off, he'd landed more-or-less on his feet this time. He made a lunge at the dangling reins, but his sorrel mare shied away from his grab. Dea jumped back as she swung on her haunches and then, realizing her freedom, bounced back down the trail, tail bannering, horse body-language for *Nyah, nyah, ya can't catch me!* Dr. Dea, red and furious, ran swearing in pursuit. She broke into a canter.

"No, no, don't run after her!" called Miles.

"How the hell am I supposed to catch her if I don't run after her?" snarled Dea. The space surgeon was not a happy man. "My medkit's on that bloody beast!"

"How do you think you can catch her if you do?" asked Miles. "She can run faster than you can."

At the end of the little column, Pym turned his horse sideways, blocking the trail. "Just wait, Harra," Miles advised the anxious hill woman in passing. "Hold your horse still. Nothing starts a horse running faster than another running horse."

The other two riders were doing rather better. The woman Harra Csurik sat her horse wearily, allowing it to plod along without interference, but at least riding on balance instead of trying to use the reins as a handle like the unfortunate Dea. Pym, bringing up the rear, was competent if not comfortable.

Miles slowed Fat Ninny to a walk, reins loose, and wandered after the mare, radiating an air of calm relaxation. *Who, me? I don't want to catch you. We're just enjoying the scenery, right. That's it, stop for a bite.* The sorrel mare paused to nibble at a weed, but kept a wary eye on Miles's approach.

At a distance just short of starting the mare bolting off again, Miles stopped Fat Ninny and slid off. He made no move toward the mare, but instead stood still and made a great show of fishing in his pockets. Fat Ninny butted his head against Miles eagerly, and Miles cooed and fed him a bit of sugar. The mare cocked her ears with interest. Fat Ninny smacked his lips and nudged for more. The mare snuffled up for her share. She lipped a cube from Miles's palm as he slid his other arm quietly through the loop of her reins.

"Here you go, Dr. Dea. One horse. No running."

"No fair," wheezed Dea, trudging up. "You had sugar in your pockets."

"Of course I had sugar in my pockets. It's called foresight and planning. The trick of handling horses isn't to be faster than the horse, or stronger than the horse. That pits your weakness against his strengths. The trick is to be smarter than the horse. That pits your strength against his weakness, eh?"

Dea took his reins. "It's snickering at me," he said suspiciously.

"That's nickering, not snickering," Miles grinned. He tapped Fat Ninny behind his left foreleg, and the horse obediently grunted down onto one knee. Miles clambered up readily to his conveniently-lowered stirrup.

"Does mine do that?" asked Dr. Dea, watching with fascination.

"Sorry, no."

Dea glowered at his horse. "This animal is an idiot. I shall lead it for a while."

As Fat Ninny lurched back to his four feet Miles suppressed a riding-instructorly comment gleaned from his Grandfather's store such as, *Be smarter than the horse, Dea*. Though Dr. Dea was officially sworn to Lord Vorkosigan for the duration of this investigation, Space Surgeon Lieutenant Dea certainly outranked Ensign Vorkosigan. To command older men who outranked one called for a certain measure of tact.

The logging road widened out here, and Miles dropped back beside Harra Csurik. Her fierceness and determination of yesterday morning at the gate seemed to be fading even as the trail rose toward her home. Or perhaps it was simply exhaustion catching up with her. She'd said little all morning, been sunk in silence all afternoon. If she was going to drag Miles all the way up to the back of beyond and then wimp out on him . . .

"What, ah, branch of the Service was your father in, Harra?" Miles began conversationally.

She raked her fingers through her hair in a combing gesture more nervousness than vanity. Her eyes looked out at him through the straw-colored wisps like skittish creatures in the protection of a hedge.

"District Militia, m'lord. I don't really remember him, he died when I was real little."

"In combat?"

She nodded. "In the fighting around Vorbarr Sultana, during Vordarian's Pretendership."

Miles refrained from asking which side he had been swept up on—most footsoldiers had had little choice, and the amnesty had included the dead as well as the living.

"Ah . . . do you have any sibs?"

"No, lord. Just me and my mother left."

A little anticipatory tension eased in Miles's neck. If this judgment indeed drove all the way through to an execution, one misstep could trigger a blood feud among the in-laws. *Not* the legacy of justice the Count intended him to leave behind. So the fewer in-laws involved, the better. "What about your husband's family?"

"He's got seven. Four brothers and three sisters."

"Hm." Miles had a mental flash of an entire team of huge, menacing hill hulks. He glanced back at Pym, feeling a trifle understaffed for his task. He had pointed out this factor to the Count, when they'd been planning this expedition last night.

"The village Speaker and his deputies will be your back-up," the Count had said, "just as for the district magistrate on court circuit."

"What if they don't want to cooperate?" Miles had asked nervously.

"An officer who expects to command Imperial troops," the Count had glinted, "should be able to figure out how to extract cooperation from a backcountry headman."

In other words, his father had decided this was a test, and wasn't going to give him any more clues. Thanks, Dad.

"You have no sibs, lord?" said Harra, snapping him back to the present.

"No. But surely that's known, even in the back-beyond."

"They *say* a lot of things about you," Harra shrugged.

Miles bit down on the morbid question in his mouth like a wedge of raw lemon. He would not ask

it, he would not . . . he couldn't help himself. "Like
what?" forced out past his stiff lips.

"Everyone knows the Count's son is a mutant."
Her eyes flicked defiant-wide. "Some said it came
from the off-worlder woman he married. Some said it
was from radiation from the wars, or a disease from,
um, corrupt practices in his youth among his brother-
officers—"

That last was a new one to Miles. His brow lifted.

"—but most say he was poisoned by his enemies."

"I'm glad most have it right. It was an assassination attempt using soltoxin gas, when my mother was
pregnant with me. But it's not—*a mutation*, his
thought hiccoughed through the well-worn grooves—
how many times had he explained this?—*it's teratogenic,
not genetic, I'm not a mutant, not. . . .* What the
hell did a fine point of biochemistry matter to this
ignorant, bereaved woman? For all practical purposes
—for her purposes—he might as well be a mutant.
"—important," he finished.

She eyed him sideways, swaying gently in the
clop-a-clop rhythm of her mount. "Some said you
were born with no legs, and lived all the time in a
float chair in Vorkosigan House. Some said you were
born with no bones—"

"—and kept in a jar in the basement, no doubt,"
Miles muttered.

"But Karal said he'd seen you with your grandfather at Hassadar Fair, and you were only sickly and
undersized. Some said your father had got you into
the Service, but others said no, you'd gone off-planet
to your mother's home and had your brain turned
into a computer and your body fed with tubes, floating in a liquid—"

"I knew there'd be a jar turn up in this story
somewhere," Miles grimaced. *You knew you'd be*

sorry you asked, too, but you went and did it anyway.
She was baiting him, Miles realized suddenly. How *dare* she . . . but there was no humor in her, only a sharp-edged watchfulness.

She had gone out, way out on a limb to lay this murder charge, in defiance of family and local authorities alike, in defiance of established custom. And what had her Count given her for a shield and support, going back to face the wrath of all her nearest and dearest? Miles. Could he handle this? She must be wondering indeed. Or would he botch it, cave and cut and run, leaving her to face the whirlwind of rage and revenge alone?

He wished he'd left her weeping at the gate.

The woodland, fruit of many generations of terraforming forestry, opened out suddenly on a vale of brown native scrub. Down the middle of it, through some accident of soil chemistry, ran a half-kilometer-wide swathe of green and pink—feral roses, Miles realized with astonishment as they rode nearer. Earth roses. The track dove into the fragrant mass of them and vanished.

He took turns with Pym, hacking their way through with their Service bush knives. The roses were vigorous and studded with thick thorns, and hacked back with a vicious elastic recoil. Fat Ninny did his part by swinging his big head back and forth and nipping off blooms and chomping them down happily. Miles wasn't sure just how many he ought to let the big roan eat—just because the species wasn't native to Barrayar didn't mean it wasn't poisonous to horses. Miles sucked at his wounds and reflected upon Barrayar's shattered ecological history.

The fifty thousand Firsters from Earth had only meant to be the spearhead of Barrayar's colonization. Then, through a gravitational anomoly, the wormhole jump through which the colonists had come shifted closed, irrevocably and without warning. The terraforming which had begun, so careful and controlled in the beginning, collapsed along with everything else. Imported Earth plant and animal species had escaped everywhere to run wild, as the humans turned their attention to the most urgent problems of survival. Biologists still mourned the mass extinctions of native species that had followed, the erosions and droughts and floods, but really, Miles thought, over the centuries of the Time of Isolation the fittest of both worlds had fought it out to a perfectly good new balance. If it was alive and covered the ground who cared where it came from?

We are all here by accident. Like the roses.

They camped that night high in the hills, and pushed on in the morning to the flanks of the true mountains. They were now out of the region Miles was personally familiar with from his childhood, and he checked Harra's directions frequently on his orbital survey map. They stopped only a few hours short of their goal at sunset of the second day. Harra insisted she could lead them on in the dusk from here, but Miles did not care to arrive after nightfall, unannounced, in a strange place of uncertain welcome.

He bathed the next morning in a stream, and unpacked and dressed carefully in his new officer's Imperial dress greens. Pym wore the Vorkosigan brown-and-silver livery, and pulled the Count's standard on a telescoping aluminum pole from the recesses of his saddlebag and mounted it on his left stirrup. *Dressed to kill*, thought Miles joylessly. Dr. Dea wore ordinary black fatigues and looked uncomfortable. If they constituted a message, Miles was damned if he knew what it was.

They pulled the horses up at midmorning before a
two-room cabin set on the edge of a vast grove of
sugar maples, planted who-knew-how-many centuries ago but now raggedly marching up the vale by
self-seeding. The mountain air was cool and pure and
bright. A few chickens stalked and bobbed in the
weeds. An algae-choked wooden pipe from the woods
dribbled water into a trough, which overflowed into
a squishy green streamlet and away.

Harra slid down and smoothed her skirt and climbed
the porch. "Karal?" she called. Miles waited high on
horseback for the initial contact. Never give up a
psychological advantage.

"Harra? Is that you?" came a man's voice from
within. He banged open the door and rushed out.
"Where have you been, girl? We've been beating
the bushes for you! Thought you'd broke your neck
in the scrub somewhere—" he stopped short before
the three silent men on horseback.

"You wouldn't write down my charges, Karal,"
said Harra rather breathlessly. Her hands kneaded
her skirt. "So I walked to the district magistrate at
Vorkosigan Surleau to Speak them myself."

"Oh, girl," Karal breathed regretfully, "that was a
stupid thing to do . . ." His head lowered and swayed,
as he stared uneasily at the riders. He was a balding
man of maybe sixty, leathery and worn, and his left
arm ended in a stump. Another veteran.

"Speaker Serg Karal?" began Miles sternly. "I am
the Voice of Count Vorkosigan. I am charged to
investigate the crime Spoken by Harra Csurik before
the Count's court, namely the murder of her infant
daughter Raina. As Speaker of Silvy Vale, you are
requested and required to assist me in all matters
pertaining to the Count's justice."

At this point Miles ran out of prescribed formalities, and was on his own. That hadn't taken long. He waited. Fat Ninny snuffled. The silver-on-brown cloth of the standard made a few soft snapping sounds, lifted by a vagrant breeze.

"The district magistrate wasn't there," put in Harra, "but the Count was."

Karal was grey-faced, staring. He pulled himself together with an effort, came to a species of attention, and essayed a creaking half-bow. "Who—who are you, sir?"

"Lord Miles Vorkosigan."

Karal's lips moved silently. Miles was no lip reader, but he was pretty sure it came to a dismayed variant of *Oh, shit*. "This is my liveried man Sergeant Pym, and my medical examiner, Lieutenant Dea of the Imperial Service."

"You are my lord Count's son?" Karal croaked.

"The one and only." Miles was suddenly sick of the posing. Surely that was a sufficient first impression. He swung down off Ninny, landing lightly on the balls of his feet. Karal's gaze followed him down, and down. *Yeah, so I'm short. But wait'll you see me dance.* "All right if we water our horses in your trough here?" Miles looped Ninny's reins through his arm and stepped toward it.

"Uh, that's for the people, m'lord," said Karal. "Just a minute and I'll fetch a bucket." He hitched up his baggy trousers and trotted off around the side of the cabin. A minute's uncomfortable silence, then Karal's voice floating faintly, "Where'd you put the goat bucket, Zed?"

Another voice, light and young, "Behind the woodstack, Da." The voices fell to a muffled undertone. Karal came trotting back with a battered aluminum bucket, which he placed beside the trough. He knocked out a wooden plug in the side and a bright stream arced out to splash and fill. Fat Ninny flickered his ears and snuffled and rubbed his big head against Miles, smearing his tunic with red and white horsehairs and nearly knocking him off his feet. Karal glanced up and smiled at the horse, though his smile fell away as his gaze passed on to the horse's owner. As Fat Ninny gulped his drink Miles caught a glimpse of the owner of the second voice, a boy of around twelve who flitted off into the woods behind the cabin.

Karal fell to, assisting Miles and Harra and Pym in securing the horses. Miles left Pym to unsaddle and feed, and followed Karal into his house. Harra stuck to Miles like glue, and Dr. Dea unpacked his medical kit and trailed along. Miles's boots rang loud and unevenly on the wooden floorboards.

"My wife, she'll be back in the nooning," said Karal, moving uncertainly around the room as Miles and Dea settled themselves on a bench and Harra curled up with her arms around her knees on the floor beside the fieldstone hearth. "I'll . . . I'll make some tea, m'lord." He skittered back out the door to fill a kettle at the trough before Miles could say, *No, thank you.* No, let him ease his nerves in ordinary movements. Then maybe Miles could begin to tease out how much of this static was social nervousness and how much was—perhaps—guilty conscience. By the time Karal had the kettle on the coals he was noticeably better controlled, so Miles began.

"I'd prefer to commence this investigation immediately, Speaker. It need not take long."

"It need not . . . take place at all, m'lord. The baby's death was natural—there were no marks on her. She was weakly, she had the cat's mouth, who knows what else was wrong with her? She died in her sleep, or by some accident."

"It is remarkable," said Miles dryly, "how often such accidents happen in this district. My father the Count himself has . . . remarked on it."

"There was no call to drag you up here." Karal looked in exasperation at Harra. She sat silent, unmoved by his persuasion.

"It was no problem," said Miles blandly.

"Truly, m'lord," Karal lowered his voice, "I believe the child might have been overlain. 'S no wonder, in her grief, that her mind rejected it. Lem Csurik, he's a good boy, a good provider. She really doesn't want to do this, her reason is just temporarily overset by her troubles."

Harra's eyes, looking out from her hair-thatch, were poisonously cold.

"I begin to see," Miles's voice was mild, encouraging.

Karal brightened slightly. "It all could still be all right. If she will just be patient. Get over her sorrow. Talk to poor Lem. I'm sure he didn't kill the babe. Not rush to something she'll regret."

"I begin to see," Miles let his tone go ice cool, "why Harra Csurik found it necessary to walk four days to get an unbiased hearing. 'You think.' 'You believe.' 'Who knows what?' Not you, it appears. I hear speculation—accusation—innuendo—assertion. I came for *facts*, Speaker Karal. The Count's justice doesn't turn on guesses. It doesn't have to. This isn't the Time of Isolation. Not even in the backbeyond.

"My investigation of the facts will begin now. No judgment will be—rushed into, before the facts are complete. Confirmation of Lem Csurik's guilt or innocence will come from his own mouth, under fast-penta, administered by Dr. Dea before two witnesses—yourself and a deputy of your choice. Simple, clean, and quick." *And maybe I can be on my way out of this benighted hole before sundown.* "I require you,

Speaker, to go now and bring Lem Csurik for questioning. Sergeant Pym will assist you."

Karal killed another moment pouring the boiling water into a big brown pot before speaking. "I'm a travelled man, lord. A twenty-year Service man. But most folks here have never been out of Silvy Vale. Interrogation chemistry might as well be magic to them. They might say it was a false confession, got that way."

"Then you and your deputy can say otherwise. This isn't exactly like the good old days, when confessions were extracted under torture, Karal. Besides, if he's as innocent as you *guess*—he'll clear himself, no?"

Reluctantly, Keral went into the adjoining room. He came back shrugging on a faded Imperial Service uniform jacket with a corporal's rank marked on the collar, the buttons of which did not quite meet across his middle anymore. Preserved, evidently, for such official functions. Even as in Barrayaran custom one saluted the uniform, and not the man in it, so might the wrath engendered by an unpopular duty fall on the office and not the individual who carried it out. Miles appreciated the nuance.

Karal paused at the door. Harra still sat wrapped in silence by the hearth, rocking slightly.

"M'lord," said Karal. "I've been Speaker of Silvy Vale for sixteen years now. In all that time nobody has had to go to the district magistrate for a Speaking, not for water rights or stolen animals or swiving or even the time Neva accused Bors of tree piracy over the maple sap. We've not had a blood feud in all that time."

"I have no intention of starting a blood feud, Karal. I just want the facts."

"That's the thing, m'lord. I'm not so in love with

facts as I used to be. Sometimes, they bite." Karal's eyes were urgent.

Really, the man was doing everything but stand on his head and juggle cats—one-handed—to divert Miles. How overt was his obstruction likely to get?

"Silvy Vale cannot be permitted to have its own little Time of Isolation," said Miles warningly. "The Count's justice is for everyone, now. Even if they're small. And weakly. And have something wrong with them. And cannot even speak for themselves—*Speaker*."

Karal flinched, white about the lips—point taken, evidently. He trudged away up the trail, Pym following watchfully, one hand loosening the stunner in his holster.

They drank the tea while they waited, and Miles pottered about the cabin, looking but not touching. The hearth was the sole source of heat for cooking and washwater. There was a beaten metal sink for washing up, filled by hand from a covered bucket but emptied through a drainpipe under the porch to join the streamlet running down out of the trough. The second room was a bedroom, with a double bed and chests for storage. A loft held three more pallets; the boy around back had brothers, apparently. The place was cramped, but swept, things put away and hung up.

On a side table sat a government-issue audio receiver, and a second and older military model, opened up, apparently in the process of getting minor repairs and a new power pack. Exploration revealed a drawer full of old parts, nothing more complex than for simple audio sets, unfortunately. Speaker Karal must double as Silvy Vale's comm link specialist. How appropriate. They must pick up broadcasts from the station in Hassadar, maybe the high-power government channels from the capital as well.

No other electricity, of course. Powersat receptors were expensive pieces of precision technology. They would come even here, in time; some communities almost as small, but with strong economic co-ops, already had them. Silvy Vale was obviously still stuck in subsistence-level, and must needs wait till there was enough surplus in the district to gift them, if the surplus was not grabbed off first by some competing want. If only the city of Vorkosigan Vashnoi had not been obliterated by Cetagandan atomics, the whole district could be years ahead, economically. . . .

Miles walked out on the porch and leaned on the rail. Karal's son had returned. Down at the end of the cleared yard Fat Ninny was standing tethered, hip-shot, ears aflop, grunting with pleasure as the grinning boy scratched him vigorously under his halter. The boy looked up to catch Miles watching him, and scooted off fearfully to vanish again in the scrub downslope. "Huh," muttered Miles.

Dr. Dea joined him. "They've been gone a long time. About time to break out the fast-penta?"

"No, your autopsy kit, I should say. I fancy that's what we'll be doing next.'

Dea glanced at him sharply. "I thought you sent Pym along to enforce the arrest."

"You can't arrest a man who's not there. Are you a wagering man, Doctor? I'll bet you a mark they don't come back with Csurik. No, hold it—maybe I'm wrong. I hope I'm wrong. Here are three coming back. . . ."

Karal, Pym, and another were marching down the trail. The third was a hulking young man, big-handed, heavy-browed, thick-necked, surly. "Harra," Miles called, "is this your husband?" He looked the part, by God, just what Miles had pictured. And four brothers just like him—only bigger, no doubt. . . .

Harra appeared by Miles's shoulder, and let out her breath. "No, m'lord. That's Alex, the Speaker's deputy."

"Oh." Miles's lips compressed in silent frustration. *Well, I had to give it a chance to be simple.*

Karal stopped beneath him and began a wandering explanation of his emptyhanded state. Miles cut him off with a lift of his eyebrows. "Pym?"

"Bolted, m'lord," said Pym laconically. "Almost certainly warned."

"I agree." He frowned down at Karal, who prudently stood silent. Facts first. Decisions, such as how much deadly force to pursue the fugitive with, second. "Harra. How far is it to your burying place?"

"Down by the stream, lord, at the bottom of the valley. About two kilometers."

"Get your kit, Doctor, we're taking a walk. Karal, fetch a shovel."

"M'lord, surely it isn't needful to disturb the peace of the dead," began Karal.

"It is entirely needful. There's a place for the autopsy report right in the Procedural I got from the district magistrate's office. Where I will file my completed report upon this case when we return to Vorkosigan Surleau. I have permission from the next-of-kin—do I not, Harra?"

She nodded numbly.

"I have the two requisite witnesses, yourself and your," *gorilla,* "deputy, we have the doctor and the daylight—if you don't stand there arguing till sundown. All we need is the shovel. Unless you're volunteering to dig with your hand, Karal." Miles's voice was flat and grating and getting dangerous.

Karal's balding head bobbed in his distress. "The—

the father is the legal next-of-kin, while he lives, and you don't have his—"

"Karal," said Miles.

"M'lord?"

"Take care the grave you dig is not your own. You've got one foot in it already."

Karal's hand opened in despair. "I'll . . . get the shovel, m'lord."

The mid-afternoon was warm, the air golden and summer-sleepy. The shovel bit with a steady *scrunch-scrunch* through the soil at the hands of Karal's deputy. Downslope, a bright stream burbled away over clean rounded stones. Harra hunkered watching, silent and grim.

When big Alex levered out the little crate—so little!—Sergeant Pym went off for a patrol of the wooded perimeter. Miles didn't blame him. He hoped the soil at that depth had been cool, these last eight days. Alex pried open the box, and Dr. Dea waved him away and took over. The deputy too went off to find something to examine at the far end of the graveyard.

Dea looked the cloth-wrapped bundle over carefully, lifted it out and set it on his tarp laid out on the ground in the bright sun. The instruments of his investigation were arrayed upon the plastic in precise order. He unwrapped the brightly-patterned cloths in their special folds, and Harra crept up to retrieve them, straighten and fold them ready for re-use, then crept back.

Miles fingered the handkerchief in his pocket, ready to hold over his mouth and nose, and went to watch over Dea's shoulder. Bad, but not too bad. He'd seen and smelled worse. Dea, filter-masked, spoke procedurals into his recorder, hovering in the air by his shoulder, and made his examination first by eye and gloved touch, then by scanner.

"Here, my lord," said Dea, and motioned Miles closer. "Almost certainly the cause of death, though I'll run the toxin tests in a moment. Her neck was broken. See here on the scanner where the spinal cord was severed, then the bones twisted back into alignment."

"Karal, Alex," Miles motioned them up to witness; they came reluctantly.

"Could this have been accidental?" said Miles.

"Very remotely possible. The re-alignment had to be deliberate, though."

"Would it have taken long?"

"Seconds only. Death was immediate."

"How much physical strength was required? A big man's or . . ."

"Oh, not much at all. Any adult could have done it, easily."

"Any sufficiently motivated adult." Miles's stomach churned at the mental picture Dea's words conjured up. The little fuzzy head would easily fit under a man's hand. The twist, the muffled cartilagenous crack—if there was one thing Miles knew by heart, it was the exact tactile sensation of breaking bone, oh yes.

"Motivation," said Dea, "is not my department." He paused. "I might note, a careful external examination could have found this. Mine did. An experienced layman—" his eye fell cool on Karal, "paying attention to what he was doing, should not have missed it."

Miles too stared at Karal, waiting.

"Overlain," hissed Harra. Her voice was ragged with scorn.

"M'lord," said Karal carefully, "it's true I suspected the possibility—"

Suspected, hell. You knew.

"But I felt—and still feel, strongly," his eye flashed a wary defiance, "that only more grief would come from a fuss. There was nothing I could do to help the baby at that point. My duties are to the living."

"So are mine, Speaker Karal. As, for example, my duty to the next small Imperial subject in mortal danger from those who should be his or her protectors, for the grave fault of being," Miles flashed an edged smile, "physically different. In Count Vorkosigan's view this is not just a case. This is a test case, fulcrum of a thousand cases. Fuss . . ." he hissed the sibilant; Harra rocked to the rhythm of his voice, "you haven't begun to see *fuss* yet."

Karal subsided as if folded.

There followed an hour of messiness yielding mainly negative data; no other bones were broken, the infant's lungs were clear, her gut and bloodstream free of toxins except those of natural decomposition. Her brain held no secret tumors. The defect for which she had died did not extend to spina bifida, Dea reported. Fairly simple plastic surgery would indeed have corrected the cat's mouth, could she somehow have won access to it. Miles wondered what comfort this confirmation was to Harra; cold, at best.

Dea put his puzzle back together, and Harra rewrapped the tiny body in intricate, meaningful folds. Dea cleaned his tools and placed them in their cases and washed his hands and arms and face thoroughly in the stream, for rather a longer time than needed for just hygiene Miles thought, while the gorilla reburied the box.

Harra made a little bowl in the dirt atop the grave and piled in some twigs and bark scraps and a sawed-off strand of her lank hair.

Miles, caught short, felt in his pockets. "I have no offering on me that will burn," he said apologetically.

Harra glanced up, surprised at even the implied offer. "No matter, m'lord." Her little pile of scraps flared briefly and went out, like her infant Raina's life.

But it does matter, thought Miles.

Peace to you, small lady, after our rude invasions. I will give you a better sacrifice, I swear by my word as Vorkosigan. And the smoke of that burning will rise and be seen from one end of these mountains to the other.

Miles charged Karal and Alex straightly with producing Lem Csurik, and gave Harra Csurik a ride home up behind him on Fat Ninny. Pym accompanied them.

They passed a few scattered cabins on the way. At one a couple of grubby children playing in the yard loped alongside the horses, giggling and making hex signs at Miles, egging each other on to bolder displays, until their mother spotted them and ran out and hustled them indoors with a fearful look over her shoulder. In a weird way it was almost relaxing to Miles, the welcome he'd expected, not like Karal's and Alex's strained, self-conscious, careful not-noticing. Raina's life would not have been an easy one.

Harra's cabin was at the head of a long draw, just before it narrowed into a ravine. It seemed very quiet and isolated, in the dappled shade.

"Are you sure you wouldn't rather go stay with your mother?" asked Miles dubiously.

Harra shook her head. She slid down off Ninny, and Miles and Pym dismounted and followed her in.

The cabin was of standard design, a single room with a fieldstone fireplace and a wide roofed front porch. Water apparently came from the rivulet in the ravine. Pym held up a hand and entered first behind Harra, his hand on his stunner. If Lem Csurik had run, might he have run home first? Pym had been making scanner checks of perfectly innocent clumps of bushes all the way here.

The cabin was deserted. Although not long deserted; it did not have the lingering, dusty silence one would expect of eight days mournful disoccupation. The remains of a few hasty meals sat on the sinkboard. The bed was slept-in, rumpled and unmade. A few man's garments were scattered about. Automatically Harra began to move about the room, straightening it up, reasserting her presence, her existence, her worth. If she could not control the events of her life, at least she might control one small room.

The one untouched item was a cradle that sat beside the bed, little blankets neatly folded. Harra had fled for Vorkosigan Surleau just a few hours after the burial.

Miles wandered about the room, checking the view from the windows. "Will you show me where you went to get your brillberries, Harra?"

She led them up the ravine; Miles timed the hike. Pym divided his attention unhappily between the brush and Miles, alert to catch any bone-breaking stumble. After flinching away from about three aborted protective grabs Miles was ready to tell him to go climb a tree. Still, there was a certain understandable self-interest at work here, if Miles broke a leg it would be Pym who'd be stuck with carrying him out.

The brillberry patch was nearly a kilometer up the ravine. Miles plucked a few seedy red berries and ate them absently, looking around, while Harra and Pym waited respectfully. Afternoon sun slanted through green and brown leaves, but the bottom of the ravine was already grey and cool with premature twilight. The brillberry vines clung to the rocks and hung down invitingly, luring one to risk one's neck reaching. Miles resisted their weedy temptations, not being all that fond of brillberries. "If someone called out from your cabin, you couldn't hear them up here, could you?" remarked Miles.

"No, m'lord."

"About how long did you spend picking?"

"About," Harra shrugged, "a basketful."

The woman didn't own a chrono. "An hour, say. And a twenty-minute climb each way. About a two hour time window, that morning. Your cabin was not locked?"

"Just a latch, m'lord."

"Hm."

Method, motive, and opportunity, the district magistrate's Procedural had emphasized. Damn. The method was established, and almost anybody could have used it. The opportunity angle, it appeared, was just as bad. Anyone at all could have walked up to that cabin, done the deed, and departed, unseen and unheard. It was much too late for an aura detector to be of use, tracing the shining ghosts of movements in and out of that room, even if Miles had brought one.

Facts, hah. They were back to motive, the murky workings of men's minds. Anybody's guess.

Miles had, as per the instructions in the district magistrate's Procedural, been striving to keep an open mind about the accused, but it was getting harder and harder to resist Harra's assertions. She'd been proved right about everything so far.

They left Harra re-installed in her little home, going through the motions of order and the normal routine of life as if they could somehow re-create it, like an act of sympathetic magic.

"Are you sure you'll be all right?" Miles asked,

gathering Fat Ninny's reins and settling himself in the saddle. "I can't help but think that if your husband's in the area, he could show up here. You say nothing's been taken, so it's unlikely he's been here and gone before we arrived. Do you want someone to stay with you?"

"No, m'lord." She hugged her broom, on the porch. "I'd . . . I'd like to be alone for a while."

"Well . . . all right. I'll, ah, send you a message if anything important happens."

"Thank you, m'lord." Her tone was unpressing; she really did want to be left alone. Miles took the hint.

At a wide place in the trail back to Speaker Karal's, Pym and Miles rode stirrup to stirrup. Pym was still painfully on the alert for boogies in the bushes.

"My lord, may I suggest that your next logical step be to draft all the able-bodied men in the community for a hunt for this Csurik? Beyond doubt, you've established that the infanticide was a murder."

Interesting turn of phrase, Miles thought dryly. *Even Pym doesn't find it redundant. Oh, my poor Barrayar.* "It seems reasonable at first glance, Sergeant Pym, but has it occurred to you that half the able-bodied men in this community are probably relatives of Lem Csurik's?"

"It might have a psychological effect. Create enough disruption, and perhaps someone would turn him in just to get it over with."

"Hm, possibly. Assuming he hasn't already left the area. He could have been halfway to the coast before we were done at the autopsy."

"Only if he had access to transport." Pym glanced at the empty sky.

"For all we know one of his sub-cousins had a rickety lightflyer in a shed somewhere. But . . . he's never been out of Silvy Vale. I'm not sure he'd know how to run, where to go. Well, if he has left the district it's a problem for Imperial Civil Security, and I'm off the hook." Happy thought. "But—one of the things that bothers me, a lot, are the inconsistencies in the picture I'm getting of our chief suspect. Have you noticed them?"

"Can't say as I have, m'lord."

"Hm. Where did Karal take you, by the way, to arrest this guy?"

"To a wild area, rough scrub and gullies. Half a dozen men were out searching for Harra. They'd just called off their search and were on their way back when we met up with them. By which I concluded our arrival was no surprise."

"Had Csurik actually been there, and fled, or was Karal just ring-leading you in a circle?"

"I think he'd actually been there, m'lord. The men claimed not, but as you point out they were relatives, and besides, they did not, ah, lie well. They were tense. Karal may begrudge you his cooperation, but I don't think he'll quite dare disobey your direct orders. He is a twenty-year man, after all."

Like Pym himself, Miles thought. Count Vorkosigan's personal guard was legally limited to a ceremonial twenty men, but given his political position their function included very practical security. Pym was typical of their number, a decorated veteran of the Imperial Service who had retired to this elite private force. It was not Pym's fault that when he had joined he had stepped into a dead man's shoes, replacing the late Sergeant Bothari. Did anyone in the universe besides himself miss the deadly and difficult Bothari? Miles wondered sadly.

"I'd like to question *Karal* under fast-penta," said Miles morosely. "He displays every sign of being a man who knows where the body's buried."

"Why don't you, then?" asked Pym logically.

"I may come to that. There is, however, a certain unavoidable degradation in a fast-penta interrogation. If the man's loyal it may not be in our best long-range interest to shame him publicly."

"It wouldn't be in public."

"No, but he would remember being turned into a drooling idiot. I need . . . more information."

Pym glanced back over his shoulder. "I thought you had all the information, by now."

"I have facts. Physical facts. A great big pile of— meaningless, useless facts." Miles brooded. "If I have to fast-penta every backbeyonder in Silvy Vale to get to the bottom of this, I will. But it's not an elegant solution."

"It's not an elegant problem, m'lord," said Pym dryly.

They returned to find Speaker Karal's wife back and in full possession of her home. She was running in frantic circles, chopping, beating, kneading, stoking, and flying upstairs to change the bedding on the three pallets, driving her three sons before her to fetch and run and carry. Dr. Dea, bemused, was following her about trying to slow her down, explaining that they had brought their own tent and food, thank you, and that her hospitality was not required. This produced a most indignant response from Ma Karal.

"My lord's own son come to my house, and I to turn him out in the fields like his horse! I'd be ashamed!" And she returned to her work.

"She seems rather distraught," said Dea, looking over his shoulder.

Miles took him by the elbow and propelled him out onto the porch. "Just get out of her way, Doctor.

We're doomed to be Entertained. It's an obligation on both sides. The polite thing to do is sort of pretend we're not here till she's ready for us."

Dea lowered his voice. "It might be better, in light of the circumstances, if we were to eat only our packaged food."

The chatter of a chopping knife, and a scent of herbs and onions, wafted enticingly through the open window. "Oh, I would imagine anything out of the common pot would be all right, wouldn't you?" said Miles. "If anything really worries you, you can wisk it off and check it, I suppose, but—discreetly, eh? We don't want to insult anyone."

They settled themselves in the homemade wooden chairs, and were promptly served tea again by a boy draftee of ten, Karal's youngest. He had apparently already received private instructions in manners from one or the other of his parents, for his response to Miles's deformities was the same flickering covert not-noticing as the adults, not quite as smoothly carried off.

"Will you be sleeping in my bed, m'lord?" he asked. "Ma says we got to sleep on the porch."

"Well, whatever your Ma says, goes," said Miles. "Ah . . . do you like sleeping on the porch?"

"Naw. Last time, Zed kicked me and I rolled off in the dark."

"Oh. Well, perhaps, if we're to displace you, you would care to sleep in our tent by way of trade."

The boy's eyes widened. "Really?"

"Certainly. Why not?"

"Wait'll I tell Zed!" He danced down the steps and shot away around the side of the house. "Zed, hey, Zed . . . !"

"I suppose," said Dea, "we can fumigate it, later. . . ."

Miles's lips twitched. "They're no grubbier than you were at the same age, surely. Or than I was. When I was permitted." The late afternoon was warm. Miles took off his green tunic and hung it on the back of his chair, and unbuttoned the round collar of his cream shirt.

Dea's brows rose. "Are we keeping shopman's hours, then, m'lord, on this investigation? Calling it quits for the day?"

"Not exactly." Miles sipped tea thoughtfully, gazing out across the yard. The trees and treetops fell away down to the bottom of this feeder valley. Mixed scrub climbed the other side of the slope. A crested fold, then the long flanks of a backbone mountain, beyond, rose high and harsh to a summit still flecked with dwindling dirty patches of snow.

"There's still a murderer loose out there somewhere," Dea pointed out helpfully.

"You sound like Pym." Pym, Miles noted, had finished with their horses and was taking his scanner for another walk. "I'm waiting."

"What for?"

"Not sure. The piece of information that will make sense of all this. Look, there's only two possibilities. Csurik's either innocent or he's guilty. If he's guilty, he's not going to turn himself in. He'll certainly involve his relations, hiding and helping him. I can call in reinforcements by comm link from Imperial Civil Security in Hassadar, if I want to. Any time. Twenty men, plus equipment, here by aircar in a couple of hours. Create a circus. Brutal, ugly, disruptive, exciting—could be quite popular. A manhunt, with blood at the end.

"Of course, there's also the possibility that Csurik's innocent, but scared. In which case . . ."

"Yes?"

"In which case, there's still a murderer out there."
Miles drank more tea. "I merely note, if you want to
catch something, running after it isn't always the
best way."

Dea cleared his throat, and drank his tea too.

"In the meantime, I have another duty to carry
out. I'm here to be seen. If your scientific spirit is
yearning for something to do to wile away the hours,
try keeping count of the number of Vor-watchers
that turn up tonight."

Miles's predicted parade began almost immediately. It was mainly women, at first, bearing gifts as
to a funeral. In the absence of a comm link system
Miles wasn't sure by what telepathy they managed to
communicate with each other, but they brought covered dishes of food, flowers, extra bedding, and of-
fers of assistance. They were all introduced to Miles
with nervous curtseys, but seldom lingered to chat;
apparently a look was all their curiosity desired. Ma
Karal was polite, but made it clear that she had the
situation well in hand, and set their culinary offer-
ings well back of her own.

Some of the women had children in tow. Most of
these were sent to play in the woods in back, but a
small party of whispering boys sneaked back around
the cabin to peek up over the rim of the porch at
Miles. Miles had obligingly remained on the porch
with Dea, remarking that it was a better view, without saying for whom. For a few moments Miles
pretended not to notice his audience, restraining
Pym with a hand signal from running them off. *Yes,
look well, look your fill,* thought Miles. *What you see
is what you're going to get, for the rest of your lives
or at any rate mine. Get used to it. . . .* Then he

caught Zed Karal's whisper, as self-appointed tour guide to his cohort—"That big one's the one that's come to kill Lem Csurik!"

"Zed," said Miles.

There was an abrupt frozen silence from under the edge of the porch. Even the animal rustlings stopped.

"Come here," said Miles.

To a muted background of dismayed whispers and nervous giggles, Karal's middle boy slouched warily up on to the porch.

"You three—" Miles's pointing finger caught them in mid-flight, "wait there." Pym added his frown for emphasis, and Zed's friends stood paralyzed, eyes wide, heads lined up at the level of the porch floor as if stuck up on some ancient battlement as a warning to kindred malefactors.

"What did you just say to your friends, Zed?" asked Miles quietly. "Repeat it."

Zed licked his lips. "I jus' said you'd come to kill Lem Csurik, lord." Zed was clearly now wondering if Miles's murderous intent included obnoxious and disrespectful boys as well.

"That is not true, Zed. That is a dangerous lie."

Zed looked bewildered. "But Da—said it."

"What is true, is that I've come to catch the person who killed Lem Csurik's baby daughter. That may be Lem. But it may not. Do you understand the difference?"

"But Harra said Lem did it, and she ought to know, he's her husband and all."

"The baby's neck was broken by someone. Harra thinks Lem, but she didn't see it happen. What you and your friends here have to understand is that I won't make a mistake. I *can't* condemn the wrong person. My own truth drugs won't let me. Lem Csurik has only to come here and tell me the truth to clear himself, if he didn't do it.

"But suppose he did. What should I do with a man who would kill a baby, Zed?"

Zed shuffled. "Well, she was only a mutie . . ." then shut his mouth and reddened, not-looking at Miles.

It was, perhaps, a bit much to ask a twelve-year-old boy to take an interest in any baby, let alone a mutie one . . . *no*, dammit. It wasn't too much. But how to get a hook into that prickly defensive surface? And if Miles couldn't even convince one surly twelve-year-old, how was he to magically transmute a whole District of adults? A rush of despair made him suddenly want to rage. These people were so bloody *impossible*. He checked his temper firmly.

"Your Da was a twenty-year man, Zed. Are you proud that he served the Emperor?"

"Yes, lord." Zed's eyes sought escape, trapped by these terrible adults.

Miles forged on. "Well, these practices—mutie-killing—shame the Emperor, when he stands for Barrayar before the galaxy. I've been out there. I know. They call us all savages, for the crimes of a few. It shames the Count my father before his peers, and Silvy Vale before the District. A soldier gets honor by killing an armed enemy, not a baby. This matter touches my honor as a Vorkosigan, Zed. Besides," Miles's lips drew back on a mirthless grin, and he leaned forward intently in his chair—Zed recoiled as much as he dared—"you will all be astonished at what *only a mutie* can do. *That* I have sworn on my grandfather's grave."

Zed looked more suppressed than enlightened, his slouch now almost a crouch. Miles slumped back in his chair and released him with a weary wave of his hand. "Go play, boy."

Zed needed no urging. He and his companions

shot away around the house as though released from springs.

Miles drummed his fingers on the chair arm, frowning into the silence that neither Pym nor Dea dared break.

"These hill-folk are ignorant, lord," offered Pym after a moment.

"These hill-folk are *mine*, Pym. Their ignorance is . . . a shame upon my house." Miles brooded. How had this whole mess become his anyway? He hadn't created it. Historically, he'd only just got here himself. "Their continued ignorance, anyway," he amended in fairness. It still made a burden like a mountain. "Is the message so complex? So difficult? 'You don't have to kill your children anymore.' It's not like we're asking them all to learn—5-Space navigational math." That had been the plague of Miles's last Academy semester.

"It's not easy for them," shrugged Dea. "It's easy for the central authorities to make the rules, but these people have to live every minute of the consequences. They have so little, and the new rules force them to give their margin to marginal people who can't pay back. The old ways were wise, in the old days. Even now you have to wonder how many premature reforms we can afford, trying to ape the galactics."

And what's your definition of a marginal person, Dea? "But the margin is growing," Miles said aloud. "Places like this aren't up against famine every winter any more. They're not isolated in their disasters, relief can get from one district to another under the Imperial seal . . . we're all getting more connected, just as fast as we can. Besides," Miles paused, and added rather weakly, "perhaps you underestimate them."

Dea's brows rose ironically. Pym strolled the length of the porch, running his scanner in yet another pass over the surrounding scrubland. Miles, turning in his chair to pursue his cooling teacup, caught a slight movement, a flash of eyes, behind the casement-hung front window swung open to the summer air—Ma Karal, standing frozen, listening. For how long? Since he'd called her boy Zed, Miles guessed, arresting her attention. She raised her chin as his eyes met hers, sniffed, and shook out the cloth she'd been holding with a snap. They exchanged a nod. She turned back to her work before Dea, watching Pym, noticed her.

Karal and Alex returned, understandably, around suppertime.

"I have six men out searching," Karal reported cautiously to Miles on the porch, now well on its way to becoming Miles's official HQ. Clearly, Karal had covered ground since midafternoon. His face was sweaty, lined with physical as well as the underlying emotional strain. "But I think Lem's gone into the scrub. It could take days to smoke him out. There's hundreds of places to lie low out there."

Karal ought to know. "You don't think he's gone to some relative's?" asked Miles. "Surely, if he intends to evade us for long, he has to take a chance on re-supply, on information. Will they turn him in when he surfaces?"

"It's hard to say." Karal turned his hand palm-out. "It's . . . a hard problem for 'em, m'lord."

"Hm."

How long would Lem Csurik hang around out there in the scrub, anyway? His whole life—his blown-to-bits life—was all here in Silvy Vale. Miles considered the contrast. A few weeks ago, Csurik had been a young man with everything going for him; a home, a wife, a family on the way, happiness; by Silvy Vale standards, comfort and security. His cabin, Miles had not failed to note, though simple, had been kept with love and energy, and so redeemed from the potential squalor of its poverty. Grimmer in the winter, to be sure. Now Csurik was a hunted fugitive, all the little he had torn away in the twinkling of an eye. With nothing to hold him, would he run away and keep running? With nothing to run to, would he linger near the ruins of his life?

The police force available to Miles a few hours away in Hassadar was an itch in his mind. Was it not time to call them in, before he fumbled this into a worse mess? But . . . if he were meant to solve this by a show of force, why hadn't the Count let him come by aircar on the first day? Miles regretted that two-and-a-half-day ride. It had sapped his forward momentum, slowed him down to Silvy Vale's walking pace, tangled him with time to doubt. Had the Count foreseen it? What did he know that Miles didn't? What *could* he know? Dammit, this test didn't need to be made harder by artificial stumbling blocks, it was bad enough all on its own. *He wants me to be clever*, Miles thought morosely. *Worse, he wants me to be seen to be clever, by everyone here.* He prayed he was not about to be spectacularly stupid instead.

"Very well, Speaker Karal. You've done all you can for today. Knock off for the night. Call your men off too. You're not likely to find anything in the dark."

Pym held up his scanner, clearly about to volunteer its use, but Miles waved him down. Pym's brows rose, editorially. Miles shook his head slightly.

Karal needed no further urging. He dispatched Alex to call off the night search with torches. He remained wary of Miles. Perhaps Miles puzzled him as much as he puzzled Miles? Dourly, Miles hoped so.

Miles was not sure at what point the long summer evening segued into a party. After supper the men began to drift in, Karal's cronies, Silvy Vale's elders. Some were apparently regulars who shared the evening government news broadcasts on Karal's audio set. Too many names, and Miles daren't forget a one. A group of amateur musicians arrived with their homemade mountain instruments, rather breathless, obviously the band tapped for all the major weddings and wakes in Silvy Vale; this all seemed more like a funeral to Miles every minute.

The musicians stood in the middle of the yard and played. Miles's porch-HQ now became his aristocratic box seat. It was hard to get involved with the music when the audience was all so intently watching him. Some songs were serious, some—rather carefully at first—funny. Miles's spontaneity was frequently frozen in mid-laugh by a faint sigh of relief from those around him; his stiffening froze them in turn, self-stymied like two people trying to dodge each other in a corridor.

But one song was so hauntingly beautiful—a lament for lost love—that Miles was struck to the heart. *Elena.* . . . In that moment, old pain transformed to melancholy, sweet and distant; a sort of healing, or at least the realization that a healing had taken place, unwatched. He almost had the singers stop there, while they were perfect, but feared they might think him displeased. But he remained quiet and inward for a time afterward, scarcely hearing their next offering in the gathering twilight.

At least the piles of food that had arrived all afternoon were thus accounted for. Miles had been afraid

Ma Karal and her cronies had expected him to get around that culinary mountain all by himself.

At one point Miles leaned on the rail and glanced down the yard to see Fat Ninny at tether, making more friends. A whole flock of pubescent girls were clustered around him, petting him, brushing his fetlocks, braiding flowers and ribbons in his mane and tail, feeding him tidbits, or just resting their cheeks against his warm silky side. Ninny's eyes were half-closed in smug content.

God, thought Miles jealously, *if I had half the sex-appeal of that bloody horse I'd have more girlfriends than my cousin Ivan.* Miles considered, very briefly, the pros and cons of making a play for some unattached female. The striding lords of old and all that . . . no. There were some kinds of stupid he didn't have to be, and that was definitely one of them. The service he had already sworn to one small lady of Silvy Vale was surely all he could bear without breaking; he could feel the strain of it all around him now, like a dangerous pressure in his bones.

He turned to find Speaker Karal presenting a woman to him, far from pubescent; she was perhaps fifty, lean and little, work-worn. She was carefully clothed in an aging best-dress, her greying hair combed back and bound at the nape of her neck. She bit at her lips and cheeks in quick tense motions, half-suppressed in her self-consciousness.

" 'S Ma Csurik, m'lord. Lem's mother." Speaker Karal ducked his head and backed away, abandoning Miles without aid or mercy—*Come back, you coward!*

"Ma'am," Miles said. His throat was dry. Karal had set him up, dammit, a public play—no, the other guests were retreating out of earshot too, most of them.

"M'lord," said Ma Csurik. She managed a nervous curtsey.

"Uh . . . do sit down." With a ruthless jerk of his chin Miles evicted Dr. Dea from his chair and motioned the hill woman into it. He turned his own chair to face hers. Pym stood behind them, silent as a statue, tight as a wire. Did he imagine the old woman was about to whip a needler-pistol from her skirts? No—it was Pym's job to imagine things like that for Miles, so that Miles might free his whole mind for the problem at hand. Pym was almost as much an object of study as Miles himself. Wisely, he'd been holding himself apart, and would doubtless continue to do so till the dirty work was over.

"M'lord," said Ma Csurik again, and stumbled again to silence. Miles could only wait. He prayed she wasn't about to come unglued and weep on his knees or some damn thing. This was excruciating. *Stay strong, woman*, he urged silently.

"Lem, he . . ." she swallowed, "I'm sure he didn't kill the babe. There's never been any of that in our family, I swear it! He says he didn't, and I believe him."

"Good," said Miles affably. "Let him come say the same thing to me under fast-penta, and I'll believe him too."

"Come away, Ma," urged a lean young man who had accompanied her and now stood waiting by the steps, as if ready to bolt into the dark at a motion. "It's no good, can't you see." He glowered at Miles.

She shot the boy a quelling frown—another of her five sons?—and turned back more urgently to Miles, groping for words. "My Lem. He's only twenty, lord."

"*I'm* only twenty, Ma Csurik," Miles felt compelled to point out. There was another brief impasse.

"Look, I'll say it again," Miles burst out impatiently. "And again, and again, till the message penetrates all the way back to its intended recipient. I *cannot* condemn an innocent person. My truth drugs won't let me. Lem can clear himself. He has only to come in. Tell him, will you? Please?"

She went stony, guarded. "I . . . haven't seen him, m'lord."

"But you might."

She tossed her head. "So? I might not." Her eyes shifted to Pym and away, as if the sight of him burned. The silver Vorkosigan logos embroidered on Pym's collar gleamed in the twilight like animal eyes, moving only with his breathing. Karal was now bringing lighted lamps onto the porch, but keeping his distance still.

"Ma'am," said Miles tightly. "The Count my father has ordered me to investigate the murder of your granddaughter. If your son means so much to you, how can his child mean so little? Was she . . . your first grandchild?"

Her face was sere. "No, lord. Lem's older sister, she has two. *They're* all right," she added with emphasis.

Miles sighed. "If you truly believe your son is innocent of this crime, you must help me prove it. Or—do you doubt?"

She shifted uneasily. There was doubt in her eyes— she didn't know, blast it. Fast-penta would be useless on her, for sure. As Miles's magic wonder drug, much counted-upon, fast-penta seemed to be having wonderfully little utility in this case so far.

"Come away, Ma," the young man urged again. "It's no good. The mutie lord came up here for a killing. They have to have one. It's a show."

Damn straight, thought Miles acidly. He was a perceptive young lunk, that one.

Ma Csurik let herself be persuaded away by her

angry and embarrassed son plucking at her arm. She paused on the steps, though, and shot bitterly over her shoulder, "It's all so easy for you, isn't it?"

My head hurts, thought Miles.

There was worse to come before the evening ended.

The new woman's voice was grating, low and angry. "Don't you talk down to me, Serg Karal. I got a right for one good look at this mutie lord."

She was tall and stringy and tough. *Like her daughter,* Miles thought. She had made no attempt to freshen up. A faint reek of summer sweat hung about her working dress. And how far had she walked? Her grey hair hung in a switch down her back, a few strands escaping the tie. If Ma Csurik's bitterness had been a stabbing pain behind the eyes, this one's rage was a wringing knot in the gut.

She shook off Karal's attempted restraint and stalked up to Miles in the lamplight. "So."

"Uh . . . this is Ma Mattulich, m'lord," Karal introduced her. "Harra's mother."

Miles rose to his feet, managed a short formal nod. "How do you do, madam." He was very conscious of being a head shorter. She had once been of a height with Harra, Miles estimated, but her aging bones were beginning to pull her down.

She merely stared. She was a gum-leaf chewer, by the faint blackish stains around her mouth. Her jaw worked now on some small bit, tiny chomps, grinding too hard. She studied him openly, without subterfuge or the least hint of apology, taking in his head, his neck, his back, his short and crooked legs. Miles had the unpleasant illusion that she saw right through to all the healed cracks in his brittle bones as well. Miles's chin jerked up twice in the twitchy, nervous-involuntary tic that he was sure made him look spastic, before he controlled it with an effort.

"All right," said Karal roughly, "you've seen. Now come away, for God's sake, Mara." His hand opened in apology to Miles. "Mara, she's been pretty distraught over all this, m'lord. Forgive her."

"Your only grandchild," said Miles to her, in an effort to be kind, though her peculiar anguish repelled kindness with a scraped and bleeding scorn. "I understand your distress, ma'am. But there will be justice for little Raina. That I have sworn."

"How can there be justice *now?*" she raged, thick and low. "It's too late—a world too late—for justice, mutie lordling. What use do I have for your damned justice *now?*"

"Enough, Mara!" Karal insisted. His brows drew down and his lips thinned, and he forced her away and escorted her firmly off his porch.

The last lingering remnant of visitors parted for her with an air of respectful mercy, except for two lean teenagers hanging on the fringes who drew away as if avoiding poison. Miles was forced to revise his mental image of the Brothers Csurik. If those two were another sample, there was no team of huge menacing hill hulks after all. They were a team of little skinny menacing hill squirts instead. Not really an improvement, they looked like they could move as fast as striking ferrets if they had to. Miles's lips curled in frustration.

The evening's entertainments ended finally, thank God, close to midnight. Karal's last cronies marched off into the woods by lantern light. The repaired and re-powered audio set was carried off by its owner with many thanks to Karal. Fortunately it had been a mature and sober crowd, even somber, no drunken brawls or anything. Pym got the Karal boys settled in the tent, took a last patrol around the cabin, and joined Miles and Dea in the loft. The pallets' stuffing had been spiked with fresh scented native herbs, to which Miles hoped devoutly he was not allergic. Ma Karal had wanted to turn her own bedroom over to Miles's exclusive lordly use, exiling herself and her husband to the porch too, but fortunately Pym had been able to persuade her that putting Miles in the loft, flanked by Dea and himself, was to be preferred from a security standpoint.

Dea and Pym were soon snoring, but sleep eluded Miles. He tossed on his pallet as he turned his ploys of the day, such as they had been, over and over in his mind. Was he being too slow, too careful, too conservative? This wasn't exactly good assault tactics, surprise with a superior force. The view he'd gained of the terrain from Karal's porch tonight had been ambiguous at best.

On the other hand, it did no good to charge off across a swamp, as his fellow cadet and cousin Ivan Vorpatril had demonstrated so memorably once on summer maneuvers. It had taken a heavy hovercab with a crane to crank the six big, strong, healthy, fully field-equipped young men of Ivan's patrol out of the chest-high, gooey black mud. Ivan had got his revenge simultaneously, though, when the cadet "sniper" they had been attacking fell out of his tree and broke his arm while laughing hysterically as they sank slowly and beautifully into the ooze. Ooze that a little guy, with his laser rifle wrapped in his loin-cloth, could swim across like a frog. The war games umpire had ruled it a draw. Miles rubbed his forearm and grinned in memory, and faded out at last.

Miles awoke abruptly and without transition deep in the night with a sense of something wrong. A faint orange glow shimmered in the blue darkness of the loft. Quietly, so as not to disturb his sleeping companions, he rose on his pallet and peered over the edge into the main room. The glow was coming through the front window.

Miles swung onto the ladder and padded downstairs for a look out doors. "Pym," he called softly.

Pym shot awake with a snort. "M'lord?" he said, alarmed.

"Come down here. Quietly. Bring your stunner."

Pym was by his side in seconds. He slept in his trousers with his stunner holster and boots by his pillow. "What the hell—?" Pym muttered, looking out too.

The glow was from fire. A pitchy torch, flung to the top of Miles's tent set up in the yard, was burning quietly. Pym lurched toward the door, then controlled his movements as the same realization came to him as had to Miles. Theirs was a Service-issue tent, and its combat-rated synthetic fabric would neither melt nor burn.

Miles wondered if the person who'd heaved the torch had known that. Was this some arcane warning, or a singularly inept attack? If the tent had been ordinary fabric, and Miles in it, the intended result might not have been trivial. Worse with Karal's boys in it—a bursting blossom of flame—Miles shuddered.

Pym loosened his stunner in his holster and stood poised by the front door. "How long?"

"I'm not sure. Could have been burning like that for ten minutes before it woke me."

Pym shook his head, took a slight breath, raised his scanner, and vaulted into the fire-gilded darkness.

"Trouble, m'lord?" Speaker Karal's anxious voice came from his bedroom door.

"Maybe. Wait—" Miles halted him as he plunged for the door. "Pym's running a patrol with a scanner and a stunner. Wait'll he calls the all-clear, I think. Your boys may be safer inside the tent."

Karal came up to the window, caught his breath, and swore.

Pym returned in a few minutes. "There's no one within a kilometer, now," he reported shortly. He helped Karal take the goat bucket and douse the torch. The boys, who had slept through the fire, woke at its quenching.

"I think maybe it was a bad idea to lend them my tent," said Miles from the porch in a choked voice. "I am profoundly sorry, Speaker Karal. I didn't think."

"This should never . . ." Karal was spluttering with anger and delayed fright, "this should *never* have happened, m'lord. I apologize for . . . for Silvy Vale." He turned helplessly, peering into the darkness. The night sky, star-flecked, lovely, was threatening now.

The boys, once the facts penetrated their sleepiness, thought it was all just great, and wanted to return to the tent and lie in wait for the next assassin. Ma Karal, shrill and firm, herded them indoors instead and made them bed down in the main room. It was an hour before they stopped complaining at the injustice of it and went back to sleep.

Miles, keyed up nearly to the point of gibbering, did not sleep at all. He lay stiffly on his pallet, listening to Dea, who slept breathing heavily, and Pym, feigning sleep for courtesy and scarcely seeming to breathe at all.

Miles was about to suggest to Pym that they give up and go out on the porch for the rest of the night when the silence was shattered by a shrill squeal, enormously loud, pain-edged, from outside.

"The horses!" Miles spasmed to his feet, heart

racing, and beat Pym to the ladder. Pym cut ahead
of him by dropping straight over the side of the loft
into an elastic crouch, and beat him to the door.
There, Pym's trained bodyguard's reflexes compelled
him to try and thrust Miles back inside. Miles almost
bit him. "Go, dammit! I've got a weapon!"

Pym, good intentions frustrated, swung out the
cabin door with Miles on his heels. Halfway down
the yard they split to each side as a massive snorting
shape loomed out of the darkness and nearly ran
them down; the sorrel mare, loose again. Another
squeal pierced the night from the lines where the
horses were tethered.

"Ninny?" Miles called, panicked. It was Ninny's
voice making those noises, the like of which Miles
had not heard since the night a shed had burned
down at Vorkosigan Surleau with a horse trapped
inside. "Ninny!"

Another grunting squeal, and a thunk like someone
splitting a watermelon with a mallet. Pym staggered
back, inhaling with difficulty, a resonant deep stut-
ter, and tripped to the ground where he lay curled
up around himself. Not killed outright, apparently,
because between gasps he was managing to swear
lividly. Miles dropped to the ground beside him,
checked his skull—no, thank God it had been Pym's
chest Ninny's hoof had hit with that alarming sound.
The bodyguard only had the wind knocked out of
him, maybe a cracked rib. Miles more sensibly ran
around to the *front* of the horse lines. "Ninny!"

Fat Ninny was jerking his head against his rope,
attempting to rear. He squealed again, his white-
rimmed eyes gleaming in the darkness. Miles ran to
his head. "Ninny, boy! What is it?" His left hand slid
up the rope to Ninny's halter, his right stretched to
stroke Ninny's shoulder soothingly. Fat Ninny flinched,

but stopped trying to rear, and stood trembling. The horse shook his head. Miles's face and chest were suddenly spattered with something hot and dark and sticky.

"Dea!" Miles yelled. *"Dea!"*

Nobody slept through this uproar. Six people tumbled off the porch and down the yard, and not one of them thought to bring a light . . . no, the brilliant flare of a cold light sprang from between Dr. Dea's fingers, and Ma Karal was struggling even now to light a lantern. "Dea, get that damn light over here!" Miles demanded, and stopped to choke his voice back down an octave to its usual carefully-cultivated deeper register.

Dea galloped up and thrust the light toward Miles, then gasped, his face draining. "My lord! Are you shot?" In the flare the dark liquid soaking Miles's shirt glowed suddenly scarlet.

"Not me," Miles said, looking down at his chest in horror. A flash of memory turned his stomach over, cold at the vision of another blood-soaked death, that of the late Sergeant Bothari whom Pym had replaced. Would never replace.

Dea spun. "Pym?"

"He's all right," said Miles. A long inhaling wheeze rose from the grass a few meters off, the exhalation punctuated with obscenities. "But he got kicked by the horse. Get your medkit!" Miles peeled Dea's fingers off the cold light, and Dea dashed back to the cabin.

Miles held the light up to Ninny, and swore in a sick whisper. A huge cut, a third of a meter long and of unknown depth, scored Ninny's glossy neck. Blood soaked his coat and runneled down his foreleg. Miles's fingers touched the wound fearfully; his hands spread on either side, trying to push it closed, but the horse's skin was elastic and it pulled apart and bled profusely as Fat Ninny shook his head in pain. Miles grabbed the horse's nose—"Hold still, boy!" Somebody had been going for Ninny's jugular. And had almost made it; Ninny—tame, petted, friendly, trusting Ninny—would not have moved from the touch until the knife bit deep.

Karal was helping Pym to his feet as Dr. Dea returned. Miles waited while Dea checked Pym over, then called, "Here, Dea!"

Zed, looking quite as horrified as Miles, helped to hold Ninny's head as Dea made inspection of the cut. "I took tests," Dea complained *sotto voce* as he worked. "I beat out twenty-six other applicants, for the honor of becoming the Prime Minister's personal physician. I have practiced the procedures of seventy separate possible medical emergencies, from coronary thrombosis to attempted assassination. Nobody— *nobody*—told me my duties would include sewing up a damned horse's neck in the middle of the night in the middle of a howling wilderness. . . ." But he kept working as he complained, so Miles didn't quash him, but kept gently petting Ninny's nose, and hypnotically rubbing the hidden pattern of his muscles, to soothe and still him. At last Ninny relaxed enough to rest his slobbery chin on Miles's shoulder.

"Do horses get anesthetics?" asked Dea plaintively, holding his medical stunner as if not sure just what to do with it.

"This one does," said Miles stoutly. "You treat him just like a person, Dea. This is the last animal that the Count my grandfather personally trained. He named him. I watched him get born. We trained him together. Grandfather had me pick him up and hold him every day for a week after he was foaled, till he got too big. Horses are creatures of habit,

Grandfather said, and take first impressions to heart. Forever after Ninny thought I was bigger than he was."

Dea sighed and made busy with anesthetic stun, cleansing solution, antibiotics, muscle relaxants, and biotic glue. With a surgeon's touch he shaved the edges of the cut and placed the reinforcing net. Zed held the light anxiously.

"The cut is clean," said Dea, "but it will undergo a lot of flexing—I don't suppose it can very well be immobilized, in this position? No, hardly. This should do. If he were a human, I'd tell him to rest at this point."

"He'll be rested," Miles promised firmly. "Will he be all right now?"

"I suppose so. How the devil should I know?" Dea looked highly aggrieved, but his hand sneaked out to re-check his repairs.

"General Piotr," Miles assured him, "would have been very pleased with your work." Miles could hear him in his head now, snorting, *Damned technocrats. Nothing but horse doctors with a more expensive set of toys.* Grandfather would have loved being proved right. "You, ah . . . never met my grandfather, did you?"

"Before my time, my lord," said Dea. "I've studied his life and campaigns, of course."

"Of course."

Pym had a hand-light now, and was limping with Karal in a slow spiral around the horse lines, inspecting the ground. Karal's eldest boy had recaptured the sorrel mare and brought her back and re-tethered her. Her tether had been torn loose, not cut; had the mysterious attacker's choice of equine victim been random, or calculated? How calculated? Was Ninny attacked as a mere symbol of his master, or had the person known how passionately Miles loved the animal? Was this vandalism, a political statement, or an act of precisely-directed, subtle cruelty?

What have I ever done to you? Miles's thought howled silently to the surrounding darkness.

"They got away, whoever it was," Pym reported. "Out of scanner range before I could breathe again. My apologies, m'lord. They don't seem to have dropped anything on the ground."

There had to have been a knife, at least. A knife, its haft gory with horse blood in a pattern of perfect fingerprints, would have been extremely convenient just now. Miles sighed.

Ma Karal drifted up and eyed Dea's medkit, as he cleaned and re-packed it. "All that," she muttered under her breath, "for a horse. . . ."

Miles refrained, barely, from leaping to a hot defense of the value of this particular horse. How many people in Silvy Vale had Ma Karal seen suffer and die, in her lifetime, for lack of no more medical technology than what Dea was carrying under his arm just now?

Guarding his horse, Miles watched from the porch as dawn crept over the landscape. He had changed his shirt and washed off. Pym was inside getting his ribs taped. Miles sat with his back to the wall and a stunner on his lap as the night mists slowly grew grey. The valley was a grey blur, fog-shrouded, the hills darker rolls of fog beyond. Directly overhead, grey thinned to a paling blue. The day would be fine and hot once the fog burned away.

It was surely time now to call out the troops from Hassadar. This was getting just too weird. His bodyguard was half out of commission—true, it was Miles's horse that had rendered him so, not the mystery

attacker. But just because the attacks hadn't been
fatal didn't mean they hadn't been intended so. Perhaps a third attack would be brought off more ex-
pertly. Practice makes perfect.

Miles felt unstrung with nervous exhaustion. How
had he let a mere horse become such a handle on his
emotions? Bad, that, almost unbalanced—yet Ninny's was surely one of the truly innocent pure souls
Miles had ever known. Miles remembered the other
innocent in the case then, and shivered in the damp.
It was cruel, lord, something cruel. . . . Pym was
right, the bushes could be crawling with Csurik assassins right now.

Dammit, the bushes *were* crawling—over there, a
movement, a damping wave of branch lashing in
recoil from—what? Miles's heart lurched in his chest.
He adjusted his stunner to full power, slipped silently off the porch, and began his stalk, crouching
low, taking advantage of cover wherever the long
grasses of the yard had not been trampled flat by the
activities of the last day, and night. Miles froze like a
predatory cat as a shape seemed to coalesce out of
the mist.

A lean young man, not too tall, dressed in the
baggy trousers that seemed to be standard here,
stood wearily by the horse lines, staring up the yard
at Karal's cabin. He stood so for a full two minutes
without moving. Miles held a bead on him with his
stunner. If he dared make one move toward Ninny. . . .

The young man walked back and forth uncertainly,
then crouched on his heels, still gazing up the yard.
He pulled something from the pocket of his loose
jacket—Miles's finger tightened on the trigger—but
he only put it to his mouth and bit. An apple. The
crunch carried clearly in the damp air, and the faint
perfume of its juices. He ate about half, then stopped,

seeming to have trouble swallowing. Miles checked the knife at his belt, made sure it was loose in its sheath. Ninny's nostrils widened, and he nickered hopefully, drawing the young man's attention. He rose and walked over to the horse.

The blood pulsed in Miles's ears, louder than any other sound. His grip on the stunner was damp and white-knuckled. The young man fed Ninny his apple. The horse chomped it down, big jaw rippling under his skin, then cocked his hip, dangled one hind hoof, and sighed hugely. If he hadn't seen the man eat off the fruit first Miles might have shot him on the spot. It couldn't be poisoned. . . . The man made to pet Ninny's neck, then his hand drew back in startlement as he encountered Dea's dressing. Ninny shook his head uneasily. Miles rose slowly and stood waiting. The man scratched Ninny's ears instead, looked up one last time at the cabin, took a deep breath, stepped forward, saw Miles, and stood stock still.

"Lem Csurik?" said Miles.

A pause, a frozen nod. "Lord Vorkosigan?" said the young man. Miles nodded in turn.

Csurik swallowed. "Vor lord," he quavered, "do you keep your word?"

What a bizarre opening. Miles's brows climbed. Hell, go with it. "Yes. Are you coming in?"

"Yes and no, m'lord."

"Which?"

"A bargain, lord. I must have a bargain, and your word on it."

"If you killed Raina . . ."

"No, lord. I swear it. I didn't."

"Then you have nothing to fear from me."

Lem Csurik's lips thinned. What the devil could this hill man find ironic? How dare he find irony in Miles's confusion? Irony, but no amusement.

"Oh, lord," breathed Csurik, "I wish that were so. But I have to prove it to Harra. Harra must believe me—you have to make her believe me, lord!"

"You have to make me believe you first. Fortunately, that isn't hard. You come up to the cabin and make that same statement under fast-penta, and I will rule you cleared."

Csurik was shaking his head.

"Why not?" said Miles patiently. That Csurik had turned up at all was strong circumstantial indication of his innocence. Unless he somehow imagined he could beat the drug. Miles would be patient for, oh, three or four seconds at least. Then, by God, he'd stun him, drag him inside, tie him up till he came round, and get to the bottom of this before breakfast.

"The drug—they say you can't hold anything back."

"It would be pretty useless if you could."

Csurik stood silent a moment.

"Are you trying to conceal some lesser crime on your conscience? Is that the bargain you wish to strike? An amnesty? It . . . might be possible. If it's short of another murder, that is."

"No, lord. I've never killed anybody!"

"Then maybe we can deal. Because if you're innocent, I need to know as soon as possible. Because it means my work isn't finished here."

"That's . . . that's the trouble, m'lord." Csurik shuffled, then seemed to come to some internal decision and stood sturdily. "I'll come in and risk your drug. And I'll answer anything about me you want to ask. But you have to promise—swear!—you won't ask me about . . . about anything else. Anybody else."

"Do you know who killed your daughter?"

"Not for sure." Csurik threw his head back defiantly. "I didn't see it. I have guesses."

"I have guesses too."

"That's as may be, lord. Just so's they don't come from my mouth. That's all I ask."

Miles holstered his stunner, and rubbed his chin. "Hm." A very slight smile turned one corner of his lip. "I admit, it would be more—elegant—to solve this case by reason and deduction than brute force. Even so tender a force as fast-penta."

Csurik's head lowered. "I don't know elegant, lord. But I don't want it to be from my mouth."

Decision bubbled up in Miles, straightening his spine. Yes. He *knew*, now. He had only to run through the proofs, step by chained step. Just like 5-Space math. "Very well. I swear by my word as Vorkosigan, I shall confine my questions to the facts to which you were an eyewitness. I will not ask you for conjectures about persons or events for which you were not present. There, will that do?"

Csurik bit his lip. "Yes, lord. If you keep your word."

"Try me," suggested Miles. His lips wrinkled back on a vulpine smile, absorbing the implied insult without comment.

Csurik climbed the yard beside Miles as if to an executioner's block. Their entrance created a tableau of astonishment among Karal and his family, clustered around their wooden table where Dea was treating Pym. Pym and Dea looked rather blanker, till Miles made introduction: "Dr. Dea, get out your fast-penta. Here's Lem Csurik come to talk with us."

Miles steered Lem to a chair. The hill man sat with his hands clenched. Pym, a red and purpling bruise showing at the edges of the white tape circling his chest, took up his stunner and stepped back.

Dr. Dea muttered under his breath to Miles as he got out the hypospray. "How'd you *do* that?"

Miles's hand brushed his pocket. He pulled out a

sugar cube and held it up, and grinned through the C of his thumb and finger. Dea snorted, but pursed his lips with reluctant respect.

Lem flinched as the hypospray hissed on his arm, as if he expected it to hurt.

"Count backwards from ten," Dea instructed. By the time Lem reached three, he had relaxed; at zero, he giggled.

"Karal, Ma Karal, Pym, gather round," said Miles. "You are my witnesses. Boys, stay back and stay quiet. No interruptions, please."

Miles ran through the preliminaries, half a dozen questions designed to set up a rhythm and kill time while the fast-penta took full effect. Lem Csurik grinned foolishly, lolling in his chair, and answered them all with sunny good will. Fast-penta interrogation had been part of Miles's military intelligence course at the Service Academy. The drug seemed to be working exactly as advertised, oddly enough.

"Did you return to your cabin that morning, after you spent the night at your parents'?"

"Yes, m'lord," Lem smiled.

"About what time?"

"Midmorning."

Nobody here had a chrono, that was probably as precise an answer as Miles was likely to get. "What did you do when you got there?"

"Called for Harra. She was gone, though. It frightened me that she was gone. Thought she might've run out on me." Lem hiccoughed. "I want my Harra."

"Later. Was the baby asleep?"

"She was. She woke up when I called for Harra. Started crying again. It goes right up your spine."

"What did you do then?"

Lem's eyes widened. "I got no milk. She wanted Harra. There's nothing I could do for her."

"Did you pick her up?"

"No, lord, I let her lay. There was nothing I could do for her. Harra, she'd hardly let me touch her, she was that nervous about her. Told me I'd drop her or something."

"You didn't shake her, to stop her screaming?"

"No, lord, I let her lay. I left to look down the path for Harra."

"Then where did you go?"

Lem blinked. "My sister's. I'd promised to help haul wood for a new cabin. Bella—m'other sister—is getting married, y'see, and—"

He was beginning to wander, as was normal for this drug. "Stop," said Miles. Lem fell silent obediently, swaying slightly in his chair. Miles considered his next question carefully. He was approaching the fine line, here. "Did you meet anyone on the path? Answer yes or no."

"Yes."

Dea was getting excited. "Who? Ask him who!"

Miles held up his hand. "You can administer the antagonist now, Dr. Dea."

"Aren't you going to ask him? It could be vital!"

"I can't. I gave my word. Administer the antagonist now, doctor!"

Fortunately, the confusion of two interrogators stopped Lem's mumbled willing reply to Dea's question. Dea, bewildered, pressed his hypospray against Lem's arm. Lem's eyes, half-closed, snapped open within seconds. He sat up straight and rubbed his arm, and his face.

"Who did you meet on the path?" Dea asked him directly.

Lem's lips pressed tight; he looked for rescue to Miles.

Dea looked too. "Why won't you ask him?"

"Because I don't need to," said Miles. "I know precisely who Lem met on the path, and why he went on and not back. It was Raina's murderer. As I shall shortly prove. And—witness this, Karal, Ma Karal—that information did not come from Lem's mouth. Confirm!"

Karal nodded slowly. "I . . . see, m'lord. That was . . . very good of you."

Miles gave him a direct stare, his mouth set in a tight smile. "And when is a mystery no mystery at all?"

Karal reddened, not replying for a moment. Then he said, "You may as well keep on like you're going, m'lord. There's no stopping you now, I suppose."

"No."

Miles sent runners to collect the witnesses, Ma Karal in one direction, Zed in a second, Speaker Karal and his eldest in a third. He had Lem wait with Pym, Dea, and himself. Having the shortest distance to cover, Ma Karal arrived back first, with Ma Csurik and two of her sons in tow.

His mother fell on Lem, embracing him and then looking fearfully over her shoulder at Miles. The younger brothers hung back, but Pym had already moved between them and the door.

"It's all right, Ma," Lem patted her on the back. "Or . . . anyway, I'm all right. I'm clear. Lord Vorkosigan believes me."

She glowered at Miles, still holding Lem's arm. "You didn't let the mutie lord give you that poison drug, did you?"

"Not poison," Miles denied. "In fact, the drug may have saved his life. That damn near makes it a medicine, I'd say. However," he turned toward Lem's two younger brothers, and folded his arms sternly, "I

would like to know which of you young morons threw
the torch on my tent last night?"

The younger one whitened; the elder, hotly indignant, noticed his brother's expression and cut his
denial off in mid-syllable. "You didn't!" he hissed in
horror.

"Nobody," said the white one. "Nobody did."

Miles raised his eyebrows. There followed a short,
choked silence.

"Well, *nobody* can make his apologies to Speaker
and Ma Karal, then," said Miles, "since it was their
sons who were sleeping in the tent last night. I and
my men were in the loft."

The boy's mouth opened in dismay. The youngest
Karal stared at the pale Csurik brother, his age-
mate, and whispered importantly, "You, Dono! You
idiot, didn't ya know that tent wouldn't burn? It's
real Imperial Service issue!"

Miles clasped his hands behind his back, and
fixed the Csuriks with a cold eye. "Rather more to
the point, it was attempted assassination upon your
Count's heir, which carries the same capital charge
of treason as an attempt upon the Count himself. Or
perhaps Dono didn't think of that?"

Dono was thrown into flummoxed confusion. No
need for fast-penta here, the kid couldn't carry off a
lie worth a damn. Ma Csurik now had hold of Dono's
arm too, without letting go of Lem's; she looked as
frantic as a hen with too many chicks, trying to
shelter them from a storm.

"I wasn't trying to kill you, lord!" cried Dono.

"What were you trying to do, then?"

"You'd come to kill Lem. I wanted to . . . make
you go away. Frighten you away. I didn't think anyone would really get hurt—I mean, it was only a
tent!"

"You've never seen anything burn down, I take it. Have you, Ma Csurik?"

Lem's mother nodded, lips tight, clearly torn between a desire to protect her son from Miles, and a desire to beat Dono till he bled for his potentially lethal stupidity.

"Well, but for a chance, you could have killed or horribly injured three of your friends. Think on that, please. In the meantime, in view of your youth and ah, apparent mental defectiveness, I shall hold the treason charge. In return, Speaker Karal and your parents shall be responsible for your good behavior in future, and decide what punishment is appropriate."

Ma Csurik melted with relief and gratitude. Dono looked like he'd rather have been shot. His brother poked him, and whispered, "Mental defective!" Ma Csurik slapped the taunter on the side of his head, suppressing him effectively.

"What about your horse, m'lord?" asked Pym.

"I . . . do not suspect them of the business with the horse," Miles replied slowly. "The attempt to fire the tent was plain stupidity. The other was . . . a different order of calculation altogether."

Zed, who had been permitted to take Pym's horse, returned then with Harra up behind him. Harra entered Speaker Karal's cabin, saw Lem, and stopped with a bitter glare. Lem stood openhanded, his eyes wounded, before her.

"So, lord," Harra said. "You caught him." Her jaw was clenched in joyless triumph.

"Not exactly," said Miles. "He came here and turned himself in. He's made his statement under fast-penta, and cleared himself. Lem did not kill Raina."

Harra turned from side to side. "But I saw he'd been there! He'd left his jacket, and took his good

saw and wood planer away with him. I knew he'd
been back while I was out! There must be something
wrong with your drug!"

Miles shook his head. "The drug worked fine.
Your deduction was correct as far as it went, Lem
did visit the cabin while you were out. But when he
left, Raina was still alive, crying vigorously. It wasn't
Lem."

She swayed. "Who, then?"

"I think you know. I think you've been working
very hard to deny that knowledge, hence your excessive focus on Lem. As long as you were sure it was
Lem, you didn't have to think about the other
possibilities."

"But who else would care?" Harra cried. "Who
else would bother?"

"Who, indeed?" sighed Miles. He walked to the
front window and glanced down the yard. The fog
was clearing in the full light of morning. The horses
were moving uneasily. "Dr. Dea, would you please
get a second dose of fast-penta ready?" Miles turned,
paced back to stand before the fireplace, its coals still
banked for the night. The faint heat was pleasant on
his back.

Dea was staring around, the hypospray in his hand,
clearly wondering to whom to administer it. "My
lord?" he queried, brows lowering in demand for
explanation.

"Isn't it obvious to you, Doctor?" Miles asked
lightly.

"*No,* my lord." His tone was slightly indignant.

"Nor to you, Pym?"

"Not . . . entirely, m'lord." Pym's glance, and stunner aim, wavered uncertainly to Harra.

"I suppose it's because neither of you ever met my
grandfather," Miles decided. "He died just about a

year before you entered my father's service, Pym. He was born at the very end of the Time of Isolation, and lived through every wrenching change this century has dealt to Barrayar. He was called the last of the Old Vor, but really, he was the first of the new. He changed with the times, from the tactics of horse cavalry to that of flyer squadrons, from swords to atomics, and he changed *successfully*. Our present freedom from the Cetagandan occupation is a measure of how fiercely he could adapt, then throw it all away and adapt again. At the end of his life he was called a conservative, only because so much of Barrayar had streamed past him in the direction he had led, prodded, pushed, and pointed all his life.

"He changed, and adapted, and bent with the wind of the times. Then, in his age—for my father was his youngest and sole surviving son, and did not himself marry till middle-age—in his age, he was hit with me. And he had to change again. And he couldn't.

"He begged for my mother to have an abortion, after they knew more or less what the fetal damage would be. He and my parents were estranged for five years after I was born. They didn't see each other or speak or communicate. Everyone thought my father moved us to the Imperial Residence when he became Regent because he was angling for the throne, but in fact it was because the Count my grandfather denied him the use of Vorkosigan House. Aren't family squabbles jolly fun? Bleeding ulcers run in my family, we give them to each other." Miles strolled back to the window and looked out. Ah, yes. Here it came.

"The reconciliation was gradual, when it became quite clear there would be no other son," Miles went on. "No dramatic denouement. It helped when the medics got me walking. It was essential that I tested out bright. Most important of all, I never let him see me give up."

Nobody had dared interrupt this lordly monologue, but it was clear from several expressions that the point of it was escaping them. Since half the point was to kill time, Miles was not greatly disturbed by their failure to track. Footsteps sounded on the wooden porch outside. Pym moved quietly to cover the door with an unobscured angle of fire.

"Dr. Dea," said Miles, sighting through the window, "would you be so kind as to administer that fast-penta to the first person through the door, as they step in?"

"You're not waiting for a volunteer, my lord?"

"Not this time."

The door swung inward, and Dea stepped forward, raising his hand. The hypospray hissed. Ma Mattulich wheeled to face Dea, the skirts of her work dress swirling around her veined calves, hissing in return—"You dare!" Her arm drew back as if to strike him, but slowed in mid-swing and failed to connect as Dea ducked out of her way. This unbalanced her, and she staggered. Speaker Karal, coming in behind, caught her by the arm and steadied her. "You dare!" she wailed again, then turned to see not only Dea but all the other witnesses waiting; Ma Csurik, Ma Karal, Lem, Harra, Pym. Her shoulders sagged, and then the drug cut in and she just stood, a silly smile fighting with anguish for possession of her harsh face.

The smile made Miles ill, but it was the smile he needed. "Sit her down, Dea, Speaker Karal."

They guided her to the chair lately vacated by Lem Csurik. She was fighting the drug desperately, flashes of resistance melting into flaccid docility. Gradually the docility became ascendant, and she sat draped in the chair, grinning helplessly. Miles sneaked a peek at Harra. She stood white and silent, utterly closed.

For several years after the reconciliation Miles had never been left with his grandfather without his personal bodyguard. Sergeant Bothari had worn the Count's livery, but been loyal to Miles alone, the one man dangerous enough—some said, crazy enough—to stand up to the great General himself. There was no need, Miles decided, to spell out to these fascinated people just what interrupted incident had made his parents think Sergeant Bothari a necessary precaution. Let General Piotr's untarnished reputation serve—Miles, now. As *he* willed. Miles's eyes glinted.

Lem lowered his head. "If I had known—if I had guessed—I wouldn't have left them alone together, m'lord. I thought—Harra's mother would take care of her. I couldn't have—I didn't know *how*—"

Harra did not look at him. Harra did not look at anything.

"Let us conclude this," Miles sighed. Again, he requested formal witness from the crowd in the room, and cautioned against interruptions, which tended to unduly confuse a drugged subject. He moistened his lips and turned to Ma Mattulich.

Again, he began with the standard neutral questions, name, birthdate, parents' names, checkable biographical facts. Ma Mattulich was harder to lull than the cooperative Lem had been, her responses scattered and staccato. Miles controlled his impatience with difficulty. For all its deceptive ease, fast-penta interrogation required skill, skill and patience. He'd got too far to risk a stumble now. He worked his questions up gradually to the first critical ones.

"Were you there, when Raina was born?"

Her voice was low and drifting, dreamy. "The birth came in the night. Lem, he went for Jean the midwife. The midwife's son was supposed to go for me but he fell back to sleep. I didn't get there till morning, and then it was too late. They'd all seen."

"Seen what?"

"The cat's mouth, the dirty mutation. Monsters in us. Cut them out. Ugly little man." This last, Miles realized, was an aside upon himself. Her attention had hung up on him, hypnotically. "Muties make more muties, they breed faster, overrun . . . I saw you watching the girls. You want to make mutie babies on clean women, poison us all . . ."

Time to steer her back to the main issue. "Were you ever alone with the baby after that?"

"No, Jean she hung around. Jean knows me, she knew what I wanted. None of her damn business. And Harra was always there. Harra must not know. Harra must not . . . why should she get off so soft? The poison must be in her. Must have come from her Da, I lay only with her Da and they were all wrong but the one."

Miles blinked. "What were all wrong?" Across the room Miles saw Speaker Karal's mouth tighten. The headman caught Miles's glance and stared down at his own feet, absenting himself from the proceedings. Lem, his lips parted in absorption, and the rest of the boys were listening with alarm. Harra hadn't moved.

"All my babies," Ma Mattulich said.

Harra looked up sharply at that, her eyes widening.

"Was Harra not your only child?" Miles asked. It was an effort to keep his voice cool, calm; he wanted to shout. He wanted to be gone from here. . . .

"No, of course not. She was my only clean child, I thought. I thought, but the poison must have been hidden in her. I fell on my knees and thanked God when she was born clean, a clean one at last, after so many, so much pain. . . . I thought I had finally been punished enough. She was such a pretty baby, I thought it was over at last. But she must have been mutie after all, hidden, tricksy, sly. . . ."

"How many," Miles choked, "babies did you have?"

"Four, besides Harra my last."

"And you killed all four of them?" Speaker Karal, Miles saw, gave a slow nod to his feet.

"No!" said Ma Mattulich. Indignation broke through the fast-penta wooze briefly. "Two were born dead already, the first one, and the twisted-up one. The one with too many fingers and toes, and the one with the bulgy head, those I cut. Cut out. My mother, she watched over me to see I did it right. Harra, I made it soft for Harra. I did it for her."

"So you have in fact murdered not one infant, but three?" said Miles frozenly. The younger witnesses in the room, Karal's boys and the Csurik brothers, looked horrified. The older ones, Ma Mattulich's contemporaries, who must have lived through the events with her, looked mortified, sharing her shame. Yes, they all must have known.

"Murdered?" said Ma Mattulich. "No! I cut them out. I had to. I had to do the right thing." Her chin lifted proudly, then drooped. "Killed my babies, to please, to please . . . I don't know who. And now you call me a murderer? Damn you! What use is your justice to me *now?* I needed it then—where were you *then?*" Suddenly, shockingly, she burst into tears, which wavered almost instantly into rage. "If mine must die then so must hers! Why should she get off so soft? Spoiled her . . . I tried my best, I did my best, it's not fair . . ."

The fast-penta was not keeping up with this . . .

no, it was working, Miles decided, but her emotions were too overwhelming. Upping the dose might level her emotional surges, at some risk of respiratory arrest, but it would not elicit any more complete a confession. Miles's belly was trembling, a reaction he trusted he concealed. It had to be completed now.

"Why did you break Raina's neck, instead of cutting her throat?"

"Harra, she must not know," said Ma Mattulich. "Poor baby. It would look like she just died. . . ."

Miles eyed Lem, Speaker Karal. "It seems a number of others shared your opinion that Harra should not know."

"I didn't want it to be from my mouth," repeated Lem sturdily.

"I wanted to save her double grief, m'lord," said Karal. "She'd had so much. . . ."

Miles met Harra's eyes at that. "I think you all underestimate her. Your excessive tenderness insults both her intelligence and will. She comes from a tough line, that one."

Harra inhaled, controlling her own trembling. She gave Miles a short nod, as if to say *Thank you, little man*. He returned her a slight inclination of the head, *Yes, I understand*.

"I'm not sure yet where justice lies in this case," said Miles, "but this I swear to you, the days of cooperative concealment are over. No more secret crimes in the night. Daylight's here. And speaking of crimes in the night," he turned back to Ma Mattulich, "*was* it you who tried to cut my horse's throat last night?"

"I tried," said Ma Mattulich, calmer now in a wave of fast-penta mellowness, "but it kept rearing up on me."

"Why my *horse?*" Miles could not keep exasperation from his voice, though a calm, even tone was enjoined upon fast-penta interrogators by the training manual.

"I couldn't get at you," said Ma Mattulich simply.

Miles rubbed his forehead. "Retroactive infanticide by proxy?" he muttered.

"You," said Ma Mattulich, and her loathing came through even the nauseating fast-penta cheer, "*you* are the worst. All I went through, all I did, all the grief, and you come along at the end. A mutie made lord over us all, and all the rules changed, betrayed at the end by an off-worlder woman's weakness. You make it all for *nothing*. Hate you. Dirty mutie . . ." her voice trailed off in a drugged mumble.

Miles took a deep breath, and looked around the room. The stillness was profound, and no one dared break it.

"I believe," he said, "that concludes my investigation into the facts of this case."

The mystery of Raina's death was solved.

The problem of justice, unfortunately, remained.

Miles took a walk.

The graveyard, though little more than a crude clearing in the woodland, was a place of peace and beauty in the morning light. The stream burbled endlessly, shifting green shadows and blinding brilliant reflections. The faint breeze that had shredded away the last of the night fog whispered in the trees, and the tiny, short-lived creatures that everyone on Barrayar but biologists called bugs sang and twittered in the patches of native scrub.

"Well, Raina," Miles sighed, "and what do I do now?" Pym lingered by the borders of the clearing, giving Miles room. "It's all right," Miles assured the tiny grave, "Pym's caught me talking to dead people before. He may think I'm crazy, but he's far too well-trained to say so."

Pym in fact did not look happy, nor altogether well. Miles felt rather guilty for dragging him out; by rights the man should be resting in bed, but Miles had desperately needed this time alone. Pym wasn't just suffering the residual effect of having been kicked by Ninny. He had been silent ever since Miles had extracted the confession from Ma Mattulich. Miles was unsurprised. Pym had steeled himself to play executioner to their imagined hill bully; the substitution of a mad grandmother as his victim had clearly given him pause. He would obey whatever order Miles gave him, though, Miles had no doubt of that.

Miles considered the peculiarities of Barrayaran law, as he wandered about the clearing, watching the stream and the light, turning over an occasional rock with the toe of his boot. The fundamental principle was clear; the spirit was to be preferred over the letter, truth over technicalities. Precedent was held subordinate to the judgment of the man on the spot. Alas, the man on the spot was himself. There was no refuge for him in automated rules, no hiding behind *the law says* as if the law were some living overlord with a real Voice. The only voice here was his own.

And who would be served by the death of that half-crazed old woman? Harra? The relationship between mother and daughter had been wounded unto death by this, Miles had seen that in their eyes, yet still Harra had no stomach for matricide. Miles rather preferred it that way, having her standing by his ear crying for bloody revenge would have been enormously distracting just now. The obvious justice made a damn poor reward for Harra's courage in reporting the crime. Raina? Ah. That was more difficult.

"I'd like to lay the old gargoyle right there at your

feet, small lady," Miles muttered to her. "Is it your desire? Does it serve you? What *would* serve you?" Was this the great burning he had promised her?

What judgment would reverberate along the entire Dendarii mountain range? Should he indeed sacrifice these people to some larger political statement, regardless of their wants? Or should he forget all that, make his judgment serve only those directly involved? He scooped up a stone and flung it full force into the stream. It vanished invisibly in the rocky bed.

He turned to find Speaker Karal waiting by the edge of the graveyard. Karal ducked his head in greeting and approached cautiously.

"So, m'lord," said Karal.

"Just so," said Miles.

"Have you come to any conclusion?"

"Not really." Miles gazed around. "Anything less than Ma Mattulich's death seems . . . inadequate justice, and yet . . . I cannot see who her death would serve."

"Neither could I. That's why I took the position I did in the first place."

"No . . ." said Miles slowly, "no, you were wrong in that. For one thing, it very nearly got Lem Csurik killed. I was getting ready to pursue him with deadly force at one point. It almost destroyed him with Harra. Truth is better. Slightly better. At least it isn't a fatal error. Surely I can do . . . something with it."

"I didn't know what to expect of you, at first," admitted Karal.

Miles shook his head. "I meant to make changes. A difference. Now . . . I don't know."

Speaker Karal's balding forehead wrinkled. "But we are changing."

"Not enough. Not fast enough."

"You're young yet, that's why you don't see how much, how fast. Look at the difference between Harra and her mother. God—look at the difference between Ma Mattulich and *her* mother. *There* was a harridan." Speaker Karal shuddered. "I remember her, all right. And yet, she was not so unusual, in her day. So far from having to make change, I don't think you could stop it if you tried. The minute we finally get a powersat receptor up here, and get on the comm net, the past will be done and over. As soon as the kids see the future—their future—they'll be mad after it. They're already lost to the old ones like Ma Mattulich. The old ones know it, too, don't believe they don't know it. Why d'you think we haven't been able to get at least a small unit up here yet? Not just the cost. The old ones are fighting it. They call it off planet corruption, but it's really the future they fear."

"There's so much still to be done."

"Oh, yes. We are a desperate people, no lie. But we have hope. I don't think you realize how much you've done, just by coming up here."

"I've done nothing," said Miles bitterly. "Sat around, mostly. And now, I swear, I'm going to end up doing more nothing. And then go home. Hell!"

Speaker Karal pursed his lips, looked at his feet, at the high hills. "You are doing something for us every minute. Mutie lord. Do you think you are invisible?"

Miles grinned wolfishly. "Oh, Karal, I'm a one-man band, I am. I'm a parade."

"As you say, just so. Ordinary people need extraordinary examples. So they can say to themselves, well, if he can do *that*, I can surely do *this*. No excuses."

"No quarter, yes, I know that game. Been playing it all my life."

"I think," said Karal, "Barrayar needs you. To go on being just what you are."

"Barrayar will eat me, if it can."

"Yes," said Karal, his eyes on the horizon, "so it will." His gaze fell to the graves at his feet. "But it swallows us all in the end, doesn't it? You will out-live the old ones."

"Or in the beginning." Miles pointed down. "Don't tell *me* who I'm going to outlive. Tell Raina."

Karal's shoulders slumped. "True. S'truth. Make your judgment, lord. I'll back you."

Miles assembled them all in Karal's yard for his Speaking, the porch now having become his podium. The interior of the cabin would have been impossibly hot and close for this crowd, suffocating with the afternoon sun beating on the roof, though outdoors the light made them squint. They were all here, everyone they could round up, Speaker Karal, Ma Karal, their boys, all the Csuriks, most of the cronies who had attended last night's funereal festivities, men, women, and children. Harra sat apart. Lem kept trying to hold her hand, though from the way she flinched it was clear she didn't want to be touched. Ma Mattulich sat displayed by Miles's side, silent and surly, flanked by Pym and an uncomfortable-looking Deputy Alex.

Miles jerked up his chin, settling his head on the high collar of his dress greens, as polished and formal as Pym's batman's expertise could make him. The Imperial Service uniform that Miles had earned. Did these people know he had earned it, or did they all imagine it a mere gift from his father, nepotism at work? Damn what they thought. He knew. He stood before his people, and gripped the porch rail.

"I have concluded the investigation of the charges laid before the Count's Court by Harra Csurik of the murder of her daughter Raina. By evidence, witness, and her own admission, I find Mara Mattulich guilty of this murder, she having twisted the infant's neck until it broke, and then attempted to conceal that crime. Even when that concealment placed her son-in-law Lem Csurik in mortal danger from false charges. In light of the helplessness of the victim, the cruelty of the method, and the cowardly selfishness of the attempted concealment, I can find no mitigating excuse for the crime.

"In addition, Mara Mattulich by her own admission testifies to two previous infanticides, some twenty years ago, of her own children. These facts shall be announced by Speaker Karal in every corner of Silvy Vale, until every subject has been informed."

He could feel Ma Mattulich's glare boring into his back. *Yes, go on and hate me, old woman. I will bury you yet, and you know it.* He swallowed, and continued, the formality of the language a sort of shield before him.

"For this unmitigated crime, the only proper sentence is death. And I so sentence Mara Mattulich. But in light of her age and close relation to the next-most-injured party in the case, Harra Csurik, I choose to hold the actual execution of that sentence. Indefinitely." Out of the corner of his eye Miles saw Pym let out, very carefully and covertly, a sigh of relief. Harra combed at her straw-colored bangs with her fingers and listened intently.

"But she shall be as dead before the law. All her property, even to the clothes on her back, now belongs to her daughter Harra, to dispose of as she wills. Mara Mattulich may not own property, enter contracts, sue for injuries, nor exert her will after

death in any testament. She shall not leave Silvy
Vale without Harra's permission. Harra shall be given
power over her as a parent over a child, or as in
senility. In Harra's absence Speaker Karal will be
her deputy. Mara Mattulich shall be watched to see
she harms no other child.

"Further. She shall die without sacrifice. No one,
not Harra nor any other, shall make a burning for
her when she goes into the ground at last. As she
murdered her future, so her future shall return only
death to her spirit. She will die as the childless do,
without remembrance."

A low sigh swept the older members of the crowd
before Miles. For the first time, Mara Mattulich
bent her stiff neck.

Some, Miles knew, would find this only spiritually
symbolic. Others would see it as literally lethal, according to the strength of their beliefs. The literal-
minded, such as those who saw mutation as a sin to
be violently expiated. But even the less superstitious, Miles saw in their faces, found the meaning
clear. So.

Miles turned to Ma Mattulich, and lowered his
voice. "Every breath you take from this moment on
is by my mercy. Every bite of food you eat, by
Harra's charity. By charity and mercy—such as you
did not give—you shall live. Dead woman."

"Some mercy. Mutie lord." Her growl was low,
weary, beaten.

"You get the point," he said through his teeth. He
swept her a bow, infinitely ironic, and turned his
back on her. "I am the Voice of Count Vorkosigan.
This concludes my Speaking."

Miles met Harra and Lem afterwards, in Speaker
Karal's cabin.

"I have a proposition for you." Miles controlled his nervous pacing and stood before them. "You're free to turn it down, or think about it for a while. I know you're very tired right now." *As are we all.* Had he really been in Silvy Vale only a day and a half? It seemed like a century. His head ached with fatigue. Harra was red-eyed too. "First of all, can you read and write?"

"Some," Harra admitted. "Speaker Karal taught us some, and Ma Lannier."

"Well, good enough. You wouldn't be starting completely blind. Look. A few years back Hassadar started a teacher's college. It's not very big yet, but it's begun. There are some scholarships. I can swing one your way, if you will agree to live in Hassadar for three years of intense study."

"Me!" said Harra. "I couldn't go to a college! I barely know . . . any of that stuff."

"Knowledge is what you're supposed to have coming out, not going in. Look, they know what they're dealing with in this district. They have a lot of remedial courses. It's true, you'd have to work harder, to catch up with the town-bred and the lowlanders. But I know you have courage, and I know you have will. The rest is just picking yourself up and ramming into the wall again and again until it falls down. You get a bloody forehead, so what? You can do it, I swear you can."

Lem, sitting beside her, looked worried. He captured her hand again. "Three years?" he said in a small voice. "Gone away?"

"The school stipend isn't that much," said Miles. "But Lem, I understand you have carpenter's skills. There's a building boom going on in Hassadar right now. Hassadar's going to be the next Vorkosigan Vashnoi, I think. I'm certain you could get a job. Between you, you could live."

Lem looked at first relieved, then extremely worried. "But they all use power tools—computers—robots. . . ."

"By no means. And they weren't all born knowing how to use that stuff either. If they can learn it, you can. Besides, the rich pay well for hand-work, unique one-off items, if the quality's good. I can see you get a start, which is usually the toughest moment. After that you should be able to figure it out all right."

"To leave Silvy Vale . . ." said Harra in a dismayed tone.

"Only in order to return. That's the other half of the bargain. I can send a comm unit up here, a small one with a portable power pack that lasts a year. Somebody'd have to hump down to Vorkosigan Surleau to replace it annually, no big problem. The whole set up wouldn't cost much more than oh, a new lightflyer." Such as the shiny red one Miles had coveted in a dealer's showroom in Vorbarr Sultana, very suitable for a graduation present, he had pointed out to his parents. The credit chit was sitting in the top drawer of his dresser in the lake house at Vorkosigan Surleau right now. "It's not a massive project like installing a powersat receptor for the whole of Silvy Vale or anything. The holovid would pick up the educational satellite broadcasts from the capital; set it up in some central cabin, add a couple of dozen lap-links for the kids, and you've got an instant school. All the children would be required to attend, with Speaker Karal to enforce it, though once they'd discovered the holovid you'd probably have to beat them to make them go home. I, ah," Miles cleared his throat, "thought you might name it the Raina Csurik Primary School."

"Oh," said Harra, and began to cry for the first time that grueling day. Lem patted her clumsily. She returned the grip of his hand at last.

"I can send a lowlander up here to teach," said Miles. "I'll get one to take a short-term contract, till you're ready to come back. But he or she won't understand Silvy Vale like you do. Wouldn't understand *why*. You—you already know. You know what they can't teach in any lowland college."

Harra scrubbed her eyes, and looked up—not very far up—at him. "You went to the Imperial Academy."

"I did." His chin jerked up.

"Then I," she said shakily, "can manage . . . Hassadar Teacher's College." The name was awkward in her mouth. At first. "At any rate—I'll try, m'lord."

"I'll bet on you," Miles agreed. "Both of you. Just, ah," a smile sped across his mouth and vanished, "stand up straight and speak the truth, eh?"

Harra blinked understanding. An answering half-smile lit her tired face, equally briefly. "I will. Little man."

Fat Ninny rode home by air the next morning, in a horse van, along with Pym. Dr. Dea went along with his two patients, and his nemesis the sorrel mare. A replacement bodyguard had been sent with the groom who flew the van from Vorkosigan Surleau, who stayed with Miles to help him ride the remaining two horses back down. Well, Miles thought, he'd been considering a camping trip in the mountains with his cousin Ivan as part of his home leave anyway. The liveried man was the laconic veteran Esterhazy, whom Miles had known most of his life; excellent company for a man who didn't want to talk about it, unlike Ivan you could almost forget he was there. Miles wondered if Esterhazy's assignment had been random chance, or a mercy of the Count's. Esterhazy was good with horses.

They camped overnight by the river of roses. Miles walked up the vale in the evening light, desultorily looking for the spring of it; indeed, the floral barrier did seem to peter out a couple of kilometers upstream, merging into slightly less impassable scrub. Miles plucked a rose, checked to make sure that Esterhazy was nowhere in sight, and bit into it curiously. Clearly, he was not a horse. A cut bunch would probably not survive the trip back as a treat for Ninny. Ninny could settle for oats.

Miles watched the evening shadows flowing up along the backbone of the Dendarii range, high and massive in the distance. How small those mountains looked from space! Little wrinkles on the skin of a globe he could cover with his hand, all their crushing mass made invisible. Which was illusory, distance or nearness? Distance, Miles decided. Distance was a damned lie. Had his father known this? Miles suspected so.

He contemplated his urge to throw all his money, not just a lightflyer's worth, at those mountains; to quit it all and go teach children to read and write, to set up a free clinic, a powersat net, or all of these at once. But Silvy Vale was only one of hundreds of such communities buried in these mountains, one of thousands across the whole of Barrayar. Taxes squeezed from this very district helped maintain the very elite military school he'd just spent—how much of their resources in? How much would he have to give back just to make it even, now? He was himself a planetary resource, his training had made him so, and his feet were set on their path.

What God means you to do, Miles's theist mother claimed, could be deduced from the talents He gave you. The academic honors, Miles had amassed by sheer brute work. But the war games, outwitting his opponents, staying one step ahead—a necessity, true, he had no margin for error—the war games had been an unholy joy. War had been no game here once, not so long ago. It might be so again. What you did best, that was what was wanted from you. God seemed to be lined up with the Emperor on that point, at least, if no other.

Miles had sworn his officer's oath to the Emperor less than two weeks ago, puffed with pride at his achievement. In his secret mind he had imagined himself keeping that oath through blazing battle, enemy torture, what-have-you, even while sharing cynical cracks afterwards with Ivan about archaic dress swords and the sort of people who insisted on wearing them.

But in the dark of subtler temptations, those which hurt without heroism for consolation, he forsaw, the Emperor would no longer be the symbol of Barrayar in his heart.

Peace to you, small lady, he thought to Raina. *You've won a twisted poor modern knight, to wear your favor on his sleeve. But it's a twisted poor world we were both born into, that rejects us without mercy and ejects us without consultation. At least I won't just tilt at windmills for you. I'll send in sappers to mine the twirling suckers, and blast them into the sky. . . .*

He knew who he served now. And why he could not quit. And why he must not fail.

TWO

"Are you feeling better?" said Illyan cautiously.

"Somewhat," Miles replied carefully, and waited. He could outwait Illyan now, oh yes.

The security chief pulled up a chair and settled himself by Miles's bedside, regarded Miles, and pursed his lips. "My . . . apologies, Lord Vorkosigan, for doubting your word."

"You owe me that," Miles agreed.

"Yes. Nevertheless," Illyan frowned into the middle distance. "I wonder, Miles, if you've ever realized the extent that, in your position as your father's son, it is not only necessary to be honest, but to appear so."

"As my father's son—no," said Miles flatly.

Illyan snorted involuntarily. "Ha. Perhaps not." His fingers drummed. "Be that as it may, Count Vorvolk has seized on two discrepancies in your mercenary covert ops reports. Wild cost overruns in what should have been the simplest of tasks, personnel pick-ups. I realize Dagoola blew up on you, but what about the first time?"

"The first time what?"

"They're looking again at the pick-up you made from Jackson's Whole. Their theory being that your successfully-concealed initial peculation there tempted you to larger efforts at Dagoola."

"That was almost two years ago!" Miles protested.

"They're reaching," Illyan agreed. "They're looking hard. They want to nail you to the wall in public if they possibly can. I am, as it were, trying to confiscate the hammer. Dammit," he added irritably, "don't look at me like that. There's nothing personal in it. If you were anyone else's son the matter would not have arisen—you know it, I know it, and they know it. Financial oversight audits by untouchable Vor bores are not my idea of an amusement. My one hope is to tire him out and make him go away. So give."

Miles sighed. "Sir, I am at your disposal, as always. What d'you want to know?"

"Explain the equipment bill for the Jackson's Whole pick-up."

"It was all accounted for in my report at the time, I thought." Miles tried to remember.

"Accounted for, yes. Explained, no."

"We left half a cargo of high-class weaponry on the dock at Fell Station. If we hadn't, you might have been out a scientist, a ship, and a subordinate."

"Yes?" said Illyan. He templed his fingers and leaned back in his chair. "Why?"

"Ah . . . it's a long story. Complicated, y'know." Despite himself, Miles smiled in memory. "Can this still be just between you and me?"

Illyan tilted his head. "All right. . . ."

Labyrinth

Miles contemplated the image of the globe glowing above the vid plate, crossed his arms, and stifled queasiness. The planet of Jackson's Whole, glittering, wealthy, corrupt. . . . Jacksonians claimed their corruption was entirely imported—if the galaxy were willing to pay for virtue what it paid for vice, the place would be a pilgrimage shrine. In Miles's view this seemed rather like debating which was superior, maggots or the rotten meat they fed off. Still, if Jackson's Whole didn't exist, the galaxy would probably have had to invent it. Its neighbors might feign horror, but they wouldn't permit the place to exist if they didn't find it a secretly useful interface with the sub-economy.

The planet possessed a certain liveliness, anyway. Not as lively as a century or two back, to be sure, in its hijacker-base days. But its cutthroat criminal gangs had senesced into Syndicate monopolies, almost as structured and staid as little governments. An aristocracy, of sorts. Naturally. Miles wondered how much longer the major Houses would be able to fight off the creeping tide of integrity.

House Dyne, detergent banking—launder your money on Jackson's Whole. House Fell, weapons deals with no questions asked. House Bharaputra, illegal genetics. Worse, House Ryoval, whose motto was "Dreams Made Flesh," surely the damndest— Miles used the adjective precisely—procurer in history. House Hargraves, the galactic fence, prim-faced middlemen for ransom deals—you had to give them credit, hostages exchanged through their good offices came back alive, mostly. And a dozen smaller syndicates, variously and shiftingly allied.

Even we find you useful. Miles touched the control and the vid image vanished. His lip curled in suppressed loathing, and he called up his ordnance inventory for one final check of his shopping list. A subtle shift in the vibrations of the ship around him told him they were matching orbits—the fast cruiser *Ariel* would be docking at Fell Station within the hour.

His console was just extruding the completed data disk of weapons orders when his cabin door chimed, followed by an alto voice over its comm, "Admiral Naismith?"

"Enter." He plucked off the disk and leaned back in his station chair.

Captain Thorne sauntered in with a friendly salute. "We'll be docking in about thirty minutes, sir."

"Thank you, Bel."

Bel Thorne, the *Ariel*'s commander, was a Betan hermaphrodite, man/woman descendant of a centuries-past genetic-social experiment every bit as bizarre, in Miles's private opinion, as anything rumored to be done for money by House Ryoval's ethics-free surgeons. A fringe effort of Betan egalitarianism run

amok, hermaphroditism had not caught on, and the
original idealists' hapless descendants remained a mi-
nority on hyper-tolerant Beta Colony. Except for a
few stray wanderers like Bel. As a mercenary officer
Thorne was conscientious, loyal, and aggressive, and
Miles liked him/her/it—Betan custom used the neu-
ter pronoun—a lot. *However. . . .*

Miles could smell Bel's floral perfume from here.
Bel was emphasizing the female side today. And had
been, increasingly, for the five days of this voyage.
Normally Bel chose to come on ambiguous-to-male,
soft short brown hair and chiselled, beardless facial
features counteracted by the grey-and-white Dendarii
military uniform, assertive gestures, and wicked humor. It worried Miles exceedingly to sense Bel soften
in his presence.

Turning to his computer console's holovid plate,
Miles again called up the image of the planet they
were approaching. Jackson's Whole looked demure
enough from a distance, mountainous, rather cold—
the populated equator was only temperate—ringed
in the vid by a lacy schematic net of colored satellite
tracks, orbital transfer stations, and authorized approach vectors. "Have you ever been here before,
Bel?"

"Once, when I was a lieutenant in Admiral Oser's
fleet," said the mercenary. "House Fell has a new
baron since then. Their weaponry still has a good
reputation, as long as you know what you're buying.
Stay away from the sale on neutron hand grenades."

"Heh. For those with strong throwing arms. Fear
not, neutron hand grenades aren't on the list." He
handed the data disk to Bel.

Bel sidled up and leaned over the back of Miles's
station chair to take it. "Shall I grant leaves to the
crew while we're waiting for the baron's minions to

load cargo? How about yourself? There used to be a
hostel near the docks with all the ameneties, pool,
sauna, great food . . ." Bel's voice lowered. "I could
book a room for two."

"I'd only figured to grant day passes." Necessarily,
Miles cleared his throat.

"I *am* a woman, too," Bel pointed out in a murmur.
"Among other things."

"You're so hopelessly monosexual, Miles."

"Sorry." Awkwardly, he patted the hand that had
somehow come to rest on his shoulder.

Bel sighed and straightened. "So many are."

Miles sighed too. Perhaps he ought to make his
rejection more emphatic—this was only about the
seventh time he'd been round with Bel on this subject. It was almost ritualized by now, almost, but not
quite, a joke. You had to give the Betan credit for either
optimism or obtuseness . . . or, Miles's honesty added,
genuine feeling. If he turned round now, he knew,
he might surprise an essential loneliness in the hermaphrodite's eyes, never permitted on the lips. He
did not turn round.

And who was he to judge another, Miles reflected
ruefully, whose own body brought him so little joy?
What did Bel, straight and healthy and of normal
height, if unusual genital arrangements, find so at-
tractive in a little half-crippled part-time crazy man?
He glanced down at the grey Dendarii officer's
uniform he wore. The uniform he had won. *If you
can't be seven feet tall, be seven feet smart.* His
reason had so far failed to present him with a solution to the problem of Thorne, though.

"Have you ever thought of going back to Beta
Colony, and seeking one of your own?" Miles asked
seriously.

Thorne shrugged. "Too boring. That's why I left. It's so very safe, so very narrow. . . ."

"Mind you, a great place to raise kids." One corner of Miles's mouth twisted up.

Thorne grinned. "You got it. You're an almost perfect Betan, y'know? Almost. You have the accent, the in-jokes . . ."

Miles went a little still. "Where do I fail?"

Thorne touched Miles's cheek; Miles flinched.

"Reflexes," said Thorne.

"Ah."

"I won't give you away."

"I know."

Bel was leaning in again. "I could polish that last edge . . ."

"Never mind," said Miles, slightly flushed. "We have a mission."

"Inventory," said Thorne scornfully.

"That's not a mission," said Miles, "that's a cover."

"Ah ha." Thorne straightened up. "At last."

"At last?"

"It doesn't take a genius. We came to purchase ordnance, but instead of taking the ship with the biggest cargo capacity, you chose the *Ariel*—the fleet's fastest. There's no deader dull routine than inventory, but instead of sending a perfectly competent quartermaster, you're overseeing it personally."

"I do want to make contact with the new Baron Fell," said Miles mildly. "House Fell is the biggest arms supplier this side of Beta Colony, and a lot less picky about who its customers are. If I like the quality of the initial purchase, they could become a regular supplier."

"A quarter of Fell's arms are Betan manufacture, marked up," said Thorne. "Again, ha."

"And while we're here," Miles went on, "a certain

middle-aged man is going to present himself and sign on to the Dendarii Mercenaries as a medtech. At that point all Station passes are cancelled, we finish loading cargo as quickly as possible, and we leave."

Thorne grinned in satisfaction. "A pick-up. Very good. I assume we're being well-paid?"

"Very. If he arrives at his destination alive. The man happens to be the top research geneticist of House Bharaputra's Laboratories. He's been offered asylum by a planetary government capable of protecting him from the long arms of Baron Luigi Bharaputra's enforcers. His soon-to-be-former employer is expected to be highly irate at the lack of a month's notice. We are being paid to deliver him to his new masters alive and not, ah, forcibly debriefed of all his trade secrets.

"Since House Bharaputra could probably buy and sell the whole Dendarii Free Mercenary Fleet twice over out of petty cash, I would prefer we not have to deal with Baron Luigi's enforcers either. So we shall be innocent suckers. All we did was hire a bloody medtech, sir. And we shall be irate ourselves when he deserts after we arrive at fleet rendezvous off Escobar."

"Sounds good to me," conceded Thorne. "Simple."

"So I trust," Miles sighed hopefully. Why, after all, shouldn't things run to plan, just this once?

The purchasing offices and display areas for House Fell's lethal wares were situated not far from the docks, and most of House Fell's smaller customers never penetrated further into Fell Station. But shortly after Miles and Thorne placed their order—about as long as needed to verify a credit chit—an obsequious person in the green silk of House Fell's uniform appeared, and pressed an invitation into Admiral

Naismith's hand to a reception in the Baron's personal quarters.

Four hours later, giving up the pass cube to Baron Fell's major domo at the sealed entrance to the station's private sector, Miles checked Thorne and himself over for their general effect. Dendarii dress uniform was a grey velvet tunic with silver buttons on the shoulders and white edging, matching grey trousers with white side piping, and grey synthasuede boots—perhaps just a trifle effete? Well, he hadn't designed it, he'd just inherited it. Live with it.

The interface to the private sector was highly interesting. Miles's eye took in the details while the major domo scanned them for weapons. Life-support —in fact, all systems—appeared to be run separately from the rest of the station. The area was not only sealable, it was detachable. In effect, not Station but Ship—engines and armament around here somewhere, Miles bet, though it could be lethal to go looking for them unescorted. The major domo ushered them through, pausing to announce them on his wrist comm: "Admiral Miles Naismith, commanding, Dendarii Free Mercenary Fleet. Captain Bel Thorne, commanding the fast cruiser *Ariel*, Dendarii Free Mercenary Fleet." Miles wondered who was on the other end of the comm.

The reception chamber was large and gracefully appointed, with iridescent floating staircases and levels creating private spaces without destroying the illusions of openness. Every exit (Miles counted six) had a large green-garbed guard by it trying to look like a servant and not succeeding very well. One whole wall was a vertigo-inducing transparent viewport overlooking Fell Station's busy docks and the bright curve of Jackson's Whole bisecting the star-spattered horizon beyond. A crew of elegant women in green silk saris rustled among the guests offering food and drink.

Grey velvet, Miles decided after one glance at the other guests, was a positively demure choice of garb. He and Bel would blend right into the walls. The thin scattering of fellow privileged customers wore a wide array of planetary fashions. But they were a wary bunch, little groups sticking together, no mingling. Guerrillas, it appeared, did not speak to mercenaries, nor smugglers to revolutionaries; the Gnostic Saints, of course, spoke only to the One True God, and perhaps to Baron Fell.

"Some party," commented Bel. "I went to a pet show with an atmosphere like this once. The high point was when somebody's Tau Cetan beaded lizard got loose and ate the Best-In-Show from the canine division."

"Hush," Miles grinned out of the corner of his mouth. "This is business."

A green-sari'd woman bowed silently before them, offering a tray. Thorne raised a brow at Miles—*do we. . . ?*

"Why not?" Miles murmured. "We're paying for it, in the long run. I doubt the baron poisons his customers, it's bad for business. Business is emperor, here. Laissez-faire capitalism gone completely over the edge." He selected a pink tid-bit in the shape of a lotus and a mysterious cloudy drink. Thorne followed suit. The pink lotus, alas, turned out to be some sort of raw fish. It squeaked against his teeth. Miles, committed, swallowed it anyway. The drink was potently alcoholic, and after a sip to wash down the lotus he regretfully abandoned it on the first level surface he could find. His dwarfish body refused to handle alcohol, and he had no desire to meet Baron Fell while either semi-comatose or gig-

gling uncontrollably. The more metabolically fortunate Thorne kept beverage in hand.

A most extraordinary music began from somewhere,
a racing rich complexity of harmonics. Miles could
not identify the instrument—instruments, surely.
He and Thorne exchanged a glance, and by mutual
accord drifted toward the sound. Around a spiraling
staircase, backed by the panoply of station, planet,
and stars, they found the musician. Miles's eyes widened. *House Ryoval's surgeons have surely gone too
far this time.* . . .

Little decorative colored sparkles defined the spher-
ical field of a large null-gee bubble. Floating within
it was a woman. Her ivory arms flashed against her
green silk clothes as she played. All *four* of her ivory
arms. . . . She wore a flowing, kimono-like belted
jacket and matching shorts, from which the second
set of arms emerged where her legs should have
been. Her hair was short and soft and ebony black.
Her eyes were closed, and her rose-tinted face bore
the repose of an angel, high and distant and terrifying.

Her strange instrument was fixed in air before her,
a flat polished wooden frame strung across both top
and bottom with a bewildering array of tight gleaming wires, soundboard between. She struck the wires
with four felted hammers with blinding speed, both
sides at once, her upper hands moving at counter-
point to her lowers. Music poured forth in a cascade.

"Good God," said Thorne, "it's a quaddie."

"It's a what?"

"A quaddie. She's a long way from home."

"She's—not a local product?"

"By no means."

"I'm relieved. I think. Where the devil does she
come from, then?"

"About two hundred years ago—about the time

hermaphrodites were being invented," a peculiar wryness flashed across Thorne's face, "there was this rush of genetic experimentation on humans, in the wake of the development of the practical uterine replicator. Followed shortly by a rush of laws restricting such, but meanwhile, somebody thought they'd make a race of free fall dwellers. Then artificial gravity came in and blew them out of business. The quaddies fled—their descendants ended up on the far side of nowhere, way beyond Earth from us in the Nexus. They're rumored to keep to themselves, mostly. Very unusual, to see one this side of Earth. H'sh." Lips parted, Thorne tracked the music.

As unusual as finding a Betan hermaphrodite in a free mercenary fleet, Miles thought. But the music deserved undivided attention, though few in this paranoid crowd seemed to even be noticing it. A shame. Miles was no musician, but even he could sense an intensity of passion in the playing that went beyond talent, reaching for genius. An evanescent genius, sounds woven with time and, like time, forever receding beyond one's futile grasp into memory alone.

The outpouring of music dropped to a haunting echo, then silence. The four-armed musician's blue eyes opened, and her face came back from the ethereal to the merely human, tense and sad.

"Ah," breathed Thorne, stuck its empty glass under its arm, raised hands to clap, then paused, hesitant to become conspicuous in this indifferent chamber.

Miles was all for being inconspicuous. "Perhaps you can speak to her," he suggested by way of an alternative.

"You think?" Brightening, Thorne tripped forward, swinging down to abandon the glass on the nearest handy floor and raising splayed hands against the sparkling bubble. The hermaphrodite mustered an entranced, ingratiating smile. "Uh . . ." Thorne's chest rose and fell.

Good God, Bel, tongue-tied? Never thought I'd see it. "Ask her what she calls that thing she plays," Miles supplied helpfully.

The four-armed woman tilted her head curiously, and starfished gracefully over her boxy instrument to hover politely before Thorne on the other side of the glittering barrier. "Yes?"

"What do you call that extraordinary instrument?" Thorne asked.

"It's a double-sided hammer dulcimer, ma'am—sir . . ." her servant-to-guest dull tone faltered a moment, fearing to give insult, "Officer."

"Captain Bel Thorne," Bel supplied instantly, beginning to recover accustomed smooth equilibrium. "Commanding the Dendarii fast cruiser *Ariel*. At your service. How ever did you come to be here?"

"I had worked my way to Earth. I was seeking employment, and Baron Fell hired me." She tossed her head, as if to deflect some implied criticism, though Bel had offered none.

"You are a true quaddie?"

"You've heard of my people?" Her dark brows rose in surprise. "Most people I encounter here think I am a *manufactured* freak." A little sardonic bitterness edged her voice.

Thorne cleared its throat. "I'm Betan, myself. I've followed the history of the early genetics explosion with a rather more personal interest." Thorne cleared its throat again, "Betan hermaphrodite, you see," and waited anxiously for the reaction.

Damn. Bel never waited for reactions, Bel sailed on and let the chips fall anyhow. I wouldn't interfere with this for all the world. Miles faded back slightly, rubbing his lips to wipe off a twitching grin as all Thorne's most masculine mannerisms reasserted themselves from spine to fingertips and outward into the aether.

Her head tilted in interest. One upper hand rose to rest on the sparkling barrier not far from Bel's. "*Are* you? You're a genetic too, then."

"Oh, yes. And tell me, what's your name?"

"Nicol."

"Nicol. Is that all? I mean, it's lovely."

"My people don't use surnames."

"Ah. And, uh, what are you doing after the party?"

At this point, alas, interference found them. "Heads up, *Captain*," Miles murmured. Thorne drew up instantly, cool and correct, and followed Miles's gaze. The quaddie floated back from the force barrier and bowed her head over her hands held palm-to-palm and palm-to-palm as a man approached. Miles too came to a polite species of attention.

Georish Stauber, Baron Fell, was a surprisingly old man to have succeeded so recently to his position, Miles thought. In the flesh he looked older than the holovid Miles had viewed of him at his own mission briefing. The baron was balding, with a white fringe of hair around his shiny pate, jovial and fat. He looked like somebody's grandfather. Not Miles's; Miles's grandfather had been lean and predatory even in his great age. And the old Count's title had been as real as such things got, not the courtesy-nobility of a Syndicate survivor. Jolly red cheeks or no, Miles reminded himself, Baron Fell had climbed a pile of bodies to attain this high place.

"Admiral Naismith. Captain Thorne. Welcome to Fell Station," rumbled the baron, smiling.

Miles swept him an aristocratic bow. Thorne somewhat awkwardly followed suit. Ah. He must copy that awkwardness next time. Of such little details were cover identities made. And blown.

"Have my people been taking care of your needs?"

"Thank you, yes." So far the proper businessmen.

"So glad to meet you at last," the baron rumbled on. "We've heard a great deal about you here."

"Have you," said Miles encouragingly. The baron's eyes were strangely avid. *Quite a glad-hand for a little tin-pot mercenary, eh?* This was a little more stroke than was reasonable even for a high-ticket customer. Miles banished all hint of wariness from his return smile. *Patience. Let the challenge emerge, don't rush to meet what you cannot yet see.* "Good things, I hope."

"Remarkable things. Your rise has been as rapid as your origins are mysterious."

Hell, hell, what kind of bait was this? Was the baron hinting that he actually knew "Admiral Naismith's" real identity? This could be sudden and serious trouble. No—fear outran its cause. Wait. Forget that such a person as Lieutenant Lord Vorkosigan, Barrayaran Imperial Security, ever existed in this body. *It's not big enough for the two of us anyway, boy.* Yet why was this fat shark smiling so ingratiatingly? Miles cocked his head, neutrally.

"The story of your fleet's success at Vervain reached us even here. So unfortunate about its former commander."

Miles stiffened. "I regret Admiral Oser's death."

The baron shrugged philosophically. "Such things happen in the business. Only one can command."

"He could have been an outstanding subordinate."

"Pride is so dangerous," smiled the baron.

Indeed. Miles bit his tongue. *So he thinks I "arranged" Oser's death. So let him.* That there was one less mercenary than there appeared in this room,

that the Dendarii were now through Miles an arm of
the Barrayaran Imperial Service so covert most of
them didn't even know it themselves . . . it would
be a dull Syndicate baron who couldn't find profit in
those secrets somewhere. Miles matched the baron's
smile and added nothing.

"You interest me exceedingly," continued the baron.
"For example, there's the puzzle of your apparent
age. And your prior military career."

If Miles had kept his drink, he'd have knocked it
back in one gulp right then. He clasped his hands
convulsively behind his back instead. Dammit, the
pain lines just didn't age his face enough. If the
baron was indeed seeing right through the pseudo-
mercenary to the twenty-three-year-old Security
lieutenant—and yet, he usually carried it off—

The baron lowered his voice. "Do the rumors run
equally true about your Betan rejuvenation treatment?"

So *that's* what he was on about. Miles felt faint
with relief. "What interest could you have in such
treatments, my lord?" he gibbered lightly. "I thought
Jackson's Whole was the home of practical immortal-
ity. It's said there are some here on their third
cloned body."

"I am not one of them," said the baron rather
regretfully.

Miles's brows rose in genuine surprise. Surely this
man didn't spurn the process as murder. "Some unfortunate medical impediment?" he said, injecting
polite sympathy into his voice. "My regrets, sir."

"In a manner of speaking." The baron's smile revealed a sharp edge. "The brain transplant operation
itself kills a certain irreducible percentage of patients—"

Yeah, thought Miles, *starting with 100% of the
clones, whose brains are flushed to make room. . . .*

"—another percentage suffer varying sorts of permanent damage. Those are the risks anyone must take for the reward."

"But the reward is so great."

"But then there are a certain number of patients, indistinguishable from the first group, who do not die on the operating table by accident. If their enemies have the subtlety and clout to arrange it. I have a number of enemies, Admiral Naismith."

Miles made a little who-would-think-it gesture, flipping up one hand, and continued to cultivate an air of deep interest.

"I calculate my present chances of surviving a brain transplant to be rather worse than the average," the baron went on. "So I've an interest in alternatives." He paused expectantly.

"Oh," said Miles. Oh, indeed. He regarded his fingernails and thought fast. "It's true, I once participated in an . . . unauthorized experiment. A premature one, as it happens, pushed too eagerly from animal to human subjects. It was not successful."

"No?" said the baron. "You appear in good health."

Miles shrugged. "Yes, there was some benefit to muscles, skin tone, hair. But my bones are the bones of an old man, fragile." *True.* "Subject to acute osteo-inflammatory attacks—there are days when I can't walk without medication." *Also true, dammit.* A recent and unsettling medical development. "My life expectancy is not considered good." *For example, if certain parties here ever figure out who "Admiral Naismith" really is, it could go down to as little as fifteen minutes.* "So unless you're extremely fond of pain and think you would enjoy being crippled, I fear I must dis-recommend the procedure."

The baron looked him up and down. Disappointment pulled down his mouth. "I see."

Bel Thorne, who knew quite well there was no

such thing as the fabled "Betan rejuvenation treatment," was listening with well-concealed enjoyment and doing an excellent job of keeping the smirk off its face. Bless its little black heart.

"Still," said the baron, "your . . . scientific acquaintance may have made some progress in the intervening years."

"I fear not," said Miles. "He died." He spread his hands helplessly. "Old age."

"Oh." The baron's shoulders sagged slightly.

"Ah, there you are, Fell," a new voice cut across them. The baron straightened and turned.

The man who had hailed him was as conservatively dressed as Fell, and flanked by a silent servant with "bodyguard" written all over him. The bodyguard wore a uniform, a high-necked red silk tunic and loose black trousers, and was unarmed. Everyone on Fell Station went unarmed except Fell's men; the place had the most strictly-enforced weapons regs Miles had ever encountered. But the pattern of calluses on the lean bodyguard's hands suggested he might not need weapons. His eyes flickered and his hands shook just slightly, a hyper-alertness induced by artificial aids—if ordered, he could strike with blinding speed and adrenalin-insane strength. He would also retire young, metabolically crippled for the rest of his short life.

The man he guarded was also young—some great lord's son? Miles wondered. He had long shining black hair dressed in an elaborate braid, smooth dark olive skin, and a high-bridged nose. He couldn't be older than Miles's real age, yet he moved with a mature assurance.

"Ryoval," Baron Fell nodded in return, as a man to an equal, not a junior. Still playing the genial host, Fell added, "Officers, may I introduce Baron

Ryoval of House Ryoval. Admiral Naismith, Captain Thorne. They belong to that Illyrican-built mercenary fast cruiser in dock, Ry, that you may have noticed."

"Haven't got your eye for hardware, I'm afraid, Georish." Baron Ryoval bestowed a nod upon them, of a man being polite to his social inferiors for the principle of it. Miles bowed clumsily in return.

Dropping Miles from his attention with an almost audible thump, Ryoval stood back with his hands on his hips and regarded the null-gee bubble's inhabitant. "My agent didn't exaggerate her charms."

Fell smiled sourly. Nicol had withdrawn—recoiled—when Ryoval first approached, and now floated behind her instrument, fussing with its tuning. Pretending to be fussing with its tuning. Her eyes glanced warily at Ryoval, then returned to her dulcimer as if it might put some magic wall between them.

"Can you have her play—" Ryoval began, and was interrupted by a chime from his wrist comm. "Excuse me, Georish." Looking slightly annoyed, he turned half-away from them and spoke into it. "Ryoval. And this had better be important."

"Yes, m'lord," a thin voice responded. "This is Manager Deem in Sales and Demonstrations. We have a problem. That creature House Bharaputra sold us has savaged a customer."

Ryoval's greek-statue lips rippled in a silent snarl. "I told you to chain it with duralloy."

"We did, my lord. The chains held, but it tore the bolts right out of the wall."

"Stun it."

"We have."

"Then punish it suitably when it awakes. A sufficiently long period without food should dull its aggression—its metabolism is unbelievable."

"What about the customer?"

"Give him whatever comforts he asks for. On the House."

"I . . . don't think he'll be in shape to appreciate them for quite some time. He's in the clinic now. Still unconscious."

Ryoval hissed. "Put my personal physician on his case. I'll take care of the rest when I get back downside, in about six hours. Ryoval out." He snapped the link closed. "Morons," he growled. He took a controlled, meditative breath, and recalled his social manner as if booting it up out of some stored memory bank. "Pardon the interruption, please, Georish."

Fell waved an understanding hand, as if to say, *Business*.

"As I was saying, can you have her play something?" Ryoval nodded to the quaddie.

Fell clasped his hands behind his back, his eyes glinting in a falsely benign smile. "Play something, Nicol."

She gave him an acknowledging nod, positioned herself, and closed her eyes. The frozen worry tensing her face gradually gave way to an inner stillness, and she began to play, a slow, sweet theme that established itself, rolled over, and began to quicken.

"Enough!" Ryoval flung up a hand. "She's precisely as described."

Nicol stumbled to a halt in mid-phrase. She inhaled through pinched nostrils, clearly disturbed by her inability to drive the piece through to its destined finish, the frustration of artistic incompletion. She stuck her hammers into their holders on the side of the instrument with short, savage jerks, and crossed her upper and lower arms both. Thorne's mouth tightened, and it crossed its arms in unconscious echo. Miles bit his lip uneasily.

"My agent conveyed the truth," Ryoval went on.

"Then perhaps your agent also conveyed my regrets," said Fell dryly.

"He did. But he wasn't authorized to offer more than a certain standard ceiling. For something so unique, there's no substitute for direct contact."

"I happen to be enjoying her skills where they are," said Fell. "At my age, enjoyment is much harder to obtain than money."

"So true. Yet other enjoyments might be substituted. I could arrange something quite special. Not in the catalog."

"Her *musical* skills, Ryoval. Which are more than special. They are unique. Genuine. Not artificially augmented in any way. Not to be duplicated in your laboratories."

"My laboratories can duplicate anything sir." Ryoval smiled at the implied challenge.

"Except originality. By definition."

Ryoval spread his hands in polite acknowledgment of the philosophical point. Fell, Miles gathered, was not just enjoying the quaddie's musical talent, he was vastly enjoying the possession of something his rival keenly wanted to buy, that he had absolutely no need to sell. One-upsmanship was a powerful pleasure. It seemed even the famous Ryoval was having a tough time coming up with a better—and yet, if Ryoval could find Fell's price, what force on Jackson's Whole could save Nicol? Miles suddenly realized he knew what Fell's price could be. Would Ryoval figure it out too?

Ryoval pursued his lips. "Let's discuss a tissue sample, then. It would do her no damage, and you could continue to enjoy her unique services uninterrupted."

"It would damage her uniqueness. Circulating counterfeits always brings down the value of the real thing, you know that, Ry," grinned Baron Fell.

"Not for some time," Ryoval pointed out. "The lead time for a mature clone is at least ten years—ah, but you know that." He reddened and made a little apologetic bow, as if he realized he'd just committed some faux paux.

By the thinning of Fell's lips, he had. "Indeed," said Fell coldly.

At this point Bel Thorne, tracking the interplay, interrupted in hot horror, "You can't sell her tissues! You don't own them. She's not some Jackson's Whole construct, she's a freeborn galactic citizen!"

Both barons turned to Bel if the mercenary were a piece of furniture that had suddenly spoken. Out of turn. Miles winced.

"He can sell her contract," said Ryoval, mustering a glassy tolerance. "Which is what we are discussing. A *private* discussion."

Bel ignored the hint. "On Jackson's Whole, what practical difference does it make if you call it a contract or call it flesh?"

Ryoval smiled a little cool smile. "None whatsoever. Possession is rather more than nine points of the law, here."

"It's totally illegal!"

"Legal, my dear—ah—you are Betan, aren't you? That explains it," said Ryoval. "And illegal, is whatever the planet you are on chooses to call so and is able to enforce. I don't see any Betan enforcers around here to impose their peculiar version of morality on us all, do you, Fell?"

Fell was listening with raised brows, caught between amusement and annoyance.

Bel twitched. "So if I were to pull out a weapon and blow your head off, it would be perfectly legal?"

The bodyguard tensed, balance and center-of-gravity flowing into launch position.

"Quash it, Bel," Miles muttered under his breath.

But Ryoval was beginning to enjoy baiting his Betan interrupter. "You have no weapon. But legality aside, my subordinates have instructions to avenge me. It is, as it were, a natural or virtual law. In effect you'd find such an ill-advised impulse to be illegal indeed."

Baron Fell caught Miles's eye and tilted his head just slightly. Time to intervene. "Time to move on, Captain," Miles said. "We aren't the baron's only guests here."

"Try the hot buffet," suggested Fell affably.

Ryoval pointedly dropped Bel from his attention and turned to Miles. "Do stop by my establishment if you get downside, Admiral. Even a Betan could stand to expand the horizons of his experience. I'm sure my staff could find something of interest in your price range."

"Not any more," said Miles. "Baron Fell already has our credit chit."

"Ah, too bad. Your next trip, perhaps." Ryoval turned away in easy dismissal.

Bel didn't budge. "You can't sell a galactic citizen down there," gesturing jerkily to the curve of the planet beyond the viewport. The quaddie Nicol, watching from behind her dulcimer, had no expression at all upon her face, but her intense blue eyes blazed.

Ryoval turned back, feigning sudden surprise. "Why, Captain, I just realized. Betan—you must be a genuine genetic hermaphrodite. You possess a marketable rarity yourself. I can offer you an eye-opening employment experience at easily twice your current rate of pay. And you wouldn't even have to get shot at. I guarantee you'd be extremely popular. Group rates."

Miles swore he could see Thorne's blood pressure skyrocketing as the meaning of what Ryoval had just said sunk in. The hermaphrodite's face darkened, and it drew breath. Miles reached up and grasped Bel by the shoulder, hard. The breath held.

"No?" said Ryoval, cocking his head. "Oh, well. But seriously, I would pay well for a tissue sample, for my files."

Bel's breath exploded. "My clone-siblings, to be— be—some sort of sex-slaves into the next century! Over my dead body—or yours—you—"

Bel was so mad it was stuttering, a phenomenon Miles had never seen in seven years' acquaintance including combat.

"So Betan," smirked Ryoval.

"Stop it, Ry," growled Fell.

Ryoval sighed. "Oh, very well. But it's so easy."

"We can't win, Bel," hissed Miles. "It's time to withdraw." The bodyguard was quivering.

Fell gave Miles an approving nod.

"Thank you for your hospitality, Baron Fell," Miles said formally. "Good day, Baron Ryoval."

"Good day, Admiral," said Ryoval, regretfully giving up what was obviously the best sport he'd had all day. "You seem a cosmopolitan sort, for a Betan. Perhaps you can visit us sometime without your moral friend, here."

A war of words should be won with words. "I don't think so," Miles murmured, racking his brain for some stunning insult to withdraw on.

"What a shame," said Ryoval. "We have a dog-and-dwarf act I'm sure you'd find *fascinating.*"

There was a moment's absolute silence.

"Fry 'em from orbit," Bel suggested tightly.

Miles grinned through clenched teeth, bowed, and backed off, Bel's sleeve clutched firmly in his hand. As he turned he could hear Ryoval laughing.

Fell's majordomo appeared at their elbows within moments. "This way to the exit, please, officers," he smiled. Miles had never before been thrown out of any place with such exquisite politeness.

Back aboard the *Ariel* in dock, Thorne paced the wardroom while Miles sat and sipped coffee as hot and black as his own thoughts.

"Sorry I lost my temper with that squirt Ryoval," Bel apologized gruffly.

"Squirt, hell," said Miles. "The brain in that body has got to be at least a hundred years old. He played you like a violin. No. We couldn't expect to count coup on him. I admit, it would have been nice if you'd had the sense to shut up." He sucked air to cool his scalded tongue.

Bel made a disturbed gesture of acknowledgement and paced on. "And that poor girl, trapped in that bubble—I had one chance to talk to her, and I blew it—I *blithered*. . . ."

She really had brought out the male in Thorne, Miles reflected wryly. "Happens to the best of us," he murmured. He smiled into his coffee, then frowned. No. Better not to encourage Thorne's interest in the quaddie after all. She was clearly much more than just one of Fell's house servants. They had one ship here, a crew of twenty; even if he had the whole Dendarii fleet to back him he'd want to think twice about offending Baron Fell in Fell's own territory. They had a mission. Speaking of which, where was their blasted pick-up? Why hadn't he yet contacted them as arranged?

The intercom in the wall bleeped.

Thorne strode to it. "Thorne here."

"This is Corporal Nout at the portside docking hatch. There's a . . . woman here who's asking to see you."

Thorne and Miles exchanged a raised-brows glance. "What's her name?" asked Thorne.

An off-side mumble, then, "She says it's Nicol."

Thorne grunted in surprise. "Very well. Have her escorted to the wardroom."

"Yes, Captain." The corporal failed to kill his intercom before turning away, and his voice drifted back, ". . . stay in this outfit long enough, you see one of *everything*."

Nicol appeared in the doorway balanced in a float chair, a hovering tubular cup that seemed to be looking for its saucer, enameled in a blue that precisely matched her eyes. She slipped it through the doorway as easily as a woman twitching her hips, zipped to a halt near Miles's table, and adjusted the height to that of a person sitting. The controls, run by her lower hands, left her uppers entirely free. The lower body support must have been custom-designed just for her. Miles watched her manuever with great interest. He hadn't been sure she could even live outside her null-gee bubble. He'd expected her to be weak. She didn't look weak. She looked determined. She looked at Thorne.

Thorne looked all cheered up. "Nicol. How nice to see you again."

She nodded shortly. "Captain Thorne. Admiral Naismith." She glanced back and forth between them, and fastened on Thorne. Miles thought he could see why. He sipped coffee and waited for developments.

"Captain Thorne. You are a mercenary, are you not?"

"Yes. . . ."

"And . . . pardon me if I misunderstood, but it seemed to me you had a certain . . . empathy, for my situation. An understanding of my position."

Thorne rendered her a slightly idiotic bow. "I understand you are dangling over a pit."

Her lips tightened, and she nodded mutely.

"She got herself into it," Miles pointed out.

Her chin lifted. "And I intend to get myself out of it."

Miles turned a hand palm-out, and sipped again.

She readjusted her float chair, a nervous gesture ending at about the same altitude it began.

"It seems to me," said Miles, "that Baron Fell is a formidable protector. I'm not sure you have anything to fear from Ryoval's, er, carnal interest in you as long as Fell's in charge."

"Baron Fell is dying." She tossed her head. "Or at any rate, he thinks he is."

"So I gathered. Why doesn't he have a clone made?"

"He did. It was all set up with House Bharaputra. The clone was fourteen years old, full-sized. Then a couple of months ago, somebody assassinated the clone. The baron still hasn't found out for sure who did it, though he has a little list. Headed by his half-brother."

"Thus trapping him in his aging body. What a . . . fascinating tactical maneuver," Miles mused. "What's this unknown enemy going to do next, I wonder? Just wait?"

"I don't know," said Nicol. "The Baron's had another clone started, but it's not even out of the replicator yet. Even with growth accelerators it'd be years before it would be mature enough to transplant. And . . . it has occurred to me that there are a number of ways the baron could die besides ill health between now and then."

"An unstable situation," Miles agreed.

"I want out. I want to buy passage out."

"Then why, he asked," said Miles dryly, "don't you just go plunk your money down at the offices of one of the three galactic commercial passenger lines that dock here, and buy a ticket?"

"It's my contract," said Nicol. "When I signed it back on Earth, I didn't realize what it would mean once I got to Jackson's Whole. I can't even buy my way out of it, unless the baron chooses to let me. And somehow . . . it seems to cost more and more just to live here. I ran a calculation . . . it gets much worse before my time is up."

"How much time?" asked Thorne.

"Five more years."

"Ouch," said Thorne sympathetically.

"So you, ah, want us to help you jump a Syndicate contract," said Miles, making little wet coffee rings on the table with the bottom of his mug. "Smuggle you out in secret, I suppose."

"I can pay. I can pay more right now than I'll be able to next year. This wasn't the gig I expected, when I came here. There was talk of recording a vid demo . . . it never happened. I don't think it's ever going to happen. I have to be able to reach a wider audience, if I'm ever to pay my way back home. Back to my people. I want . . . *out* of here, before I fall down that gravity well." She jerked an upper thumb in the general direction of the planet they orbited. "People go downside here, who never come up again." She paused. "Are you *afraid* of Baron Fell?"

"No!" said Thorne, as Miles said, "Yes." They exchanged a sardonic look.

"We are inclined to be careful of Baron Fell," Miles suggested. Thorne shrugged agreement.

She frowned, and maneuvered to the table. She drew a wad of assorted planetary currencies out of her green silk jacket and laid it in front of Miles. "Would this bolster your nerve?"

Thorne fingered the stack, flipped through it. At least a couple thousand Betan dollars worth, at conservative estimate, mostly in middle denominations, though a Betan single topped the pile, camouflaging its value to a casual glance. "Well," said Thorne, glancing at Miles, "and what do we mercenaries think of that?"

Miles leaned back thoughtfully in his chair. The kept secret of Miles's identity wasn't the only favor Thorne could call in if it chose. Miles remembered the day Thorne had helped capture an asteroid mining station and the pocket dreadnought *Triumph* for him with nothing but sixteen troops in combat armor and a hell of a lot of nerve. "I encourage creative financing on the part of my commanders," he said at last. "Negotiate away, Captain."

Thorne smiled, and pulled the Betan dollar off the stack. "You have the right idea," Thorne said to the musician, "but the amount is wrong."

Her hand went uncertainly to her jacket and paused, as Thorne pushed the rest of the stack of currency, minus the single, back to her. "What?"

Thorne picked up the single and snapped it a few times. "This is the right amount. Makes it an official contract, you see." Bel extended a hand to her; after a bewildered moment, she shook it. "Deal," said Thorne happily.

"Hero," said Miles, holding up a warning finger, "beware, I'll call in my veto if you can't come up with a way to bring this off in dead secret. That's my cut of the price."

"Yes, *sir*," said Thorne.

*   *   *

Several hours later, Miles snapped awake in his cabin aboard the *Ariel* to an urgent bleeping from his comconsole. Whatever he had been dreaming was gone in the instant, though he had the vague idea it had been something unpleasant. Biological and unpleasant. "Naismith here."

"This is the duty officer in Nav and Com, sir. You have a call originating from the downside commercial comm net. He says to tell you it's Vaughn."

Vaughn was the agreed-upon code name of their pick-up. His real name was Dr. Canaba. Miles grabbed his uniform jacket and shrugged it on over his black T-shirt, passed his hands futilely through his hair, and slid into his console station chair. "Put him through."

The face of a man on the high side of middle age materialized above Miles's vid plate. Tan-skinned, racially indeterminate features, short wavy hair greying at the temples; more arresting was the intelligence that suffused those features and quickened the brown eyes. *Yep, that's my man,* thought Miles with satisfaction. *Here we go.* But Canaba looked more than tense. He looked distraught.

"Admiral Naismith?"

"Yes. Vaughn?"

Canaba nodded.

"Where are you?" asked Miles.

"Downside."

"You were to meet us up here."

"I know. Something's come up. A problem."

"What sort of problem? Ah—is this channel secure?"

Canaba laughed bitterly. "On this planet, nothing is secure. But I don't think I'm being traced. But I can't come up yet. I need . . . help."

"Vaughn, we aren't equipped to break you out against superior forces—if you've become a prisoner—"

He shook his head. "No, it's not that. I've . . . lost something. I need help to get it back."

"I'd understood you were to leave everything. You would be compensated later."

"It's not a personal possession. It's something your employer wants very badly. Certain . . . samples, have been removed from my . . . power. They won't take me without them."

Dr. Canaba took Miles for a mercenary hireling, entrusted with minimum classified information by Barrayaran Security. So. "All I was asked to transport was you and your skills."

"They didn't tell you everything."

The hell they didn't. Barrayar would take you stark naked, and be grateful. What was this?

Canaba met Miles's frown with a mouth set like iron. "I *won't* leave without them. Or the deal's off. And you can whistle for your pay, mercenary."

He meant it. Damn. Miles's eyes narrowed. "This is all a bit mysterious."

Canaba shrugged acknowledgment. "I'm sorry. But I *must* . . . Meet with me, and I'll tell you the rest. Or go, I don't care which. But a certain thing must be accomplished, must be . . . expiated." He trailed off in agitation.

Miles took a deep breath. "Very well. But every complication you add increases your risk. And mine. This had better be worth it."

"Oh, Admiral," breathed Canaba sadly, "it is to me. It is to me."

Snow sifted through the little park where Canaba met them, giving Miles something new to swear at if only he hadn't run out of invective hours ago. He

was shivering even in his Dendarii-issue parka by
the time Canaba walked past the dingy kiosk where
Miles and Bel roosted. They fell in behind him without a word.

Bharaputra Laboratories were headquartered in a
downside town Miles frankly found worrisome;
guarded shuttleport, guarded Syndicate buildings,
guarded municipal buildings, guarded walled resi-
dential compounds; in between, a crazy disorder of
neglected aging structures that didn't seem to be
guarded by anyone, occupied by people who *slunk*.
It made Miles wonder if the two Dendarii troopers
he'd detailed to shadow them were quite enough.
But the slithery people gave them a wide berth; they
evidently understood what guards meant. At least
during daylight.

Canaba led them into one of the nearby buildings.
Its lift tubes were out-of-order, its corridors unheated.
A darkly-dressed maybe-female person scurried out
of their way in the shadows, reminding Miles uncomfortably of a rat. They followed Canaba dubiously
up the safety ladder set in the side of a dead lift
tube, down another corridor, and through a door
with a broken palm-lock into an empty dirty room,
greyly lit by an unpolarized but intact window. At
least they were out of the wind.

"I think we can talk safely here," said Canaba,
turning and pulling off his gloves.

"Bel?" said Miles.

Thorne pulled an assortment of anti-surveillance
detectors from its parka and ran a scan, as the two
guards prowled the perimeters. One stationed himself in the corridor, the second near the window.

"It scans clean," said Bel at last, as if reluctant to
believe its own instruments. "For now." Rather pointedly, Bel walked around Canaba and scanned him

too. Canaba waited with bowed head, as if he felt he deserved no better. Bel set up the sonic baffler.

Miles shrugged back his hood and opened his parka, the better to reach his concealed weapons in the event of a trap. He was finding Canaba extraordinarily hard to read. What were the man's motivations anyway? There was no doubt House Bharaputra had assured his comfort—his coat, the rich cut of his clothing beneath it, spoke of that—and though his standard of living surely would not drop when he transferred his allegience to the Barrayaran Imperial Science Institute, he would not have nearly the opportunities to amass wealth on the side that he had here. So, he wasn't in it for the money. Miles could understand that. But why work for a place like House Bharaputra in the first place unless greed overwhelmed integrity?

"You puzzle me, Dr. Canaba," said Miles lightly. "Why this mid-career switch? I'm pretty well acquainted with your new employers, and frankly, I don't see how they could out-bid House Bharaputra."

There, that was a properly mercenary way to put it.

"They offered me protection from House Bharaputra. Although, if *you're* it . . ." he looked doubtfully down at Miles.

Ha. And, hell. The man really was ready to bolt. Leaving Miles to explain the failure of his mission to Chief of Imperial Security Illyan in person. "They bought our services," said Miles, "and therefore you command our services. They want you safe and happy. But we can't begin to protect you when you depart from a plan designed to maximize your safety, throw in random factors, and ask us to operate in the dark. I need full knowledge of what's going on if I'm to take full responsibility for the results."

"No one is asking you to take responsibility."

"I beg your pardon, doctor, but they surely have."

"Oh," said Canaba. "I . . . see." He paced to the window, back. "But will you do what I ask?"

"I will do what I can."

"Happy," Canaba snorted. "God . . ." he shook his head wearily, inhaled decisively. "I never came here for the money. I came here because I could do research I couldn't do anywhere else. Not hedged round with outdated legal restrictions. I dreamed of breakthroughs . . . but it became a nightmare. The freedom became slavery. The things they wanted me to do. . . ! Constantly interrupting the things I wanted to do. Oh, you can always find someone to do anything for money, but they're second-raters. These labs are full of second raters. The very best can't be bought. I've done things, unique things, that Bharaputra won't develop because the profit would be too small, never mind how many people it would benefit—I get no credit, no standing for my work—every year, I see in the literature of my field galactic honors going to lesser men, because I cannot publish my results . . ." He stopped, lowered his head. "I doubtless sound like a megalomaniac to you."

"Ah . . ." said Miles, "you sound quite frustrated."

"The frustration," said Canaba, "woke me from a long sleep. Wounded ego—it was only wounded ego. But in my pride, I rediscovered shame. And the weight of it stunned me, stunned me where I stood. *Do* you understand? Does it matter if you understand? Ah!" He paced away to the wall, and stood facing it, his back rigid.

"Uh," Miles scratched the back of his head ruefully, "yeah. I'd be glad to spend many fascinating hours listening to you explain it to me—on my ship. Outbound."

Canaba turned with a crooked smile. "You are a

practical man, I perceive. A soldier. Well, God knows I need a soldier now."

"Things are that screwed up, eh?"

"It . . . happened suddenly. I thought I had it under control."

"Go on," sighed Miles.

"There were seven synthesized gene-complexes. One of them is a cure for a certain obscure enzyme disorder. One of them will increase oxygen-generation in space station algae twenty-fold. One of them came from outside Bharaputra Labs, brought in by a man— we never found out who he really was, but death followed him. Several of my colleagues who had worked on his project were murdered all in one night, by the commandos who pursued him—their records destroyed —I never told anyone I'd borrowed an unauthorized tissue sample to study. I've not unravelled it fully yet, but I can tell you, it's absolutely unique."

Miles recognized that one, and almost choked, reflecting upon the bizarre chain of circumstances that had placed an identical tissue sample in the hands of Dendarii Intelligence a year ago. Terrence See's telepathy complex—and the main reason *why* His Imperial Majesty suddenly wanted a top geneticist. Dr. Canaba was in for a little surprise when he arrived at his new Barrayaran laboratory. But if the other six complexes came anywhere near matching the value of the known one, Security Chief Illyan would peel Miles with a dull knife for letting them slip through his fingers. Miles's attention to Canaba abruptly intensified. This side-trip might not be as trivial as he'd feared.

"Together, these seven complexes represent tens of thousands of hours of research time, mostly mine, some of others—my life's work. I'd planned from the beginning to take them with me. I bundled them up in a viral insert and placed them, bound and dormant, in a live . . ." Canaba faltered, "organism, for storage. An organism, I thought, that no one would think to look at for such a thing."

"Why didn't you just store them in your own tissue?" Miles asked irritably. "Then you couldn't lose 'em."

Canaba's mouth opened. "I . . . never thought of that. How elegant. Why didn't I think of that?" His hand touched his forehead wonderingly, as if probing for systems failure. His lips tightened again. "But it would have made no difference. I would still need to . . ." he fell silent. "It's about the organism," he said at last. "The . . . creature." Another long silence.

"Of all the things I did," Canaba continued lowly, "of all the interruptions this vile place imposed on me, there is one I regret the most. You understand, this was years ago. I was younger, I thought I still had a future here to protect. And it wasn't all my doing—guilt by committee, eh? Spread it around, make it easy, say it was *his* fault, *her* doing . . . well, it's mine now."

You mean it's *mine* now, thought Miles grimly. "Doctor, the more time we spend here, the greater the chance of compromising this operation. Please get to the point."

"Yes . . . yes. Well, a number of years ago, House Bharaputra Laboratories took on a contract to manufacture a . . . new species. Made to order."

"I thought it was House Ryoval that was famous for making people, or whatever, to order," said Miles.

"They make slaves, one-off. They are very specialized. And small—their customer base is surprisingly small. There are many rich men, and there are, I suppose, many depraved men, but a House Ryoval customer has to be a member of both sets, and the overlap isn't as large as you'd think. Anyway, our contract was supposed to lead to a major production run, far beyond Ryoval's capabilities. A certain subplanetary government, hard-pressed by its neighbors, wanted us to engineer a race of super-soldiers for them."

"What, again?" said Miles. "I thought that had been tried. More than once."

"This time, we thought we could do it. Or at least, the Bharaputran hierarchy was willing to take their money. But the project suffered from too much input. The client, our own higher-ups, the genetics project members, everybody had ideas they were pushing. I swear it was doomed before it ever got out of the design committee."

"A super-soldier. Designed by a committee. Ye gods. The mind boggles." Miles's eyes were wide in fascination. "So then what happened?"

"It seemed to . . . several of us, that the physical limits of the merely human had already been reached. Once a, say, muscle system has been brought to perfect health, stimulated with maximum hormones, exercised to a certain limit, that's all you can do. So we turned to other species for special improvements. I, for instance, became fascinated by the aerobic and anaerobic metabolism in the muscles of the thoroughbred horse—"

"What?" said Thorne, shocked.

"There were other ideas. Too many. I swear, they weren't all mine."

"You mixed human and animal genes?" breathed Miles.

"Why not? Human genes have been spliced into animals from the crude beginnings—it was almost the first thing tried. Human insulin from bacteria and the like. But till now, no one dared do it in reverse. I broke the barrier, cracked the codes . . . It looked good at first. It was only when the first ones reached puberty that all the errors became fully apparent. Well, it was only the initial trial. They were meant to be formidable. But they ended up monstrous."

"Tell me," Miles choked, "were there any actual combat-experienced soldiers on the committee?"

"I assume the client had them. They supplied the parameters," said Canaba.

Said Thorne in a suffused voice, "*I* see. They were trying to re-invent the *enlisted* man."

Miles shot Thorne a quelling glower, and tapped his chrono. "Don't let us interrupt, doctor."

There was a short silence. Canaba began again. "We ran off ten prototypes. Then the client . . . went out of business. They lost their war—"

"Why am I not surprised?" Miles muttered under his breath.

"—funding was cut off, the project was dropped before we could apply what we had learned from our mistakes. Of the ten prototypes, nine have since died. There was one left. We were keeping it at the labs due to . . . difficulties, in boarding it out. I placed my gene complexes in it. They are there still. The last thing I meant to do before I left was kill it. A mercy . . . a responsibility. My expiation, if you will."

"And then?" prodded Miles.

"A few days ago, it was suddenly sold to House Ryoval. As a novelty, apparently. Baron Ryoval collects oddities of all sorts, for his tissue banks—"

Miles and Bel exchanged a look.

"—I had no idea it was to be sold. I came in in the morning and it was gone. I don't think Ryoval has any idea of its real value. It's there now, as far as I know, at Ryoval's facilities."

Miles decided he was getting a sinus headache. From the cold, no doubt. "And what, pray, d'you want us soldiers to do about it?"

"Get in there, somehow. Kill it. Collect a tissue sample. Only then will I go with you."

And stomach twinges. "What, both ears and the tail?"

Canaba gave Miles a cold look. "The left gastrocnemius muscle. That's where I injected my complexes. These storage viruses aren't virulent, they won't have migrated far. The greatest concentration should still be there."

"I see." Miles rubbed his temples, and pressed his eyes. "All right. We'll take care of it. This personal contact between us is very dangerous, and I'd rather not repeat it. Plan to report to my ship in forty-eight hours. Will we have any trouble recognizing your critter?"

"I don't think so. This particular specimen topped out at just over eight feet. I . . . want you to know, the fangs were *not* my idea."

"I . . . see."

"It can move very fast, if it's still in good health. Is there any help I can give you? I have access to painless poisons . . ."

"You've done enough, thank you. Please leave it to us professionals, eh?"

"It would be best if its body can be destroyed entirely. No cells remaining. If you can."

"That's why plasma arcs were invented. You'd best be on your way."

"Yes." Canaba hesitated. "Admiral Naismith?"

"Yes. . . ."

"I . . . it might also be best if my future employer didn't learn about this. They have intense military interests. It might excite them unduly."

"Oh," said Miles/Admiral Naismith/Lieutenant Lord Vorkosigan of the Barrayaran Imperial Service, "I don't think you have to worry about that."

"Is forty-eight hours enough for your commando raid?" Canaba worried. "You understand, if you don't get the tissue, I'll go right back downside. I will not be trapped aboard your ship."

"You will be happy. It's in my contract," said Miles. "Now you'd better get gone."

"I must rely on you, sir." Canaba nodded in suppressed anguish, and withdrew.

They waited a few minutes in the cold room, to let Canaba put some distance between them. The building creaked in the wind; from an upper corridor echoed an odd shriek, and later, a laugh abruptly cut off. The guard shadowing Canaba returned. "He made it to his ground car all right, sir."

"Well," said Thorne, "I suppose we'll need to get hold of a plan of Ryoval's facilities, first—"

"I think not," said Miles.

"If we're to raid—"

"Raid, hell. I'm not risking my men on anything so idiotic. I said I'd slay his sin for him. I didn't say how."

The commercial comconsole net at the downside shuttleport seemed as convenient as anything. Miles slid into the booth and fed the machine his credit card while Thorne lurked just outside the viewing angle and the guards, outside, guarded. He encoded the call.

In a moment, the vid plate produced the image of a sweet-faced receptionist with dimples and a white fur crest instead of hair. "House Ryoval, Customer Services. How may I help you, sir?"

"I'd like to speak to Manager Deem, in Sales and

Demonstrations," said Miles smoothly, "about a possible purchase for my organization."

"Who may I say is calling?"

"Admiral Miles Naismith, Dendarii Free Mercenary Fleet."

"One moment, sir."

"You really think they'll just sell it?" Bel muttered from the side as the girl's face was replaced by a flowing pattern of colored lights and some syrupy music.

"Remember what we overheard yesterday?" said Miles. "I'm betting it's *on* sale. Cheap." He must try not to look too interested.

In a remarkably short time, the colored glop gave way to the face of an astonishingly beautiful young man, a blue-eyed albino in a red silk shirt. He had a huge livid bruise up one side of his white face. "This is Manager Deem. May I help you, Admiral?"

Miles cleared his throat carefully. "A rumor has been brought to my attention that House Ryoval may have recently acquired from House Bharaputra an article of some professional interest to me. Supposedly, it was the prototype of some sort of new improved fighting man. Do you know anything about it?"

Deem's hand stole to his bruise and palpated it gently, then twitched away. "Indeed, sir, we do have such an article."

"Is it for sale?"

"Oh, *ye*—I mean, I think some arrangement is pending. But it may still be possible to bid on it."

"Would it be possible for me to inspect it?"

"Of course," said Deem with suppressed eagerness. "How soon?"

There was a burst of static, and the vid image split, Deem's face abruptly shrinking to one side.

The new face was only too familiar. Bel hissed under its breath.

"I'll take this call, Deem," said Baron Ryoval.

"Yes, my lord." Deem's eyes widened in surprise, and he cut out. Ryoval's image swelled to occupy the space available.

"So, Betan," Ryoval smiled, "it appears I have something you want after all."

Miles shrugged. "Maybe," he said neutrally. "If it's in my price range."

"I thought you gave all your money to Fell."

Miles spread his hands. "A good commander always has hidden reserves. However, the actual value of the item hasn't yet been established. In fact, its existence hasn't even been established."

"Oh, it exists, all right. And it is . . . impressive. Adding it to my collection was a unique pleasure. I'd hate to give it up. But for you," Ryoval smiled more broadly, "it may be possible to arrange a special cut rate." He chuckled, as at some secret pun that escaped Miles.

A special cut throat is more like it. "Oh?"

"I propose a simple trade," said Ryoval. "Flesh for flesh."

"You may overestimate my interest, Baron."

Ryoval's eyes glinted. "I don't think so."

He knows I wouldn't touch him with a stick if it weren't something pretty compelling. So. "Name your proposal, then."

"I'll trade you even, Bharaputra's pet monster—ah, you should see it, Admiral!—for three tissue samples. Three tissue samples that will, if you are clever about it, cost you nothing." Ryoval held up one finger. "One from your Betan hermaphrodite," a second finger, "one from yourself," a third finger, making a W, "and one from Baron Fell's quaddie musician."

Over in the corner, Bel Thorne appeared to be suppressing an apopleptic fit. Quietly, fortunately.

"That third could prove extremely difficult to obtain," said Miles, buying time to think.

"Less difficult for you than me," said Ryoval. "Fell knows my agents. My overtures have put him on guard. You represent a unique opportunity to get in under that guard. Given sufficient motivation, I'm certain it's not beyond you, mercenary."

"Given sufficient motivation, very little is beyond me, Baron," said Miles semi-randomly.

"Well, then. I shall expect to hear from you within—say—twenty-four hours. After that time my offer will be withdrawn." Ryoval nodded cheerfully. "Good day, Admiral." The vid blanked.

"Well, then," echoed Miles.

"Well what?" said Thorne with suspicion. "You're not actually seriously considering that—vile proposal, are you?"

"What does he want my tissue sample for, for God's sake?" Miles wondered aloud.

"For his dog and dwarf act, no doubt," said Thorne nastily.

"Now, now. He'd be dreadfully disappointed when my clone turned out to be six feet tall, I'm afraid." Miles cleared his throat. "It wouldn't actually hurt anyone, I suppose. To take a small tissue sample. Whereas a commando raid risks lives."

Bel leaned back against the wall and crossed its arms. "Not true. You'd have to fight me for mine. And *hers*."

Miles grinned sourly. "So."

"So?"

"So let's go find a map of Ryoval's flesh pit. It seems we're going hunting."

*　　　*　　　*

House Ryoval's palatial main biologicals facility wasn't a proper fortress, just some guarded buildings. Some bloody big guarded buildings. Miles stood on the roof of the lift-van and studied the layout through his night-glasses. Fog droplets beaded in his hair. The cold damp wind searched for chinks in his jacket much as he searched for chinks in Ryoval's security.

The white complex loomed against the dark forested mountainside, its front gardens floodlit and fairy-like in the fog and frost. The utility entrances on the near side looked more promising. Miles nodded slowly to himself and climbed down off the rented lift-van, artistically broke-down on the little mountain side-trail overlooking Ryoval's. He swung into the back, out of the piercing wind.

"All right, people, listen up." His squad hunkered around as he set up the holovid map in the middle. The colored lights of the display sheened their faces, tall Ensign Murka, Thorne's second-in-command, and two big troopers. Sergeant Laureen Anderson was the van driver, assigned to outside back-up along with Trooper Sandy Hereld and Captain Thorne. Miles harbored a secret Barrayaran prejudice against taking female troops inside Ryoval's, that he trusted he concealed. It went double for Bel Thorne. Not that one's sex would necessarily make any difference to the adventures that might follow in the event of capture, if even a tenth of the bizarre rumors he'd heard were true. Nevertheless . . . Laureen claimed to be able to fly any vehicle made by man through the eye of a needle, not that Miles figured she'd ever done anything so domestic as thread a needle in her life. She would not question her assignment.

"Our main problem remains, that we still don't know where exactly in this facility Bharaputra's creature is being kept. So first we penetrate the fence, the outer courts, and the main building, here and here." A red thread of light traced their projected route at Miles's touch on the control board. "Then we quietly pick up an inside employee and fast-penta him. From that point on we're racing time, since we must assume he'll be promptly missed.

"The key word is quietly. We didn't come here to kill *people*, and we are not at war with Ryoval's employees. You carry your stunners, and keep those plasma arcs and the rest of the toys packed till we locate our quarry. We dispatch it fast and quietly, I get my sample," his hand touched his jacket, beneath which rested the collection case that would keep the tissue alive till they got back to the *Ariel*. "Then we fly. If anything goes wrong before I get that very expensive cut of meat, we don't bother to fight our way out. Not worth it. They have peculiar summary ways of dealing with murder charges here, and I don't see the need for any of us to end up as spare parts in Ryoval's tissue banks. We wait for Captain Thorne to arrange a ransom, and then try something else. We hold a lever or two on Ryoval in case of emergencies."

"Dire emergencies," Bel muttered.

"If anything goes wrong after the butcher-mission is accomplished, it's back to combat rules. That sample will then be irreplaceable, and must be got back to Captain Thorne at all costs. Laureen, you sure of our emergency pickup spot?"

"Yes, sir." She pointed on the vid display.

"Everybody else got that? Any questions? Suggestions? Last-minute observations? Communications check, then, Captain Thorne."

Their wrist comms all appeared to be in good working order. Ensign Murka shrugged on the weapons pack. Miles carefully pocketed the blueprint map cube, that had cost them a near-ransom from a certain pliable construction company just a few hours ago. The four members of the penetration team slipped from the van and merged with the frosty darkness.

They slunk off through the woods. The frozen crunchy layer of plant detritus tended to slide underfoot, exposing a layer of slick mud. Murka spotted a spy eye before it spotted them, and blinded it with a brief burst of microwave static while they scurried past. The useful big guys made short work of boosting Miles over the wall. Miles tried not to think about the ancient pub sport of dwarf tossing. The inner court was stark and utilitarian, loading docks with big locked doors, rubbish collection bays, and a few parked vehicles.

Footsteps echoed, and they ducked down in a rubbish bay. A red-clad guard passed, slowly waving an infra-red scanner. They crouched and hid their faces in their infra-red blank ponchos, looking like so many bags of garbage no doubt. Then it was tiptoe up to the loading docks.

Ducts. The key to Ryoval's facility had turned out to be ducts, for heating, for access to power-optics cables, for the comm system. Narrow ducts. Quite impassable to a big guy. Miles slipped out of his poncho and gave it to a trooper to fold and pack.

Miles balanced on Murka's shoulders and cut his way through the first ductlet, a ventilation grille high on the wall above the loading dock doors. Miles handed the grille down silently, and after a quick visual scan for unwanted company, slithered through. It was a tight fit even for him. He let himself down gently to the concrete floor, found the door control box, shorted the alarm, and raised the door about a meter. His team rolled through, and he let the door back down as quietly as he could. So far so good; they hadn't yet had to exchange a word.

They made it to cover on the far side of the receiving bay just before a red-coveralled employee wandered through, driving an electric cart loaded with cleaning robots. Murka touched Miles's sleeve, and looked his inquiry—*This one?* Miles shook his head, *Not yet.* A maintenance man seemed less likely than an employee from the inner sanctum to know where their quarry was kept, and they didn't have time to litter the place with the unconscious bodies of false trials. They found the tunnel to the main building, just as the map cube promised. The door at the end was locked as expected.

It was up on Murka's shoulders again. A quick zizz of Miles's cutters loosened a panel in the ceiling, and he crawled through—the frail supporting framework would surely not have held a man of greater weight—and found the power cables running to the door lock. He was just looking over the problem and pulling tools out of his pocketed uniform jacket when Murka's hand reached up to thrust the weapons pack beside him and quietly pull the panel back into place. Miles flung himself to his belly and pressed his eye to the crack as a voice from down the corridor bellowed, "Freeze!"

Swear words screamed through Miles's head. He clamped his jaw on them. He looked down on the tops of his troopers' heads. In a moment, they were surrounded by half-a-dozen red-clad black-trousered armed guards. "What are you doing here?" snarled the guard sergeant.

"Oh, shit!" cried Murka. "*Please*, mister, don't tell my CO you caught us in here. He'd bust me back to private!"

"Huh?" said the guard sergeant. He prodded Murka with his weapon, a lethal nerve disruptor. "Hands up! Who are you?"

"M'name's Murka. We came in on a mercenary ship to Fell Station, but the captain wouldn't grant us downside passes. Think of it—we come all the way to Jackson's Whole, and the sonofabitch wouldn't let us go downside! Bloody pure-dick wouldn't let us see Ryoval's!"

The red-tunic'd guards were doing a fast scan-and-search, none too gently, and finding only stunners and the portion of security-penetration devices that Murka had carried.

"I made a bet we could get in even if we couldn't afford the front door." Murka's mouth turned down in great discouragement. "Looks like I lost."

"Looks like you did," growled the guard sergeant, drawing back.

One of his men held up the thin collection of baubles they'd stripped off the Dendarii. "They're not equipped like an assassination team," he observed.

Murka drew himself up, looking wonderfully offended. "We aren't!"

The guard sergeant turned over a stunner. "AWOL, are you?"

"Not if we make it back before midnight." Murka's tone went wheedling. "Look, m' CO's a right bastard. Suppose there's any way you could see your way clear that he doesn't find out about this?" One of Murka's hands drifted suggestively past his wallet pocket.

The guard sergeant looked him up and down, smirking. "Maybe."

Miles listened with open-mouthed delight. *Murka, if this works I'm promoting you. . . .*

Murka paused. "Any chance of seeing inside first? Not the girls even, just the place? So I could say that I'd seen it."

"This isn't a whorehouse, soldier boy!" snapped the guard sergeant.

Murka looked stunned. "What?"

"This is the *biologicals* facility."

"Oh," said Murka.

"You *idiot*," one of the troopers put in on cue. Miles sprinkled silent blessings down upon his head. None of the three so much as flicked an eyeball upward.

"But the man in town told me—" began Murka.

"What man?" said the guard sergeant.

"The man who took m'money," said Murka.

A couple of the red tunic'd guards were beginning to grin. The guard sergeant prodded Murka with his nerve disruptor. "Get going, soldier boy. Back that way. This is your lucky day."

"You mean we get to see inside?" said Murka hopefully.

"No," said the guard sergeant, "I mean we aren't going to break both your legs before we throw you out on your ass." He paused and added more kindly, "There's a whorehouse back in town." He slipped Murka's wallet out of his pocket, checked the name on the credit card and put it back, and removed all the loose currency. The guards did the same to the outraged-looking troopers, dividing the assorted cash up among them. "They take credit cards, and you've still got till midnight. Now move!"

And so Miles's squad was chivvied, ignominiously but intact, down the tunnel. Miles waited till the whole mob was well out of earshot before keying his wrist comm. "Bel?"

"Yes," came back the instant reply.

"Trouble. Murka and the troops were just picked up by Ryoval's security. I believe the boy genius has just managed to bullshit them into throwing them out the back door, instead of rendering them down for parts. I'll follow as soon as I can, we'll rendezvous and regroup for another try." Miles paused. This was a total bust, they were now worse off than when they'd started. Ryoval's security would be stirred up for the rest of the long Jacksonian night. He added to the comm, "I'm going to see if I can't at least find out the location of the critter before I withdraw. Should improve our chances of success next round."

Bel swore in a heartfelt tone. "Be careful."

"You bet. Watch for Murka and the boys. Naismith out."

Once he'd identified the right cables it was the work of a moment to make the door slide open. He then had an interesting dangle by his fingertips while coaxing the ceiling panel to fall back into place before he dropped from maximum downward extension, fearful for his bones. Nothing broke. He slipped across the portal to the main building and took to the ducts as soon as possible, the corridors having been proved dangerous. He lay on his back in the narrow tube and balanced the blueprint holocube on his belly, picking out a new and safer route not necessarily passable to a couple of husky troopers. And where did one look for a monster? A closet?

It was at about the third turn, inching his way through the system dragging the weapon pack, that he became aware that the territory no longer matched the map. Hell and damnation. Were these changes in the system since its construction, or a subtly sabotaged map? Well, no matter, he wasn't really lost, he could still retrace his route.

He crawled along for about thirty minutes, discovering and disarming two alarm sensors before they discovered him. The time factor was getting seriously pressing. Soon he would have to—ah, there! He peered through a vent grille into a dim room filled with holovid and communications equipment.

Small Repairs, the map cube named it. It didn't look like a repairs shop. Another change since Ryoval had moved in? But a man sat alone with his back to Miles's wall. Perfect, too good to pass up.

Breathing silently, moving slowly, Miles eased his dart-gun out of the pack and made sure he loaded it with the right cartridge, fast-penta spiked with a paralyzer, a lovely cocktail blended for the purpose by the *Ariel's* medtech. He sighted through the grille, aimed the needle-nose of the dart gun with tense precision, and fired. Bullseye. The man slapped the back of his neck once and sat still, hand falling nervelessly to his side. Miles grinned briefly, cut his way through the grille, and lowered himself to the floor.

The man was well-dressed in civilian-type clothes— one of the scientists, perhaps? He lolled in his chair, a little smile playing around his lips, and stared with unalarmed interest at Miles. He started to fall over.

Miles caught him and propped him back upright. "Sit up now, that's right, you can't talk with your face in the carpet now, can you?"

"Nooo . . ." The man bobbled his head and smiled agreeably.

"Do you know anything about a genetic construct, a monstrous creature, just recently bought from House Bharaputra and brought to this facility?"

The man blinked and smiled. "Yes."

Fast-penta subjects did tend to be literal, Miles reminded himself. "Where is it being kept?"

"Downstairs."

"Where exactly downstairs?"

"In the sub-basement. The crawl-space around the foundations. We were hoping it would catch some of the rats, you see." The man giggled. "Do cats eat rats? Do rats eat cats. . . ?"

Miles checked his map-cube. Yes. That looked good, in terms of the penetration team getting in and out, though it was still a large search area, broken up into a maze by structural elements running down into the bedrock, and specially-set low-vibration support columns running up into the laboratories. At the lower edge, where the mountainside sloped away, the space ran high-ceilinged and very near the surface, a possible break-out point. The space thinned to head-cracking narrowness and then to bedrock at the back where the building wedged into the slope. All right. Miles opened his dart case to find something that would lay his victim out cold and non-questionable for the rest of the night. The man pawed at him and his sleeve slipped back to reveal a wrist-comm almost as thick and complex as Miles's own. A light blinked on it. Miles looked at the device, suddenly uneasy. This room . . . "By the way, who are you?"

"Moglia, Chief of Security, Ryoval Biologicals," the man recited happily. "At your service, sir."

"Oh, indeed you are." Miles's suddenly-thick fingers scrabbled faster in his dart case. Damn, damn, *damn.*

The door burst open. "Freeze, mister!"

Miles hit the tight-beam alarm/self-destruct on his own wrist comm and flung his hands up, and the wrist comm off, in one swift motion. Not by chance, Moglia sat between Miles and the door, inhibiting the trigger reflexes of the entering guards. The comm melted as it arced through the air—no chance of Ryoval security tracing the outside squad through it now, and Bel would at least know something had gone wrong.

The security chief chuckled to himself, temporarily fascinated by the task of counting his own fingers.

The red-clad guard sergeant, backed by his squad, thundered into what was now screamingly obvious to Miles as the Security Operations Room, to jerk Miles around, slam him face-first into the wall, and begin frisking him with vicious efficiency. Within moments he had separated Miles from a clanking pile of incriminating equipment, his jacket, boots, and belt. Miles clutched the wall and shivered with the pain of several expertly-applied nerve jabs and the swift reversal of his fortune.

The security chief, when un-penta'd at last, was not at all pleased with the guard sergeant's confession about the three uniformed men he had let go with a fine earlier in the evening. He put the whole guard shift on full alert, and sent an armed squad out to try and trace the escaped Dendarii. Then, with an apprehensive expression on his face very like the guard-sergeant's during his mortified admission— compounded with sour satisfaction, contemplating Miles, and drug-induced nausea—he made a vid call.

"My lord?" said the security chief carefully.

"What is it, Moglia?" Baron Ryoval's face was sleepy and irritated.

"Sorry to disturb you sir, but I thought you might like to know about the intruder we just caught here. Not an ordinary thief, judging from his clothes and equipment. Strange-looking fellow, sort of a tall dwarf. He squeezed in through the ducts." Moglia held up tissue-collection kit, chip-driven alarm-disarming tools, and Miles's weapons, by way of evidence. The guard sergeant bundled Miles, stumbling, into range of the vid's pick-up. "He was asking a lot of questions about Bharaputra's monster."

Ryoval's lips parted. Then his eyes lit, and he threw back his head and laughed. "I should have guessed. Stealing when you should be buying, Admiral?" he chortled. "Oh, very good, Moglia!"

The security chief looked fractionally less nervous. "Do you know this little mutant, my lord?"

"Yes, indeed. He calls himself Miles Naismith. A mercenary—bills himself as an admiral. Self-promoted, no doubt. Excellent work, Moglia. Hold him, and I'll be there in the morning and deal with him personally."

"Hold him how, sir?"

Ryoval shrugged. "Amuse yourselves. Freely."

When Ryoval's image faded, Miles found himself pinned between the speculative glowers of both the security chief and the guard sergeant.

Just to relieve feelings, a burly guard held Miles while the security chief delivered a blow to his belly. But the chief was still too ill to really enjoy this as he should. "Came to see Bharaputra's toy soldier, did you?" he gasped, rubbing his own stomach.

The guard sergeant caught his chief's eye. "You know, I think we should give him his wish."

The security chief smothered a belch, and smiled as at a beatific vision. "Yes . . . "

Miles, praying they wouldn't break his arms, found himself being frog-marched down a complex of corridors and lift tubes by the burly guard, followed by the sergeant and the chief. They took a last lift-tube to the very bottom, a dusty basement crowded with stored and discarded equipment and supplies. They made their way to a locked hatch set in the floor. It swung open on a metal ladder descending into obscurity.

"The last thing we threw down there was a rat," the guard sergeant informed Miles cordially. "Nine bit its head right off. Nine gets very hungry. Got a metabolism like an ore furnace."

The guard forced Miles onto the ladder and down

it a meter or so by the simple expedient of striking at his clinging hands with a truncheon. Miles hung just out of range of the stick, eyeing the dimly-lit stone below. The rest was pillars and shadows and a cold dankness.

"Nine!" called the guard sergeant into the echoing darkness. "Nine! Dinner! Come and catch it!"

The security chief laughed mockingly, then clutched his head and groaned under his breath.

Ryoval had said he'd deal with Miles personally in the morning, surely the guards understood their boss wanted a live prisoner. Didn't they? Didn't he? "Is this the dungeon?" Miles spat blood and peered around.

"No, no, just a basement," the guard sergeant assured him cheerily. "The dungeon is for the *paying* customers. Heh, heh, heh." Still chortling at his own humor, he kicked the hatch closed. The chink of the locking mechanism rained down; then silence.

The bars of the ladder bit chill through Miles's socks. He hooked an arm around an upright and tucked one hand into the armpit of his black T-shirt to warm it briefly. His grey trousers had been emptied of everything but a ration bar, his handkerchief, and his legs.

He clung there for a long time. Going up was futile; going down, singularly uninviting. Eventually the startling ganglial pain began to dull, and the shaking physical shock to wear off. Still he clung. Cold.

It could have been worse, Miles reflected. The sergeant and his squad could have decided they wanted to play Lawrence of Arabia and the Six Turks. Commodore Tung, Miles's Dendarii chief of staff and a certified military history nut, had been plying Miles with a series of classic military memoirs lately. How had Colonel Lawrence escaped an analogous tight spot? Ah, yes, played dumb and persuaded his captors to throw him out in the mud. Tung must have pressed that book-fax on Murka, too.

The darkness, Miles discovered as his eyes adjusted, was only relative. Faint luminescent panels in the ceiling here and there shed a sickly yellow glow. He descended the last two meters to stand on solid rock.

He pictured the newsfax, back home on Barrayar— *Body of Imperial Officer Found in Flesh-Czar's Dream Palace. Death From Exhaustion?* Dammit, this wasn't the glorious sacrifice in the Emperor's service he'd once vowed to risk, this was just embarrassing. Maybe Bharaputra's creature would eat the evidence.

With this morose comfort in mind, he began to limp from pillar to pillar, pausing, listening, looking around. Maybe there was another ladder somewhere. Maybe there was a hatch someone had forgotten to lock. Maybe there was still hope.

Maybe there was something moving in the shadows just beyond that pillar. . . .

Miles's breath froze, then eased again, as the movement materialized into a fat albino rat the size of an armadillo. It shied as it saw him and waddled rapidly away, its claws clicking on the rock. Only an escaped lab rat. A bloody big rat, but still, only a rat.

The huge rippling shadow struck out of nowhere, at incredible speed. It grabbed the rat by its tail and swung it squealing against a pillar, dashing out its brains with a crunch. A flash of a thick claw-like fingernail, and the white furry body was ripped open from sternum to tail. Frantic fingers peeled the skin away from the rat's body as blood splattered. Miles first saw the fangs as they bit and tore and buried themselves in the rat's tissues.

They were functional fangs, not just decorative, set in a protruding jaw, with long lips and a wide mouth; yet the total effect was lupine rather than simian. A flat nose, ridged, powerful brows, high cheekbones. Hair a dark matted mess. And yes, fully eight feet tall, a rangy, tense-muscled body.

Climbing back up the ladder would do no good, the creature could pluck him right off and swing him just like the rat. Levitate up the side of a pillar? Oh, for suction-cup fingers and toes, something the bio-engineering committee had missed somehow. Freeze and play invisible? Miles settled on this last defense by default—he was paralyzed with terror.

The big feet, bare on the cold rock, also had claw-like toenails. But the creature was dressed, in clothes made of green lab-cloth, a belted kimono-like coat and loose trousers. And one other thing.

They didn't tell me it was female.

She was almost finished with the rat when she looked up and saw Miles. Bloody-faced, bloody-handed, she froze as still as he.

In a spastic motion, Miles whipped the squashed ration bar from his trouser thigh-pocket and extended it toward her in his outstretched hand. "Dessert?" he smiled hysterically.

Dropping the rat's stripped carcass, she snatched the bar out of his hand, ripped off the cover, and devoured it in four bites. Then she stepped forward, grabbed him by an arm and his black T-shirt, and lifted him up to her face. The clawed fingers bit into his skin, and his feet dangled in air. Her breath was about what he would have guessed. Her eyes were raw and burning. "Water!" she croaked.

They didn't tell me she talked.

"Um, um—water," squeaked Miles. "Quite. There ought to be water around here—look, up at the ceiling, all those pipes. If you'll, um, put me down, good girl, I'll try and spot a water pipe or something. . . ."

Slowly, she lowered him back to his feet and released him. He backed carefully away, his hands held out open at his sides. He cleared his throat, and tried to bring his voice back down to a low, soothing tone. "Let's try over here. The ceiling gets lower, or rather, the bedrock rises . . . over near that light panel, there, that thin composite plastic tube—white's the usual color-code for water. We don't want grey, that's sewage, or red, that's the power-optics . . ." No telling what she understood, tone was everything with creatures. "If you, uh, could hold me up on your shoulders like Ensign Murka, I could have a go at loosening that joint there . . ." He made pantomime gestures, uncertain if anything was getting through to whatever intelligence lay behind those terrible eyes.

The bloody hands, easily twice the size of his own, grabbed him abruptly by the hips and boosted him upward. He clutched the white pipe, inched along it to a screw-joint. Her thick shoulders beneath his feet moved along under him. Her muscles trembled, it wasn't all his own shaking. The joint was tight—he needed tools—he turned with all his strength, in danger of snapping his fragile finger bones. Suddenly the joint squeaked and slid. It gave, the plastic collar was moving, water began to spray between his fingers. One more turn and it sheared apart, and water arced in a bright stream down onto the rock beneath.

She almost dropped him in her haste. She put her mouth under the stream, wide open, let the water splash straight in and all over her face, coughing and guzzling even more frantically than she'd gone at the rat. She drank, and drank, and drank. She let it run over her hands, her face and head, washing away the blood, and then drank some more. Miles began to think she'd never quit, but at last she backed away and pushed her wet hair out of her eyes, and stared down at him. She stared at him for what seemed like a full minute, then suddenly roared, "Cold!"

Miles jumped. "Ah . . . cold . . . right. Me too, my socks are wet. Heat, you want heat. Lessee. Uh, let's try back this way, where the ceiling's lower. No point here, the heat would all collect up there out of reach, no good . . ." She followed him with all the intensity of a cat tracking a . . . well . . . rat, as he skittered around pillars to where the crawl space's floor rose to genuine crawl-height, about four feet. There, that one, that was the lowest pipe he could find. "If we could get this open," he pointed to a plastic pipe about as big around as his waist, "it's full of hot air being pumped along under pressure. No handy joints though, this time." He stared at his puzzle, trying to think. This composite plastic was extremely strong.

She crouched and pulled, then lay on her back and kicked up at it, then looked at him quite woefully.

"Try this." Nervously, he took her hand and guided it to the pipe, and traced long scratches around the circumference with her hard nails. She scratched and scratched, then looked at him again as if to say, *This isn't working!*

"Try kicking and pulling again now," he suggested.

She must have weighed three hundred pounds, and she put it all behind the next effort, kicking then grabbing the pipe, planting her feet on the ceiling and arching with all her strength. The pipe split along the scratches. She fell with it to the floor, and hot air began to hiss out. She held her hands, her face to it, nearly wrapped herself around it, sat on her knees and let it blow across her. Miles crouched down and stripped off his socks and flopped them over the warm pipe to dry. Now would be a good opportunity to run, if only there were anywhere to run to. But he was reluctant to let his prey out of his sight. His prey? He considered the incalcuable value of her left calf muscle, as she sat on the rock and buried her face in her knees.

They didn't tell me she wept.

He pulled out his regulation handkerchief, an archaic square of cloth. He'd never understood the rationale for the idiotic handkerchief, except, perhaps, that where soldiers went there would be weeping. He handed it to her. "Here. Mop your eyes with this."

She took it, and blew her big flat nose in it, and made to hand it back.

"Keep it," Miles said. "Uh . . . what do they call you, I wonder?"

"Nine," she growled. Not hostile, it was just the way her strained voice came out of that big throat. ". . . What do they call you?"

Good God, a complete sentence. Miles blinked. "Admiral Miles Naismith." He arranged himself cross-legged.

She looked up, transfixed. "A soldier? A *real offi-cer?*" And then more doubtfully, as if seeing him in detail for the first time, "You?"

Miles cleared his throat firmly. "Quite real. A bit down on my luck just at the moment," he admitted.

"Me, too," she said glumly, and sniffled. "I don't know how long I've been in this basement, but that was my first drink."

"Three days, I think," said Miles. "Have they not, ah, given you any food, either?"

"No." She frowned; the effect, with the fangs, was

quite overpowering. "This is worse than anything they did to me in the lab, and I thought that was bad."

It's not what you don't know that'll hurt you, the old saying went. *It's what you do know that isn't so.* Miles thought of his map cube; Miles looked at Nine. Miles pictured himself taking this entire mission's carefully-worked-out strategy plan delicately between thumb and forefinger and flushing it down a waste-disposal unit. The ductwork in the ceiling niggled at his imagination. Nine would never fit through it. . . .

She clawed her wild hair away from her face and stared at him with renewed fierceness. Her eyes were a strange light hazel, adding to the wolfish effect. "What are you *really* doing here? Is this another test?"

"No, this is real life." Miles's lips twitched. "I, ah, made a mistake."

"Guess I did too," she said, lowering her head.

Miles pulled at his lip and studied her through narrowed eyes. "What sort of life have you had, I wonder?" he mused, half to himself.

She answered literally. "I lived with hired fosterers till I was eight. Like the clones do. Then I started to get big and clumsy and break things—they brought me to live at the lab after that. It was all right, I was warm and had plenty to eat."

"They can't have simplified you too much if they seriously intended you to be a soldier. I wonder what your IQ is?" he speculated.

"A hundred and thirty-five."

Miles fought off stunned paralysis. "I . . . see. Did you ever get . . . any training?"

She shrugged. "I took a lot of tests. They were . . . OK. Except for the aggression experiments. I don't like electric shocks." She brooded a moment.

"I don't like experimental psychologists, either. They lie a lot." Her shoulders slumped. "Anyway, I failed. We all failed."

"How can they know if you failed if you never had any proper training?" Miles said scornfully. "Soldiering entails some of the most complex, cooperative learned behavior ever invented—I've been studying strategy and tactics for years, and I don't know half yet. It's all up *here*." He pressed his hands urgently to his head.

She looked across at him sharply. "If that's so," she turned her huge clawed hands over, staring at them, "then why did they do *this* to me?"

Miles stopped short. His throat was strangely dry. *So, admirals lie too. Sometimes, even to themselves.* After an unsettled pause he asked, "Did you never think of breaking open a water pipe?"

"You're punished, for breaking things. Or I was. Maybe not you, you're human."

"Did you ever think of escaping, breaking out? It's a soldier's duty, when captured by the enemy, to escape. Survive, escape, sabotage, in that order."

"Enemy?" She looked upward at the whole weight of House Ryoval pressing overhead. "Who are my friends?"

"Ah. Yes. There is that . . . point." And where would an eight-foot-tall genetic cocktail with fangs run to? He took a deep breath. No question what his next move must be. Duty, expediency, survival, all compelled it. "Your friends are closer than you think. Why do you think I came here?" *Why, indeed?*

She shot him a silent, puzzled frown.

"I came for you. I'd heard of you. I'm . . . recruiting. Or I was. Things went wrong, and now I'm escaping. But if you came with me, you could join the Dendarii Mercenaries. A top outfit—always looking for a few good men, or whatever. I have this master-sergeant who . . . who *needs* a recruit like you." Too true. Sergeant Dyeb was infamous for his sour attitude about women soldiers, insisting that they were too soft. Any female recruit who survived his course came out with her aggression highly developed. Miles pictured Dyeb being dangled by his toes from a height of about eight feet. . . . He controlled his runaway imagination in favor of concentration on the present crisis. Nine was looking . . . unimpressed.

"Very funny," she said coldly, making Miles wonder for a wild moment if she'd been equipped with the telepathy gene complex— no, she pre-dated that—"but I'm not even human. Or hadn't you heard?"

Miles shrugged carefully. "Human is as human does." He forced himself to reach out and touch her damp cheek. "Animals don't weep, Nine."

She jerked, as from an electric shock. "Animals don't lie. Humans do. All the time."

"Not *all* the time." He hoped the light was too dim for her to see the flush in his face. She was watching his face intently.

"Prove it." She tilted her head as she sat cross-legged. Her pale gold eyes were suddenly burning, speculative.

"Uh . . . sure. How?"

"Take off your clothes."

". . . what?"

"Take off your clothes, and lie down with me as *humans* do. Men and women." Her hand reached out to touch his throat.

The pressing claws made little wells in his flesh. "Blrp?" choked Miles. His eyes felt wide as saucers.

A little more pressure, and those wells would spring forth red fountains. *I am about to die. . . .*

She stared into his face with a strange, frightening, bottomless hunger. Then abruptly, she released him. He sprang up and cracked his head on the low ceiling, and dropped back down, the stars in his eyes unrelated to love at first sight.

Her lips wrinkled back on a fanged groan of despair. "Ugly," she wailed. Her clawed nails raked across her cheeks leaving red furrows. "Too *ugly* . . . animal . . . you *don't* think I'm human—" She seemed to swell with some destructive resolve.

"No, no, no!" gibbered Miles, lurching to his knees and grabbing her hands and pulling them down. "It's not that. It's just, uh—how old are you, anyway?"

"Sixteen."

Sixteen. God. He remembered sixteen. Sex-obsessed and dying inside every minute. A horrible age to be trapped in a twisted, fragile, abnormal body. God only knew how he had survived his own self-hatred then. No—he remembered how. *He'd* been saved by one who loved him. "Aren't you a little young for this?" he tried hopefully.

"How old were you?"

"Fifteen," he admitted, before thinking to lie. "But . . . it was traumatic. Didn't work out at all in the long run."

Her claws turned toward her face again.

"Don't *do* that!" he cried, hanging on. It reminded him entirely too much of the episode of Sergeant Bothari and the knife. The Sergeant had taken Miles's knife away from him by superior force. Not an option open to Miles here. "Will you *calm down?*" he yelled at her.

She hesitated.

"It's just that, uh, an officer and gentleman doesn't

just fling himself onto his lady on the bare ground. One . . . one sits down. Gets comfortable. Has a little conversation, drinks a little wine, plays a little music . . . slows down. You're hardly warm yet. Here, sit over here where it's warmest." He positioned her nearer the broken duct, got up on his knees behind her, tried rubbing her neck and shoulders. Her muscles were tense, they felt like rocks under his thumbs. Any attempt on his part to strangle her would clearly be futile.

I can't believe this. Trapped in Ryoval's basement with a sex-starved teenage werewolf. There was nothing about this in any of my Imperial Academy training manuals. . . . He remembered his mission, which was to get her left calf muscle back to the *Ariel* alive. *Dr. Canaba, if I survive you and I are going to have a little talk about this.* . . .

Her voice was muffled with grief and the odd shape of her mouth. "You think I'm too tall."

"Not at all." He was getting hold of himself a bit, he could lie faster. "I adore tall women, ask anyone who knows me. Besides, I made the happy discovery some time back that height difference only matters when we're standing up. When we're lying down it's, ah, less of a problem. . . ." A rapid mental review of everything he'd ever learned by trial and error, mostly error, about women was streaming uninvited through his mind. It was harrowing. What did women *want*?

He shifted around and took her hand, earnestly. She stared back equally earnestly, waiting for . . . *instruction*. At this point the realization came over Miles that he was facing his first virgin. He smiled at her in total paralysis for several seconds. "Nine . . . you've never done this before, have you?"

"I've seen vids." She frowned introspectively.

"They usually start with kisses, but . . ." a vague gesture toward her misshapen mouth, "maybe you don't want to."

Miles tried not to think about the late rat. She'd been systematically starved, after all. "Vids can be very misleading. For women—especially the first time—it takes practice to learn your own body responses, woman friends have told me. I'm afraid I might hurt you." *And then you'll disembowel me.*

She gazed into his eyes. "That's all right. I have a very high pain threshold."

But I don't.

This was mad. She was mad. *He* was mad. Yet he could feel a creeping fascination for the—proposition— rising from his belly to his brain like a fey fog. No doubt about it, she was the tallest female thing he was ever likely to meet. More than one woman of his acquaintance had accused him of wanting to go mountain-climbing. He could get that out of his system once for all. . . .

Damn, I do believe she'd clean up good. She was not without a certain . . . charm was *not* the word— whatever beauty there was to be found in the strong, the swift, the leanly athletic, the functioning form. Once you got used to the *scale* of it. She radiated a smooth heat he could feel from here—*animal magnetism?* the suppressed observer in the back of his brain supplied. Power? Whatever else it was, it would certainly be *astonishing*.

One of his mother's favorite aphorisms drifted through his head. *Anything worth doing,* she always said, *is worth doing well.*

Dizzy as a drunkard, he abandoned the crutch of logic for the wings of inspiration. "Well then, doctor," he heard himself muttering insanely, "let us experiment."

Kissing a woman with fangs was indeed a novel sensation. Being kissed back—she was clearly a fast learner—was even more novel. Her arms circled him ecstatically, and from that point on he lost control of the situation, somehow. Though some time later, coming up for air, he did look up to ask, "Nine, have you ever heard of the black widow spider?"

"No . . . what is it?"

"Never mind," he said airily.

It was all very awkward and clumsy, but sincere, and when he was done the water in her eyes was from joy, not pain. She seemed enormously (how else?) pleased with him. He was so unstrung he actually fell asleep for a few minutes, pillowed on her body.

He woke up laughing.

"You really do have the most elegant cheekbones," he told her, tracing their line with one finger. She leaned into his touch, cuddled up equally to him and the heat pipe. "There's a woman on my ship who wears her hair in a sort of woven braid in the back— it would look just great on you. Maybe she could teach you how."

She pulled a wad of her hair forward and looked cross-eyed at it, as if trying to see past the coarse tangles and filth. She touched his face in turn. "You are very handsome, Admiral."

"Huh? Me?" He ran a hand over the night's beard stubble, sharp features, the old pain lines . . . *she must be blinded by my putative rank, eh?*

"Your face is very . . . alive. And your eyes see what they're looking at."

"Nine . . ." he cleared his throat, paused. "Dammit, that's not a name, that's a number. What happened to Ten?"

"He died." *Maybe I will too*, her strange-colored eyes added silently, before her lids shuttered them.

"Is Nine all they ever called you?"

"There's a long biocomputer code-string that's my actual designation."

"Well, we all have serial numbers," Miles had two, now that he thought of it, "but this is absurd. I can't call you Nine, like some robot. You need a proper name, a name that fits you." He leaned back onto her warm bare shoulder—she was like a furnace, they had spoken truly about her metabolism—and his lips drew back on a slow grin. "Taura."

"Taura?" Her long mouth gave it a skewed and lilting accent. ". . . it's too beautiful for me!"

"Taura," he repeated firmly. "Beautiful but strong. Full of secret meaning. Perfect. Ah, speaking of secrets . . ." Was now the time to tell her about what Dr. Canaba had planted in her left calf? Or would she be hurt, as someone falsely courted for her money—or his title—Miles faltered. "I think, now that we know each other better, that it's time for us to blow out of this place."

She stared around, into the grim dimness. "How?"

"Well, that's what we have to figure out, eh? I confess, ducts rather spring to my mind." Not the heat pipe, obviously. He'd have to go anorexic for months to fit in it, besides, he'd cook. He shook out and pulled on his black T-shirt—he'd put on his trousers immediately after he'd woke, that stone floor sucked heat remorselessly from any flesh that touched it—and creaked to his feet. God. He was getting too old for this sort of thing already. The sixteen-year-old, clearly, possessed the physical resilience of a minor goddess. What was it he'd gotten into at sixteen? Sand, that was it. He winced in memory of what it had done to certain sensitive body folds and crevices. Maybe cold stone wasn't so bad after all.

She pulled her pale green coat and trousers out from under herself, dressed, and followed him in a crouch until the space was sufficient for her to stand upright.

They quartered and re-quartered the underground chamber. There were four ladders with hatches, all locked. There was a locked vehicle exit to the outside on the downslope side. A direct breakout might be simplest, but if he couldn't make immediate contact with Thorne it was a twenty-seven-kilometer hike to the nearest town. In the snow, in his sock feet—her bare feet. And if they got there, he wouldn't be able to use the vidnet anyway because his credit card was still locked in the Security Ops office upstairs. Asking for charity in Ryoval's town was a dubious proposition. So, break straight out and be sorry later, or linger and try to equip themselves, risking recapture, and be sorry sooner? Tactical decisions were such fun.

Ducts won. Miles pointed upward to the most likely one. "Think you can break that open and boost me in?" he asked Taura.

She studied it, nodded slowly, the expression closing on her face. She stretched up and moved along to a soft metal clad joint, slipped her claw-hard fingernails under the strip, and yanked it off. She worked her fingers into the exposed slot and hung on it as if chinning herself. The duct bent open under her weight. "There you go," she said.

She lifted him up as easily as a child, and he squirmed into the duct. This one was a particularly close fit, though it was the largest he had spotted as accessible in this ceiling. He inched along it on his back. He had to stop twice to suppress a residual, hysteria-tinged laughing fit. The duct curved upward, and he slithered around the curve in the darkness only to find that it split here into a Y, each branch half-sized. He cursed and backed out.

Taura had her face turned up to him, an unusual angle of view.

"No good that way," he gasped, reversing direction gymnastically at the gap. He headed the other way. This too curved up, but within moments he found a grille. A tightly-fitted, unbudgable, unbreakable, and with his bare hands uncuttable grille. Taura might have the strength to rip it out of the wall, but Taura couldn't fit through the duct to reach it. He contemplated it a few moments. "Right," he muttered, and backed out again.

"So much for ducts," he reported to Taura. "Uh . . . could you help me down?" She lowered him to the floor, and he dusted himself futilely. "Let's look around some more."

She followed him docilely enough, though something in her expression hinted she might be losing faith in his admiralness. A bit of detailing on a column caught his eye, and he went to take a closer look in the dim light.

It was one of the low-vibration support columns. Two meters in diameter, set deep in the bedrock in a well of fluid, it ran straight up to one of the labs, no doubt, to provide an ultra-stable base for certain kinds of crystal generation projects and the like. Miles rapped on the side of the column. It rang hollow. *Ah yes, makes sense, concrete doesn't float too well, eh?* A groove in the side outlined . . . an access port? He ran his fingers around it, probing. There was a concealed . . . something. He stretched his arms and found a twin spot on the opposite side.

The spots yielded slowly to the hard pressure of his thumbs. There was a sudden pop and hiss, and the whole panel came away. He staggered, and barely kept from dropping it down the hole. He turned it sideways and drew it out.

"Well, well," Miles grinned. He stuck his head through the port, looked down and up. Black as pitch. Rather gingerly, he reached his arm in and felt around. There was a ladder running up the damp inside, for access for cleaning and repairs; the whole column could apparently be filled with fluid of whatever density at need. Filled, it would have been self-pressure-sealed and unopenable. Carefully, he examined the inner edge of the hatch. Openable from either side, by God. "Let's go see if there's any more of these, further up."

It was slow going, feeling for more grooves as they ascended in the blackness. Miles tried not to think about the fall, should he slip from the slimy ladder. Taura's deep breathing, below him, was actually rather comforting. They had gone up perhaps three stories when Miles's chilled and numbing fingers found another groove. He'd almost missed it, it was on the opposite side of the ladder from the first. He then discovered, the hard way, that he didn't have nearly the reach to keep one arm hooked around the ladder and press both release catches at the same time. After a terrifying slip, trying, he clung spasmodically to the ladder till his heart stopped pounding. "Taura?" he croaked. "I'll move up, and you try it." Not much up was left, the column ended a meter or so above his head.

Her extra arm length was all that was needed—the catches surrendered to her big hands with a squeak of protest.

"What do you see?" Miles whispered.

"Big dark room. Maybe a lab."

"Makes sense. Climb back down and put that lower panel back on, no sense advertising where we went."

Miles slipped through the hatch into the darkened laboratory while Taura accomplished her chore. He dared not switch on a light in the windowless room, but a few instrument readouts on the benches and walls gave enough ghostly glow for his dark-adapted eyes that at least he didn't trip over anything. One glass door led to a hallway. A heavily electronically-monitored hallway. With his nose pressed to the glass Miles saw a red shape flit past a cross-corridor; guards here. What did they guard?

Taura oozed out of the access hatch to the column —with difficulty—and sat down heavily on the floor, her face in her hands. Concerned, Miles nipped back to her. "You all right?"

She shook her head. "No. Hungry."

"What, already? That was supposed to be a twenty-four hour rat—er, ration bar." Not to mention the two or three kilos of meat she'd had for an appetizer.

"For you, maybe," she wheezed. She was shaking.

Miles began to see why Canaba had dubbed his project a failure. Imagine trying to feed a whole army of such appetites. Napoleon would quail. Maybe the raw-boned kid was still growing. Daunting thought.

There was a refrigerator at the back of the lab. If he knew lab techs . . . ah, ha. Indeed, in among the test tubes was a package with half a sandwich and a large, if bruised, pear. He handed them to Taura. She looked vastly impressed, as if he'd conjured them from his sleeve by magic, and devoured them at once, and grew less pale.

Miles foraged further for his troop. Alas, the only other organics in the fridge were little covered dishes of gelatinous stuff with unpleasant multi-colored fuzz growing in them. But there were three big shiny walk-in wall freezers lined up in a row. Miles peered through a glass square in one thick door, and risked pressing the wall pad that turned on the light inside. Within were row on row on row of labelled drawers, full of clear plastic trays. Frozen samples of some kind. Thousands—Miles looked again, and calculated more carefully—hundreds of thousands. He glanced at the lighted control panel by the freezer drawer. The temperature inside was that of liquid nitrogen. Three freezers . . . *Millions* of. . . . Miles sat down abruptly on the floor himself. "Taura, do you know where we *are*?" he whispered intensely.

"Sorry, no," she whispered back, creeping over.

"That was a rhetorical question. *I* know where we are."

"Where?"

"Ryoval's treasure chamber."

"What?"

"That," Miles jerked his thumb at the freezer, "is the baron's hundred-year-old tissue collection. My God. Its value is almost incalculable. Every unique, irreplaceable, mutant bizarre bit he's begged, bought, borrowed or stolen for the last three-fourths of a century, all lined up in neat little rows, waiting to be thawed and cultured and cooked up into some poor new slave. This is the living heart of his whole human biologicals operation." Miles sprang to his feet and pored over the control panels. His heart raced, and he breathed open-mouthed, laughing silently, feeling almost like he was about to pass out. "Oh, shit. Oh, God." He stopped, swallowed. Could it be done?

These freezers had to have an alarm system, monitors surely, piped up to Security Ops at the very least. Yes, there was a complex device for opening the door—that was fine, he didn't want to open the door. He left it untouched. It was systems readout he was after. If he could bugger up just one sensor. . . . Was the thing broadcast-output to several outside monitor locations, or did they run an optic thread to just one? The lab benches supplied him with a small hand light, and drawers and drawers of assorted tools and supplies. Taura watched him in puzzlement as he darted here, there, taking inventory.

The freezer monitor *was* broadcast output, inaccessible; could he hit it on the input side? He levered off a smoke-dark plastic cover as silently as he could. There, *there*, the optic thread came out of the wall, pumping continuous information about the freezer's interior environment. It fit into a simple standard receiver plug on the more daunting black box that controlled the door alarm. There'd been a whole drawer full of assorted optic threads with various ends and Y-adaptors. . . . Out of the spaghetti-tangle he drew what he needed, discarding several with broken ends or other damage. There were three optical data recorders in the drawer. Two didn't work. The third did.

A quick festoon of optic thread, a swift unplugging and plugging, and he had one freezer talking to two control boxes. He set the freed thread to talking to the datacorder. He simply had to chance the blip during transfer. If anyone checked they'd find all seemed well again. He gave the datacorder several minutes to develop a nice continuous replay loop, crouching very still with even the tiny hand light extinguished. Taura waited with the patience of a predator, making no noise.

One, two, three, and he set the datacorder to talking to all three control boxes. The real thread plugs hung forlornly loose. Would it work? There were no alarms going off, no thundering herd of irate security troops. . . .

"Taura, come here."

She loomed beside him, baffled.

"Have you ever met Baron Ryoval?" asked Miles.

"Yes, once . . . when he came to buy me."

"Did you like him?"

She gave him an are-you-out-of-your-mind? look.

"Yeah, I didn't much care for him either." Restrained murder, in point of fact. He was now meltingly grateful for that restraint. "Would you like to rip his lungs out, if you could?"

Her clawed hands clenched. "Try me!"

"Good!" He smiled cheerily. "I want to give you your first lesson in tactics." He pointed. "See that control? The temperature in these freezers can be raised to almost 200 degrees centigrade, for heat sterilization during cleaning. Give me your finger. One finger. Gently. More gently than that." He guided her hand. "The least possible pressure you can apply to the dial, and still move . . . Now the next," he pulled her to the next panel, "and the last." He exhaled, still not quite able to believe it.

"And the lesson is," he breathed, "it's not how much force you use. It's where you apply it."

He resisted the urge to scrawl something like *The Dwarf Strikes Back* across the front of the freezer with a flow pen. The longer the baron in his mortal rage took to figure out who to pursue, the better. It would take several hours to bring all that mass in there from liquid nitrogen temperature up to *well-done*, but if no one came in till morning shift, the destruction would be absolute.

Miles glanced at the time on the wall digital. Dear God, he'd spent a lot of time in that basement. Well-spent, but still . . . "Now," he said to Taura, who was still meditating on the dial, and her hand, with her gold eyes glowing, "we have to get out of here. Now we *really* have to get out of here." Lest her next tactics lesson turn out to be, Don't blow up the bridge you're standing on, Miles allowed nervously.

Contemplating the door-locking mechanism more closely, plus what lay beyond—among other things, the sound-activated wall-mounted monitors in the halls featured automatic laser fire—Miles almost went to turn the freezer temperatures back down. His chip-driven Dendarii tools, now locked in the Security Ops office, might barely have handled the complex circuitry in the pried-open control box. But of course, he couldn't get at his tools without his tools . . . a nice paradox. It shouldn't surprise Miles, that Ryoval saved his most sophisticated alarm system for this lab's one and only door. But it made the room a much worse trap than even the sub-basement.

He made another tour of the lab with the filched hand light, checking drawers again. No computer-keys came to hand, but he did find a big, crude pair of cutters in a drawer full of rings and clamps, and bethought him of the duct grille that had lately defeated him in the basement. So. The passage up to this lab had merely been the illusion of progress toward escape.

"There's no shame in a strategic retreat to a better position," he whispered to Taura when she balked at re-entering the support column's dark tube. "This is a dead-end, here. Maybe literally." The doubt in her tawny eyes was strangely unsettling, a weight in his heart. *Still don't trust me, eh? Well, maybe those who have been greatly betrayed need great proof.* "Stick with me, kid," he muttered under his breath, swinging into the tube. "We're going places." Her doubt was merely masked under lowered eyelids, but she followed him, sealing the hatch behind them.

With the hand light, the descent was slightly less nasty than the ascent into the unknown had been. There were no other exits to be found, and shortly they stood on the stone they had started from. Miles checked the progress of their ceiling waterspout, while Taura drank again. The splattering water ran off in a flat greasy trickle downslope; given the vast size of the chamber, it would be some days before the pool collecting slowly against the lower wall offered any useful strategic possibilities, though there was always the hope it might do a bit to undermine the foundations.

Taura boosted him back into the duct. "Wish me luck," he murmured over his shoulder, muffled by the close confines.

"Goodbye," she said. He could not see the expression on her face; there was none in her voice.

"See you later," he corrected firmly.

A few minutes of vigorous wriggling brought him back to his grille. It opened onto a dark room stacked with stuff, part of the basement proper, quiet and unoccupied. The snip of his cutters, biting through the grille, seemed loud enough to bring down Ryoval's entire security force, but none appeared. Maybe the security chief was sleeping off his drug hangover. A scrabbling noise, not of Miles's own making, echoed thinly through the duct and Miles froze. He flashed his light down a side-branching tube. Twin red jewels flashed back, the eyes of a huge rat. He briefly considered trying to clout it and haul it back to Taura. No. When they got back to the *Ariel*, he'd give her a steak dinner. Two steak dinners. The rat saved itself by turning and scampering away.

The grille parted at last, and he squeezed into the

storage room. What time was it, anyway? Late, very
late. The room gave onto a corridor, and on the floor
at the end, one of the access hatches gleamed dully.
Miles's heart rose in serious hope. Once he'd got
Taura, they must next try to reach a vehicle. . . .

This hatch, like the first, was manual, no sophisticated electronics to disarm. It re-locked automatically upon closing, however. Miles jammed it with
his clippers before descending the ladder. He aimed
his light around—"Taura!" he whispered. "Where
are you?"

No immediate answer; no glowing gold eyes flashing in the forest of pillars. He was reluctant to shout.
He slapped down the rungs and began a silent fast
trot through the chamber, the cold stone draining
the heat through his socks and making him long for
his lost boots.

He came upon her sitting silently at the base of a
pillar, her head turned sideways resting on her knees.
Her face was pensive, sad. Really, it didn't take long
at all to begin reading the subtleties of feeling in her
wolfish features.

"Time to march, soldier girl," Miles said.

Her head lifted. "You came back!"

"What did you think I was going to do? Of course I
came back. You're my recruit, aren't you?"

She scrubbed her face with the back of a big
paw—hand, Miles corrected himself severely—and
stood up, and up. "Guess I must be." Her outslung
mouth smiled slightly. If you didn't have a clue what
the expression was, it could look quite alarming.

"I've got a hatch open. We've got to try to get out
of this main building, back to the utility bay. I saw
several vehicles parked there earlier. What's a little
theft, after—"

With a sudden whine, the outside vehicle entrance, downslope to their right, began to slide upward. A rush of cold dry air swept through the dankness, and a thin shaft of yellow dawn light made the shadows blue. They shielded their eyes in the unexpected glare. Out of the bright squinting haze coalesced half-a-dozen red-clad forms, double-timing it, weapons at the ready.

Taura's hand was tight on Miles's. *Run*, he started to cry, and bit back the shout; no way could they outrun a nerve disruptor beam, a weapon which at least two of the guards now carried. Miles's breath hissed out through his teeth. He was too infuriated even to swear. They'd been so *close*. . . .

Security Chief Moglia sauntered up. "What, still in one piece, Naismith?" he smirked unpleasantly. "Nine must have finally realized it's time to start cooperating, eh, Nine?"

Miles squeezed her hand hard, hoping the message would be properly understood as, *Wait*.

She lifted her chin. "Guess so," she said coldly.

"It's about time," said Moglia. "Be a good girl, and we'll take you upstairs and feed you breakfast after this."

Good, Miles's hand signalled. She was watching him closely for cues, now.

Moglia prodded Miles with his truncheon. "Time to go, dwarf. Your friends have actually made ransom. Surprised me."

Miles was surprised himself. He moved toward the exit, still towing Taura. He didn't look at her, did as little as possible to draw unwanted attention to their, er, togetherness, while still maintaining it. He let go of her hand as soon as their momentum was established.

What the hell. . . ? Miles thought as they emerged into the blinking dawn, up the ramp and onto a circle of tarmac slick with glittering rime. A most peculiar tableau was arranged there.

Bel Thorne and one Dendarii trooper, armed with stunners, shifted uneasily—not prisoners? Half a dozen armed men in the green uniform of House Fell stood at the ready. A float truck emblazoned with Fell's logo was parked at the tarmac's edge. And Nicol the quaddie, wrapped in white fur against the frost, hovered in her float chair at the stunner-point of a big green-clad guard. The light was grey and gold and chilly as the sun, lifting over the dark mountains in the distance, broke through the clouds.

"Is that the man you want?" the green-uniformed guard captain asked Bel Thorne.

"That's him." Thorne's face was white with an odd mixture of relief and distress. "Admiral, are you all right?" Thorne called urgently. Its eyes widened, taking in Miles's tall companion. "What the hell's *that?*"

"*She* is Recruit-trainee Taura," Miles said firmly, hoping 1) Bel would unravel the several meanings packed in that sentence and 2) Ryoval's guards wouldn't. Bel looked stunned, so evidently Miles had got at least partly through; Security Chief Moglia looked suspicious, but baffled. Miles was clearly a problem Moglia thought he was about to get rid of, however, and he thrust his bafflement aside to deal with the more important person of Fell's guard captain.

"What *is* this?" Miles hissed at Bel, sidling closer until a red-clad guard lifted his nerve disruptor and shook his head. Moglia and Fell's captain were exchanging electronic data on a report panel, heads bent together, evidently the official documentation.

"When we lost you last night, I was in a panic," Bel pitched its voice low toward Miles. "A frontal assault was out of the question. So I ran to Baron

Fell to ask for help. But the help I got wasn't quite what I expected. Fell and Ryoval cooked up a deal between them to exchange Nicol for you. I swear, I only found out the details an hour ago!" Bel protested at Nicol's thin-lipped glower in its direction.

"I . . . see." Miles paused. "Are we planning to refund her dollar?"

"*Sir,*" Bel's voice was anguished, "we had *no idea* what was happening to you in there. We were expecting Ryoval to start beaming up a holocast of obscene and ingenious tortures, starring you, at any minute. Like Commodore Tung says, on hemmed-in ground, use subterfuge."

Miles recognized one of Tung's favorite Sun Tzu aphorisms. On bad days Tung had a habit of quoting the 4000-year-dead general in the original Chinese; when Tung was feeling benign they got a translation. Miles glanced around, adding up weapons, men, equipment. Most of the green guards carried stunners. Thirteen to . . . three? Four? He glanced at Nicol. Maybe five? *On desperate ground,* Sun Tzu advised, *fight.* Could it get much more desperate than this?

"Ah . . ." said Miles. "Just what the devil did we offer Baron Fell in exchange for this extraordinary charity? Or is he doing it out of the goodness of his heart?"

Bel shot him an exasperated look, then cleared its throat. "I promised you'd tell him the real truth about the Betan rejuvenation treatment."

"*Bel* . . ."

Thorne shrugged unhappily. "I thought, once we'd got you back, we'd figure something out. But I never thought he'd offer Nicol to Ryoval, I swear!"

Down in the long valley, Miles could see a bead moving on the thin gleam of monorail. The morning shift of bioengineers and technicians, janitors and office clerks and cafeteria cooks, was due to arrive soon. Miles glanced at the white building looming above, pictured the scene to come in that third floor lab as the guards deactivated the alarms and let them in to work, as the first one through the door sniffed and wrinkled his nose and said plaintively, "What's that awful *smell*?"

"Has 'Medtech Vaughn' signed aboard the *Ariel* yet?" Miles asked.

"Within the hour."

"Yeah, well . . . it turns out we didn't need to kill his fatted calf after all. It comes with the package." Miles nodded toward Taura.

Bel lowered its voice still further. "*That's* coming with us?"

"You'd better believe it. Vaughn didn't tell us everything. To put it mildly. I'll explain later," Miles added as the two guard captains broke up their tete-a-tete. Moglia swung his truncheon jauntily, heading toward Miles. "Meantime, you made a slight miscalculation. This isn't hemmed-in ground. This is *desperate* ground. Nicol, I want you to know, the Dendarii don't give refunds."

Nicol frowned in bewilderment. Bel's eyes widened, as it checked out the odds—calculating them thirteen to three, Miles could tell.

"Truly?" Bel choked. A subtle hand signal, down by its trouser seam, brought the trooper to full alert.

"Truly desperate," Miles reiterated. He inhaled deeply. "Now! Taura, attack!"

Miles launched himself toward Moglia, not so much actually expecting to wrestle his truncheon from him as hoping to maneuver Moglia's body between himself and the fellows with the nerve disruptors. The Dendarii trooper, who had been paying attention to details, dropped one of the nerve disruptor wielders with his first stunner shot, then rolled away from the second's return fire. Bel dropped the second nerve disruptor man and leapt aside. Two red guards, aiming their stunners at the running hermaphrodite, were lifted abruptly by their necks. Taura cracked their heads together, unscientifically but hard; they fell to hands and knees, groping blindly for their lost weapons.

Fell's green guards hesitated, not certain just whom to shoot, until Nicol, her angel's face alight, suddenly shot skyward in her float chair and dropped straight down again on the head of her guard, who was distracted by the fight. He fell like an ox. Nicol flipped her floater sideways as green-guard stunner fire found her, shielding herself from its flare, and shot upwards again. Taura picked up a red guard and threw him at a green one; they both went down in a tangle of arms and legs.

The Dendarii trooper closed on a green guard hand-to-hand, to shield himself from stunner blast. Fell's captain wouldn't buy the maneuver, and ruthlessly stunned them both, a sound tactic with the numbers on his side. Moglia got his truncheon up against Miles's windpipe and started to press, meanwhile yelling into his wrist comm, calling for back-up from Security Ops. A green guard screamed as Taura yanked his arm out of its shoulder socket and swung him into the air by the dislocated joint at another one aiming his stunner at her.

Colored lights danced before Miles's eyes. Fell's captain, focusing on Taura as the biggest threat, dropped to stunner fire from Bel Thorne as Nicol whammed her float chair into the back of the last green guard left standing.

"The float truck!" Miles croaked. "Go for the float truck!" Bel cast him a desperate look and sprinted toward it. Miles fought like an eel until Moglia got a hand down to his boot, drew a sharp, thin knife, and pressed it to Miles's neck.

"Hold still!" snarled Moglia. "That's better . . ." He straightened in the sudden silence, realizing he'd just pulled domination from disaster. "*Everybody* hold still." Bel froze with its hand on the float-truck's door pad. A couple of the men splayed on the tarmac twitched and moaned.

"Now stand away from—glk," said Moglia.

Taura's voice whispered past Moglia's ear, a soft, soft growl. "Drop the knife. Or I'll rip your throat out with my bare hands."

Miles's eyes wrenched sideways, trying to see around his own clamped head, as the sharp edge sang against his skin.

"I can kill him, before you do," croaked Moglia.

"The little man is mine," Taura crooned. "You gave him to me yourself. He came *back* for me. Hurt him one little bit, and I'll tear your head off and then I'll drink your blood."

Miles felt Moglia being lifted off his feet. The knife clattered to the pavement. Miles sprang away, staggering. Taura held Moglia by his neck, her claws biting deep. "I still want to rip his head off," she growled petulantly, remembrance of abuse sparking in her eyes.

"Leave him," gasped Miles. "Believe me, in a few hours he's going to be suffering a more artistic vengeance than anything we can dream up."

Bel galloped back to stun the security chief at can't miss range while Taura held him out like a wet cat. Miles had Taura throw the unconscious Dendarii over her shoulder while he ran around to the back of the float truck and released the doors for Nicol, who zipped her chair inside. They tumbled within, dropped the doors, and Bel at the controls

shot them into the air. A siren was going off somewhere in Ryoval's.

"Wrist comm, wrist comm," Miles babbled, strip-
ping his unconscious trooper of the device. "Bel,
where is our drop shuttle parked?"

"We came in at a little commercial shuttleport just
outside Ryoval's town, about forty kilometers from
here."

"Anybody left manning it?"

"Anderson and Nout."

"What's their scrambled comm channel?"

"Twenty-three."

Miles slid into the seat beside Bel and opened the
channel. It took a small eternity for Sergeant Anderson to answer, fully thirty or forty seconds, while the
float-truck streaked above the treetops and over the
nearest ridge.

"Laureen, I want you to get your shuttle into the
air. We need an emergency pick-up, soonest. We're
in a House Fell float truck, heading—" Miles thrust
his wrist under Bel's nose.

"North from Ryoval Biologicals," Bel recited. "At
about two hundred sixty kilometers per hour, which
is all the faster this crate will go."

"Home in on our screamer," Miles set the wrist
comm emergency signal. "Don't wait for clearance
from Ryoval's shuttleport traffic control, 'cause you
won't get it. Have Nout patch my comm through to
the *Ariel*."

"You got it, sir," Anderson's thin voice came cheerily back over his comm.

Static, and another few seconds excruciating delay.
Then an excited voice, "Murka here. I thought you
were coming out right behind us last night! You all
right, sir?"

"Temporarily. Is 'Medtech Vaughn' aboard?"

"Yes, sir."

"All right. Don't let him off. Assure him I have his tissue sample with me."

"Really! How'd you—"

"Never mind how. Get all the troops back aboard and break from the station into free orbit. Plan to make a flying pick-up of the drop shuttle, and tell the pilot-officer to plot a course for the Escobar wormhole jump at max acceleration as soon as we're clamped on. Don't wait for clearance."

"We're still loading cargo. . . ."

"Abandon any that's still unloaded."

"Are we in serious shit, sir?"

"Mortal, Murka."

"Right, sir. Murka out."

"I thought we were all supposed to be as quiet as mice here on Jackson's Whole," Bel complained. "Isn't this all a bit splashy?"

"The situation's changed. There'd be no negotiating with Ryoval for Nicol, or for Taura either, after what we did last night. I struck a blow for truth and justice back there that I may live to regret, briefly. Tell you about it later. Anyway, do you really want to stick around while I explain to Baron Fell the real truth about the Betan rejuvenation treatment?"

"Oh," Thorne's eyes were alight, as it concentrated on its flying, "I'd pay money to watch that, sir."

"Ha. No. For one last moment back there, all the pieces were in our hands. Potentially, anyway." Miles began exploring the readouts on the float-truck's simple control panel. "We'd never get everybody together again, never. One maneuvers to the limit, but the golden moment demands action. If you miss it, the gods damn you forever. And vice versa. . . . Speaking of action, did you see Taura take out *seven* of those guys?" Miles chortled in memory. "What's she going to be like after basic training?"

Bel glanced uneasily over its shoulder, to where Nicol had her float chair lodged and Taura hunkered in the back along with the body of the unconscious trooper. "I was too busy to keep count."

Miles swung out of his seat, and made his way into the back to check on their precious live cargo.

"Nicol, you were great," he told her. "You fought like a falcon. I may have to give you a discount on that dollar."

Nicol was still breathless, ivory cheeks flushed. An upper hand shoved a strand of black hair out of her sparkling eyes. "I was afraid they'd break my dulcimer." A lower hand stroked a big box-shaped case jammed into the float-chair's cup beside her. "Then I was afraid they'd break Bel. . . ."

Taura sat leaning against the truck wall, a bit green.

Miles knelt beside her. "Taura dear, are you all right?" He gently lifted one clawed hand to check her pulse, which was bounding. Nicol gave him a rather strange look at his tender gesture, her float chair was wedged as far from Taura as it could get.

"Hungry," Taura gasped.

"Again? But of course, all that energy expenditure. Anybody got a ration bar?" A quick check found an only-slightly-nibbled rat bar in the stunned trooper's thigh pocket, which Miles immediately liberated. Miles smiled benignly at Taura as she wolfed it down; she smiled back as best she could with her mouth full. *No more rats for you after this*, Miles promised silently. *Three steak dinners when we get back to the* Ariel, *and a couple of chocolate cakes for dessert. . . .*

The float-truck jinked. Taura, reviving somewhat, extended her feet to hold Nicol's dented cup in place against the far wall and keep it from bouncing around. "Thank you," said Nicol warily. Taura nodded.

"Company," Bel Thorne called over its shoulder. Miles hastened forward.

Two aircars were coming up fast behind them. Ryoval's security. Doubtless beefed up tougher than the average civilian police car—yes. Bel jinked again as a plasma bolt boiled past, leaving bright green streaks across Miles's retinas. Quasi-military and seriously annoyed, their pursuers were.

"This is one of Fell's trucks, we ought to have *something* to fling back at them." There was nothing in front of Miles that looked like any kind of weapons-control.

A *whoomp*, a scream from Nicol, and the float-truck staggered in air, righted itself under Bel's hands. A roar of air and vibration—Miles cranked his head around frantically—one top back corner of the truck's cargo area was blown away. The rear door was fused shut on one side, whanging loose along the opposite edge. Taura still braced the float chair, Nicol now had her upper hands wrapped around Taura's ankles. "Ah," said Thorne. "No armor."

"What did they think this was going to be, a peaceful mission?" Miles checked his wrist comm. "Laureen, are you in the air yet?"

"Coming, sir."

"Well, if you've ever itched to red-line it, now's your chance. Nobody's going to complain about your abusing the equipment this time."

"*Thank* you, sir," she responded happily.

They were losing speed and altitude. "Hang on!" Bel yelled over its shoulder, and suddenly reversed thrust. Their closing pursuers shot past them, but immediately began climbing turns. Bel accelerated again; another scream from the back as their live cargo was thus shifted toward the now-dubious rear doors.

The Dendarii hand stunners were of no use at all. Miles clambered into the back again, looking for some sort of luggage compartment, gun rack, anything—surely Fell's people did not rely only on the fearsome reputation of their House for protection. . . .

The padded benches along each side of the cargo compartment, upon which Fell's guard squad had presumably sat, swung up on storage space. The first was empty, the second contained personal luggage— Miles had a brief flash of strangling an enemy with someone's pajama pants, flinging underwear into thruster air-intakes—the third compartment was also empty. The fourth was locked.

The float-truck rocked under another blast, part of the top peeled away in the wind, Miles grabbed for Taura, and the truck plummeted downward. Miles's stomach, and the rest of him, seemed to float upward. They were all flattened to the floor again as Bel pulled up. The float truck shivered and lurched, and all, Miles and Taura, the unconscious trooper, Nicol in her float chair, were flung forward in a tangle as the truck plowed to a tilted stop in a copse of frost-blackened scrub.

Bel, blood streaming down its face, clambered back to them crying "Out, out, out!" Miles stretched for the new opening in the roof, jerked his hand back at the burning touch of hot slagged metal and plastics. Taura, standing up, stuck her head out through the hole, then crouched back down to boost Miles through. He slithered to the ground, looked around. They were in an unpeopled valley of native vegetation, flanked by ropy, ridgy hills. Flying up the slot toward them came the two pursuing aircars, swelling, slowing—coming in for a capture, or just taking careful aim?

The *Ariel's* combat drop shuttle roared up over the ridge and descended like the black hand of God. The pursuing aircars looked suddenly *much* smaller. One veered off and fled, the second was smashed to the ground not by plasma fire but by a swift swat from a tractor beam. Not even a trickle of smoke marked where it went down. The drop shuttle settled demurely beside them in a deafening crackling crush of shrubbery. Its hatch extended and unfolded itself in a sort of suave, self-satisfied salute.

"Show-off," Miles muttered. He pulled the woozy Thorne's arm over his shoulder, Taura carried the stunned man, Nicol's battered cup stuttered through the air, and they all staggered gratefully to their rescue.

Subtle noises of protest emanated from the ship around him as Miles stepped into the *Ariel's* shuttle hatch corridor. His stomach twitched queasily from an artificial gravity not quite in synch with overloaded engines. They were on their way, breaking orbit already. Miles wanted to get to Nav and Com as quickly as possible, though the evidence so far suggested that Murka was carrying on quite competently. Anderson and Nout hauled in the downed trooper, now moaning his way to consciousness, and turned him over to the medtech waiting with a float pallet. Thorne, who had acquired a temporary plas dressing for the forehead cut during the shuttle flight, sent Nicol in her damaged float chair after them and wisked off toward Nav and Com. Miles turned to encounter the man he least wanted to see. Dr. Canaba hovered anxiously in the corridor, his tanned face strained.

"You," said Miles to Canaba, in a voice dark with rage. Canaba stepped back involuntarily. Miles wanted, but was too short, to pin Canaba to the wall by his neck, and regretfully dismissed the idea of ordering Trooper Nout to do it for him. Miles pinned Canaba with a glare instead. "You cold-blooded double-dealing son-of-a-bitch. You set me up to murder a sixteen-year-old girl!"

Canaba raised his hands in protest. "You don't understand—"

Taura ducked through the shuttle hatch. Her tawny eyes widened in a surprise only exceeded by Canaba's. "Why, Dr. Canaba! What are you doing here?"

Miles pointed to Canaba. "You, stay there," he ordered thickly. He tampered his anger down and turned to the shuttle pilot. "Laureen?"

"Yes, sir?"

Miles took Taura by the hand and led her to Sergeant Anderson. "Laureen, I want you to take Recruit-trainee Taura here in tow and get her a square meal. All she can eat, and I do mean all. Then help her get a bath, a uniform, and orient her to the ship."

Anderson eyed the towering Taura warily. "Er . . . yes, sir."

"She's had a hell of a time," Miles felt compelled to explain, then paused and added, "Do us proud. It's important."

"Yes, sir," said Anderson sturdily, and led off, Taura following with an uncertain backward glance to Miles and Canaba.

Miles rubbed his stubbled chin, conscious of his stains and stink, fear-driven weariness stretching his nerves taut. He turned to the stunned geneticist. "All right, doctor," he snarled, "make me understand. Try real hard."

"I couldn't leave her in Ryoval's hands!" said Canaba in agitation. "To be made a victim, or worse, an agent of his, his merchandised depravities . . ."

"Didn't you ever think of asking us to rescue her?"

"But," said Canaba, confused, "why should you? It wasn't in your contract—a mercenary—"

"Doctor, you've been living on Jackson's Whole too damn long."

"I knew that back when I was throwing up every morning before going to work." Canaba drew himself up with a dry dignity. "But Admiral, you don't understand." He glanced down the corridor in the direction Taura had gone. "I couldn't leave her in Ryoval's hands. But I can't possibly take her to Barrayar. They kill mutants there!"

"Er . . ." said Miles, given pause. "They're attempting to reform those prejudices. Or so I understand. But you're quite right. Barrayar is not the place for her."

"I had hoped, when you came along, not to have to do it, to kill her myself. Not an easy task. I've known her . . . too long. But to leave her down there would have been the most vile condemnation . . ."

"That's no lie. Well, she's out of there now. Same as you." *If we can keep so. . . .* Miles was frantic to get to Nav and Com and find out what was happening. Had Ryoval launched pursuit yet? Had Fell? Would the space station guarding the distant wormhole exit be ordered to block their escape?

"I didn't want to just abandon her," dithered Canaba, "but I couldn't take her with me!"

"I should hope not. You're totally unfit to have charge of her. I'm going to urge her to join the Dendarii Mercenaries. It would seem to be her ge-

netic destiny. Unless you know some reason why
not?"

"But she's going to die!"

Miles stopped short. "And you and I are not?" he
said softly after a moment, then more loudly, "Why?
How soon?"

"It's her metabolism. Another mistake, or concate-
nation of mistakes. I don't know when, exactly. She
could go another year, or two, or five. Or ten."

"Or fifteen?"

"Or fifteen, yes, though not likely. But early, still."

"And yet you wanted to take from her what little
she had? Why?"

"To spare her. The final debilitation is rapid, but
very painful, to judge from what some of the other
. . . prototypes, went through. The females were
more complex than the males, I'm not certain . . .
But it's a ghastly death. Especially ghastly as Ryoval's
slave."

"I don't recall encountering a lovely death yet.
And I've seen a variety. As for duration, I tell you we
could all go in the next fifteen minutes, and where is
your tender mercy then?" He *had* to get to Nav and
Com. "I declare your interest in her forfeit, doctor.
Meanwhile, let her grab what life she can."

"But she was my project—I must answer for her—"

"No. She's a free woman now. She must answer
for herself."

"How free can she ever be, in that body, driven
by that metabolism, that face—a freak's life—better
to die painlessly, than to have all that suffering in-
flicted on her—"

Miles spoke through his teeth. With emphasis.
"No. It's. Not."

Canaba stared at him, shaken out of the rutted
circle of his unhappy reasoning at last.

That's right, doctor, Miles's thought glittered. *Get your head out of your ass and look at me. Finally.*

"Why should . . . you care?" asked Canaba.

"I like her. Rather better than I like you, I might add." Miles paused, daunted by the thought of having to explain to Taura about the gene complexes in her calf. And sooner or later they'd have to retrieve them. Unless he could fake it, pretend the biopsy was some sort of medical standard operating procedure for Dendarii induction—no. She deserved more honesty than that.

Miles was highly annoyed at Canaba for putting this false note between himself and Taura and yet— without the gene complexes, would he have indeed gone in after her as his boast implied? Extended and endangered his assigned mission just out of the goodness of his heart, yeah? Devotion to duty, or pragmatic ruthlessness, which was which? He would never know, now. His anger receded, and exhaustion washed in, the familiar post-mission down— too soon, the mission was far from over, Miles reminded himself sternly. He inhaled. "You can't save her from being alive, Dr. Canaba. Too late. Let her go. Let *go.*"

Canaba's lips were unhappily tight, but, head bowing, he turned his hands palm-out.

"Page the Admiral," Miles heard Thorne say as he entered Nav and Com, then "Belay that," as heads swivelled toward the swish of the doors and they saw Miles. "Good timing, sir."

"What's up?" Miles swung into the com station chair Thorne indicated. Ensign Murka was monitoring ship's shielding and weapons systems, while their Jump pilot sat at the ready beneath the strange crown of his headset with its chemical cannulae and wires.

Pilot Padget's expression was inward, controlled and meditative; his consciousness fully engaged, even merged, with the *Ariel*. Good man.

"Baron Ryoval is on the com for you," said Thorne. "Personally."

"I wonder if he's checked his freezers yet?" Miles settled in before the vid link. "How long have I kept him waiting?"

"Less than a minute," said the com officer.

"Hm. Let him wait a little longer, then. What's been launched in pursuit of us?"

"Nothing, so far," reported Murka.

Miles's brows rose at this unexpected news. He took a moment to compose himself, wishing he'd had time to clean up, shave, and put on a fresh uniform before this interview, just for the psychological edge. He scratched his itching chin and ran his hands through his hair, and wriggled his damp sock toes against the deck matting, which they barely reached. He lowered his station chair slightly, straightened his spine as much as he could, and brought his breathing under control. "All right, bring him up."

The rather blurred background to the face that formed over the vid plate seemed faintly familiar—ah yes, the Security Ops room at Ryoval Biologicals. Baron Ryoval had arrived personally on that scene as promised. It took only one glance at the dusky, contorted expression on Ryoval's youthful face to fill in the rest of the scenario. Miles folded his hands and smiled innocently. "Good morning, Baron. What can I do for you?"

"*Die*, you little mutant!" Ryoval spat. "You! There isn't going to be a bunker deep enough for you to burrow in. I'll put a price on your head that will have every bounty hunter in the galaxy all over you like a second skin—you'll not eat or sleep—I'll have you—"

Yes, the baron had seen his freezers all right. Recently. Gone entirely was the suave contemptuous dismissal of their first encounter. Yet Miles was puzzled by the drift of his threats. It seemed the baron expected them to escape Jacksonian local space. True, House Ryoval owned no space fleet, but why not rent a dreadnought from Baron Fell and attack now? That was the ploy Miles had most expected and feared, that Ryoval and Fell, and maybe Bharaputra too, would combine against him as he attempted to carry off their prizes.

"Can you afford to hire bounty hunters now?" asked Miles mildly. "I thought your assets were somewhat reduced. Though you still have your surgical specialists, I suppose."

Ryoval, breathing heavily, wiped spittle from his mouth. "Did my dear little brother put you up to this?"

"Who?" said Miles, genuinely startled. Yet another player in the game . . . ?

"Baron Fell."

"I was . . . not aware you were related," said Miles. "*Little* brother?"

"You lie badly," sneered Ryoval. "I knew he had to be behind this."

"You'll have to ask him," Miles shot at random, his head spinning as the new datum rearranged all his estimates. *Damn* his mission briefing, which had never mentioned this connection, concentrating in detail only on House Bharaputra. Half-brothers only, surely—yes, hadn't Nicol mentioned something about 'Fell's half-brother'?

"I'll have your head for this," foamed Ryoval. "Shipped back frozen in a box. I'll have it encased in plastic and hang it over my—no, better. Double the money for the man who brings you in alive. You will die slowly, after infinite degradation—"

In all, Miles was glad the distance between them was widening at high acceleration.

Ryoval interrupted his own tirade, dark brows snapping down in sudden suspicion. "Or was it Bharaputra who hired you? Trying to block me from cutting in on their biologicals monopoly at the last, not merging as they promised?"

"Why, now," drawled Miles, "would Bharaputra really mount a plot against the head of another House? Do you have personal evidence that they do that sort of thing? Or—who did kill your, ah, brother's clone?" The connections were locking into place at last. Ye gods. It seemed Miles and his mission had blundered into the middle of an on-going power struggle of byzantine complexity. Nicol had testified that Fell had never pinned down the killer of his young duplicate. . . . "Shall I guess?"

"You know bloody well," snapped Ryoval. "But which of them hired you? Fell, or Bharaputra? Which?"

Ryoval, Miles realized, knew absolutely nothing yet of the real Dendarii mission against House Bharaputra. And with the atmosphere among the Houses being what it apparently was, it could be quite a long time before they got around to comparing notes. The longer the better, from Miles's point of view. He began to suppress, then deliberately released, a small smile. "What, can't you believe it was just my personal blow against the genetic slave trade? A deed in honor of my lady?"

This reference to Taura went straight over Ryoval's head; he had his idea-fixee now, and its ramifications and his rage were an effective block against incoming data. Really, it should not be at all hard to convince a man who had been conspiring deeply against his rivals, that those rivals were conspiring against him in turn.

"Fell, or Bharaputra?" Ryoval reiterated furiously. "Did you think to conceal a theft for Bharaputra with that wanton destruction?"

Theft? Miles wondered intently. Not of Taura, surely—of some tissue sample Bharaputra had been dealing for, perhaps? Oh *ho*. . . .

"Isn't it obvious?" said Miles sweetly. "You gave your brother the motive, in your sabotage of his plans to extend his life. And you wanted too much from Bharaputra, so they supplied the method, placing their super-soldier inside your facility where I could rendezvous with her. They even made you pay for the privilege of having your security screwed! You played right into our hands. The master plan, of course," Miles buffed his fingernails on his T-shirt, "was mine."

Miles glanced up through his eyelashes. Ryoval seemed to be having trouble breathing. The baron cut the vid connection with an abrupt swat of his shaking hand. Blackout.

Humming thoughtfully, Miles went to get a shower.

He was back in Nav and Com in fresh grey-and-whites, full of salicylates for his aches and contusions and with a mug of hot black coffee in his hands as antidote to his squinting red eyes, when the next call came in.

So far from breaking into a tirade like his half-brother, Baron Fell sat silent a moment in the vid, just staring at Miles. Miles, burning under his gaze, felt extremely glad he'd had the chance to clean up. So, had Baron Fell missed his quaddie at last? Had Ryoval communicated to him yet any part of the smouldering paranoid misconceptions Miles had so lately fanned to flame? No pursuit had yet been launched from Fell Station—it must come soon, or not at all, or any craft light enough to match the *Ariel*'s acceleration would be too light to match its firepower. Unless Fell planned to call in favors from the consortium of Houses that ran the Jumppoint Station. . . . One more minute of this heavy silence, Miles felt, and he would break into uncontrollable blither. Fortunately, Fell spoke at last.

"You seem, Admiral Naismith," Baron Fell rumbled, "whether accidentally or on purpose, to be carrying off something that does not belong to you."

Quite a few somethings, Miles reflected, but Fell referred only to Nicol if Miles read him right. "We were compelled to leave in rather a hurry," he said in an apologetic tone.

"So I'm told." Fell inclined his head ironically. He must have had a report from his hapless squad commander. "But you may yet save yourself some trouble. There was an agreed-upon price for my musician. It's of no great difference to me, if I give her up to you or to Ryoval, as long as I get that price."

Captain Thorne, working the *Ariel*'s monitors, flinched under Miles's glance.

"The price you refer to, I take it, is the secret of the Betan rejuvenation technique," said Miles.

"Quite."

"Ah . . . hum." Miles moistened his lips. "Baron, I cannot."

Fell turned his head. "Station commander, launch pursuit ships—"

"Wait!" Miles cried.

Fell raised his brows. "You reconsider? Good."

"It's not that I *will* not tell you," said Miles desperately, "it's just that the truth would be of no use to you. None whatsoever. Still, I agree you deserve some compensation. I have another piece of information I could trade you, more immediately valuable."

"Oh?" said Fell. His voice was neutral but his expression was black.

"You suspected your half-brother Ryoval in the murder of your clone, but could not chain any evidence to him, am I right?"

Fell looked fractionally more interested. "All my agents and Bharaputra's could not turn up a connection. We tried."

"I'm not surprised. Because it was Bharaputra's agents who did the deed." Well, it was possible, anyway.

Fell's eyes narrowed. "Killed their own product?" he said slowly.

"I believe Ryoval struck a deal with House Bharaputra to betray you," said Miles rapidly. "I believe it involved the trade of some unique biological samples in Ryoval's possession; I don't think cash alone would have been worth their risk. The deal was done on the highest levels, obviously. I don't know how they figured to divide the spoils of House Fell after your eventual death—maybe they didn't mean to divide it at all. They seem to have had some ultimate plan of combining their operations for some larger monopoly of biologicals on Jackson's Whole. A corporate merger of sorts." Miles paused to let this sink in. "May I suggest you may wish to reserve your forces and favors against enemies more, er, intimate and immediate than myself? Besides, you have all our credit chit but we have only half our cargo. Will you call it even?"

Fell glowered at him for a full minute, the face of a man thinking in three different directions at once. Miles knew the feeling. He then turned his head, and grated out of the corner of his mouth, "Hold pursuit ships."

Miles breathed again.

"I thank you for this information, Admiral," said Fell coldly, "but not very much. I shall not impede your swift exit. But if you or any of your ships appear in Jacksonian space again—"

"Oh, Baron," said Miles sincerely, "staying far, far away from here is fast becoming one of my dearest ambitions."

"You're wise," Fell growled, and moved to cut the link.

"Baron Fell," Miles added impulsively. Fell paused. "For your future information—is this link secured?"

"Yes."

"The true secret of the Betan rejuvenation technique —is that there is none. Don't be taken in again. I look the age I do, because it is the age I am. Make of it what you will."

Fell said absolutely nothing. After a moment a faint, wintry smile moved his lips. He shook his head and cut the com.

Just in case, Miles lingered on in sort of a glassy puddle in one corner of Nav and Com until the Comm Officer reported their final clearance from Jumppoint Station traffic control. But Miles calculated Houses Fell, Ryoval, and Bharaputra were going to be too busy with each other to concern themselves with him, at least for a while. His late transfer of information both true and false among the combatants —to each according to his measure—had the feel of throwing one bone to three starving, rabid dogs. He almost regretted not being able to stick around and see the results. Almost.

Hours after the Jump he woke in his cabin, fully dressed but with his boots set neatly by his bed, with no memory of how he'd got there. He rather fancied Murka must have escorted him. If he'd fallen asleep while walking alone he'd surely have left the boots on.

Miles first checked with the duty officer as to the *Ariel's* situation and status. It was refreshingly dull. They were crossing a blue star system between Jump points on the route to Escobar, unpeopled and empty of everything but a smattering of routine commercial traffic. Nothing pursued them from the direction of Jackson's Whole. Miles had a light meal, not sure if it was breakfast, lunch, or dinner, his bio-rhythm being thoroughly askew from shiptime after his downside adventures. He then sought out Thorne and Nicol. He found them in Engineering. A tech was just polishing out the last dent in Nicol's float chair.

Nicol, now wearing a white tunic and shorts trimmed with pink piping, lay sprawled on her belly on a bench watching the repairs. It gave Miles an odd sensation to see her out of her cup, it was like looking at a hermit crab out of its shell, or a seal on the shore. She looked strangely vulnerable in one-gee, yet in null gee she'd looked so right, so clearly at ease, he'd stopped noticing the oddness of the extra arms very quickly. Thorne helped the tech fit the float cup's blue shell over its reconditioned anti-grav mechanism, and turned to greet Miles as the tech proceeded to lock it in place.

Miles sat down-bench from Nicol. "From the looks of things," he told her, "you should be free of pursuit from Baron Fell. He and his half-brother are going to be fully occupied avenging themselves on each other for a while. Makes me glad I'm an only child."

"Hm," she said pensively.

"You should be safe," Thorne offered encouragingly.

"Oh—no, it's not that," Nicol said. "I was just thinking about my sisters. Time was I couldn't wait to get away from them. Now I can't wait to see them again."

"What are your plans now?" Miles asked.

"I'll stop at Escobar, first," she replied. "It's a good nexus crossing, from there I should be able to work my way back to Earth. From Earth I can get to Orient IV, and from there I'm sure I can get home."

"Is home your goal now?"

"There's a lot more galaxy to be seen out this way," Thorne pointed out. "I'm not sure if Dendarii rosters can be stretched to include a ship's musician, but—"

She was shaking her head. "Home," she said firmly. "I'm tired of fighting one-gee all the time. I'm tired of being alone. I'm starting to have nightmares about growing legs."

Thorne sighed faintly.

"We do have a little colony of downsiders living among us now," she added suggestively to Thorne. "They've fitted out their own asteroid with artificial gravity—quite like the real thing downside, only not as drafty."

Miles was faintly alarmed—to lose a ship commander of proven loyalty—

"Ah," said Thorne in a pensive tone to match Nicol's. "A long way from my home, your asteroid belt."

"Will you return to Beta Colony, then, someday?" she asked. "Or are the Dendarii Mercenaries your home and family?"

"Not quite that passionate, for me," said Thorne. "I mainly stick around due to an overwhelming curiosity to see what happens next." Thorne favored Miles with a peculiar smile.

Thorne helped load Nicol back into her blue cup. After a brief systems check she was hovering upright again, as mobile—more mobile—than her legged companions. She rocked and regarded Thorne brightly.

"It's only three more days to Escobar orbit," said Thorne to Nicol rather regretfully. "Still—seventy-two hours. 4,320 minutes. How much can you do in 4,320 minutes?"

Or how often, thought Miles dryly. *Especially if you don't sleep.* Sleep, per se, was not what Bel had in mind, if Miles recognized the signs. Good luck—to both of them.

"Meanwhile," Thorne maneuvered Nicol into the corridor, "let me show you around my ship. Illyrican-built—that's out your way a bit, I understand. It's quite a story, how the *Ariel* first fell into Dendarii hands—we were the Oseran Mercenaries, back then—"

Nicol made encouraging noises. Miles suppressed an envious grin, and turned the other way up the corridor, to search out Dr. Canaba and arrange the discharge of his last unpleasant duty.

Bemusedly, Miles set aside the hypospray he'd been turning over in his hands as the door to sickbay sighed open. He swivelled in the medtech's station chair and glanced up as Taura and Sergeant Anderson entered. "My *word*," he murmured.

Anderson sketched a salute. "Reporting as ordered, sir." Taura's hand twitched, uncertain whether to attempt to mimic this military greeting or not. Miles gazed up at Taura and his lips parted with involuntary delight. Taura's transformation was all he'd dreamed of and more.

He didn't know how Anderson had persuaded the
stores computer to so exceed its normal parameters,
but somehow she'd made it disgorge a complete
Dendarii undress kit in Taura's size: crisp grey-and-
white pocketed jacket, grey trousers, polished ankle-
topping boots. Taura's face and hair were clean enough
to outshine her boots. Her dark hair was now drawn
back in a thick, neat, and rather mysterious braid
coiling up the back of her head—Miles could not
make out where the ends went—and glinting with
unexpected mahogany highlights.

She looked, if not exactly well-fed, at least less
rawly starving, her eyes bright and interested, not
the haunted yellow flickers in bony caverns he'd first
seen. Even from this distance he could tell that
re-hydration and the chance to brush her teeth and
fangs had cured the ketone-laced breath that several
days in Ryoval's sub-basement on a diet of raw rats
and nothing had produced. The dirt-encrusted scale
was smoothed away from her huge hands, and—
inspired touch—her clawed nails had been, not
blunted, but neatened and sharpened, and then en-
amelled with an iridescent pearl-white polish that
complemented her grey-and-whites like a flash of
jewelry. The polish had to have been shared out of
some personal stock of the sergeant's.

"Outstanding, Anderson," said Miles in admiration.

Anderson smirked proudly. "That about what you
had in mind, sir?"

"Yes, it was." Taura's face reflected his delight
straight back at him. "What did you think of your
first wormhole jump?" he asked her.

Her long lips rippled, what happened when she
tried to purse them, Miles guessed. "I was afraid I
was getting sick, I was so dizzy all of a sudden, till
Sergeant Anderson explained what it was."

"No little hallucinations, or odd time-stretching effects?"

"No, but it wasn't—well, it was quick, anyway."

"Hm. It doesn't sound like you're one of the fortunates—or unfortunates—to be screened for Jump pilot aptitudes. From the talents you demonstrated on Ryoval's landing pad yesterday morning, Tactics should be loathe to lose you to Nav and Com." Miles paused. "Thank you, Laureen. What did my page interrupt?"

"Routine systems checks on the drop shuttles, putting them to bed. I was having Taura look over my shoulder while I worked."

"Right, carry on. I'll send Taura back to you when she's done here."

Anderson exited reluctantly, clearly curious. Miles waited till the doors swished closed to speak again. "Sit down, Taura. So your first twenty-four hours with the Dendarii have been satisfactory?"

She grinned, settling herself carefully in a station chair, which creaked. "Just fine."

"Ah." He hesitated. "You understand, when we reach Escobar, you do have the option to go your own way. You're not compelled to join us. I could see you got some kind of start, downside there."

"What?" Her eyes widened in dismay. "No! I mean . . . do I eat too much?"

"Not at all! You fight like four men, we can bloody well afford to feed you like three. But . . . I need to set a few things straight, before you make your trainee's oath." He cleared his throat. "I didn't come to Ryoval's to recruit you. A few weeks before Bharaputra sold you, do you remember Dr. Canaba injecting something into your leg? With a needle, not a hypospray."

"Oh, yes." She rubbed her calf half-consciously. "It made a knot."

"What, ah, did he tell you it was?"

"An immunization."

She'd been right, Miles reflected, when they'd first met. Humans did lie a lot. "Well, it wasn't an immunization. Canaba was using you as a live repository for some engineered biological material. Molecularly bound, dormant material," he added hastily as she twisted around and looked at her leg in disquiet. "It can't activate spontaneously, he assures me. My original mission was only to pick up Dr. Canaba. But he wouldn't leave without his gene complexes."

"He planned to take me with him?" she said in thrilled surprise. "So I should thank *him* for sending you to me!"

Miles wished he could see the look on Canaba's face if she did. "Yes and no. Specifically, no." He rushed roughly on before his nerve failed him. "You have nothing to thank him for, nor me either. He meant to take only your tissue sample, and sent me to get it."

"Would you rather have left me at—is that why Escobar—" she was still bewildered.

"It was your good luck," Miles plunged on, "that I'd lost my men and was disarmed when we finally met. Canaba lied to me, too. In his defense, he seems to have had some dim idea of saving you from a brutal life as Ryoval's slave. He sent me to kill you, Taura. He sent me to slay a monster, when he should have been begging me to rescue a princess in disguise. I'm not too pleased with Dr. Canaba. Nor with myself. I lied through my teeth to you down in Ryoval's basement, because I thought I had to, to survive and win."

Her face was confused, congealing, the light in her

eyes fading. "Then you didn't . . . really think I was human—"

"On the contrary. Your choice of test was an excellent one. It's much harder to lie with your body than with your mouth. When I, er, demonstrated my belief, it had to be real." Looking at her, he still felt a twinge of lurching, lunatic joy, somatic residual from that adventure-of-the-body. He supposed he always would feel something—male conditioning, no doubt. "Would you like me to demonstrate it again?" he asked half-hopefully, then bit his tongue. "No," he answered his own question. "If I am to be your commander—we have these non-fraternization rules. Mainly to protect those of lower rank from exploitation, though it can work both—ahem!" He was digressing dreadfully. He picked up the hypospray, fiddled with it nervously, and put it back down.

"Anyway, Dr. Canaba has asked me to lie to you again. He wanted me to sneak up on you with a general anesthetic, so he could biopsy back his sample. He's a coward, you may have noticed. He's outside now, shaking in his shoes for fear you'll find out what he intended for you. I think a local zap with a medical stunner would suffice. I'd sure want to be conscious and watching if he were working on *me*, anyway." He flicked the hypospray contemptuously with one finger.

She sat silent, her strange wolfish face—though Miles was getting used to it—unreadable. "You want me to let him . . . cut into my leg?" she said at last.

"Yes."

"Then what?"

"Then nothing. That will be the last of Dr. Canaba for you, and Jackson's Whole and all the rest of it. That, I promise. Though if you're doubtful of my promises, I can understand why."

"The last . . ." she breathed. Her face lowered, then rose, and her shoulders straightened. "Then let's get it over with." There was no smile to her long mouth now.

Canaba, as Miles expected, was not happy to be presented with a conscious subject. Miles truly didn't care how unhappy Canaba was about it, and after one look at his cold face, Canaba didn't argue. Canaba took his sample wordlessly, packaged it carefully in the biotainer, and fled with it back to the safety and privacy of his own cabin as soon as he decently could.

Miles sat with Taura in sickbay till the medical stun wore off enough for her to walk without stumbling. She sat without speaking for a long time. He watched her still features, wishing beyond measure he knew how to re-light those gold eyes.

"When I first saw you," she said softly, "it was like a miracle. Something magic. Everything I'd wished for, longed for. Food. Water. Heat. Revenge. Escape." She gazed down at her polished claws, "Friends . . ." and glanced up at him, ". . . touching."

"What else do you wish for, Taura?" Miles asked earnestly

Slowly she replied. "I wish I were normal."

Miles was silent too. "I can't give you what I don't possess myself," he said at length. The words seemed to lie in inadequate lumps between them. He roused himself to a better effort. "No. Don't wish that. I have a better idea. Wish to be yourself. To the hilt. Find out what you're best at, and develop it. Hopscotch your weaknesses. There isn't time for them. Look at Nicol—"

"So beautiful," sighed Taura.

"Or look at Captain Thorne, and tell me what

'normal' is, and why I should give a damn for it.
Look at me, if you will. Should I kill myself trying to
overcome men twice my weight and reach in unarmed combat, or should I shift the ground to where
their muscle is useless, 'cause it never gets close
enough to apply its strength? I haven't got *time* to
lose, and neither have you."

"Do you know how little time?" demanded Taura
suddenly.

"Ah . . ." said Miles cautiously, "do you?"

"I am the last survivor of my creche mates. How
could I not know?" Her chin lifted defiantly.

"Then don't wish to be normal," said Miles passionately, rising to pace. "You'll only waste your
precious time in futile frustration. Wish to be great!
That at least you have a fighting chance for. Great at
whatever you are. A great trooper, a great sergeant.
A great quartermaster, for God's sake, if that's what
comes with ease. A great musician like Nicol—only
think how horrible if she were wasting her talents
trying to be merely normal." Miles paused self-
consciously in his pep talk, thinking, *Easier to preach
than practice. . . .*

Taura studied her polished claws, and sighed. "I
suppose it's useless for me to wish to be beautiful,
like Sergeant Anderson."

"It is useless for you to try to be beautiful *like*
anyone but yourself," said Miles. "Be beautiful like
Taura, ah, that you can do. Superbly well." He found
himself gripping her hands, and ran one finger across
an iridescent claw, "Though Laureen seems to have
grasped the principle, you might be guided by her
taste."

"Admiral," said Taura slowly, not releasing his
hands, "are you actually my commander yet? Ser-

geant Anderson said something about orientation, and induction tests, and an oath. . . ."

"Yes, all that will come when we make fleet rendezvous. Till then, technically, you're our guest."

A certain sparkle was beginning to return to her gold eyes. "Then—till then—it wouldn't break any Dendarii rules, would it, if you showed me again how human I am? One more time?"

It must be, Miles thought, akin to the same drive that used to propel men to climb sheer rock faces without an antigrav belt, or jump out of ancient aircraft with nothing to stop them going splat but a wad of silk cloth. He felt the fascination rising in him, the death-defying laugh. "Slowly?" he said in a strangled voice. "Do it right this time? Have a little conversation, drink a little wine, play a little music? Without Ryoval's guard squad lurking overhead, or ice cold rock under my . . ."

Her eyes were huge and gold and molten. "You did say you liked to practice what you were great at."

Miles had never realized how susceptible he was to flattery from tall women. A weakness he must guard against. Sometime.

They retired to his cabin and practiced assiduously till halfway to Escobar.

THREE

"Whatever happened to the wolf girl?" inquired Illyan after a long, fascinated silence.

"Ah. She's doing well, I'm glad to say. She made sergeant not long ago. My Dendarii fleet surgeon has her on some meds to slow her metabolism down a bit. Somewhat experimental."

"Will they increase her life-span, then?"

Miles shrugged. "I wish we knew. Maybe. We're hoping."

"Well." Illyan shifted. "That leaves Dagoola, about which, I might remind you, the only report I had from you before the other operatives took over was that, er, excessively succinct one you filed from Mahata Solaris."

"That was only meant to be preliminary. I thought I'd be reporting home sooner than this."

"That's not a problem—or at any rate, not a problem for Count Vorvolk. Dagoola, Miles. Cough it up, and then you can get some sleep."

Miles frowned wearily. "It started out so simply. Almost as simple as the Jackson's Whole job. Then things went wrong. Then things went very wrong. . . ."

"So begin at the beginning."

"The beginning. God. Well . . ."

"The Borders of Infinity"

How could I have died and gone to hell without noticing the transition?

The opalescent force dome capped a surreal and alien landscape, frozen for a moment by Miles's disorientation and dismay. The dome defined a perfect circle, half a kilometer in diameter. Miles stood just inside its edge, where the glowing concave surface dove into the hard-packed dirt and disappeared. His imagination followed the arc buried beneath his feet to the far side, where it erupted again to complete the sphere. It was like being trapped inside an eggshell. An unbreakable eggshell.

Within was a scene from an ancient limbo. Dispirited men and women sat, or stood, or mostly lay down, singly or in scattered irregular groups, across the breadth of the arena. Miles's eye searched anxiously for some remnant of order or military grouping, but the inhabitants seemed splashed randomly as a liquid across the ground.

Perhaps he had been killed just now, just entering this prison camp. Perhaps his captors had betrayed

him to his death, like those ancient Earth soldiers
who had lured their victims sheeplike into poisoned
showers, diverting and soothing their suspicions with
stone soap, until their final enlightenment burst upon
them in a choking cloud. Perhaps the annihilation of
his body had been so swift, his neurons had not had
time to carry the information to his brain. Why else
did so many antique myths agree that hell was a
circular place?

Dagoola IV Top Security Prison Camp #3. This
was it? This naked . . . dinner plate? Miles had
vaguely visioned barracks, marching guards, daily
head counts, secret tunnels, escape committees.

It was the dome that made it all so simple, Miles
realized. What need for barracks to shelter prisoners
from the elements? The dome did it. What need for
guards? The dome was generated from without. Nothing inside could breach it. No need for guards, or
head counts. Tunnels were a futility, escape committees an absurdity. The dome did it all.

The only structures were what appeared to be big
grey plastic mushrooms evenly placed about every
hundred meters around the perimeter of the dome.
What little activity there was seemed clustered around
them. Latrines, Miles recognized.

Miles and his three fellow prisoners had entered
through a temporary portal, which had closed behind
them before the brief bulge of force dome containing
their entry vanished in front of them. The nearest
inhabitant of the dome, a man, lay a few meters away
upon a sleeping mat identical to the one Miles now
clutched. He turned his head slightly to stare at the
little party of newcomers, smiled sourly, and rolled
over on his side with his back to them. Nobody else
nearby even bothered to look up.

"Holy shit," muttered one of Miles's companions.

He and his two buddies drew together unconsciously.
The three had been from the same unit once, they'd
said. Miles had met them bare minutes ago, in their
final stages of processing, where they had all been
issued their total supply of worldly goods for life in
Dagoola #3.

A single pair of loose grey trousers. A matching
short-sleeved grey tunic. A rectangular sleeping mat,
rolled up. A plastic cup. That was all. That, and the
new numbers encoded upon their skins. It bothered
Miles intensely that their captors had chosen to locate the numbers in the middle of their backs, where
they couldn't see them. He resisted a futile urge to
twist and crane his neck anyway, though his hand
snaked up under his shirt to scratch a purely psycho-
somatic itch. You couldn't feel the encode either.

Some motion appeared in the tableau. A group of
four or five men approaching. The welcoming committee at last? Miles was desperate for information.
Where among all these countless grey men and
women—no, not countless, Miles told himself firmly.
They were all accounted for here.

The battered remnants of the 3rd and 4th Armored All-Terrain Rangers. The ingenious and tenacious civilian defenders of Garson Transfer Station.
Winoweh's 2nd Battalion had been captured almost
intact. And the 14th Commandos, survivors of the
high-tech fortress at Fallow Core. Particularly the
survivors of Fallow Core. Ten thousand, two hundred fourteen exactly. The planet Marilac's finest.
Ten thousand, two hundred fifteen, counting himself. Ought he to count himself?

The welcoming committee drew up in a ragged
bunch a few meters away. They looked tough and tall
and muscular and not noticeably friendly. Dull, sul-

len eyes, full of a deadly boredom that even their present calculation did not lighten.

The two groups, the five and the three, sized each other up. The three turned, and started walking stiffly and prudently away. Miles realized belatedly that he, not a part of either group, was thus left alone.

Alone and immensely conspicuous. Self-consciousness, body-consciousness, normally held at bay by the simple fact that he didn't have time to waste on it, returned to him with a rush. Too short, too odd-looking—his legs were even in length now, after the last operation, but surely not long enough to outrun these five. And where did one run to, in this place? He crossed off flight as an option.

Fight? Get serious.

This isn't going to work, he realized sadly, even as he started walking toward them. But it was more dignified than being chased down with the same result.

He tried to make his smile austere rather than foolish. No telling whether he succeeded. "Hi, there. Can you tell me where to find Colonel Guy Tremont's 14th Commando Division?"

One of the five snorted sardonically. Two moved behind Miles.

Well, a snort was almost speech. Expression, anyway. A start, a toehold. Miles focused on that one. "What's your name and rank and company, soldier?"

"No ranks in here, mutant. No companies. No soldiers. No nothing."

Miles glanced around. Surrounded, of course. Naturally. "You got some friends, anyway."

The talker almost smiled. "You don't."

Miles wondered if perhaps he had been premature in crossing off flight as an option. "I wouldn't count on that if I were—*unh!*" The kick to his kidneys, from behind, cut him off—he damn near bit his tongue—he fell, dropping bedroll and cup and landing in a tangle. A barefoot kick, no combat boots this time, thank God—by the rules of Newtonian physics, his attackers' foot ought to hurt just as much as his back. Fine. Jolly. Maybe they'd bruise their knuckles, punching him out. . . .

One of the gang gathered up Miles's late wealth, cup and bedroll. "Want his clothes? They're too little for me."

"Naw."

"Yeah," said the talker. "Take 'em anyway. Maybe bribe one of the women."

The tunic was jerked off over Miles's head, the pants over his feet. Miles was too busy protecting his head from random kicks to fight much for his clothes, trying obliquely to take as many hits as possible on his belly or ribcage, not arms or legs or jaw. A cracked rib was surely the most injury he could afford right now, here, at the beginning. A broken jaw would be the worst.

His assailants desisted only a little before they discovered by experimentation the secret weakness of his bones.

"*That's* how it is in here, mutant," said the talker, slightly winded.

"I was born naked," Miles panted from the dirt. "Didn't stop me."

"Cocky little shit," said the talker.

"Slow learner," remarked another.

The second beating was worse than the first. Two cracked ribs at least—his jaw barely escaped being smashed, at the cost of something painfully wrong in his left wrist, flung up as a shield. This time Miles resisted the impulse to offer any verbal parting shots.

He lay in the dirt and wished he could pass out.

He lay a long time, cradled in pain. He was not
sure how long. The illumination from the force dome
was even and shadowless, unchanging. Timeless, like
eternity. Hell was eternal, was it not? This place had
too damn many congruencies with hell, that was
certain.

And here came another demon. . . . Miles blinked
the approaching figure into focus. A man, as bruised
and naked as Miles himself, gaunt-ribbed, starveling,
knelt in the dirt a few meters away. His face was
bony, aged by stress—he might have been forty, or
fifty—or twenty-five.

His eyes were unnaturally prominent, due to the
shrinking of his flesh. Their whites seemed to gleam
feverishly against the dirt darkening his skin. Dirt,
not beard stubble—every prisoner in here, male and
female, had their hair cut short and the hair follicles
stunned to prevent re-growth. Perpetually clean-
shaved and crew-cut. Miles had undergone the same
process bare hours ago. But whoever had processed
this fellow must have been in a hurry. The hair
stunner had missed a line on his cheek and a few
dozen hairs grew there like a stripe on a badly-mown
lawn. Even curled as they were, Miles could see
they were several centimeters long, draggling down
past the man's jaw. If only he knew how fast hair
grew, he could calculate how long this fellow had
been here. *Too long, whatever the numbers*, Miles
thought with an inward sigh.

The man had the broken-off bottom half of a plastic cup, which he pushed cautiously toward Miles.
His breath whistled raggedly past his yellowish teeth,
from exertion or excitement or disease—probably
not disease, they were all well immunized here.

Escape, even through death, was not that easy. Miles rolled over and propped himself stiffly on his elbow, regarding his visitor through the thinning haze of his aches and pains.

The man scrabbled back slightly, smiled nervously. He nodded toward the cup. "Water. Better drink. The cup's cracked, and it all leaks out if you wait too long."

"Thanks," croaked Miles. A week ago, or in a previous lifetime, depending on how you counted time, Miles had dawdled over a selection of wines, dissatisfied with this or that nuance of flavor. His lips cracked as he grinned in memory. He drank. It was perfectly ordinary water, lukewarm, faintly redolent of chlorine and sulfur. *A refined body, but the bouquet is a bit presumptuous.* . . .

The man squatted in studied politeness until Miles finished drinking, then leaned forward on his knuckles in restrained urgency. "Are you the One?"

Miles blinked. "Am I the what?"

"The One. The *other* one, I should say. The scripture says there has to be two."

"Uh," Miles hesitated cautiously, "what exactly does the scripture say?"

The man's right hand wrapped over his knobby left wrist, around which was tied a rag screwed into a sort of rope. He closed his eyes; his lips moved a moment, and then he recited aloud, ". . . but the pilgrims went up that hill with ease, because they had these two men to lead them by the arms; also they had left their garments behind them, for though they went in with them, they came out without them." His eyes popped back open to stare hopefully at Miles.

So, now we begin to see why this guy seems to be

all by himself. . . . "Are you, perchance, the other One?" Miles shot at a venture.

The man nodded shyly.

"I see. Um . . ." How was it that he always attracted the nut cases? He licked the last drops of water from his lips. The fellow might have some screws loose, but he was certainly an improvement over the last lot, always presuming he didn't have another personality or two of the homicidal loonie variety tucked away in his head. No, in that case he'd be introducing himself as the Chosen Two, and not be looking for outside assistance. "Um . . . what's your name?"

"Suegar."

"Suegar. Right, all right. My name is Miles, by the way."

"Huh." Suegar grimaced in a sort of pleased irony. "Your name means 'soldier,' did you know?"

"Uh, yeah, so I've been told."

"But you're not a soldier . . . ?"

No subtle expensive trick of clothing line or uniform style here to hide from himself, if no one else, the peculiarities of his body. Miles flushed. "They were taking anything, toward the end. They made me a recruiting clerk. I never did get to fire my gun. Listen, Suegar—how did you come to know you were the One, or at any rate one of the Ones? Is it something you've always known?"

"It came on me gradually," confessed Suegar, shifting to sit cross-legged. "I'm the only one in here with the words, y'see." He caressed his rag rope again. "I've hunted all up and down the camp, but they only mock me. It was a kind of process of elimination, y'see, when they all gave up but me."

"Ah." Miles too sat up, only gasping a little in pain. Those ribs were going to be murder for the next few days. He nodded toward the rope bracelet. "Is that where you keep your scripture? Can I see it?" And how the hell had Suegar ever gotten a plastic flimsy, or loose piece of paper or whatever, in here?

Suegar clutched his arms protectively to his chest and shook his head. "They've been trying to take them from me for months, y'see. I can't be too careful. Until you prove you're the One. The devil can quote scripture, y'know."

Yes, that was rather what I had in mind. . . . Who knew what opportunities Suegar's "scripture" might contain? Well, maybe later. For now, keep dancing. "Are there any other signs?" asked Miles. "You see, I don't know that I'm your One, but on the other hand I don't know I'm not, either. I just got here, after all."

Suegar shook his head again. "It's only five or six sentences, y'see. You have to interpolate a lot."

I'll bet. Miles did not voice the comment aloud. "However did you come by it? Or get it in here?"

"It was at Port Lisma, y'see, just before we were captured," said Suegar. "House-to-house fighting. One of my boot heels had come a bit loose, and it clicked when I walked. Funny, with all that barrage coming down around our ears, how a little thing like that can get under your skin. There was this bookcase with a glass front, real antique books made of paper—I smashed it open with my gun butt and tore out part of a page from one, and folded it up to stick in my boot heel, to make a sort of shim, y'see, and stop the clicking. Didn't look at the book. Didn't even know it was scripture till later. At least, I think it's scripture. It sounds like scripture, anyway. It must be scripture."

Suegar twisted his beard hairs nervously around

his finger. "When we were waiting to be processed, I'd pulled it out of my boot, just idle-like, y'know. I had it in my hand—the processing guard saw it, but he just didn't take it away from me. Probably thought it was just a harmless piece of paper. Didn't know it was scripture. I still had it in my hand when we were dumped in here. D'you know, it's the only piece of writing in this whole camp?" he added rather proudly. "It must be scripture."

"Well . . . you take good care of it, then," advised Miles kindly. "If you've preserved it this long, it was obviously meant to be your job."

"Yeah . . ." Suegar blinked. Tears? "I'm the only one in here with a job, aren't I? So I must be one of the Ones."

"Sounds good to me," said Miles agreeably. "Say, ah," he glanced around the vast featureless dome, "how do you find your way around in here, anyway?" The place was decidedly undersupplied with landmarks. It reminded Miles of nothing so much as a penguin rookery. Yet penguins seemed able to find their rocky nests. He was going to have to start thinking like a penguin—or get a penguin to direct him. He studied his guide bird, who had gone absent and was doodling in the dirt. Circles, naturally.

"Where's the mess hall?" Miles asked more loudly. "Where did you get that water?"

"Water taps are on the outside of the latrines," said Suegar, "but they only work part of the time. No mess hall. We just get rat bars. Sometimes."

"Sometimes?" said Miles angrily. He could count Suegar's ribs. "Dammit, the Cetagandans are claiming loudly to be treating their POW's by Interstellar Judiciary Commission rules. So many square meters of space per person, 3,000 calories a day, at least fifty grams of protein, two liters of drinking water—you should be getting at least two IJC standard ration bars a day. Are they starving you?"

"After a while," Suegar sighed, "you don't really care if you get yours or not." The animation that his interest in Miles as a new and hopeful object in his world had lent Suegar seemed to be falling away. His breathing had slowed, his posture slumped. He seemed about to lie down in the dirt. Miles wondered if Suegar's sleeping mat had suffered the same fate as his own. Quite some time ago, probably.

"Look, Suegar—I think I may have a relative in this camp somewhere. A cousin of my mother's. D'you think you could help me find him?"

"It might be good for you, to have a relative," Suegar agreed. "It's not good to be by yourself, here."

"Yeah, I found that out. But how can you find anyone? It doesn't look too organized."

"Oh, there's—there's groups and groups. Everyone pretty much stays in the same place after a while."

"He was in the 14th Commandos. Where are they?"

"None of the *old* groups are left, much."

"He was Colonel Tremont. Colonel Guy Tremont."

"Oh, an officer." Suegar's forehead wrinkled in worry. "That makes it harder. You weren't an officer, were you? Better not let on, if you were—"

"I was a clerk," repeated Miles.

"—because there's groups here who don't like officers. A clerk. You're probably OK, then."

"Were you an officer, Suegar?" asked Miles curiously.

Suegar frowned at him, twisted his beard hairs. "Marilac Army's gone. If there's no army, it can't have officers, can it?"

Miles wondered briefly if he might get farther faster by just walking away from Suegar and trying to strike up a conversation with the next random prisoner he came across. Groups and groups. And, presumably, groups, like the five burly surly brothers. He decided to stick with Suegar for a while longer. For one thing, he wouldn't feel quite so naked if he wasn't naked by himself.

"Can you take me to anybody who used to be in the 14th?" Miles urged Suegar anew. "Anybody, who might know Tremont by sight."

"You don't know him?"

"We'd never met in person. I've seen vids of him. But I'm afraid his appearance may be . . . changed, by now."

Suegar touched his own face pensively. "Yeah, probably."

Miles clambered painfully to his feet. The temperature in the dome was just a little cool, without clothes. A voiceless draft raised the hairs on his arms. If he could just get one garment back, would he prefer his pants, to cover his genitals, or his shirt, to disguise his crooked back? Screw it. No time. He held out a hand to help Suegar up. "Come on."

Suegar glanced up at him. "You can always tell a newcomer. You're still in a hurry. In here, you slow down. Your brain slows down. . . ."

"Your scripture got anything to say on that?" inquired Miles impatiently.

" '. . . they therefore went up here with much agility and speed, through the foundation of the city . . .' " Twin verticals appeared between Suegar's eyebrows, as he frowned speculatively at Miles.

Thank you, thought Miles. *I'll take it*. He pulled Suegar up. "Come on, then."

Neither agility nor speed, but at least progress. Suegar led him on a shambling walk across a quarter of the camp, through some groups, in wide arcs around others. Miles saw the surly brothers again at a distance, sitting on their collection of mats. Miles upped his estimation of the size of the tribe from five to about fifteen. Some men sat in twos or threes or sixes, a few sat alone, as far as possible from any others, which still wasn't very far.

The largest group by far consisted entirely of women. Miles studied them with electric interest as soon as his eye picked up the size of their unmarked boundary. There were several hundred of them at least. None were matless, although some shared. Their perimeter was actually patrolled, by groups of half a dozen or so strolling slowly about. They apparently defended two latrines for their exclusive use.

"Tell me about the girls, Suegar," Miles urged his companion, with a nod toward their group.

"Forget the girls." Suegar's grin actually had a sardonic edge. "They do not put out."

"What, not at all? None of them? I mean, here we all are, with nothing to do but entertain each other. I'd think at least some of them would be interested." Miles's reason raced ahead of Suegar's answer, mired in unpleasantness. How unpleasant did it get in here?

For answer, Suegar pointed upward to the dome. "You know we're all monitored in here. They can see everything, pick up every word if they want. That is, if there's still anybody out there. They may have all gone away, and just forgotten to turn the dome off. I have dreams about that, sometimes. I dream that I'm here, in this dome, forever. Then I wake up, and I'm here, in this dome. . . . Sometimes I'm not sure if I'm awake or asleep. Except that the food is still coming, and once in while—not so often, anymore—somebody new, like you. The food could be automated, though, I suppose. You could be a dream. . . ."

"They're still out there," said Miles grimly.

Suegar sighed. "You know, in a way, I'm almost glad."

Monitored, yes. Miles knew all about the monitoring. He put down an urge to wave and call *Hi, Mom!* Monitoring must be a stultifying job for the goons out there. He wished they might be bored to death. "But what's that got to do with the girls, Suegar?"

"Well, at first everybody was pretty inhibited by that—" he pointed skywards again. "Then after a while we discovered that they didn't interfere with anything we did. At all. There were some rapes. . . . Since then things have been—deteriorating."

"Hm. Then I suppose the idea of starting a riot, and breaching the dome when they bring troops inside to restore order, is a no-go?"

"That was tried once, a long time ago. Don't know how long." Suegar twisted his hairs. "They don't have to come inside to stop a riot. They can reduce the dome's diameter—they reduced it to about a hundred meters, that time. Nothing to stop them reducing it down to one meter, with all of us still inside, if they choose. It stopped the riot, anyway. Or they can reduce the gas permeability of the dome to zilch and just let us breathe ourselves into a coma. That's happened twice."

"I see," said Miles. It made his neck crawl.

A bare hundred or so meters away, the side of the dome began to bulge inward like an aneurysm. Miles touched Suegar's arm. "What's happening there? More new prisoners being delivered?"

Suegar glanced around. "Uh oh. We're not in a real good position, here." He hovered a moment, as if uncertain whether to go forward or back.

A wave of movement rippled through the camp from the bulge outward, of people getting to their feet. Faces turned magnetically toward the side of the dome. Little knots of men came together; a few sprinters began running. Some people didn't get up at all. Miles glanced back towards the women's group. About half of them were forming rapidly into a sort of phalanx.

"We're so close—what the hell, maybe we've got a chance," said Suegar. "Come on!" He started toward the bulge at his most rapid pace, a jog. Miles perforce jogged too, trying to jar his ribs as little as possible. But he was quickly winded, and his rapid breathing added an excruciating torque to his torso.

"What are we doing?" Miles started to pant to Suegar, before the dome's extruding bulge dissolved with a fading twinkle, and he saw what they were doing, saw it all.

Before the force dome's shimmering barrier now sat a dark brown pile, roughly a meter high, two meters deep, three meters wide. IJC standard ration bars, Miles recognized. Rat bars, apocryphally named after their supposed principal ingredient. Fifteen hundred calories each. Twenty-five grams of protein, fifty percent of the human MDR for vitamins A, B, C, and the rest of the alphabet—tasted like a shingle sprinkled with sugar and would sustain life and health forever or for as long as you could stand to keep eating them.

Shall we have a contest, children, to guess how many rat bars are in that pile? Miles thought. *No contest. I don't even have to measure the height and divide by three centimeters. It has to be 10,215 exactly. How ingenious.*

The Cetagandan Psy Ops corps must contain some remarkable minds. If they ever fell into his hands, Miles wondered, should he recruit them—or exterminate them? This brief fantasy was overwhelmed by the need to keep to his feet in the present reality, as

10,000 or so people, minus the wholly despairing and those too weak to move, all tried to descend on the same six square meters of the camp at once.

The first sprinters reached the pile, grabbed up armloads of rat bars, and started to sprint off. Some made it to the protection of friends, divided their spoils, and started to move away from the center of the growing human maelstrom. Others failed to dodge clots of operators like the burly surly brothers, and were violently relieved of their prizes. The second wave of sprinters, who didn't get away in time, were pinned up against the side of the dome by the incoming bodies.

Miles and Suegar, unfortunately, were in this second category. Miles's view was reduced to a sweating, heaving, stinking, swearing mass of elbows and chests and backs.

"Eat, eat!" Suegar urged around stuffed cheeks as he and Miles were separated by the pack. But the bar Miles had grabbed was twisted out of his hands before he had gathered his wits enough to follow Suegar's advice. Anyway, his hunger was nothing to his terror of being crushed, or worse, falling underfoot. His own feet pummeled over something soft, but he was unable to push back with enough strength to give the person—man, woman, who knew?—a chance to get up again.

In time the press lessened, and Miles found the edge of the crowd and broke free again. He staggered a little way off and fell to the dirt to sit, shaken and shaking, pale and cold. His breath rasped unevenly in his throat. It took him a long time to get hold of himself again.

Sheer chance, that this had hit his rawest nerve, his darkest fears, threatened his most dangerous weakness. *I could die here*, he realized, *without ever seeing the enemy's face.* But there seemed to be no new bones broken, except possibly in his left foot. He was not too sure about his left foot. The elephant who had trod on it was surely getting more than his fair share of rat bars.

All right, Miles thought at last. *That's enough time spent on R&R. On your feet, soldier.* It was time to go find Colonel Tremont.

Guy Tremont. The real hero of the siege of Fallow Core. The defiant one, the one who'd held, and held, and held, after General Xian fled, after Baneri was killed.

Xian had sworn to return, but then Xian had run into that meat grinder at Vassily Station. HQ had promised re-supply, but then HQ and its vital shuttleport had been taken by the Cetagandans.

But by this time Tremont and his troops had lost communication. So they held, waiting, and hoping. Eventually resources were reduced to hope and rocks. Rocks were versatile, they could either be boiled for soup or thrown at the enemy. At last Fallow Core was taken. Not surrendered. Taken.

Guy Tremont. Miles wanted very much to meet Guy Tremont.

On his feet and looking around, Miles spotted a distant shambling scarecrow being pelted off from a group with clods of dirt. Suegar paused out of range of their missiles, still pointing to the rag on his wrist and talking. The three or four men he was haranguing turned their backs to him by way of a broad hint.

Miles sighed and started trudging toward him. "Hey, Suegar!" he called and waved when he got closer.

"Oh, there you are." Suegar turned and brightened, and joined him. "I lost you." Suegar rubbed dirt out of his eyebrows. "Nobody wants to listen, y'know?"

"Yeah, well, most of them have heard you at least once by now, right?"

"Pro'bly twenty times. I keep thinking I might have missed one, y'see. Maybe the very One, the other One."

"Well, I'd be glad to listen to you, but I've really got to find Colonel Tremont first. You said you knew somebody . . . ?"

"Oh, right. This way." Suegar led off again.

"Thanks. Say, is every chow call like that last one?"

"Pretty much."

"What's to keep some—group—from just taking over that arc of the dome?"

"It's never issued at the same place twice. They move it all around the perimeter. There was a lot of strategy debated at one time, as to whether it was better to be at the center, so's you're never more than half a diameter away, or near the edge, so's to be up front at least part of the time. Some guys had even worked out the mathematics of it, probabilities and all that."

"Which do you favor?"

"Oh, I don't have a spot, I move around and take my chances." His right hand touched his rag. "It's not the most important thing, anyway. Still, it was good to eat—today. Whatever day this is."

"Today is November 2, '97, Earth Common Era."

"Oh? Is that all?" Suegar pulled his beard strands out straight and rolled his eyes, attempting to look across his face at them. "Thought I'd been here longer than that. Why, it hasn't even been three years. Huh." He added apologetically, "In here it's always today."

"Mm," said Miles. "So the rat bars are always delivered in a pile like that, eh?"

"Yeah."

"Damned ingenious."

"Yeah," Suegar sighed. Rage, barely breathed, was camouflaged in that sigh, in the twitch of Suegar's hands. *So, my madman is not so simple. . . .*

"Here we are," Suegar added. They paused before a group defined by half a dozen sleeping mats in a rough circle. One man looked up and glowered.

"Go away, Suegar. I ain't in the mood for a sermon."

"That the colonel?" whispered Miles.

"Naw, his name's Oliver. I knew him—a long time ago. He was at Fallow Core, though," Suegar whispered back. "He can take you to him."

Suegar bundled Miles forward. "This is Miles. He's new. Wants to talk to you." Suegar himself backed away. Helpfully, Miles realized. Suegar was aware of his unpopularity, it seemed.

Miles studied the next link in his chain. Oliver had managed to retain his grey pajamas, sleeping mat, and cup intact, which reminded Miles again of his own nakedness. On the other hand, Oliver did not seem to be in possession of any ill-gotten duplicates. Oliver might be as burly as the surly brothers, but was not otherwise related. That was good. Not that Miles in his present state need have any more worries about thievery.

Oliver stared at Miles without favor, then seemed to relent. "What d'you want?" he growled.

Miles opened his hands. "I'm looking for Colonel Guy Tremont."

"Ain't no colonels in here, boy."

"He was a cousin of my mother's. Nobody in the family—nobody in the outside world—has heard anything from or about him since Fallow Core fell.

I—I'm not from any of the other units or pieces of units that are in here. Colonel Tremont is the only person I know anything about at all." Miles clasped his hands together and tried to look waif-like. Real doubt shook him, drew down his brows. "Is he still alive, even?"

Oliver frowned. "Relative, eh?" He scratched the side of his nose with a thick finger. "I suppose you got a right. But it won't do you any good, boy, if that's what you're thinking."

"I . . ." Miles shook his head. "At this point, I just want to *know*."

"Come on, then." Oliver levered himself to his feet with a grunt and lumbered off without looking over his shoulder.

Miles limped in his wake. "Are you taking me to him?"

Oliver made no answer until they'd finished their journey, only a few dozen meters, among and between sleeping mats. One man swore, one spat; most ignored them.

One mat lay at the edge of a group, almost far enough away to look alone. A figure lay curled up on his side with his back to them. Oliver stood silent, big fists on hips, and regarded it.

"Is that the colonel?" Miles whispered urgently.

"No, boy." Oliver sucked on his lower lip. "Only his remains."

Miles, alarmed, knelt down. Oliver was speaking poetically, Miles realized with relief. The man breathed. "Colonel Tremont? Sir?"

Miles's heart sank again, as he saw that breathing was about all that Tremont did. He lay inert, his eyes open but fixed on nothing. They did not even flick toward Miles and dismiss him with contempt. He was thin, thinner than Suegar even. Miles traced the angle of his jaw, the shape of his ear, from the holovids he'd studied. The remains of a face, like the ruined fortress of Fallow Core. It took nearly an archeologist's insight to recognize the connections between past and present.

He was dressed, his cup sat upright by his head, but the dirt around his mat was churned to acrid, stinking mud. From urine, Miles realized. Tremont's elbows were marked with lesions, the beginning of decubiti, bedsores. A damp patch on the grey fabric of his trousers over his bony hips hinted at more advanced and horrible sores beneath.

Yet somebody must be tending him, Miles thought, *or he wouldn't be looking even this good.*

Oliver knelt beside Miles, bare toes squishing in the mud, and pulled a hunk of rat bar from beneath the elastic waistband of his trousers. He crumbled a bit between his thick fingers and pushed it between Tremont's lips. "Eat," he whispered. The lips almost moved; the crumbs dribbled to the mat. Oliver tried again, seemed to become conscious of Miles's eyes upon him, and stuffed the rest of the rat bar back into his pants with an unintelligible grumble.

"Was—was he injured when Fallow Core was overrun?" asked Miles. "Head injury?"

Oliver shook his head. "Fallow Core wasn't stormed, boy."

"But it fell on October 6th, it was reported, and—"

"It fell on October 5th. Fallow Core was betrayed." Oliver turned and walked away before his stiffened face could betray any emotion.

Miles knelt in the mud and let his breath trickle out slowly.

So. And so.

Was this the end of his quest, then?

*   *   *

He wanted to pace and think, but walking still hurt too much. He hobbled a little way off, trying not to accidentally infringe upon the territory of any sizeable group, and sat, then lay in the dirt with his hands behind his head, staring up at the pearly glow of the dome sealed like a lid over them all.

He considered his options, one, two, three. He considered them carefully. It didn't take long.

I thought you didn't believe in good guys and bad guys? He had cauterized his emotions, he'd thought, coming in here, for his own protection, but he could feel his carefully cultivated impartiality slipping. He was beginning to hate that dome in a really intimate, personal way. Aesthetically elegant, form united with function as perfectly as an eggshell, a marvel of physics—perverted into an instrument of torture.

Subtle torture . . . Miles reviewed the Interstellar Judiciary Commission's rules for the treatment of POW's, to which Cetaganda was a signatory. So many square meters of space per person, yes, they were certainly supplied with that. No prisoner to be solitarily confined for a period exceeding twenty-four hours—right, no solitude in here except by withdrawal into madness. No dark periods longer than twelve hours, that was easy, no dark periods at all, the perpetual glare of noon instead. No beatings—indeed, the guards could say with truth that they never laid a hand on their prisoners. They just watched, while the prisoners beat each other up instead. Rapes, even more strictly forbidden, doubtless handled the same way.

Miles had seen what they could do with their issue of two IJC standard ration bars per person per day. The rat bar riot was a particularly neat touch, he thought. No one could fail to participate (he rubbed his growling stomach). The enemy might have seeded the initial breakdown by sending in a short pile. But maybe not—the first person who snatched two instead of one left another foodless. Maybe next time that one took three, to make up for it, and so it quickly snowballed. Breaking down any hope of order, pitting group against group, person against person in a scrambling dogfight, a twice-a-day reminder of their powerlessness and degradation. None could afford for long to hold themselves aloof unless they wished to embrace slow starvation.

No forced labor—hah, check. That would require the imposition of order. Access to medical personnel—right, the various units' own medics must be mixed in out there somewhere. He re-ran the wording of that paragraph through his memory again—by God, it *did* say "personnel," didn't it? No medicine, just medical personnel. Empty-handed, naked doctors and medtechs. His lips drew back in a mirthless grin. Accurate lists of prisoners taken had been duly dispatched, as required. But no other communication . . .

Communication. This lack of word from the outside world might drive even him crazy shortly. It was as bad as prayer, talking to a God who never talked back. No wonder they all seemed touched with a sort of solipsistic schizophrenia here. Their doubts infected him. *Was* anybody still out there? Could his voice be heard and understood?

Ah, blind faith. The leap of faith. His right hand clenched, as if crushing an eggshell. "This," he enunciated clearly, "calls for a major change of plans."

He drove himself to his feet to go find Suegar again.

Miles found him not far off, hunkered in the dirt doodling. Suegar looked up with a brief smile. "Did Oliver take you to—to your cousin?"

"Yes, but I came too late. He's dying."

"Yeah . . . I was afraid that might be the case. Sorry."

"Me too." Miles was momentarily distracted from his purpose by a practical curiosity. "Suegar, what do they do with dead bodies here?"

"There's a rubbish pile of sorts, over against one side of the dome. The dome sort of extrudes and laps it up every once in a while, same way as food and new prisoners are introduced. Usually by the time a body swells and starts to stink, somebody'll drag it over there. I take 'em sometimes."

"No chance of anybody sneaking out in the rubbish pile, I suppose?"

"They microwave-incinerate it all before the portal's opened."

"Ah." Miles took a deep breath, and launched himself. "Suegar, it's come to me. I *am* the other One."

Suegar nodded serenely, unsurprised. "I'd had it figured."

Miles paused, nonplussed. Was that all the response . . . ? He had expected something more energetic, either pro or con. "It came to me in a vision," he declared dramatically, following his script anyway.

"Oh, yeah?" Suegar's attention sharpened gratifyingly. "I've never gotten a vision," he added with envy. "Had to figure it all out, y'know, from context. What's it like? A trance?"

Shit, and here I thought this guy talked with elves and angels. . . . Miles backed down slightly. "No, it's like a thought, only more compelling. It storms your will—burns like lust, only not so easy to satisfy. Not like a trance, because it drives you outward, not inward." He hesitated, unsettled, having spoken more truth than he'd intended.

Suegar looked vastly encouraged. "Oh, good. I was afraid for a second you might be one of those guys who start talking to people nobody else can see."

Miles glanced upward involuntarily, returned his gaze straightly to Suegar.

"—so that's a vision. Why, I've felt like that." His eyes seemed to focus and intensify.

"Didn't you recognize it in yourself?" asked Miles blandly.

"Not by name . . . it's not a comfortable thing, to be chosen so. I tried to evade it for a long time, but God finds ways of dealing with draft dodgers."

"You're too modest, Suegar. You've believed in your scripture, but not in yourself. Don't you know that when you're given a task, you're given the power to accomplish it as well?"

Suegar sighed in joyous satisfaction. "I knew it was a job for two. It's just like the scripture said."

"Uh, right. So now we are two. But we must be more. I guess we'd better start with your friends."

"That won't take much time," said Suegar wryly. "You got a step two in mind, I hope?"

"Then we'll start with your enemies. Or your nodding acquaintances. We'll start with the first bleeding body that crosses our path. It doesn't matter where we start, because I mean to have them all, in the end. All, to the last and least." A particularly apt quote shot across his memory, and he declaimed vigorously, " 'Those who have ears, let them hear.' All." Miles sent a real prayer up from his heart with that one.

"All right," Miles pulled Suegar to his feet, "let's go preach to the unconverted."

Suegar laughed suddenly. "I had a top kick once

who used to say, 'Let's go kick some ass,' in just that tone of voice."

"That, too," Miles grimaced. "You understand, universal membership in this congregation won't come all voluntary. But you leave the recruiting to me, hear?"

Suegar stroked his beard hairs, regarded Miles from beneath raised brows. "A clerk, eh?"

"Right."

"Yes, sir."

They started with Oliver.

Miles gestured. "May we step into your office?"

Oliver rubbed his nose with the back of his hand and sniffed. "Let me give you a piece of advice, boy. You ain't gonna make it in here as a stand-up comic. Every joke that can possibly be made has been run into the ground. Even the sick ones."

"Very well." Miles sat cross-legged, near Oliver's mat but not too near. Suegar hunkered down behind Miles's shoulder, not so welded to the ground, as if ready to skip backwards if necessary. "I'll lay it out straight, then. I don't like the way things are run around here."

Oliver's mouth twisted sardonically; he did not comment aloud. He didn't need to.

"I'm going to change them," Miles added.

"Shit," said Oliver, and rolled back over.

"Starting here and now."

After a moment's silence Oliver added, "Go away or I'll pound you."

Suegar started to get up; Miles irritably motioned him back down.

"He was a commando," Suegar whispered worriedly. "He can break you in half."

"Nine-tenths of the people in this camp can break

me in half, including the girls," Miles whispered back. "It's not a significant consideration."

Miles leaned forward, grasped Oliver's chin, and twisted his face back toward him. Suegar sucked his breath through his teeth with a whistle at this dangerous tactic.

"Now, there's this about cynicism, Sergeant. It's the universe's most supine moral position. Real comfortable. If nothing can be done, then you're not some kind of shit for not doing it, and you can lie there and stink to yourself in perfect peace."

Oliver batted Miles's hand down, but did not turn away again. Rage flared in his eyes. "Suegar tell you I was a sergeant?" he hissed.

"No, it's written on your forehead in letters of fire. Listen up, Oliver—"

Oliver rolled over and up as far as supporting his upper body with his knuckles on his sleeping mat. Suegar flinched, but did not flee.

"You listen up, mutant," Oliver snarled. "We've done it all already. We've done drill, and games, and clean living, exercise, and cold showers, except there ain't no cold showers. We've done group sings and floor shows. We've done it by the numbers, by the book, by candlelight. We've done it by force, and made real war on each other. After that we did sin and sex and sadism till we were ready to puke. We've done it all at least ten times. You think you're the first reformer to come through here?"

"No, Oliver," Miles leaned into his face, his eyes boring into Oliver's burning eyes unscorched. His voice fell to a whisper. "I think I'm the last."

Oliver was silent a moment, then barked a laugh. "By God, Suegar has found his soul-mate at last. Two loonies together, just like his scripture says."

Miles paused thoughtfully, sat up as straight as his

spine would allow. "Read me your scripture again, Suegar. The full text." He closed his eyes for total concentration, also to discourage interruptions from Oliver.

Suegar rustled around and cleared his throat nervously. " 'For those that shall be the heirs of salvation,' " he began. " 'Thus they went along toward the gate. Now you must note that the city stood upon a mighty hill, but the pilgrims went up that hill with ease, because they had these two men to lead them by the arms; also they had left their mortal garments behind them in the river, for though they went in with them, they came out without them. They therefore went up here with much agility and speed, through the foundation upon which the city was framed higher than the clouds. They therefore went up through the regions of the air . . .' " He added apologetically, "It breaks off there. That's where I tore the page. Not sure what that signifies."

"Probably means that after that you're supposed to improvise for yourself," Miles suggested, opening his eyes again. So, that was the raw material he was building on. He had to admit the last line in particular gave him a turn, a chill like a bellyfull of cold worms. So be it. Forward.

"There you are, Oliver. That's what I'm offering. The only hope worth breathing for. Salvation itself."

"Very uplifting," sneered Oliver.

" 'Uplifted' is just what I intend you all to be. You've got to understand, Oliver, I'm a fundamentalist. I take my scriptures *very* literally."

Oliver opened his mouth, then closed it with a snap. Miles had his utter attention.

Communication at last, Miles breathed inwardly. *We have connected.*

"It would take a miracle," said Oliver at last, "to uplift this whole place."

"Mine is not a theology of the elect. I intend to preach to the masses. Even," he was definitely getting into the swing of this, "the sinners. Heaven is for everyone.

"But miracles, by their very nature, must break in from outside. We don't carry them in our pockets—"

"You don't, that's for sure," muttered Oliver with a glance at Miles's undress.

"—we can only pray, and prepare ourselves for a better world. But miracles come only to the prepared. Are you prepared, Oliver?" Miles leaned forward, his voice vibrating with energy.

"Sh . . ." Oliver's voice trailed off. He glanced for confirmation, oddly enough, at Suegar. "Is this guy for real?"

"He thinks he's faking it," said Suegar blandly, "but he's not. He's the One, all right and tight."

The cold worms writhed again. Dealing with Suegar, Miles decided, was like fencing in a hall of mirrors. Your target, though real, was never quite where it looked like it should be.

Oliver inhaled. Hope and fear, belief and doubt, intermingled in his face. "How shall we be saved, Rev'rend?"

"Ah—call me Brother Miles, I think. Yes. Tell me—how many converts can you deliver on your own naked, unsupported authority?"

Oliver looked extremely thoughtful. "Just let them see *that* light, and they'll follow it anywhere."

"Well . . . well . . . salvation is for all, to be sure, but there may be certain temporary practical advantages to maintaining a priesthood. I mean, blessed also are they who do not see, and yet believe."

"It's true," agreed Oliver, "that if your religion failed to deliver a miracle, that a human sacrifice would certainly follow."

"Ah . . . quite," Miles gulped. "You are a man of acute insight."

"That's not an insight," said Oliver. "That's a personal guarantee."

"Yes, well . . . to return to my question. How many followers can you raise? I'm talking bodies here, not souls."

Oliver frowned, cautious still. "Maybe twenty."

"Can any of them bring in others? Branch out, hook in more?"

"Maybe."

"Make them your corporals, then. I think we had better disregard any previous ranks here. Call it, ah, the Army of the Reborn. No. The Reformation Army. That scans better. We shall be re-formed. The body has disintegrated like the caterpillar in its chrysalis, into nasty green gook, but we shall re-form into the butterfly and fly away."

Oliver sniffed again. "Just what reforms you planning?"

"Just one, I think. The food."

Oliver gave him a disbelieving stare. "You sure this isn't just a scam to get yourself a free meal?"

"True, I *am* getting hungry . . ." Miles backed off from the joke as Oliver remained icily unimpressed. "But so are a lot of other people. By tomorrow, we can have them all eating out of our hands."

"When would you want these twenty guys?"

"By the next chow call." Good, he'd startled the man.

"That soon?"

"You understand, Oliver, the belief that you have all the time in the world is an illusion this place fosters on purpose. Resist it."

"You're sure in a hurry."

"So, you got a dental appointment? I think not.

Besides, I'm only half your mass. I gotta move twice as fast just to keep up the momentum. Twenty, plus. By next chow call."

"What the hell do you think you're gonna be able to do with twenty guys?"

"We're going to take the food pile."

Oliver's lips tightened in disgust. "Not with twenty guys, you're not. No go. Besides, it's been done. I told you we'd made real war in here. It'd be a quick massacre."

"—and then, after we've taken it—we re-distribute it. Fair and square, one rat bar per customer, all controlled and quartermasterly. To sinners and all. By the next chow call everybody who's ever been shorted will be coming over to us. And then we'll be in a position to deal with the hard cases."

"You're nuts. You can't do it. Not with twenty guys."

"Did I say we were only going to have twenty guys? Suegar, did I say that?"

Suegar, listening in rapt fascination, shook his head.

"Well, I ain't sticking my neck out to get pounded unless you can produce some visible means of support," said Oliver. "This could get us killed."

"Can do," Miles promised recklessly. One had to start lifting somewhere; his imaginary bootstraps would do well enough. "I will deliver 500 troops to the sacred cause by chow call."

"You do that, and I'll walk the perimeter of this camp naked on my hands," retorted Oliver.

Miles grinned. "I may hold you to that, Sergeant. Twenty plus. By chow call." Miles stood. "Come on, Suegar."

Oliver waved them off irritably. They retreated in good order. When Miles looked back over his shoulder, Oliver had arisen, and was walking toward a group of occupied mats tangential to his own, waving down an apparent acquaintance.

"So where do we get 500 troops before next chow call?" Suegar asked. "I better warn you, Oliver was the best thing I had. The next is bound to be tougher."

"What," said Miles, "is your faith wavering so soon?"

"I believe," said Suegar, "I just don't see. Maybe that makes me blessed, I dunno."

"I'm surprised. I thought it was pretty obvious. There." Miles pointed across the camp toward the unmarked border of the women's group.

"Oh." Suegar stopped short. "Oh, oh. I don't think so, Miles."

"Yes. Let's go."

"You won't get in there without a change-of-sex operation."

"What, as God-driven as you are, haven't you tried to preach your scripture to them?"

"I tried. Got pounded. Tried elsewhere after that."

Miles paused, and pursed his lips, studying Suegar. "It wasn't defeat, or you wouldn't have hung on long enough to meet me. Was it—ah, shame, that drained your usual resolve? You got something to work off in that quarter?"

Suegar shook his head. "Not personally. Except maybe, sins of omission. I just didn't have the heart to harass 'em any more."

"This whole place is suffering from sins of omission." A relief, that Suegar wasn't some sort of self-confessed rapist. Miles's eyes swept the scene, teasing out the pattern from the limited cues of position, grouping, activity. "Yes . . . predator pressure produces herd behavior. Social—fragmentation here being what it is, the pressure must be pretty high, to hold a group of that size together. But I hadn't noticed any incidents since I got here. . . ."

"It comes and goes," said Suegar. "Phases of the moon or something."

Phases of the moon, right. Miles sent up a prayer of thanks in his heart to whatever gods might be—to Whom it may concern—that the Cetagandans appeared to have implanted some standard time-release anti-ovulant in all their female prisoners, along with their other immunizations. Bless the forgotten individual who'd put *that* clause in the IJC rules, forcing the Cetagandans into more subtle forms of legal torture. And yet, would the presence of pregnancies, infants, and children among the prisoners have been another destabilizing stress—or a stabilizing force deeper and stronger than all the previous loyalties the Cetagandans seemed to have so successfully broken down? From a purely logistical viewpoint, Miles was elated that the question was theoretical.

"Well . . ." Miles took a deep breath, and pulled an imaginary hat down over his eyes at an aggressive angle. "I'm new here, and so temporarily unembarrassed. Let he who is without sin cast the first lure. Besides, I have an advantage for this sort of negotiation. I'm clearly not a threat." He marched forward.

"I'll wait for you here," called Suegar helpfully, and hunkered down where he was.

Miles timed his forward march to intersect a patrol of six women strolling down their perimeter. He arranged himself in front of them and swept off his imaginary hat to hold strategically over his crotch. "Good afternoon, ladies. Allow me to apologize for m'beh—"

His opening line was interrupted by a mouthful of dirt abruptly acquired as his legs were swept backward and his shoulders forward by the four women who had parted around him, dumping him neatly on his face. He had not even managed to spit it out when he found himself plucked up and whirled dizzily through the air, still face-down, by hands grasping his arms and legs. A muttered count of three, and he was soaring in a short forlorn arc, to land in a heap not far from Suegar. The patrollers walked on without another word.

"See what I mean?" said Suegar.

Miles turned his head to look at him. "You had that trajectory calculated to the centimeter, didn't you?" he said smearily.

"Just about," agreed Suegar. "I figured they could heave you quite a bit farther than usual, on account of your size."

Miles scrambled back up to a sitting position, still trying to get his wind. Damn the ribs, which had grown almost bearable, but which now wrung his chest with electric agony at every breath. In a few minutes he got up and brushed himself off. As an afterthought, he picked up his invisible hat, too. Dizzied, he had to brace his hands on his knees a moment.

"All right," he muttered, "back we go."

"Miles—"

"It's gotta be done, Suegar. No other choice. Anyway, I can't quit, once I've started. I've been told I'm pathologically persistent. I *can't* quit."

Suegar opened his mouth to object, then swallowed his protest. "Right," he said. He settled down cross-legged, his right hand unconsciously caressing his rag rope library. "I'll wait till you call me in." He seemed to fall into a reverie, or meditation—or maybe a doze.

Miles's second foray ended precisely like the first, except that his trajectory was perhaps a little wider and a little higher. The third attempt went the same way, but his flight was much shorter.

"Good," he muttered to himself. "Must be tiring 'em out."

This time he skipped in parallel to the patrol, out of reach but well within hearing. "Look," he panted, "you don't have to do this piecemeal. Let me make it easy for you. I have this teratogenic bone disorder —I'm not a mutant, you understand, my genes are normal, it's just their expression got distorted, from my mother being exposed to a certain poison while she was pregnant—it was a one-shot thing, won't affect any children *I* might have—I always felt it was easier to get dates when that was clearly understood, *not* a mutant—anyway, my bones are brittle, in fact any one of you could probably break every one in my body. You may wonder why I'm telling you all this—in fact, I usually prefer not to advertise it—you have to stop and listen to me. I'm not a threat—do I look like a threat?—a challenge, maybe, not a threat—are you going to make me run all around this camp after you? Slow down, for God's sake—" He would be out of wind, and therefore verbal ammunition, very shortly at this rate. He hopped around in front of them and planted himself, arms outstretched.

"—so if you *are* planning to break every bone in my body, please do it now and get it over with, because I'm going to keep coming back here until you do."

At a brief hand signal from their leader the patrol stopped, facing him.

"Take him at his word," suggested a tall redhead. Her short brush of electric copper hair fascinated Miles to distraction; he pictured missing masses of it having fallen to the floor at the clippers of the ruthless Cetagandan prison processors. "I'll break the left arm if you'll break the right, Conr," she continued.

"If that's what it takes to get you to stop and listen to me for five minutes, so be it," Miles responded, not retreating. The redhead stepped forward and braced herself, locking his left elbow in an arm bar, putting on the pressure.

"Five minutes, right?" Miles added desperately as the pressure mounted. Her stare scorched his profile. He licked his lips, closed his eyes, held his breath, and waited. The pressure reached critical—he rose on his toes . . .

She released him abruptly, so that he staggered. "Men," she commented disgustedly. "Always gotta make everything a peeing contest."

"Biology is Destiny," gasped Miles, popping his eyes back open.

"—or are you some kind of pervert—do you get off on being beaten up by women?"

God, I hope not. He remained unbetrayed by unauthorized salutes from his nether parts, just barely. If he was going to be around that redhead much he was definitely going to have to get his pants back somehow. "If I said yes, would you refrain, just to punish me?" he offered.

"Shit, no."

"It was just a thought—"

"Cut the crap, Beatrice," said the patrol leader. At a jerk of her head the redhead stepped back into formation. "All right, runt, you've got your five minutes. Maybe."

"Thank you, ma'am." Miles took a breath, and reordered himself as best he could with no uniform to adjust. "First, let me apologize for intruding upon your privacy in this undress. Practically the first persons I met upon entering this camp were a self-help group—they helped themselves to my clothes, among other things—"

"I saw that," confirmed Beatrice-the-redhead un-expectedly. "Pitt's bunch."

Miles pulled off his hat and swept her a bow with it. "Yes, thank you."

"You moon people behind you when you do that," she commented dispassionately.

"That's their look-out," responded Miles. "For my-self, I want to talk to your leader, or leaders. I have a serious plan for improving the tone of this place with which I wish to invite your group to collaborate. Bluntly, you are the largest remaining pocket of civil-ization, not to mention military order, in here. I'd like to see you expand your borders."

"It takes everything we've got to keep our borders from being overrun, son," replied the leader. "No can do. So take yourself off."

"Jack yourself off, too," suggested Beatrice. "You ain't gettin' any in here."

Miles sighed, and turned his hat around in his hands by its wide brim. He spun it for a moment on one finger, and locked eyes with the redhead. "Note my hat. It was the one garment I managed to keep from the ravages of the burly surly brothers—Pitt's bunch, you say."

She snorted at the turn of phrase. "Those jerks . . . why just a hat? Why not pants? Why not a full-dress uniform while you're at it?" she added sarcastically.

"A hat is a more useful object for communicating. You can make broad gestures," he did so, "denote sincerity," he held it over his heart, "or indicate embarrassment," over his genitals, with a hang-dog crouch, "or rage—" he flung it to earth as if he might drive it into the ground, then picked it up and brushed it off carefully, "or determination—" he jammed it on his head and yanked the brim down over his eyes, "or make courtesies." He swept it off again in salute to her. "Do you see the hat?"

She was beginning to be amused. "Yes . . ."

"Do you see the feathers on the hat?"

"Yes . . ."

"Describe them."

"Oh—plumey things."

"How many?"

"Two. Bunched together."

"Do you see the color of the feathers?"

She drew back, suddenly self-conscious again, with a sidewise glance at her companions. "No."

"When you can see the color of the feathers," said Miles softly, "you'll also understand how you can expand your borders to infinity."

She was silent, her face closed and locked. But the patrol leader muttered, "Maybe this little runt better talk to Tris. Just this once."

The woman in charge had clearly been a front line trooper once, not a tech like the majority of the females. She had certainly not acquired the muscles that flowed like braided leather cords beneath her skin from crouching by the hour in front of a holovid display in some rear-echelon underground post. She had toted the real weapons that spat real death, and sometimes broke down; had rammed against the limits of what could really be done by flesh and bone and metal, and been marked by that deforming press. Illusion had been burned out of her like an infection, leaving a cauterized scar. Rage burned permanently in her eyes like a fire in a coal seam, underground and unquenchable. She might be thirty-five, or forty.

God, I'm in love, thought Miles. *Brother Miles wants YOU for the Reformation Army* . . . then got hold of his thoughts. Here, now, was the make-or-break point for his scheme, and all the persiflage, verbal misdirection, charm, chutzpah, and bullshit he could muster weren't going to be enough, not even tied up with a big blue bow.

The wounded want power, nothing else; they think it will keep them from being hurt again. This one will not be interested in Suegar's strange message—at least, not yet. . . . Miles took a deep breath.

"Ma'am, I'm here to offer you command of this camp."

She stared at him as if he were something she'd found growing on the walls in a dark corner of the latrine. Her eyes raked over his nudity; Miles could feel the claw marks glowing from his chin to his toes.

"Which you store in your duffel bag, no doubt," she growled. "Command of this camp doesn't exist, mutant. So it's not yours to give. Deliver him to our perimeter in pieces, Beatrice."

He ducked the redhead. He would pursue correction of the mutant business later. "Command of this camp is mine to *create*," he asserted. "Note, please, that what I offer is power, not revenge. Revenge is too expensive a luxury. Commanders can't afford it."

Tris uncoiled from her sleeping mat to her full height, then had to bend her knees to bring her face level to his, hissing, "Too bad, little turd. You almost interest me. Because I *want* revenge. On every man in this camp."

"Then the Cetagandans have succeeded; you've forgotten who your real enemy is."

"Say, rather, that I've discovered who my real enemy is. Do you want to know the things they've done to us—our own guys—"

"The Cetagandans want you to believe this," a wave of his hand embraced the camp, "is something you're doing to each other. So fighting each other, you become their puppets. They watch you all the time, you know, voyeurs of your humiliation."

Her glance flicked upward, infinitesimally; good. It was almost a disease among these people, that they would look in any direction at all in preference to up at the dome.

"Power is better than revenge," suggested Miles, not flinching before her snake-cold, set face, her hot coal eyes. "Power is a live thing, by which you reach out to grasp the future. Revenge is a dead thing, reaching out from the past to grasp you."

"—and you're a bullshit artist," she interrupted, "reaching out to grasp whatever's going down. I've got you pegged now. *This* is power." She flexed her arm under his nose, muscles coiling and loosing. "This is the only power that exists in here. You haven't got it, and you're looking for some to cover your ass. But you've come to the wrong store."

"No," Miles denied, and tapped his forehead. "*This* is power. And I own the store. This controls that," he slapped his bunched fist. "Men may move mountains, but ideas move men. Minds can be reached through bodies—what else is the point of all this," he waved at the camp, "but to reach your minds through your bodies. But that power flows both ways, and the outflow is the stronger tide.

"When you have allowed the Cetagandans to reduce your power to *that* alone," he squeezed her bicep for emphasis—it was like squeezing a rock covered in velvet, and she tensed, enraged at the liberty, "then you have allowed them to reduce you to your weakest part. And they win."

"They win anyway," she snapped, shrugging him off. He breathed relief that she hadn't chosen to break his arm. "Nothing that we do within this circle will result in any net change. We're still prisoners, whatever we do. They can cut off the food, or the damn air, or squeeze us to mush. And time's on their side. If we spill our guts restoring order—if that's what you're trying to work up to—all they have to do is wait for it to break down again. We're *beaten*. We're *taken*. There's nobody left *out there*. We're here forever. And you'd better start getting used to the idea."

"I've heard that song before," said Miles. "Use your head. If they meant to keep you forever, they could have incinerated you at the start, and saved the considerable expense of operating this camp. No. It's your minds they want. You are all here because you were Marilac's best and brightest, the hardest fighters, the strongest, baddest, most dangerous. The ones any potential resisters to the occupation would look to for leadership. It's the Cetagandans' plan to break you, and then return you to your world like little innoculated infections, counseling surrender to your people.

"When this is killed," he touched her forehead, oh so lightly, "then the Cetagandans have nothing more to fear from this," one finger on her bicep, "and you will all go free. To a world whose horizon will encircle you just like this dome, and just as inescapably. The war's not over. You are *here* because the Cetagandans are still waiting for the surrender of Fallow Core."

He thought for a moment she might murder him, strangle him on the spot. She must certainly prefer ripping him apart to letting him see her weep.

She regained her protective bitter tension with a toss of her head, a gulp of air. "If that's true, then following you puts us farther from freedom, not closer."

Damn, a logician to boot. She didn't have to pound

him, she could parse him to death if he didn't scramble. He scrambled. "There is a subtle difference between being a prisoner and being a slave. I don't mistake either for being free. Neither do you."

She fell silent, staring at him through slitted eyes, pulling unconsciously on her lower lip. "You're an odd one," she said at last. "Why do you say 'you' and not 'we'?"

Miles shrugged casually. Blast—he rapidly reviewed his pitch—she was right, he had. A little too close to the edge, there. He might yet make an opportunity of the mistake, though. "Do I look like the flower of Marilac's military might? I'm an outsider, trapped in a world I never made. A traveller—a pilgrim—just passing through. Ask Suegar."

She snorted. "That loonie."

She'd missed the catch. Rats, as Elli would say. He missed Elli. Try again later. "Don't discount Suegar. He has a message for you. I found it fascinating."

"I've heard it. I find it irritating. . . . So, what do you want out of this? And don't tell me 'nothing,' 'cause I won't believe you. Frankly, I think you're after command of the camp yourself, and I'm not volunteering to be your stepping stone in some empire-building scheme."

She was thinking at speed now, and constructively, actually following out trains of thought besides that of having him removed to her border in bits. He was getting warmer. . . .

"I only wish to be your spiritual advisor. I do not want—indeed, can't use—command. Just an advisor."

It must have been something about the term "advisor" that clicked, some old association of hers. Her eyes flicked fully open suddenly. He was close enough to see her pupils dilate. She leaned forward, and her index finger traced the faint indentations on his face beside his nose caused by certain control leads in a space armor helmet. She straightened again, and her first two fingers in a V caressed the deeper marks permanently flanking her own nose. "What did you say you were, before?"

"A clerk. Recruiting office," Miles replied sturdily.

"I . . . see."

And if what she saw was the absurdity of someone claiming to be a rear-echelon clerk having worn combat armor often and long enough to have picked up its stigmata, he was in. Maybe.

She coiled herself back up on her sleeping mat, and gestured toward its other end. "Sit down, chaplain. And keep talking."

Suegar was genuinely asleep when Miles found him again, sitting up cross-legged and snoring. Miles tapped him on the shoulder.

"Wake up, Suegar, we're home."

He snorted to consciousness. "God, I miss coffee. Huh?" He blinked at Miles. "You're still in one piece?"

"It was a near thing. Look, this garments-in-the-river bit—now that we've found each other, do we have to go *on* being naked? Or is the prophecy sufficiently fulfilled?"

"Huh?"

"Can we get dressed now?" Miles repeated patiently.

"Why—I don't know. I suppose, if we were meant to have clothes, they'd be given to us—"

Miles prodded and pointed. "There. They're given to us."

Beatrice stood a few meters away in a hip-shot pose of bored exasperation, a bundle of grey cloth under her arm. "You two loonies want this stuff or not? I'm going back."

"You got them to give you clothes?" Suegar whispered in amazement.

"Us, Suegar, us." Miles motioned to Beatrice. "I think it's all right."

She fired the bundle at him, sniffed, and stalked away.

"Thanks," Miles called. He shook out the fabric. Two sets of grey pajamas, one small, one large. Miles had only to turn up the bottoms of the pants legs one fold to keep them from catching under his heels. They were stained and stiff with old sweat and dirt, and had probably been peeled off a corpse, Miles reflected. Suegar crawled into his and stood fingering the grey fabric in wonder.

"They gave us clothes. *Gave* us," he muttered. "How'd you do that?"

"They gave us everything, Suegar. Come on, I've got to talk to Oliver again." Miles dragged Suegar off determinedly. "I wonder how much time we've actually got before the next chow call? Two in each twenty-four-hour cycle, to be sure, but I wouldn't be surprised if it's irregular, to increase your temporal disorientation—after all, it's the only clock in here . . ."

Movement caught Miles's eye, a man running. It wasn't the occasional flurry of someone outrunning a hostile group; this one just ran, head down, flat out, bare feet thumping the dirt in frantic rhythm. He followed the perimeter generally, except for a detour around the border of the women's group. As he ran, he wept.

"What's this?" Miles asked Suegar, with a nod at the approaching figure.

Suegar shrugged. "It takes you like that sometimes. When you can't stand sitting in here any more. I saw a guy run till he died, once. Around and around and around . . ."

"Well," Miles decided, "this one's running to us."

"He's gonna be running away from us in a second . . ."

"Then help me catch him."

Miles hit him low and Suegar high. Suegar sat on his chest. Miles sat on his right arm, halving his effective resistance. He must have been a very young soldier when he was captured—maybe he had lied about his age at induction—for even now he had a boy's face, ravaged by tears and his personal eternity inside this hollow pearl. He inhaled in sobbing gasps and exhaled in garbled obscenities. After a time he quieted.

Miles leaned into his face and grinned wolfishly. "You a party animal, boy?"

"Yeah . . ." his white-rimmed eyes rolled, right and left, but no rescue approached.

"How 'bout your friends? They party animals too?"

"The best," the boy asserted, perhaps secretly shaken by the suspicion that he'd fallen into the hands of someone even crazier than himself. "You better clear off me, mutant, or they'll take you apart."

"I want to invite you and your friends to a *major* party," Miles chanted. "We gonna have a party tonight that's an his-tor-i-cal event. You know where to find Sergeant Oliver, late of the 14th Commandos?"

"Yeah . . ." the boy admitted cautiously.

"Well, you go get your friends and report to him. You better reserve your seat aboard his ve-hic-le now, 'cause if you're not on it, you gonna be *under* it. The Reformation Army is moving out. You copy?"

"Copy," he gasped, as Suegar pressed his fist into the boy's solar plexus for emphasis.

"Tell him Brother Miles sent you," Miles called as the boy staggered off, glancing nervously over his shoulder. "You can't hide in here. If you don't show, I'll send the Cosmic Commandos to find you."

Suegar shook out his cramped limbs, his new used clothes. "Think he'll come?"

Miles grinned. "Fight or flight. That one'll be all right." He stretched himself, recaptured his original orientation. "Oliver."

In the end they had not twenty, but 200. Oliver had picked up forty-six. The running boy brought in eighteen. The signs of order and activity in the area brought in the curious—a drifter at the edge of the group had only to ask, "What's going on?" to be inducted and promoted to corporal on the spot. Interest among the spectators was aroused to a fever when Oliver's troops marched up to the women's border—and were admitted within. They picked up another seventy-five volunteers instantly.

"Do you know what's going on?" Miles asked one such, as he fed them through a short gauntlet of inspection and sent them off to one of the fourteen command groups he had devised.

"No," the man admitted. He waved an arm eagerly toward the center of the women's group. "But I wanta go where *they're* going . . ."

Miles cut the admissions off at 200 total in deference to Tris's growing nervousness at this infiltration of her borders, and promptly turned the courtesy into a card in his own hand in their still-continuing strategy debate. Tris wanted to divide her group in the usual way, half for the attack, half to maintain home base and keep the borders from collapsing. Miles was insisting on an all-out effort.

"If we win, you won't need guards anymore."

"What if we lose?"

Miles lowered his voice. "We don't dare lose. This is the only time we'll have surprise on our side. Yes, we can fall back—re-group—try again—I for one am prepared—no, compelled—to keep trying till it kills me. But after this, what we're trying to do will be fully apparent to any counter-group, and they'll have time to plan counter-strategies of their own. I have a particular aversion to stalemates. I prefer winning wars to prolonging them."

She sighed, momentarily drained, tired, old. "I've been at war a long time, y'know? After a while even losing a war can start to look preferable to prolonging it."

He could feel his own resolve slip, sucked into the vortex of that same black doubt. He pointed upwards, dropping his voice to a rasping whisper. "But not, surely, to *those* bastards."

She glanced upwards. Her shoulders straightened. "No. Not to those . . ." She took a deep breath. "All right, chaplain. You'll get your all-out effort. Just once . . ."

Oliver returned from a circuit of the command groups and squatted beside them. "They've got their orders. How many's Tris contributing to each group?"

"Commandant Tris," Miles quickly corrected for her as her brows beetled. "It's gonna be an all-out shot. You'll get every walking body in here."

Oliver made a quick calculation in the dirt with his finger for a stylus. "That'll put about fifty in each group—ought to be enough . . . matter of fact, what say we set up twenty groups? It'll speed distribution when we get the lines set up. Could make the difference between bringing this off, and not."

"No," Miles cut in quickly as Tris began to nod agreement. "It has to be fourteen. Fourteen battle groups make fourteen lines for fourteen piles. Fourteen is—is a theologically significant number," he added as they stared doubtfully at him.

"Why?" asked Tris.

"For the fourteen apostles," Miles intoned, tenting his hands piously.

Tris shrugged. Suegar scratched his head, started to speak—Miles speared him with a baleful glance, and he stilled.

Oliver eyed him narrowly. "Huh." But he did not argue further.

Then came the waiting. Miles stopped worrying about his uppermost fear—that their captors would introduce the next food pile early, before his plans were in place—and started worrying about his second greatest fear, that the food pile would come so late he'd lose control of his troops and they would start to wander off, bored and discouraged. Getting them all assembled had made Miles feel like a man pulling on a goat with a rope made of water. Never had the insubstantial nature of the Idea seemed more self-apparent.

Oliver tapped him on the shoulder and pointed. "Here we go . . ."

A side of the dome about a third of the way around the edge from them began to bulge inward.

The timing was perfect. His troops were at the peak of readiness. Too perfect . . . the Centagandans had been watching all this, surely they wouldn't miss an opportunity to make life more difficult for their prisoners. If the food pile wasn't early, it had to be late. Or . . .

Miles bounded to his feet, screaming, "Wait! Wait! Wait for my order!"

His sprint groups wavered, drawn toward the anticipated goal. But Oliver had chosen his group commanders well—they held, and held their groups, and looked to Oliver. They *had* been soldiers once. Oliver looked to Tris, flanked by her lieutenant Beatrice, and Tris looked to Miles, angrily.

"What is it now? We're gonna lose our advantage . . ." she began, as the general stampede throughout the camp started toward the bulge.

"If I'm wrong," Miles moaned, "I'm going to kill myself— wait, dammit! On my order. I can't see— Suegar, give me a boost—" He clambered up on the thin man's shoulders and stared toward the bulge. The force wall had only half twinkled out when the first distant cries of disappointment met his straining ears. Miles's head swivelled frantically. How many wheels within wheels—if the Cetagandans knew, and he knew they knew, and they knew he knew they knew, and . . . He cut off his internal gibber as a second bulge began, on the opposite side of the camp from the first.

Miles's arm flung out, pointing toward it like a man rolling dice. "There! There! Go, go, go!"

Tris caught on then, whistling and shooting him a look of startled respect, before whirling and dashing off to double-time the main body of their troops after the sprint groups. Miles slithered off Suegar and started limping after.

He glanced back over his shoulder, as the rolling grey mass of humanity crashed up against the opposite side of the dome and reversed itself. He felt suddenly like a man trying to outrun a tidal wave. He indulged himself with one brief anticipatory whimper, and limped faster.

One more chance to be mortally wrong—no. His sprint groups had reached the pile, and the pile was really there. Already they were starting to break it down. The support troops surrounded them with a wall of bodies as they began to spread out along the perimeter of the dome. The Cetagandans had outfoxed themselves. This time.

Miles was reduced from the commander's eagle

overview to the grunt's worm's-eye as the tidal wave overtook him. Someone shoved him from behind, and his face hit the dirt. He thought he recognized the back of the surly Pitt, vaulting over him, but he wasn't certain—surely Pitt would have stepped on, not over him. Suegar yanked him up by the left arm, and Miles bit back a scream of pain. There was enough howling already.

Miles recognized the running boy, squaring off with another tough. Miles shoved past him with a shouted reminder—"You're supposed to be yelling *Get in line!*, NOT *Get fucked!* . . . The signal always gets degraded in combat," he muttered to himself. "Always . . ."

Beatrice materialized beside him. Miles clung to her instantly. Beatrice had personal space, her own private perimeter, maintained even as Miles watched, by a casual elbow to somebody's jaw with a quite sickening crack. It he tried that, Miles reflected enviously, not only would he smash his own elbow, but his opponent's nipple would probably be quite undamaged. Speaking of nipples, he found himself face to—well, not face—confronting the redhead. He resisted the urge to cuddle into the soft grey fabric covering home base with a contented sigh on the grounds that it would certainly get both his arms broken. He uncrossed his eyes and looked up into her face.

"C'mon," she said, and dragged him off through the mob. Was the noise level dropping? The human wall of his own troops parted just enough to let them squeeze through.

They were near the exit point of the chow line. It was working, by God it was working. The fourteen command groups, still bunched rather too closely along the dome wall—but that could be improved next run—were admitting the hungry supplicants one at a time. The expediters kept the lines moving at top speed, and channeled the already-supplied along the perimeter behind the human shield wall in a steady stream, to flow back out into the larger camp at the edge of the mob. Oliver had put his toughest-looking bravos to work in pairs, patrolling the outflow and making sure no one's rat bar was taken by force.

It was a long time since anyone here had had a chance to be a hero. Not a few of the newly-appointed policemen were approaching their work with great enthusiasm—maybe some personal grudges being worked off there—Miles recognized one of the burly surlys prone beneath a pair of patrollers, apparently getting his face beaten in. Miles, remembering what he was about, tried not to find music in the meaty thunks of fist on flesh.

Miles and Beatrice and Suegar bucked the stream of rat bar-clutching prisoners back toward the distribution piles. With a slightly regretful sigh, Miles sought out Oliver and dispatched him to the exit to restore order among his order-keepers.

Tris had the distribution piles and their immediate lines under tight control. Miles congratulated himself on having the women hand out the food. He had definitely tuned into a deep emotional resonance there. Not a few of the prisoners even muttered a sheepish "thank you" as their rat bars were shoved into their hands, and so did the ones in line behind them, when their turns came.

Nyah! Miles thought upward to the bland and silent dome. *You don't have the monopoly on psychological warfare any more, you bastards. We're gonna reverse your peristalsis, and I hope you barf your bowels out—*

An altercation at one of the food piles interrupted

his meditations. Miles's lip curled with annoyance as he saw Pitt in the middle of it. He limped hastily toward it.

Pitt, it appeared, had repaid his rat bar not with a "thank you" but with a leer, a jeer, and a filthy remark. At least three of the women within hearing were trying to rip him apart, without success; he was big and beefy and had no inhibitions about fighting back. One of the females, not much taller than Miles himself, was knocked back in a heap and didn't get up again. In the meantime, the line was jammed, and the smooth civilized flow of would-be diners totally disrupted. Miles cursed under his breath.

"You, you, you, and—you," Miles tapped shoulders, "grab that guy. Get him out of here—back to the dome wall—"

Miles's draftees were not terribly pleased with their assignment, but by this time Tris and Beatrice had run up and led the attack with rather more science. Pitt was seized and pulled away, behind the lines. Miles made sure the rat bar distribution pile was running again before turning his attention to the savage, foul-mouthed Pitt. Oliver and Suegar had joined him by this time.

"I'm gonna rip the bastard's balls off," Tris was saying. "I command—"

"A military command," Miles interrupted. "If this one is accused of disorderly conduct, you should court martial him."

"He is a rapist and a murderer," she replied icily. "Execution's too good for him. He's got to die *slowly*."

Miles pulled Suegar aside. "It's tempting, but I feel real uneasy about handing him over to her just now. And yet . . . real uneasy. Why is that?"

Suegar eyed him respectfully. "I think you're right. You see, there's—there's too many guilty."

Pitt, now in a foaming fury, spotted Miles. "You! You little cunt-licking wimp—you think *they* can protect you?" He jerked his head toward Tris and Beatrice. "They ain't got the muscle. We've run 'em over before and we'll run 'em over again. We wouldn'ta lost the damn war if we'd had real soldiers— like the Barrayarans. They didn't fill their army with cunts and cunt-lickers. And they ran the Cetagandans right off their planet—"

"Somehow," Miles growled, drawn in, "I doubt you're an expert in the Barrayarans' defense of their homeworld in the First Cetagandan War. Or you might have learned something—"

"Did Tris make you an honorary girl, mutant?" jeered Pitt in return. "It wouldn't take much—"

Why am I standing here bandying words with this low-life crazy? Miles asked himself as Pitt raved on. *No time. Let's finish it.*

Miles stepped back and folded his arms. "Has it occurred to any of you yet that this man is clearly a Cetagandan agent?"

Even Pitt was shocked to silence.

"The evidence is plain," Miles went on forcefully, raising his voice so all bystanders could hear. "He is a ringleader in your disruption. By example and guile he has corrupted the honest soldiers around him, set them one against another. You were Marilac's best. The Cetagandans could not count on your fall. So they planted a seed of evil among you. Just to make sure. And it worked—wonderfully well. You never suspected—"

Oliver grabbed Miles's ear and muttered, "Brother Miles—I know this guy. He's no Cetagandan agent. He's just one of a whole lot of—"

"Oliver," Miles hissed back through clenched teeth, "*shut up.*" And continued in his clearest parade-ground bellow, "Of course he's a Cetagandan spy. A mole. And all this time you thought this was something you were doing to *yourselves.*"

And where the devil does not exist, Miles thought to himself, *it may become expedient to invent him.* His stomach churned, but he kept his face set in righteous rage. He glanced at the faces around him. Not a few were as white as his must be, though for a different reason. A low mutter rose among them, partly bewildered, partly ominous.

"Pull off his shirt," Miles ordered, "and lay him down on his face. Suegar, give me your cup."

Suegar's plastic cup had a jagged point along its broken edge. Miles sat on Pitt's buttocks, and using the point as a stylus scratched the words

CETA

SPY

across Pitt's back in large print. He dug deep and ruthlessly, and the blood welled. Pitt screamed and swore and bucked.

Miles scrambled to his feet, shaking and breathless from more than just the physical exertion.

"Now," he ordered, "give him his rat bar and escort him to the exit."

Tris's teeth opened in objection, clicked back down. Her eyes burned into Pitt's back as he was hustled off. Her gaze turned rather more doubtfully to Miles, as she stood on one side of him and Oliver on the other.

"Do you really think he was a Cetagandan?" she asked Miles lowly.

"No way," scoffed Oliver. "What the hell's the charade all about, Brother Miles?"

"I don't doubt Tris's accusation of his other crimes," said Miles tightly. "You must know. But he couldn't be punished for them without dividing the camp, and so undermining Tris's authority. This way, Tris and the women have their revenge without half the men being set against them. The commandant's hands are clean, yet justice is done on a criminal, and a hard case who would doubtless be stockade bait outside is removed from under our feet. Furthermore, any like-minded souls are handed a warning they can't ignore. It works on every level."

Oliver's face had grown expressionless. After a silent moment he remarked, "You fight dirty, Brother Miles."

"I can't afford to lose." Miles shot him a black look from beneath his own lowered brows. "Can you?"

Oliver's lips tightened. "No."

Tris made no comment at all.

Miles personally oversaw the delivery of rat bars to all those prisoners too sick or weak or beaten to have attempted the chow line.

Colonel Tremont lay too still upon his mat, curled up, staring blankly. Oliver knelt and closed the drying, fixed eyes. The colonel might have died anytime in the last few hours.

"I'm sorry," said Miles sincerely. "Sorry I came so late."

"Well . . ." said Oliver, "well . . ." He stood, chewing on his lip, shook his head, and said no more. Miles and Suegar, Tris and Beatrice, helped Oliver carry the body, mat, clothes, cup and all, to the rubbish pile. Oliver shoved the rat bar he had reserved under the dead man's arm. No one attempted to strip the corpse after they had turned away, although another one stiffening there had already been so robbed, lying naked and tumbled.

They stumbled across Pitt's body shortly thereafter. The cause of death was most probably strangulation, but the face was so battered that its empurpling was not a certain clue.

Tris, squatting beside it, looked up at Miles in slow re-estimation. "I think you may be right about power after all, little man."

"And revenge?"

"I thought I could never get my fill of it," she sighed, contemplating the thing beside her. "Yeah . . . that too."

"Thank you." Miles prodded the body with his toe. "Make no mistake, *that* is a loss for our side."

Miles made Suegar let somebody else drag it to the rubbish pile.

Miles held a council of war immediately after chow call. Tremont's pallbearers, whom Miles had begun to think of as his general staff, and the fourteen group leaders gathered around him at a spot near the borders of the women's group. Miles paced back and forth before them, gesturing energetically.

"I commend the group leaders for an excellent job, and Sergeant Oliver for choosing them. By bringing this off, we have bought not only the allegiance of the greater part of the camp, but time as well. Each chow call after this should run a little easier, a little smoother, each become a real-life practice drill for the next.

"And make no mistake, this is a military exercise. We're at war again. We've already suckered the Cetagandans into breaking their carefully calculated routine and making a counter-move. We acted. They reacted. Strange as it may all seem to you, *we* had the offensive advantage.

"Now we start planning our next strategies. I want your thinking on what the next Cetagandan challenge will be." *Actually, I want you thinking, pe-*

riod. "So much for the sermon—Commandant Tris, take over." Miles forced himself to sit down cross-legged, yielding the floor to his chosen one whether she wanted it or not. He reminded himself that Tris had been a field officer, not a staff officer; she needed the practice more than he did.

"Of course, they can send in short piles again, like they did before," she began after clearing her throat. "It's been suggested that's how this mess got started in the first place." Her glance crossed Miles's, who nodded encouragingly. "This means we're going to have to start keeping head counts, and work out a strict rotation schedule in advance of people to divide their rations with the short-changed. Each group leader must choose a quartermaster and a couple of accountants to double-check his count."

"An equally disruptive move the Cetagandans may try," Miles couldn't help putting in, "is to send in an overstock, giving us the interesting problem of how to equitably divide the extras. I'd provide for that, too, if I were you." He smiled blandly up at Tris.

She raised an eyebrow at him, and continued. "They may also try dividing the chow pile, complicating our problem of capturing it so as to strictly control its re-distribution. Are there any other really dirty tricks any of you can anticipate?" She couldn't help glancing at Miles.

One of the group leaders raised his hand hesitantly. "Ma'am—they're listening to all this. Aren't we doing their thinking for them?"

Miles rose to answer that one, loud and clear. "Of course they're listening. We've doubtless got their quivering attention." He made a rude gesture dome-wards. "Let them. Every move they make is a message from outside, a shadow marking their shape, information about them. We'll take it."

"Suppose," said another group leader even more hesitantly, "they cut off our air again? Permanently?"

"Then," said Miles smoothly, "they lose their hard-won position one-up on the IJC, which they've gone to enormous trouble to gain. It's a propaganda coup they've been making much of lately, particularly since our side, in the stress of the way things are going back home, hasn't been able to maintain its own troops in style, let alone any captured Cetagandans. The Cetagandans, whose published view is that they're sharing their Imperial government with us out of cultural generosity, are claiming this as a demonstration of their superior civilization and good manners—"

Some jeers and catcalls marked the prisoners' view of this assertion, and Miles smiled and went on. "The death rate reported for this camp is so extraordinary, it's caught the IJC's attention. The Cetagandans have managed to account for it so far, through three separate IJC inspections, but 100% would be a bit extreme even for them to justify." A shiver of agreement, compressed rage, ran through his rapt listeners.

Miles sat again. Oliver leaned over to him to whisper, "How the hell did you come by all that information?"

Miles smirked. "Did it sound convincing? Good."

Oliver sat back, looking unnerved. "You don't have any inhibitions at all, do you?"

"Not in combat."

Tris and her group leaders spent the next two hours laying out chow call scenario flow charts, and their tactical responses at each branching. They broke up to let the group leaders pass it on to their chosen subordinates, and Oliver to his crew of supplementary Enforcers.

Tris paused before Miles, who had succumbed to gravity sometime during the second hour and now lay in the dirt staring somewhat blankly at the dome, blinking in an effort to keep his blurring eyes open. He had not slept in the day and a half before entering this place. He was not sure how much time had passed since then.

"I thought of one more scenario," Tris remarked. "What do we do if they do nothing at all? Do nothing, change nothing."

Miles smiled sleepily. "It seems most probable. That attempted double-cross on the last chow call was a slip on their part, I think."

"But in the absence of an enemy, how long can we go on pretending we're an army?" she persisted. "You scraped us up off the bottom for this. When it runs down at last, what then?"

Miles curled up on his side, drowning in weird and shapeless thoughts, and enticed by the hint of an erotic dream about a tall aggressive redhead. His yawn cracked his face. "Then we pray for a miracle. Remind me to discuss miracles with you . . . later. . . ."

He half-woke once when somebody shoved a sleeping mat under him. He gave Beatrice a sleepy bedroom smile.

"Crazy mutant," she snarled at him, and rolled him roughly onto the pad. "Don't you go thinking this was my idea."

"Why Suegar," Miles muttered, "I think she *likes* me." He cuddled back into the entwining limbs of the dream-Beatrice in fleeting peace.

To Miles's secret dismay, his analysis proved right. The Cetagandans returned to their original rat bar routine, unresponsive again to their prisoners' internal permutations. Miles was not sure he liked that. True, it gave him ample opportunity to fine-tune his distribution scheme. But some harassment from the

dome would have directed the prisoners' attention
outward, given them a foe again, above all broken
the paralyzing boredom of their lives. In the long
run, Tris must prove right.

"I hate an enemy who doesn't make mistakes,"
Miles muttered irritably, and flung his efforts into
events he could control.

He found a phlegmatic prisoner with a steady heart-
beat to lie in the dirt and count his own pulse, and
began timing distribution, and then working on reducing timing.

"It's a spiritual exercise," he announced when he
had his fourteen quartermasters start issuing the rat
bars 200 at a time, with thirty-minute breaks between groups.

"It's a change of pace," he explained in an aside to
Tris. "If we can't induce the Cetagandans to provide
some variety, we'll just have to do it ourselves." He
also finally got an accurate head count of the surviving prisoners. Miles was everywhere, exhorting, prod-
ding, pushing, restraining.

"If you really want it to go faster, make more
bleeding piles," Oliver protested.

"Don't blaspheme," said Miles, and went to work
inducing his groups to cart their rat bars away to
distribution piles spaced evenly around the perimeter.

At the end of the nineteenth chow call since he
had entered the camp, Miles judged his distribution
system complete and theologically correct. Calling
every two chow calls a "day," he had been there nine
days.

"I'm all done," he realized with a groan, "and it's
too early."

"Weeping because you have no more worlds to
conquer?" inquired Tris with a sarcastic grin.

By the thirty-second chow call, the system was
still running smoothly, but Miles was getting frayed.

"Welcome to the long haul," said Beatrice dryly. "You better start pacing yourself, Brother Miles. If what Tris says is true, we're going to be in here even longer because of you. I must remember to thank you for that properly sometime." She treated him to a threatening smirk, and Miles prudently remembered an errand on the opposite side of the camp.

She was right, Miles thought, depressed. Most prisoners here counted their captivity not in days and weeks, but months and years. He himself was likely to be gibbering nuts in a space of time that most of them would regard as a mere breath. He wondered glumly what form his madness would take, Manic, inspired by the glittering delusion that he was—say—the Conquerer of Komarr? Or depressive, like Tremont, curling up in himself until he was no one at all, a sort of human black hole?

Miracles. There had been leaders throughout history who had been wrong in their timing for armageddon, leading their shorn flocks up the mountain to await an apotheosis that never came. Their later lives were usually marked by obscurity and drinking problems. Nothing to drink in here. Miles wanted about six doubles, right now.

Now. Now. Now.

Miles took to walking the dome perimeter after each chow call, partly to make or at least pretend to inspection, partly to burn off a little of his uncomfortably accumulating nervous energy. It was getting harder and harder to sleep. There had been a period of quiet in the camp after the chow calls were successfully regulated, as if their ordering had been a crystal dropped in a supersaturated solution. But in the last few days the number of fistfights broken up by the Enforcers had risen. The Enforcers themselves were getting quicker to violence, acquiring a potentially unsavory swagger. Phases of the moon. Who could outrace the moon?

"Slow down, Miles," complained Suegar, ambling along beside him.

"Sorry." Miles restrained his stride and broke his self-absorption to look around. The glowing dome rose on his left hand, seeming to pulse to an unsettling hum just out of the range of his hearing. Quiet spread out on his right, groups of people mostly sitting. Not that much visible change since his first day in here. Maybe a little less tension, maybe a little more concerted care being taken of the injured or ill. Phases of the moon. He shook off his unease and smiled cheerfully at Suegar.

"You getting any more positive responses to your sermons these days?" Miles asked.

"Well—nobody tries to beat me up anymore," said Suegar. "But then, I haven't been preaching so often, being busy with the chow calls and all. And then, there are the Enforcers now. It's hard to say."

"You going to keep trying?"

"Oh, yes." Suegar paused. "I've seen worse places than this, y'know. I was at a mining camp once, when I was scarcely more than a kid. A fire gem strike. For a change, instead of one big company or the government muscling in, it had gotten divided up into hundreds and hundreds of little claims, usually about two meters square. Guys dug out there by hand, with trowels and whisk brooms—big fire gems are delicate, y'know, they'll shatter at a careless blow— they dug under the broiling sun, day after day. A lot of these guys had less clothes than us now. A lot of 'em didn't eat as good, or as regular. Working their butts off. More accidents, more disease than here. There were fights, too, in plenty.

"But they lived for the future. Performed the most incredible feats of physical endurance for hope, all voluntary. They were obsessed. They were—well, you remind me a lot of them. They wouldn't quit for *nothing*. They turned a mountain into a chasm in a year, with hand trowels. It was nuts. I loved it.

"This place," Suegar glanced around, "just makes me scared shitless." His right hand touched his rag rope bracelet. "It'll suck up your future, swallow you down—it's like death is just a formality, after that. Zombie town, suicide city. The day I stop trying, this place'll eat me."

"Mm," agreed Miles. They were nearing what Miles thought of as the farthest point of their circuit, across the camp from the women's group at whose now-permeable borders Miles and Suegar kept their sleeping mats.

A couple of men walking the perimeter from the opposite direction coalesced with another grey-pajama'd pair. As if casually and spontaneously, three more arose from their mats on Miles's right. He could not be sure without turning his head, but Miles thought he caught more peripheral motion closing in behind him.

The approaching four stopped a few meters in front of them. Miles and Suegar hesitated. Grey-clad men, all variously larger than Miles—who wasn't?—frowning, full of a fierce tension that arced to Miles and scree'd down his nerves. Miles recognized only one of them, an ex-surly brother he'd seen in Pitt's company. Miles didn't bother taking his eyes off Pitt's lieutenant to look around for Enforcers. For one thing, he was pretty sure one of the men in the company facing them *was* an Enforcer.

And the worst of it was, getting cornered—if you could call it that in here—was his own fault, for letting his movements fall into a predictable daily routine. A stupid, basic, beginner's mistake, that; inexcusable.

Pitt's lieutenant stepped forward, chewing on his lip, staring at Miles with hollowed eyes. *He's psyching himself up*, Miles realized. *If all he wanted was to beat me to a pulp, he could do it in his sleep*. The man slid a carefully-braided rag rope through his fingers. A strangling cord . . . no, it wasn't going to be another beating. This time, it was going to be premeditated murder.

"You," said Pitt's lieutenant hoarsely. "I couldn't figure you out at first. You're not one of us. You could never have been one of us. Mutant . . . You gave me the clue yourself. Pitt wasn't a Cetagandan spy. *You* are!" And lunged forward.

Miles dodged, overwhelmed by onslaught and insight. Damn, he'd known there must be a good reason scragging Pitt that way had felt so much like a mistake despite its efficiency. The false accusation was two-edged, as dangerous to its wielder as its victim—Pitt's lieutenant might even believe *his* accusation true—Miles had started a witch-hunt. Poetic justice, that he be its first victim, but where would it end? No wonder their captors hadn't interfered lately. Their silent Cetagandan watchers must be falling off their station chairs laughing right now—mistake piled on mistake, culminating here by dying stupidly like vermin at the hands of vermin in this verminous hole. . . .

Hands grabbed him; he contorted spasmodically, kicking out, but only half-broke their hold. Beside him Suegar whirled, kicked, struck, shouted with demonic energy. He had reach, but lacked mass. Miles lacked both reach and mass. Still Suegar managed to break an assailant's hold on Miles for a moment.

Suegar's left arm, lashing out for a backhand blow, was caught and locked. Miles winced in sympathetic anticipation of the familiar muffled crack of breaking bones, but instead the man stripped off the rag rope bracelet from Suegar's wrist.

"Hey, Suegar!" the man taunted, dancing backward. "Look what I got!"

Suegar's head swivelled, his attention wrenched from his determined defense of Miles. The man peeled the wrinkled, tattered piece of paper from its cloth covering and waved it in the air. Suegar cried out in dismay and started to plunge toward him, but found himself blocked by two other bodies. The man tore the paper in half twice, then paused, as if momentarily puzzled how to dispose of it—then, with a sudden grin, stuffed the pieces in his mouth and started chewing. Suegar screamed.

"Dammit," cried Miles furiously, "it was me you wanted! You didn't have to do that—" He jammed his fist with all his strength into the smirking face of the nearest attacker, whose attention had been temporarily distracted by Suegar's show.

He could feel his bones shatter all the way back through his wrist. He was so damn *tired* of the bones, tired of being hurt again and again. . . .

Suegar was screaming and sobbing and trying to gain on the paper chewer, who stood and chewed on through his grin. Suegar had lost all science in his attack, flailing like a windmill. Miles saw him go down, then had no attention left for anything but the anaconda coil of the strangling cord, settling over his own neck. He managed to get one hand between the cord and his throat, but it was the broken one. Cables of pain shuddered up his arm, seeming to burrow under his skin all the way to his shoulder. The pressure in his head mounted to bursting, closing down his vision. Dark purple and yellow moire-patterned clouds boiled up in his eyes like thunder heads. A flashing brush of red hair sizzled past his tunneling vision. . . .

He was on the ground then, with blood, wonderful blood, thudding back into his oxygen-starved brain. It hurt good, hot and pulsing. He lay for a moment not caring about anything else. It would be so good not to have to get up again. . . .

The damn dome, cold and white and featureless, mocked his returning vision. Miles jerked onto his knees, staring around wildly. Beatrice, some Enforcers, and some of Oliver's commando buddies were chasing Miles's would-be assassins across the camp. Miles had probably only passed out for a few seconds. Suegar lay on the ground a couple of meters off.

Miles crawled over to Suegar. The thin man lay curled up around his stomach, his face pale green and clammy, involuntary shivers coursing through his body. Not good. Shocky. Keep patient warm and administer synergine. No synergine. Miles peeled clumsily out of his tunic and laid it over Suegar. "Suegar? You all right? Beatrice chased the barbarians off . . ."

Suegar looked up and smiled briefly, but the smile was reabsorbed almost immediately by distancing pain.

Beatrice came back eventually, mussed and breathing heavily. "You loonies," she greeted them dispassionately. "You don't need a bodyguard, you need a bloody keeper." She flopped onto her knees beside Miles to stare at Suegar. Her lips thinned to a white slit. She glanced at Miles, her eyes darkening, the creases between her brows deepening.

I've changed my mind, Miles thought. *Don't*

*start caring for me, Beatrice, don't start caring for
anybody. You'll only get hurt. Over and over and
over . . .*

"You better come back to my group," said Beatrice.

"I don't think Suegar can walk."

Beatrice rounded up some muscle, and the thin
man was rolled onto a sleeping mat and carried, too
much like Colonel Tremont's corpse for Miles's taste,
back to their now-usual sleeping place.

"Find a doctor for him," Miles demanded.

Beatrice came back, strong-arming an angry, older
woman.

"He's probably got a busted belly," snarled the
doctor. "If I had a diagnostic viewer, I could tell you
just what was busted. You got a diagnostic viewer?
He needs synergine and plasma. You got any? I
could cut him, and glue him back together, and
speed his healing with electra-stim, if I had an operating theatre. Put him back on his feet in three days,
no sweat. You got an operating theatre? I thought
not.

"Stop looking at me like that. I used to think I was
a healer. It took this place to teach me I was nothing
but an interface between the technology and the
patient. Now the technology is gone, and I'm just
nothing."

"But what can we do?" asked Miles.

"Cover him up. In a few days he'll either get
better or die, depending on what got busted. That's
all." She paused, standing with folded arms and regarding Suegar with rancor, as if his injury was a
personal affront. And so it was, for her: another load
of grief and failure, grinding her hard-won healer's
pride into the dirt. "I think he's going to die," she
added.

"I think so too," said Miles.

"Then what did you want me for?" She stomped off.

Later she came back with a sleeping mat and a couple of extra rags, and helped put them around and over Suegar for added insulation, then stomped off again.

Tris reported to Miles. "We got those guys who tried to kill you rounded up. What do you want done with 'em?"

"Let them go," said Miles wearily. "They're not the enemy."

"The hell they're not!"

"They're not my enemies, anyway. It was just a case of mistaken identity. I'm just a hapless traveller, passing through."

"Wake up, little man. I don't happen to share Oliver's belief in your 'miracle.' You're not passing through here. This is the last stop."

Miles sighed. "I'm beginning to think you're right." He glanced at Suegar, breathing shallowly and too fast, beside whom he crouched in watch. "You're almost certainly right, by this time. Nevertheless— let them go."

"Why?" she wailed, outraged.

"Because I said to. Because I asked you to. Would you have me beg for them?"

"Aargh! No. All right!" She wheeled away, running her hands through her clipped hair and muttering under her breath.

A timeless time passed. Suegar lay on his side not speaking, though his eyes flicked open now and then to stare unseeing. Miles moistened his lips with water periodically. A chow call came and went without incident or Miles's participation; Beatrice passed by and dropped two rat bars beside them, stared at them with a carefully-hardened gaze of general disapproval, and stalked off.

Miles cradled his injured hand and sat cross-legged, mentally reviewing the catalogue of errors that had brought him to this pass. He contemplated his seeming genius for getting his friends killed. He had a sick premonition that Suegar's death was going to be almost as bad as Sergeant Bothari's, six years ago, and he had known Suegar only weeks, not years. Repeated pain, as he had reason to know, made one more afraid of injury, not less, a growing, gut-wrenching dread. Not again, never again . . .

He lay back and stared at the dome, the white, unblinking eye of a dead god. And had more friends than he knew already been killed by this megalomanic escapade? It would be just like the Cetagandans, to leave him in here all unknowing, and let the growing doubt and fear gradually drive him crazy.

Swiftly drive him crazy—the god's eye blinked.

Miles blinked in sympathetic nervous recoil, opened his eyes wide, stared at the dome as if his eyes could bore right through it. Had it blinked? Had the flicker been hallucinatory? Was he losing it?

It flickered again. Miles shot to his feet, inhaling, inhaling, inhaling.

The dome blinked out. For a brief instant, planetary night swept in, fog and drizzle and the kiss of a cold wet wind. This planet's unfiltered air smelled like rotten eggs. The unaccustomed dark was blinding.

"CHOW CALL!" Miles screamed at the top of his lungs.

Then limbo transmuted to chaos in the brilliant flash of a smart bomb going off beyond a cluster of buildings. Red light glared off the underside of an enormous billowing cloud of debris, blasting upward.

A racketing string of similar hits encircled the camp, peeled back the night, deafened the unprotected. Miles, still screaming, could not hear his own voice. A returning fire from the ground clawed the clouds with lines of colored light.

Tris, her eyes stunned, rocketed past him. Miles grabbed her by the arm with his good hand and dug in his heels to brake her, yanking her down so he could scream in her ear.

"This is it! Get the fourteen group leaders organized, make 'em get their first blocks of 200 lined up and waiting all around the perimeter. Find Oliver, we've *got* to get the Enforcers moving to get the rest waiting their turn under control. If this goes exactly as we drilled it, we'll all get off." *I hope.* "But if they mob the shuttles like they used to mob the rat bar pile, none of us will. You copy?"

"I never believed—I didn't think—*shuttles?*"

"You don't have to think. We've drilled this fifty times. Just follow the chow drill. The *drill!*"

"You *sneaky* little sonofabitch!" The acknowledging wave of her arm, as she dashed off, was very like a salute.

A string of flares erupted in the sky above the camp, as if a white strobe of lightning went on and on, casting a ghastly illumination on the scene below. The camp seethed like a termite mound kicked over. Men and women were running every which way in shouting confusion. Not exactly the orderly vision Miles had had in mind—why, for example, had his people chosen a night drop and not a daytime one?—he would grill his staff later on that point, after he got done kissing their feet—

"Beatrice!" Miles waved her down. "Start passing the word! We're doing the chow call drill. But instead of a rat bar, each person gets a shuttle seat.

Make 'em understand that—don't let anybody go haring off into the night or they'll miss their flight. Then come back here and stay by Suegar. I don't want him getting lost or trampled on. *Guard*, you copy?"

"I'm not a damn dog. What shuttles?"

The sound Miles's ears had been straining for penetrated the din at last, a high-pitched, multi-faceted whine that grew louder and louder. They loomed down out of the boiling scarlet-tinged clouds like monstrous beetles, carapaced and winged, feet extending even as they watched. Fully armored combat drop shuttles, two, three, six . . . seven, eight . . . Mile's lips moved as he counted. Thirteen, fourteen, by God. They *had* managed to get #B-7 out of the shop in time.

Miles pointed. "*My* shuttles."

Beatrice stood with her mouth open, staring upward. "My God. They're beautiful." He could almost see her mind start to ratchet forward. "But they're not *ours*. Not Cetagandan either. Who the hell . . . ?"

Miles bowed. "This is a paid political rescue."

"*Mercenaries?*"

"We're not something wriggling with too many legs that you found in your sleeping bag. The proper tone of voice is *Mercenaries!*—with a glad cry."

"But—but—but—"

"*Go,* dammit. Argue *later.*"

She flung up her hands and ran.

Miles himself started tackling every person within reach, passing on the order of the day. He captured one of Oliver's tall commando buddies and demanded a boost on his shoulders. A quick look around showed fourteen coagulating knots of people in the mob scattered around the perimeter in nearly the right positions. The shuttles hovered, engines howling, then thumped to the ground one by one all around the camp.

"It'll have to do," Miles muttered to himself. He slapped the commando's shoulder. "Down."

He forced himself to walk to the nearest shuttle, a run on the shuttles being just the scenario he had poured out blood and bone and pride these last— three, four?—weeks to avoid.

A quartet of fully-armed and half-armored troops were the first down the shuttle ramp, taking up guard positions. Good. They even had their weapons pointed in the right direction, toward the prisoners they were here to rescue. A larger patrol, fully armored, followed to gallop off double time, leapfrogging their own covering-fire range into the dark toward the Cetagandan installations surrounding the dome circle. Hard to judge which direction held the most danger—from the continuing fireworks, his fighter shuttles were providing plenty of external distraction for the Cetagandans.

At last came the man Miles most wanted to see, the shuttle's comm officer.

"Lieutenant, uh," he connected face and name, "Murka! Over here!"

Murka spotted him. He fumbled excitedly with his equipment and called into his audio pick-up, "Commodore Tung! He's *here*, I *got* him!"

Miles peeled the comm set ruthlessly from the lieutenant's head, who obligingly ducked down to permit the theft, and jammed it on his own head left-handed in time to hear Tung's voice reply tinnily, "Well, for God's sake don't lose him again, Murka. Sit on him if you have to."

"I want my staff," called Miles into the pick-up. "Have you retrieved Elli and Elena yet? How much time have we got for this?"

"Yes, sir, no, and about two hours—if we're lucky," Tung's voice snapped back. "Good to have you back aboard, Admiral Naismith."

"You're telling me . . . Get Elena and Elli. Priority One."

"Working. Tung out."

Miles turned to find that the rat bar group leader in this section had actually succeeded in marshalling his first group of 200, and was engaged in making the second 200 sit back down in a block to wait their turns. Excellent. The prisoners were being channeled up the ramp one at a time through a strange gauntlet. A mercenary slit the back of each grey tunic with a swift slice from a vibra-knife. A second mercenary slapped each prisoner across the back with a medical stunner. A third made a pass with a surgical hand-tractor, roughly ripping out the Cetagandan serial numbers encoded beneath the skin. He didn't bother to waste time on bandaging after. "Go to the front and sit five across, go to the front and sit five across, go to the front . . ." he chanted, droning in time to his hypnotically moving device.

Miles's sometime-adjutant Captain Thorne appeared, hurrying out of the glare and black shadows, flanked by one of the fleet's ship's surgeons and—praise be—a soldier carrying some of Miles's clothes, and boots. Miles dove for the boots, but was captured instead by the surgeon.

She ran a med stunner between his bare uneven shoulderblades, and zipped a hand-tractor across in its path.

"Ow!" Miles yelped. "Couldn't you wait one bleeding second for the stun to cut in?" The pain faded rapidly to numbness as Miles's left hand patted for the damage. "What's this all about?"

"Sorry, sir," said the surgeon insincerely. "Stop

that, your fingers are dirty." She applied a plastic bandage. Rank hath its privileges. "Captain Bothari-Jesek and Commander Quinn learned something from their fellow Cetagandan prison monitors that we hadn't known before you went in. These encodes are permeated with drug beads, whose lipid membranes are kept aligned by a low-power magnetic field the Cetagandans were generating in the dome. An hour out of the dome, and the membranes start to break down, releasing a poison. About four hours later the subject dies—very unpleasantly. A little insurance against escapes, I guess."

Miles shuddered, and said faintly, "I see." He cleared his throat, and added more loudly, "Captain Thorne, mark a commendation—with *highest* honors —to Commander Elli Quinn and Captain Elena Bothari-Jesek. The, ah, our employer's intelligence service didn't even have that one. In fact, our employer's intelligence data lacked on a truly vast number of points. I shall have to speak to them—sharply —when I present the bill for this expanded operation. Before you put that away, doctor, numb my hand, please." Miles stuck out his right hand for the surgeon's inspection.

"Did it again, did you?" muttered the surgeon. "I'd think you'd learn . . ." A pass with the medical stunner, and Miles's swollen hand disappeared from his senses entirely, nothing left from the wrist down. Only his eyes assured him it was still attached to his arm.

"Yes, but will they pay for the expanded operation?" asked Captain Thorne anxiously. "This started out as a one-shot lightning strike to hook out one guy, just the sort of thing little outfits like us specialize in—now it's straining the whole Dendarii fleet. These damn prisoners outnumber *us* two to one.

This wasn't in the original contract. What if our perennial mystery employer decides to stiff us?"

"They won't," said Miles. "My word. But—there's no doubt I'll have to deliver the bill in person."

"God help them, then," muttered the surgeon, and took herself off to continue pulling encodes from the waiting prisoners.

Commodore Ky Tung, a squat, middle-aged Eurasian in half-armor and a command channel headset, turned up at Miles's elbow as the first shuttles loaded with prisoners clapped their locks shut and screamed up into the black fog. They took off in first-come first-served positions, no waiting. Knowing Tung's passion for tight formations, Miles judged time must be their most dangerous limiting factor.

"What are we loading these guys onto, upstairs?" Miles asked Tung.

"We gutted a couple of used freighters. We can cram about 5,000 in the holds of each. The ride out is going to be fast and nasty. They'll all have to lie down and breathe as little as possible."

"What are the Cetagandans scrambling to catch us?"

"Right now, barely more than some police shuttles. Most of their local space military contingent just happens to be on the other side of their sun just now, which is why we just happened to pick this moment to drop by . . . we had to wait for their practice maneuvers again, in case you were starting to wonder what was keeping us. In other words, the same scenario as our original plan to pull Colonel Tremont."

"Except expanded by a factor of 10,000. And we've got to get in—what, four lifts? instead of one," said Miles.

"Yeah, but get this," grinned Tung. "They sited

these prison camps on this miserable outpost planet so's they wouldn't have to expend troops and equipment guarding them—counted on distance from Marilac, and the downgearing of the war there, to discourage rescue attempts. But in the period since you went in, half of their original guard complement has been pulled to other hot spots. Half!"

"They were relying on the dome." Miles eyed him. "And for the bad news?" he murmured.

Tung's smile soured. "This round, our total time window is only two hours."

"Ouch. Half their local space fleet is still too many. And they'll be back in two hours?"

"One hour, forty minutes, now." A sidewise flick of Tung's eyes betrayed the location of his ops clock, holovid-projected by his command headset into the air at a corner of his vision.

Miles did a calculation in his head, and lowered his voice. "Are we going to be able to lift the last load?"

"Depends on how fast we can lift the first three," said Tung. His ordinarily stoic face was more unreadable than ever, betraying neither hope nor fear.

Which depends in turn on how effectively I managed to drill them all . . . What was done was done; what was coming was not yet. Miles wrenched his attention to the immediate now.

"Have you found Elli and Elena yet?"

"I have three patrols out searching."

He hadn't found them yet. Miles's guts tightened. "I wouldn't have even attempted to expand this operation in midstream if I hadn't known they were monitoring me, and could translate all those oblique hints back into orders."

"Did they get 'em all right?" asked Tung. "We argued over some of their interpretations of your double-talk on the vids."

Miles glanced around. "They got 'em right . . . you got vids of all this?" A startled wave of Miles's hand took in the circle of the camp.

"Of you, anyway. Right off the Cetagandan monitors. They burst-transmitted them all daily. Very—er—entertaining, sir," Tung added blandly.

Some people would find entertainment in watching someone swallow slugs, Miles reflected. "Very dangerous . . . when was your last communication with them?"

"Yesterday." Tung's hand clamped on Miles's arm, restraining an involuntary leap. "You can't do better than my three patrols, sir, and I haven't any to spare to go looking for *you*."

"Yah, yah." Miles slapped his right fist into his left palm in frustration before remembering that was a bad idea. His two co-agents, his vital link between the dome and the Dendarii, missing. The Cetagandans shot spies with depressing consistency. After, usually, a series of interrogations that rendered death a welcome release. . . . He tried to reassure himself with logic. If they'd blown their covers as Cetagandan monitor techs, and been interrogated, Tung would have run into a meat grinder here. He hadn't, ergo, they hadn't. Of course, they might have been killed by friendly fire, just now. . . . Friends. He had too many friends to stay sane in this crazy business.

"You," Miles retrieved his clothes from the still-waiting soldier, "go over there," he pointed, "and find a redhaired lady named Beatrice and an injured man named Suegar. Bring them to me. Carry him carefully, he has internal injuries."

The soldier saluted and marched off. Ah, the pleasure again of being able to give a command without having to follow it up with a supporting theological argument. Miles sighed. Exhaustion waited to swallow him, lurking at the edge of his adrenalin-spurred bubble of hyperconsciousness. All the factors—shuttles, timing, the approaching enemy, distance to the getaway jump point, formed and reformed in all their possible permutations in his mind. Small variations in timing in particular multiplied into major troubles. But he'd known it would be like this back when he'd started. A miracle they'd got this far. No—he glanced at Tung, at Thorne—not a miracle, but the extraordinary initiative and devotion of his people. *Well done, oh, well done. . . .*

Thorne helped him as he fumbled to dress himself one-handed. "Where the hell is my command headset?" Miles asked.

"We were told you were injured, sir, and in a state of exhaustion. You were scheduled for immediate evacuation."

"Damn presumptuous of somebody . . ." Miles bit back ire. No place in this schedule for running errands topside. Besides, if he had his headset, he'd be tempted to start giving orders, and he wasn't yet sufficiently briefed on the internal complexities of the operation from the Dendarii fleet's point of view. Miles swallowed his observer status without further comment. It did free him for rear guard.

Miles's batman reappeared, with Beatrice and four drafted prisoners, carrying Suegar on his mat to lay at Miles's feet.

"Get my surgeon," Miles said. His soldier obediently trotted off and found her. She knelt beside the semi-conscious Suegar and pulled the encode from his back. A knot of tension unwound in Miles's neck at the reassuring hiss of a hypospray of synergine.

"How bad?" Miles demanded.

"Not good," the surgeon admitted, checking her diagnostic viewer. "Burst spleen, oozing hemorrhage in the stomach—this one had better go direct to surgery on the command ship. Medtech—" she motioned to a Dendarii waiting with the guards for the return of the shuttle, and gave triage instructions. The medtech swathed Suegar in a thin foil heat wrap.

"I'll make sure he gets there," promised Miles. He shivered, envying the heat wrap a little as the drizzly acid fog beaded in his hair and coiled into his bones.

Tung's expression and attention were abruptly absorbed by a message from his comm set. Miles, who had yielded Lieutenant Murka's headset back to him so that he might continue his duties, shifted from foot to foot in agony for news. *Elena, Elli, if I've killed you* . . .

Tung spoke into his pick-up. "Good. Well done. Report to the A7 drop site." A jerk of his chin switched channels. "Sim, Nout, fall back with your patrols to your shuttle drop site perimeters. They've been found."

Miles found himself bent over with his hand supported on gelid knees, waiting for his head to clear, his heart lurching in huge slow gulps. "Elli and Elena? Are they all right?"

"They didn't call for a medtech . . . you sure you don't need one yourself? You're green."

"I'm all right." Miles's heart steadied, and he straightened up, to meet Beatrice's questing eyes. "Beatrice, would you please go get Tris and Oliver for me? I need to talk to them before the next shuttle relay goes up."

She shook her head helplessly and wheeled away. She did not salute. On the other hand, she didn't argue, either. Miles was insensibly cheered.

The booming racket around the dome circle had died down to the occasional whine of small-arms fire, human cry, or blurred amplified voice. Fires burned in the distance, red-orange glows in the muffling fog. Not a surgically clean operation . . . the Cetagandans were going to be extremely pissed when they'd counted their casualties, Miles judged. Time to be gone, and long gone. He tried to keep the poisoned encodes in mind, as anodyne to the vision of Cetagandan clerks and techs crushed in the rubble of their burning buildings, but the two nightmares seemed to amplify instead of cancelling each other out.

Here came Tris and Oliver, both looking a little wild-eyed. Beatrice took up station at Tris's right shoulder.

"Congratulations," Miles began, before they could speak. He had a lot of ground to cover and not much time left. "You have achieved an army." A wave of his arm swept the orderly array of prisoners—ex-prisoners—spread across the camp in their shuttle groups. They waited quietly, most seated on the ground. Or was it the Cetagandans who had ingrained such patience in them? Whatever.

"Temporarily," said Tris. "This is the lull, I believe. If things hot up, if you lose one or more shuttles, if somebody panics and it spreads—"

"You can tell anybody who's inclined to panic they can ride up with me if it'll make them feel better. Ah—better also mention that I'm going up in the *last* load," said Miles.

Tung, dividing his attention between this confab and his headset, grimaced in exasperation at this news.

"That'll settle 'em," grinned Oliver.

"Give them something to think about, anyway," conceded Tris.

"Now I'm going to give you something to think about. The new Marilac resistance. You're it," said

Miles. "My employer originally engaged me to rescue Colonel Tremont, that he might raise a new army and carry on the fight. When I found him . . . as he was, dying, I had to decide whether to follow the letter of my contract, and deliver a catatonic or a corpse, or the spirit—and deliver an army. I chose this, and I chose you two. *You* must carry on Colonel Tremont's work."

"I was only a field lieutenant," began Tris in horror, in chorus with Oliver's, "I'm a grunt, not a staff officer. Colonel Tremont was a genius—"

"You are his heirs now. *I* say so. Look around you. Do I make mistakes in choosing my subordinates?"

After a moment's silence Tris muttered, "Apparently not."

"Build yourselves a staff. Find your tactics geniuses, your technical wizards, and put 'em to work for you. But the drive, and the decisions, and the direction, must be yours, forged in this pit. It is you two who will remember this place, and so remember what it is you are doing, and why, always."

Oliver spoke quietly. "And when do we muster out of this army, Brother Miles? My time was up during the siege of Fallow Core. If I'd been anywhere else, I could have gone home."

"Until the Cetagandan army of occupation rolled down your street."

"Even then. The odds aren't good."

"The odds were worse for Barrayar, in its day, and they ran the Cetagandans right off. It took twenty years, and more blood than either of you have seen in your lives combined, but they did it," asserted Miles.

Oliver seemed more struck by this historical precedent than Tris, who said skeptically, "Barrayar had those crazy Vor warriors. Nuts who rushed into battle, who *liked* to die. Marilac just doesn't have that sort of cultural tradition. We're civilized—or we were, once. . . ."

"Let me tell you about the Barrayaran Vor," cut in Miles. "The loonies who sought a glorious death in battle found it very early on. This rapidly cleared the chain of command of the accumulated fools. The survivors were those who learned to fight dirty, and live, and fight another day, and win, and win, and win, and for whom nothing, not comfort, or security, not family or friends or their immortal souls, was more important than winning. Dead men are losers by definition. Survival and victory. They weren't supermen, or immune to pain. They sweated in confusion and darkness. And with not one-half the physical resources Marilac possesses even now, they won. When you're Vor," Miles ran down a little, "there is no mustering out."

After a silence Tris said, "Even a volunteer patriotic army must eat. And we won't beat the Cetagandans by firing spitballs at them."

"There will be financial and military aid forthcoming through a covert channel other than myself. If there is a Resistance command to deliver it to."

Tris measured Oliver by eye. The fire in her burned closer to the surface than Miles had ever seen it, coursing down those corded muscles. The whine of the first returning shuttles pierced the fog. She spoke quite softly. "And here I thought I was the atheist, Sergeant, and you were the believer. Are you coming with me—or mustering out?"

Oliver's shoulders bowed. With the weight of history, Miles realized, not defeat, for the heat in his eyes matched Tris's. "Coming," he grunted.

Miles caught Tung's eyes. "How we doing?"

Tung shook his head, held up fingers. "About six minutes slow, unloading upstairs."

"Right." Miles turned back to Tris and Oliver. "I want you both to go up on this wave, in separate shuttles, one to each troopship. When you get there, start expediting the off-loading of your people. Lieutenant Murka will give you your shuttle assignment—" he motioned Murka over, and packed them off.

Beatrice lingered. "I'm inclined to panic," she informed Miles in a distant tone. Her bare toe smudged whorls in the dampening dirt.

"I don't need a bodyguard anymore," Miles said. He grinned. "A keeper, maybe . . ."

A smile lighted her eyes that did not yet reach her mouth. Later, Miles promised himself. Later, he would make that mouth laugh.

The second wave of shuttles began to lift, even as the remnants of the returning first wave were still landing. Miles prayed everyone's sensors were operating properly, passing each other in this fog. Their timing could only get more ragged from now on. The fog itself was coagulating into a cold rain, silver needles pelting down.

The focus of the operation was narrowing rapidly now, more of machines and numbers and timing, less of loyalties and souls and fearsome obligations. An emotionally pathological mind, devoid of love and fear, might even call it fun, Miles thought. He began jotting scores left-handed in the dirt, numbers up, down, in transit, remaining, but the dirt was turning to gluey black mud and did not retain the impressions.

"Shit," Tung hissed suddenly through clenched teeth. The air before his face blurred in a flurry of vid-projected incoming information, his eyes flicking through it with practiced rapidity. His right hand bunched and twitched, as if tempted to wrench off his headset and stamp it into the mud in frustration and disgust. "That tears it. We just lost two shuttles out of the second wave."

Which two? Miles's mind screamed. *Oliver, Tris
. . .* He forced his first question to be, "How?" *I
swear, if they crashed into each other, I'm going to
go find a wall and beat my head on it till I go
numb. . . .*

"Cetagandan fighter broke through our cordon.
He was going for the troop freighters, but we nailed
him in time. Almost in time."

"You got identifications on which two shuttles?
And were they loaded or returning?"

Tung's lips moved in subvocalization. "A-4, fully
loaded. B-7, returning empty. Loss total, no survivors. Fighter shuttle 5 from the *Triumph* is disabled
by enemy fire; pilot recovery now in progress."

He hadn't lost his commanders. His hand-picked
and carefully nurtured successors to Colonel Tremont
were safe. He opened his eyes, squeezed shut in
pain, to find Beatrice, to whom the shuttle IDs meant
nothing, waiting anxiously for interpretation.

"Two hundred dead?" she whispered.

"Two hundred six," Miles corrected. The faces,
names, voices of the six familiar Dendarii fluttered
through his memory. The 200 ciphers must have had
faces too. He blocked them out, as too crushing an
overload.

"These things happen," Beatrice muttered numbly.
"You all right?"

"Of course I'm all right. These things happen.
Inevitable. I am not a weepy wimp who folds under
fire." She blinked rapidly, lifting her chin. "Give me
. . . something to do. Anything."

Quickly, Miles added for her. *Right.* He pointed
across the camp. "Go to Pel and Liant. Divide their
remaining shuttle groups into blocks of thirty-three,
and add them to each of the remaining third-wave
shuttle groups. We'll have to send the third wave up

over-loaded. Then report back to me. Go quick, the rest will be back in minutes."

"Yessir," she saluted. For her sake, not his; for order, structure, rationality, a lifeline. He returned the salute gravely.

"They were already overloaded," objected Tung as soon as she was out of earshot. "They're going to fly like bricks with 233 squeezed on board. And they'll take longer to load on here and unload topside."

"Yes. God." Miles gave up scratching figures in the useless mud. "Run the numbers through the computer for me, Ky. I don't trust myself to add two and two just now. How far behind will we be by the time the main body of the Cetagandans comes in range? Come close as you can, no fudge factors, please."

Tung mumbled into his headset, reeled off numbers, margins, timing. Miles tracked every detail with predatory intensity. Tung concluded bluntly. "At the end of the last wave, five shuttles are still going to be waiting to unload when the Cetagandan fire fries us."

A thousand men and women . . .

"May I respectfully suggest, sir, that the time has come to start cutting our losses?" added Tung.

"You may, Commodore."

"Option One, maximally efficient; only drop seven shuttles in the last wave. Leave the last five shuttle loads of prisoners on the ground. They'll be re-taken, but at least they'll be alive." Tung's voice grew persuasive on this last line.

"Only one problem, Ky. *I* don't want to stay here."

"You can still be on the last shuttle up, just like you said. By the way, sir, have I expressed myself yet, sir, on what a genuinely dumbshit piece of grandstanding that is?"

"Eloquently, with your eyebrows, a while ago. And while I'm inclined to agree with you, have you noticed yet how closely the remaining prisoners keep watching me? Have you ever watched a cat sneaking up on a horned hopper?"

Tung stirred uneasily, eyes taking in the phenomenon Miles described.

"I don't fancy gunning down the last thousand in order to get my shuttle into the air."

"Skewed as we are, they might not realize there were no more shuttles coming till after you were in the air."

"So we just leave them standing there, waiting for us?" *The sheep look up, but are not fed* . . .

"Right."

"You like that option, Ky?"

"Makes me want to puke, but—consider the 9,000 others. And the Dendarii fleet. The idea of dropping them all down the rat hole in a pre-doomed effort to pack up all these—miserable sinners of yours, makes me want to puke a lot more. Nine-tenths of a loaf is *much* better than none."

"Point taken. Let us go on to option two, please. The flight out of orbit is calculated on the speed of the slowest ship, which is . . . ?"

"The freighters."

"And the *Triumph* remains the swiftest?"

"Betcher ass." Tung had captained the *Triumph* once.

"And the best armored."

"Yo. So?" Tung saw perfectly well where he was being driven. His obtuseness was but a form of oblique balking.

"So. The first seven shuttles up on the last wave lock onto the troop freighters and boost on schedule. We call back five of the *Triumph*'s fighter pilots and dump and destroy their craft. One's damaged already, right? The last five of these drop shuttles clamp to the *Triumph* in their place, protected from the now-arriving fire of the Cetagandan ships by the *Triumph's* full shielding. Pack the prisoners into the *Triumph's* corridors, lock shuttle hatches, boost like hell."

"The added mass of a thousand people—"

"Would be less than that of a couple of the drop shuttles. Dump and blow them too, if you have to, to fit the mass/acceleration window."

"—would overload life support—"

"The emergency oxygen will take us to the wormhole jump point. After Jump the prisoners can be distributed among the other ships at our leisure."

Tung's voice grew anguished. "Those combat drop shuttles are *brand new*. And my fighters—*five* of them—do you realize how hard it will be to recoup the funds to replace 'em? It comes to—"

"I asked you to calculate the time, Ky, not the price tag," said Miles through his teeth. He added more quietly, "I'll tack them on to our bill for services rendered."

"You ever hear the term *cost overrun*, boy? You will. . . ." Tung switched his attention back to his headset, itself but an extension of the tactics room aboard the *Triumph*. Calculations were made, new orders entered and executed.

"It flies," sighed Tung. "Buys a damned expensive fifteen minutes. If nothing else goes wrong . . ." he trailed off in a frustrated mumble, as impatient as Miles himself with his inability to be three places at once.

"There comes my shuttle back," Tung noted aloud. He glanced at Miles, plainly unwilling to leave his admiral to his own devices, as plainly itching to be out of the acid rain and dark and mud and closer to the nerve center of operations.

"Get gone," said Miles. "You can't ride up with me anyway, it's against procedure."

"Procedure, hah," said Tung blackly.

With the lift-off of the third wave, there were barely 2,000 prisoners left on the ground. Things were thinning out, winding down; the armored combat patrols were falling back now from their penetration of the surrounding Cetagandan installations, back toward their assigned shuttle landing sites. A dangerous turning of the tide, should some surviving Cetagandan officer recover enough organization to harry their retreat.

"See you aboard the *Triumph*," Tung emphasized. He paused to brace Lieutenant Murka, out of Miles's earshot. Miles grinned in sympathy for the overworked lieutenant, in no doubt about the orders Tung was now laying on him. If Murka didn't come back with Miles in tow, he'd probably be wisest not to come back at all.

Nothing left now but a little last waiting. Hurry up and wait. Waiting, Miles realized, was very bad for him. It allowed his self-generated adrenalin to wear off, allowed him to feel how tired and hurt he really was. The illuminating flares were dying to a red glow.

There was really very little time between the fading of the labored thunder of the last third wave shuttle to depart, and the screaming whine of the first fourth-wave shuttle plunging back. Alas that this had more to do with being skewed than being swift. The Marilacans still waited in their rat bar blocks, discipline still holding. Of course, nobody'd told them about the little problem in timing they faced. But the nervous Dendarii patrols, chivvying them up the ramps, kept things moving at a pace to Miles's taste. Rear guard was never a popular position to draw, even among the lunatic fringe who defaced their weapons with notches and giggled among themselves while speculating upon newer and more grotesque methods of blowing away their enemies.

Miles saw the semi-conscious Suegar carried up the ramp first. Suegar would actually reach the *Triumph*'s sickbay faster in his company, Miles calculated, on this direct flight, than had he been sent on an earlier shuttle to one of the troop freighters and had to await a safe moment to transfer.

The arena they were leaving had grown silent and dark, sodden and sad, ghostly. *I will break the doors of hell, and bring up the dead . . .* there was something not quite right about the half-remembered quote. No matter.

This shuttle's armored patrol, the last, drew back out of the fog and darkness, electronically whistled in like a pack of sheepdogs by their master Murka, who stood at the foot of the ramp as liaison between the ground patrol and the shuttle pilot, who was expressing her anxiety to be gone with little whining revs on the engines.

Then from the darkness—plasma fire, sizzling through the rain-sodden, saturated air. Some Cetagandan hero—officer, troop, tech, who knew?—had crawled up out of the rubble and found a weapon— and an enemy to fire it at. Splintered afterimages, red and green, danced in Miles's eyes. A Dendarii patroller rolled out of the dark, a glowing line across the back of his armor smoking and sparking until quenched in the black mud. His armor legs seized up, and he lay wriggling like a frantic fish in an effort to peel out of it. A second plasma burst, ill-aimed,

spent itself turning a few kilometers of fog and rain
to superheated steam on a straight line to some
unknown infinity.

Just what they needed, to be pinned down by
sniper fire *now*. . . . A pair of Dendarii rear guards
started back into the fog. An excited prisoner—ye
gods, it was Pitt's lieutenant again—grabbed up the
armor-paralyzed soldier's weapon and made to join
them.

"No! Come back later and fight on your own time,
you jerk!" Miles sloshed toward Murka. "Fall back,
load up, get in the air! Don't stop to fight! No time!"

Some of the last of the prisoners had fallen flat to
the ground, burrowing like mudpuppies, a sound
sensible reflex in any other context. Miles dashed
among them, slapping rumps. "Get *aboard*, up the
ramp, go, go, go!" Beatrice popped up out of the
mud and mimicked him, shakily driving her fellows
before her.

Miles skidded to a stop beside his fallen Dendarii
and snapped the armor clamps open left-handed.
The soldier kicked off his fatal carapace, rolled to his
feet, and limped for the safety of the shuttle. Miles
ran close behind him.

Murka and one patrolman waited at the foot of the
ramp.

"Get ready to pull in the ramp and lift on my
mark," Murka began to the shuttle pilot. "R—" his
words were lost in an explosive pop as the plasma
beam sliced across his neck. Miles could feel the
searing heat from it pass centimeters above his head
as he stood next to his lieutenant. Murka's body
crumpled.

Miles dodged, paused to yank off Murka's comm
headset. The head came too. Miles had to brace it
with his numb hand to pull the headset free. The

weight of the head, its density and roundness, hammered into his senses. The precise memory of it would surely be with him until his dying day. He let it fall by Murka's body.

He staggered up the ramp, a last armored Dendarii pulling on his arm. He could feel the ramp sag peculiarly under their feet, glanced down to see a half-melted seam across it where the plasma arc that had killed Murka had passed on.

He fell through the hatchway, clutching the headset and yelling into it, "Lift, lift! Mark, now! Go!"

"Who is this?" came the shuttle pilot's voice back.

"Naismith."

"Yes, *sir*."

The shuttle heaved off the ground, engines roaring, even before the ramp had withdrawn. The ramp mechanism labored, metal and plastic complaining—then jammed on the twisted distortion of the melt.

"Get that hatch sealed back there!" the shuttle pilot's voice yowled over the headset.

"Ramp's jammed," Miles yowled back. "Jettison it!"

The ramp mechanism skreeled and shrieked, reversing itself. The ramp shuddered, jammed again. Hands reached out to thump on it urgently. "You'll never get it that way!" Beatrice, across the hatch from Miles, yelled fiercely, and twisted around to kick at it with her bare feet. The wind of their flight screamed over the open hatchway, buffeting and vibrating the shuttle like a giant blowing across the top of a bottle.

To a chorus of shouting, thumping, and swearing, the shuttle lurched abruptly onto its side. Men, women, and loose equipment tangled across the tilting deck. Beatrice kicked bloodily at a final buggered bolt. The ramp tore loose at last. Beatrice, sliding, fell with it.

Miles dove at her, lunging across the hatchway. If he connected, he never knew, for his right hand was a senseless blob. He saw her face only as a white blur as she whipped away into the blackness.

It was like a silence, a great silence, in his head. Although the roar of wind and engines, screaming and swearing and yelling, went on as before, it was lost somewhere between his ears and his brain, and went unregistered. He saw only a white blur, smearing into the darkness, repeated again and again, replaying like a looping vid.

He found himself crouched on his hands and knees, the shuttle's acceleration sucking him to the deck. They'd gotten the hatch closed. The merely human babble within seemed muffled and thin, now that the roaring voices of the gods were silenced. He looked up into the pale face of Pitt's lieutenant, crouched beside him still clutching the unfired Dendarii weapon he'd grabbed up in that other lifetime.

"You'd better kill a whole lot of Cetagandans for Marilac, boy," Miles rasped to him at last. "You better be worth something to *some*body, 'cause I've sure paid too much for you."

The Marilacan's face twitched uncertainly, too cowed even to try to look apologetic. Miles wondered what his own face must look like. From the reflection in that mirror, strange, very strange.

Miles began to crawl forward, looking for something, somebody. . . . Formless flashes made yellow streaks in the corners of his vision. An armored Dendarii, her helmet off, pulled him to his feet.

"Sir? Hadn't you better come forward to the pilot's compartment, sir?"

"Yes, all right . . ."

She got an arm around him, under his arm, so he didn't fall down again. They picked their way forward in the crowded shuttle, through Marilacans and Dendarii mixed. Faces were drawn to him, marked him fearfully, but none dared an expression of any kind. Miles's eye was caught by a silver cocoon, as they neared the forward end.

"Wait . . ."

He fell to his knees beside Suegar. A hit of hope . . . "Suegar. Hey, Suegar!"

Suegar opened his eyes to slits. No telling how much of this he was taking in, through the pain and the shock and the drugs.

"You're on your way now. We made it, made the timing. With all ease. With agility and speed. Up through the regions of the air, higher than the clouds. You had the scripture right, you did."

Suegar's lips moved. Miles bent his head closer.

". . . wasn't really a scripture," Suegar whispered. "I knew it . . . you knew it . . . don't shit me . . ."

Miles paused, cold-stoned. Then he leaned forward again. "No, brother," he whispered. "For though we went in clothed, we have surely come out naked."

Suegar's lips puffed on a dry laugh.

Miles didn't weep until after they'd made the wormhole jump.

FOUR

Illyan sat silent.

Miles lay back, pale and exhausted, a stupid trembling concealed in his belly making his voice shake. "Sorry. Thought I'd got over it. So much craziness has happened since then, no time to think, digest. . . ."

"Combat fatigue," Illyan suggested.

"The combat only lasted a couple of hours."

"Ah? I'd reckon it at six weeks, by that account."

"Whatever. But if your Count Vorvolk wants to argue that I should have traded lives for equipment, well . . . I had maybe five minutes to make a decision, under enemy fire. If I'd had a month to study it, I'd have come to the same conclusion. And I'll stand behind it now, in a court martial or any goddamn arena he wants to fight me in."

"Calm down," Illyan advised. "*I* will deal with Vorvolk, and his shadow-advisors. I think . . . no, I *guarantee* their little plot will not intrude further on your recovery, Lieutenant Vorkosigan." His eyes glinted. Illyan had served thirty years in Imperial

Security, Miles reminded himself. Aral Vorkosigan's Dog still had teeth.

"I'm sorry my . . . carelessness shook your confidence in me, sir," said Miles. It was an odd wound that doubt had dealt him; Miles could feel it still, an invisible ache in his chest, slow to heal. So, trust was more of a feedback loop than he had ever realized. Was Illyan right, should he pay more attention to appearances? "I'll try to be more intelligent in future."

Illyan gave him an indecipherable look, his mouth set, neck oddly flushed. "So shall I, Lieutenant."

The swish of the door, the sweep of skirts. Countess Vorkosigan was a tall woman, hair gone red-roan, with a stride that had never quite accommodated itself to Barrayaran female fashions. She wore the long rich skirts of a Vor-class matron as cheerfully as a child playing dress-up, and about as convincingly.

"M'lady," Illyan nodded, rising.

"Hello, Simon. Goodbye, Simon," she grinned back. "That doctor you spooked begs me to use my superior firepower to throw you out. I know you officers and gentlemen have business, but it's time to wrap it up. Or so the medical monitors indicate." She glanced at Miles. A frown flickered across her easy-going features, a hint of steel.

Illyan caught it too, and bowed. "We're quite finished, m'lady. No problem."

"So I trust." Chin lifted, she watched him out.

Miles, studying that steady profile, realized with a sudden lurch just why the death of a certain tall aggressive redhead might still be wringing his gut, long after his reconciliation to other casualties for which he was surely no less responsible. *Ha. How late we come to our insights. And how uselessly.* Still, a tightness eased in his throat as Countess Vorkosigan turned back to him.

"You look like a defrosted corpse, love." Her lips brushed his forehead warmly.

"Thank you, Mother," Miles chirped.

"That nice Commander Quinn who brought you in says you haven't been eating properly. As usual."

"Ah." Miles brightened. "Where is Quinn? Can I see her?"

"Not here. She is excluded from classified areas, to wit this Imperial Military Hospital, on the grounds of her being foreign military personnel. Barrayarans!" That was Captain Cordelia Naismith's (Betan Astronomical Survey, retired) favorite swear word, delivered with a multitude of inflections as the occasion demanded; this time with exasperation. "I took her to Vorkosigan House to wait."

"Thank you. I . . . owe a lot to Quinn."

"So I gather." She smiled at him. "You can be at the long lake three hours after you delude that doctor into releasing you from this dismal place. I've invited Commander Quinn along— there, I thought that might motivate you to pay more serious attention to recovery."

"Yes, *ma'am*." Miles eased down into his covers. Sensation was beginning to return to his arms. Unfortunately, the sensation in question was pain. He smiled whitely. It was better than no sensation at all, oh yes.

"We will take turns, feeding and spoiling you," she envisioned. "And . . . you can tell me all about Earth."

"Ah . . . yes. I have a great deal to tell you about Earth."

"Rest, then." Another kiss, and she was gone.

MILES VORKOSIGAN/NAISMITH:
HIS UNIVERSE AND TIMES

Chronology	Events	Chronicle
Approx. 200 years before Miles's birth	Quaddies are created by genetic engineering.	*Falling Free*
During Beta-Barrayaran War	Cordelia Naismith meets Lord Aral Vorkosigan while on opposite sides of a war. Despite difficulties, they fall in love and are married.	*Shards of Honor*
The Vordarian Pretendship	While Cordelia is pregnant, an attempt to assassinate Aral by poison gas fails, but Cordelia is affected; Miles Vorkosigan is born with bones that will always be brittle and other medical problems. His growth will be stunted.	*Barrayar*
Miles is 17	Miles fails to pass physical test to get into the Service Academy. On a trip, necessities force him to improvise the Free Dendarii Mercenaries into existence; he has unintended but unavoidable adventures for four months. Leaves the Dendarii in Ky Tung's competent hands and takes Elli Quinn to Beta for	*The Warrior's Apprentice*

	rebuilding of her damaged face; returns to Barrayar to thwart plot against his father. Emperor pulls strings to get Miles into the Academy.	
Miles is 20	Ensign Miles graduates and immediately has to take on one of the duties of the Barrayaran nobility and act as detective and judge in a murder case. Shortly afterward, his first military assignment ends with his arrest. Miles has to rejoin the Dendarii to rescue the young Barrayaran emperor. Emperor accepts Dendarii as his personal secret service force.	"The Mountains of Mourning" in *Borders of Infinity* *The Vor Game*
Miles is 22	Miles sends Commander Elli Quinn, who's been given a new face on Beta, on a solo mission to Kline Station.	*Ethan of Athos*
Miles is 23	Now a Barrayaran Lieutenant, Miles goes with the Dendarii to smuggle a scientist out of Jackson's Whole. Miles's fragile leg bones have been replaced by synthetics.	"Labyrinth" in *Borders of Infinity*

Miles is 24	Miles plots from within a Cetagandan prison camp on Dagoola IV to free the prisoners. The Dendarii fleet is pursued by the Cetagandans and finally reaches Earth for repairs. Miles has to juggle both his identities at once, raise money for repairs, and defeat a plot to replace him with a double. Ky Tung stays on Earth. Commander Elli Quinn is now Miles's right-hand officer. Miles and the Dendarii depart for Sector IV on a rescue mission.	"The Borders of Infinity" in *Borders of Infinity* *Brothers in Arms*
Miles is 25	Hospitalized after previous mission, Miles's broken arms are replaced by synthetic bones. With Simon Illyan, Miles undoes yet another plot against his father while flat on his back.	*Borders of Infinity*